# The Well of Shadows

## Sabrina Blaum

**Babette B. Publishing**

## Copyright @ 2021 Sabrina Blaum

All rights reserved

The characters and events portrayed in this book are fictitious. Any similarity to real persons, living or dead, is coincidental and not intended by the author.

No part of this book may be reproduced, or stored in a retrieval system, or transmitted in any form or by any means, electronic, mechanical, photocopying, recording, or otherwise, without express written permission of the publisher.

ISBN-13: 978-1-7376851-1-1

Cover Design: 100Covers.com
Design of Morgen Family Crest: Sydney Qrys
Author Image: Willow Hyppolite

Library of Congress Control Number: 2021915542
Printed in the United States of America

*To W.B. Gerard, my late mentor and friend, who has taught me everything I know about writing.*

# foreword

This is in fact the fourth novel I've completed, though it is the first one I've chosen to publish (and we'll never talk about the first one). The first draft was the easiest, completed in three months, but then the real hard work began.

The tale you're about to encounter found its inspiration in real-world events, though I didn't realize that until my first readthrough. It's funny how that works sometimes.

I hope you'll find it an enjoyable read and time well-spent.

# map of saltung

# timeline

**Year 0:** Tyler Morgen and his beloved wife Elizabeth unite the ruling families of Saltung against the threat of the Verlohren. Faced with a rise of the deceased haunting their lands in physical form until they acknowledge and atone for their sins, Tyler founds the Council of the Living to ensure the safety of the now allied towns of Saltung. To honor Tyler's leadership, the founding members agree to keep the position of Head of the Council in the Morgen family line.

**Year 41:** Maximilian Morgen, the first Morgen heir, ascends to the Council leadership at a time of turmoil. He leads the hunt to exile the Sattran, a subset of Verlohren who no longer possess any hope of redemption, to the far reaches of the land.

**Year 116:** After years of prosperity, the Council of the Living is once again faced with a threat. The Dagen, a rebel faction of Verlohren bent on upending the rightful rule of the Morgen family, have organized in the major towns of Saltung to increase their recruitment efforts until Council Head Luce Morgen rids the land of this danger.

**Year 188:** Council Head Anson Morgen faces a new rebel group, formed in the memory of the Dagen, calling themselves Sterne. They elude capture and destruction until the end of Anson's rule in year 209.

**Year 251:** Rumors of a new rebel group rising spread across the land, but Council Head Louisa Morgen succeeds in crushing them before they can organize in the same year. She has ruled over one of the most flourishing eras of Saltung.

**Year 300:** The Tarung, the newest rebel group of Verlohren, seeks influence and is closely monitored by the Head of the Council, Anthony Morgen.

**Year 302:** The Tarung have extended their reach and now have Living sympathizers, pushing Anthony Morgen to increase raids to prevent an uprising and ensure the prosperity of the Living. Year 302 also marks the beginning of Lady Christina's Initiation to succeed as the Head of the Council of the Living.

Sabrina Blaum

# MORGEN FAMILY TREE

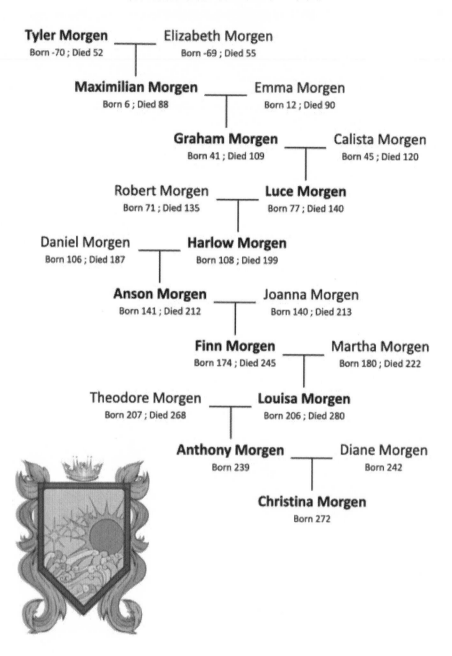

**Tyler Morgen**
Born -70 ; Died 52

Elizabeth Morgen
Born -69 ; Died 55

**Maximilian Morgen**
Born 6 ; Died 88

Emma Morgen
Born 12 ; Died 90

**Graham Morgen**
Born 41 ; Died 109

Calista Morgen
Born 45 ; Died 120

Robert Morgen
Born 71 ; Died 135

**Luce Morgen**
Born 77 ; Died 140

Daniel Morgen
Born 106 ; Died 187

**Harlow Morgen**
Born 108 ; Died 199

**Anson Morgen**
Born 141 ; Died 212

Joanna Morgen
Born 140 ; Died 213

**Finn Morgen**
Born 174 ; Died 245

Martha Morgen
Born 180 ; Died 222

Theodore Morgen
Born 207 ; Died 268

**Louisa Morgen**
Born 206 ; Died 280

**Anthony Morgen**
Born 239

Diane Morgen
Born 242

**Christina Morgen**
Born 272

# one

Aimee legs burned as she chased after Dylan's bobbing blond head. "Run, Dylan, faster!"

Four figures dressed in tight gray uniforms with intricately woven red strings stitched across their chests scurried after them with weapons drawn. Their silver blades gleamed in the reflecting light of the searing crimson sun.

"Just a little farther," Aimee huffed before twisting and rushing left while Dylan raced straight ahead.

This split their pursuers, two of them dashing after Dylan while the others sprinted after her. The throbbing pulse behind her temples resonated in her head like the clang of a monk swinging wide and drubbing a metallic gong.

Her loose-fitting clothing clung to her skin as sweat dripped down her face and neck, swirled along her arms, and slid off her fingers. She sped up and grunted in relief when the bustling marketplace of Freit, her home and the capital of Saltung, swallowed her whole. A throng of people built an unsurmountable barrier, blocking the gray-clad henchmen.

She loathed crowds; and the way she had to wriggle through them, always touching someone or something, strung a tension through her body that set her teeth on edge. This wasn't just any crowd or any marketplace—Aimee had sought refuge in the biggest bazaar of the Living. While risky, given that people weren't keen on encountering her kind, it beat getting caught by the Council guards.

She wiped her face and took a deep breath as she slunk through the crowds, hurrying toward their meeting place. Aimee trusted Dylan, and he was an excellent runner, aware of all the town's shortcuts and hiding places. Yet fear still nagged at her, forever lounging on her shoulder and muttering into her ears. Sometimes it even howled.

Nine years as a spit upon and too often hunted outcast would do that to a person. But those days could end if their lead panned out, if... But no, hope was scarce, and at the rate she was going, she might as well pour zinder on it and flick a lit match on top, for that was all that would be left if this turned into another dead end.

Not long after, Aimee rushed to Dylan who sat crouched on the floor with a map spread out in front of him. "Are you OK?"

"Yes. I lost them near the temple. Mass had just ended." He grinned and patted the ground next to him. "Look at this." His finger traced several areas on the map.

"This is it? This is what we got from your guy?"

"It's an atlas of Saltung."

"I can see that, but..." Aimee frowned. "What about these regions?" She pointed at the area behind the Thal mountain range and then at an island in the middle of the unforgiving Troken ocean. "I've never seen these on any of the charts of Saltung. Have you?"

"No. All records I've ever come across end at the mountains, and there's never a note of any islands either."

Aimee rose and paced. "But you think these places are real?"

"I trust Markus. He's helped me in the past, and he risked a lot getting this to us."

"He's a Living, though, and he might... Where did the guards come from?" Aimee halted and placed her hands on her hips.

"Markus wouldn't betray us. Not all Living are bad, and I don't think the guards knew what this was about. They just saw two... well, us, trespassing and gave chase."

"Hmm. I hope you're right. This will become much more complicated if the Council of the Living knows what we're up to."

"Agreed." Dylan stood and folded the map before putting it back in his satchel.

"There's a way—"

"No! We've discussed this. We're not doing that. Besides, they can't see me."

"Not your family, but there are others who work there who could—"

"No, Aimee. They can *never* know."

"You're so concerned with them believing the lies about us?"

"What? No. It's tempting to show them, to show my father especially but if they realized... I just have a bad feeling. The Council cannot learn the truth, and seeing me..."

"Raises all kinds of questions."

"A ton. No, to them, I've moved on. They believe that, and they need to continue to do so."

"What if I reached out to them?"

"They wouldn't talk to you. The alarms would sound as soon as you're within a hundred feet of that place. Their magic detects us."

"How would you have gotten in then?" Aimee asked.

"I would've met with them somewhere else."

"Exactly. Why can't I do that? I could tell them we were friends. Sort of. I was your tutor for two years."

"Let me think about it."

"All right. Markus could send a note to your sister, or I could talk to her."

"No! She... That's out of the question. She wouldn't listen anyway," Dylan grumbled and handed Aimee a squashed cheese sandwich. "Here. You must be starving."

"Thank you." Aimee grabbed it and tore off a big bite. "I hate this."

"Yeah," Dylan said, and his clear blue eyes held Aimee's red-hot gaze for a second before he turned his head.

\*\*\*

Chris sank onto her bed and groaned. Today had been long, longer than usual. The Initiation sessions drained the life out of her. *Good,* she thought, frowning. They might as well do that. Her parents didn't know what she'd done. A part of her wanted to rush to their room and confess everything, but they wouldn't care or understand. Perhaps both? It didn't matter.

She only had a few hours left to sleep before her meeting with Lance. She pummeled her stiff pillow into submission and burrowed under the covers. This was it. Her life. Played out in front of her before she ever lived it. She had never questioned this before, Lance notwithstanding. The rest, though? Her duty to her family, to the Council?

That was all she'd ever known, unlike her little brother. The lucky one. He never had to bear the responsibility of being the heir to the Morgen clan, the first born of Lord Anthony and Lady Diane Morgen, who would take over as the Head of the Council of the Living. Her brother had been free to do with his life as he wished, and what had he done? He'd argued for those defective... those... Chris scoffed.

She recalled their last argument, how everything had spun out of control, how her heart had clawed at her chest and her vision had blurred. Chris didn't want to relive that. She'd cried enough since then. Curled up into a taut ball under wafts of down feathers, she sniffled when hot tears once more leaked down her face. She had to get a hold of this so that tomorrow she could resume pretending to be who everyone thought she was.

The next day passed in a flurry of activities before her mother dragged Chris to the fitting room. "Yes, Mother," she said, refraining from rolling her eyes while she stood motionless in front of a full-length mirror, servants buzzing around to put the finishing touches on her flowing, light-gray dress. Cerise loops of satin ran up her arms, forming the Council's Crest on her chest, a crimson sun drowning out three stars across the ocean.

14

"I cannot comprehend your attitude. It is quite uncalled for. Lance is a gentleman, and you are very lucky indeed to be matched with him," Diane tutted, standing behind Chris and eyeing her dress. "Her hair should be up in a bun. That will take care of those unruly curls and show off her neck." She gestured at one handmaid.

"Did you love Father right away?" Chris asked, startled by the speed at which her mother's head snapped up while her green eyes widened.

"Excuse me?"

"Back when you were engaged. You... you didn't get to choose each other either. Were you in love with him from the start?"

"Your father and I have nothing to do with your relationship with Lance."

Chris slouched and smoothed her dress. "Of course not, Mother."

"Let us go. Your father and Lance are waiting."

She followed her mother through the brightly lit corridors of their mansion to the great hall.

"Lady Diane and Lady Christina," the herald announced as soon as the French doors opened and admitted them.

Anthony and Lance rose and stepped to the side, pulling out chairs for them.

"Lady Diane, Christina." Anthony smiled at his family.

"It's wonderful to see you again, Christina." Lance bowed his head. "Lady Diane, always a pleasure."

Diana took her seat. "Welcome, my dear Lance."

"Lance," Chris said and settled in her chair.

"How is the Initiation coming along?" Lance asked.

"Splendidly." Anthony raised his glass. "My Christina has always been an impeccable student, and the Initiation is no different."

"That is great to hear. Eleven more months!" Lance lifted his glass, too.

Diane laughed. "Someone appears eager for his wedding."

"Can you blame me? Christina's beauty's sole competition is her intellect."

"Hear, hear," said Anthony. "You are the perfect match."

"We're lucky. Not everyone is promised to their teenage love," Lance said and smiled at Chris who sat straight, motionless, holding his gaze.

Anthony's laughter boomed. "You have kept that secret well. My Christina does not share her feelings openly. We never knew of such a connection in your younger years, but we are all allowed our secrets, and I trust my daughter."

"We admired each other from afar, though she always seemed as taken by me as I by her," Lance stated, his gaze never leaving Chris. "To our future marriage and the fortune and wealth of House Morgen!" he said, and everyone raised their glasses, uttering the traditional salute.

Once the dreadful dinner had finished and after Chris uttered her goodbyes, she scurried back to her rooms. She clawed at her dress, barely avoiding ripping the fabric to shreds. She tossed it to the floor and exhaled in a rush before covering her face with both hands. "In and out," she breathed into her empty bedroom.

Releasing her twist, she combed her fingers through loose strands before rotating her shoulders, but the tension refused to ebb. A bath was in order. She pulled her hair up again, this time in a non-headache inducing careless bun, and stepped into her en-suite to run the water. Chris added salt and lavender leaves before undressing.

Her life wasn't her own, though she usually denied this, pushing this knowledge down, burying it to where she could almost convince herself she had a choice. Then a dinner like tonight happened and reality crashed at her feet.

She lit three azure candles and stepped into the tub, biting back a groan at the blissful heat seeping into her. Chris hated the cold, yet that was what people always called her. Cold and unfeeling. Never moving.

She was the proverbial crayfish put into clear cold water, never realizing her fate until she was cooked to death. She chuckled at her morbid thoughts. Her brother would have teased her and brought her out of her misery, away from the chill and into his warmth. Or he would have before the change, before he fought for *them*. Did he mean to abandon her, or had that just been her damaged and clouded perception? She'd never know now that Dylan had moved on.

\*\*\*

Year 302, Day 4

"I hope this doesn't blow up," Dylan mumbled, ducking behind a large rock and peering at the wooden bench close to the burbling riverbank.

"You worry too much," Aimee replied. "Martha Jenkins, that's her name, right?"

"Yes."

"What's her position?"

"She's a junior mage."

"What makes you so sure she's sympathetic to our cause?"

"I've talked to her. A lot. We were friends," Dylan said and cleared his throat.

"Friends? That's all?"

"All right, so there might have been some... affection, but it went nowhere." Dylan glanced at his feet. "We were supposed to go on a date, but then..."

Aimee squeezed his arm. "I see. I'm sorry."

"Yeah, well, we can't change that now, but I'm sure she'll be willing to help, or at least pass along a message to my sister."

"I thought that was out of the question?" Aimee frowned. "You didn't mention that part when we set this up."

17

"I had a dream last night. I... we used to be close. When we were growing up, but then they dragged her into all this 'preparing the heir' business, and she got so serious about it. Obsessed, almost. Chris is super smart, always has been, and she loves books, and studying, so this came naturally to her. But it also made her... dunno... distant? Like she entered a new world, and I wasn't part of it anymore."

"You grew apart."

"Yeah, but I'd been friends with this boy who'd passed. I didn't even understand at first, but when I found out... when I saw the markings, they wanted me to stop seeing him. I knew we shouldn't be friends, but there was no difference. It made no sense to me, and everything that they'd taught me my entire life seemed like a lie."

"Because it is."

"I know that now, but not then. I had an inkling, and I always follow my feelings, so I kept meeting Jim, my friend, in secret. I always made sure to keep him safe. He was the inspiration to establish the network when I got older, to help people like him, but back then, I set out to study and research the history of the Verlohren."

"That's when you came across the missing text?"

"Yes."

"And that dream of your sister convinced you we should send her a message?"

"Oh, right. Sorry. I got off track. Yes. I feel we need her."

"Couldn't that also just be your desire to move on? You need her for that."

"I thought about that, too. I'm not sure, which is why I'm hoping this won't blow up."

"Well, only one way to find out. There she is." Aimee pointed out the red-haired woman who, after gazing around a few times, lowered herself onto the bench. "Here goes nothing." Aimee rose but paused when Dylan touched her arm.

"Tell her to say to Chris what we've talked about last time."

"All right," Aimee said and trekked toward the riverbank.

"Hey. Nice day for a hike," she offered, sitting down next to Martha.

"Too bad I'm wearing sandals," Martha replied with the agreed upon response.

Both sat in silence for a moment. Aimee shoved her trembling hands under her legs and shifted forward. "I'm sorry. It's weird being around any..."

"Living?" Martha said, and Aimee nodded. "It's OK. The laws are clear, and tradition is even more so, but since starting my studies and allowing magic to fill my being, uh..." She rubbed her arm. "That's not what you're here for."

"No, go on, please. What happened?"

"My parents were never that harsh on the Verlohren, so I didn't have too many negative thoughts on them. On you." Martha picked at a splinter sticking out between two wood panels. "My studies made me see the world differently. There's this schism, a split, but it's hard to explain. I'm not sure it's natural and that... You don't *feel* wrong."

"Oh," Aimee exhaled, her gaze falling to her feet, and she blinked rapidly.

"I'm sorry. I'm making you uncomfortable."

"No, it's not that. I'm just... My experiences with the Living haven't been too pleasant, that is, if I interact with you at all." She raised her head and caught Martha's gaze. "I was wondering if, uh, during your studies, did you ever notice a script, or the reference to a text called the *Demise of Reason*?"

"Hmm." Martha's eyes turned vacant as she stared across the river. "No. It doesn't sound familiar, but again, I haven't studied for that long yet. I can be on the lookout."

"That would be great. Listen... Could you deliver a message to Lady Christina?

"Lady Christina Morgen?" Martha laughed. "We don't run in the same circles."

"But weren't you friends with her brother?"

"Oh, yes, well... that's... Dylan was special." Martha rubbed her neck. "I uh, I sometimes see her when she comes to the Center when we have lessons, but I've never seen her teach the early years. I could try to talk to her, but I doubt I'd ever be able to catch her alone. I'm assuming you wouldn't want anyone to overhear this message?"

"That's right. You can try, see if your studies mention the text, and if there's an opportunity..."

"I can do that. What should I say?"

"Tell her that Dylan says the night has teeth."

"That's cryptic."

Aimee folded her hands in her lap. "I'm afraid I can't explain it."

"I understand, but if this means something significant to her, she won't just let me walk away. She'd have many questions, right?"

"I doubt it. Not for you right away. And if she does, you can tell her to meet you here, and I'll join you."

"I doubt she'll be up for that. She's very busy. It's Initiation season, but again, I can't guarantee that I'll even have the chance to speak to her."

"That's OK. We weren't sure you'd even show, much less prove to be so... kind."

"All right. I'll contact you the way you've reached out and tell you if I hear anything, or if I delivered your message. Be careful. There are rumors they're planning more raids in the next few days." Martha offered an apologetic smile when Aimee flinched at the news.

"Thank you. I appreciate your help. And the warning."

\*\*\*

The clanging of wooden sticks colliding echoed through the room.

Chris lunged to her left and yanked the baton back before smashing it against the bar in Terry's hand. The impact sent vibrations through her arms, and she strained to apply more pressure and push his weapon down farther before bouncing up and circling her opponent again.

Terry bent his knees, crouched, accelerated and thrust the stick at Chris, who fell back, deflecting the blow at the last second, and almost lost her footing.

She tightened her grip on the cane with both hands and shoved against Terry, pushing him backward. Chris skipped on light feet, baiting him as she waited for his attack.

She dodged his momentum and surged forward to slam her baton down, grazing Terry's chest, whereupon he redoubled his efforts and counterattacked with rapid strides, aiming low to swipe at Chris's legs. She leaped high, swung her staff, and cracked it against Terry's neck on the downward motion.

He tumbled to the floor, and the stick slipped from his grasp. "Good fight. You're getting faster," he panted and sprang back up.

"Thank you. It's probably an unconscious effort to run away." She grabbed a towel and wiped her face and hands before returning the rod to its fastenings against the wall.

Terry raised his eyebrows. "Are you OK?"

Her gaze drifted beyond the window and locked on the shadow she had perceived in her peripheral. "What?"

"I asked if you're all right. You could tell your father you need a break. You seem stressed."

"Right." Chris laughed. "He'll like that." She seized a water bottle and took a large gulp. "Besides, you said I'm getting faster."

"Sure, but you're also tense. You almost fell earlier."

"But I didn't."

He raised his hands. "No offense. I worry about you."

"No need. That's what I've worked toward all my life. It'll be fine."

"If you say so. Is it true that Lance is leading the raids tonight?"

Chris grunted. "He wants to show my father how useful he'll be to the Council."

"Remember, you'll marry him."

"What does that have to do with any of this?"

"You're usually better at faking it. Your disdain for him is painted all over your face, so much so, any idiot would see it."

"That must be true since you noticed it." She chuckled, and Terry playfully slapped her shoulder.

"Be nice."

"That's all I ever am," she said.

"To anyone you're not sparring with, maybe."

***

Year 302, Day 6

Aimee and Dylan secured shelter in an old, ransacked, decrepit shack that the Living considered too dangerous to even enter. Pink, green, and black mold clung to the walls like psychedelic wallpaper.

She cringed when she got closer to the hairy and slimy wall ornaments while heading for the kitchen. "I'm not sure which is worse. Being in this... *place,* surrounded by that stench, or being caught during the raid."

"Oh hush," Dylan chided. "This was all I could find on such short notice. Didn't expect them to have another raid already. I wonder why they've ramped them up over the last month. Must be all the rumors about the Tarung."

"Hmm. You got something to eat?"

He rolled his eyes. "Aren't you too grossed out?"

She glared at him and crossed her arms in front of her chest.

"Figures." Dylan rummaged through his backpack, fishing out a peanut butter sandwich and an apple for Aimee, and a cheese sandwich for himself. "Have you heard from Martha?" he asked between bites.

"No. I'd tell you right away."

"Right." He sat on the floor.

"Don't be so disappointed. It's only been two days. She said that she isn't close to your sister, and she doesn't see her often. It'll take a while."

"True. And the Initiation season makes everything even more complicated."

"I've been meaning to ask about that. What's this Initiation stuff about?"

Dylan's eyes widened, and he opened his mouth only to shut it again. "You don't know?"

"Not what we covered in school. Besides, it's not like the Council shares their inner workings with its citizens. All I know is that it's the time before the heir takes over."

"Right. So, Chris became the successor the moment she was born because it's always the first born who takes over as the Head of the Council. She had extra studies growing up, but it got real when she turned eighteen."

"What additional classes did she take?"

"I'm not sure. I didn't complete them myself. But the way she explained it, they focused on history, tradition, and some philosophical ethics nonsense?"

Aimee laughed. "Aren't you interested in history?"

"True history, real history, yes, not this sham. These lies." He balled his fists.

"Does your father know the truth?"

He picked up a pebble and threw it across the room. "I can't imagine he doesn't."

"And Chris?"

"Gods, I hope not. I don't wanna go there."

"Yeah, so, Initiation?"

"They increase all the teachings, the martial arts, the magic, and she also has to teach different levels and give lectures to other instructors and Council members. Then there are meditation and reflection sessions where she has to sequester herself for a while."

"Wow. That's a lot."

"Yeah, but the best thing, they reveal all the Council secrets to her. Bit by bit."

"That's what you want her to do. Fill in the blanks?"

"If she's willing." Dylan sighed. "Chris has never been a fan of the Verlohren. She... she believes we're defective."

"Of course she does. And she's a mage?"

"A great one."

"All right, while it's sweet that you're proud of your big sister and all, this is something you should have shared, oh, I don't know, maybe *before* we sent Martha off with a message for your Verlohren-hating sister?!"

"Hey! That's not fair. I thought you knew all this stuff."

"How, Dylan? You grew up as a member of the ruling family of Saltung, and I was a tutor from the wrong side of town."

"But you were *my* tutor!"

"That was luck and circumstances. Your original tutor had had an accident, and they needed a quick replacement," Aimee said.

"Oh. I never knew."

"Why would they have told you?"

"Just sayin'," he mumbled and pulled his legs to his chest.

"Do you hear that?" Aimee breathed and crept to the window. Wooden blinds hung crookedly on the frame, but some panels were missing, and she used one gap to gaze outside. "Torches," she hissed and backed away, crouching next to Dylan on the floor. "Tell me they also taught you magic?"

"No, but even if they did, Verlohren—"

"Can't use magic, yes. Wishful thinking," she grumbled.

"We can't leave. Then they'll catch us for sure," Dylan whispered. "What do we do?"

"We wait."

\*\*\*

Year 302, Day 8

"You must concentrate and listen to your connection to the soil. Feel the energy that surrounds you. Harness it. Guide it," Chris instructed, sitting cross-legged in front of five rows of students, newbies, as they liked to call themselves. A convenient excuse for laziness and lack of ambition; an opinion that had yet to make her any friends.

They were all in their first year of education, and Chris struggled to hide her frustration with their overall lackluster attempts at magic. This education was a privilege, but they acted as if it were a burden. She had *begged* her father to start her training early, and when she *finally* had had the opportunity... Chris scoffed.

The other night's dinner and this morning's Initiation session had robbed her not only of her patience, but they also unearthed memories she preferred to hide in the presence of others.

"Focus on your breathing, follow it along, in and out, concentrate on the center of your being, and use this energy to light the candle in front of you." Chris opened her eyes and frowned when only three out of twenty candles quavered in the semi-darkness of the classroom. "Well, that's disappointing. How can you expect to progress in your studies if you cannot ignite a simple candle? How will you handle a confrontation?"

A student in the third row muttered something which caused others around him to snicker.

"Excuse me? What did you say, Timothy?"

He shifted in his seat. "I only asked what sort of conflict we are preparing for, given that Saltung has been at peace for generations."

"And I'm sure that's *exactly* how you worded it to your friends."

Most of the students dropped their heads and fidgeted with their hands in their laps.

—

"I understand that this seems elementary, and it is, but you have to align yourself with the Alder path. You *must* follow the steps that guide us, that will allow you to master magic. Without proper training, you can become a danger to yourself, and to others. Discipline, as boring as you may consider it, is essential," Chris explained. "As for your question, I suggest you get out of your own circle once in a while and pay attention to what's going on outside, otherwise you'll only see what you always see."

Wide eyes and head scratches greeted her words.

"Never mind. Here's the deal, if fifteen of you light their candle in the next ten minutes, I'll let you leave early."

A rumble went through the class, and they collectively returned their focus to their candles, and right away, two more lights sprang to life.

A knock on the door rang out and Chris ambled to answer it. "Mother. What are you doing here? I'm in the middle of teaching," she mouthed.

"Is that so? Follow me." Diane turned and stepped back into the hallway.

"Continue with your work. I'll be right back," Chris addressed her class and left the room.

"You are too easy on them. How will they ever learn discipline if you coddle them?"

"What are you talking about?"

"Their parents pay for the honor of having their offspring educated at the Council, by our family, and by the most esteemed teachers of Saltung. You cannot end their lessons early because you grow tired of their inability to cast spells. Both reflect poorly on you as an instructor."

Chris pinched the bridge of her nose. "I'm not their primary teacher, and aside from being lazy, they are… adequate. What do you want me to do? Strap them to their seats and have them memorize incantations? Their parents wouldn't approve of *that*."

"This is not the time to be facetious," Diane sniffed. "You have always been such a stickler for rules. I do not understand why you are suddenly so lax toward our traditions."

"Letting my class go ten minutes earlier is—"

A loud bang reverberated through the door behind them.

"What now? Wait here." Chris threw open the door and marched back into the classroom to find the wall tapestry with the embroidered emblem of the Council on fire. Angry, coral wisps of flame devoured the drapery while smoke billowed off the wobbling cloth. The students closest to the wall coughed and fled to the opposite side of the room.

"I asked you to light the candles, not set the room on fire." Chris barged toward the blaze and raised her hands while muttering a slow incantation that suffocated the flames.

"Leave," Chris ground out. The students hesitated for a second before filing out of the room as one seemingly inseparable conglomerate.

She returned to her desk and when she looked up after packing her belongings, a young woman had lingered behind and stood right in front of her.

"Excuse me, Lady Christina. Will you teach us from now on?"

"I've taught this class before, though your regular instructor will take over again next week. You are new, aren't you?"

"Yes," the woman said, fiddling with a pen in her hand. "I didn't... I didn't realize you teach newbie classes. With the Initiation and all..." She cleared her throat.

Chris straightened and tilted her head. "What can I do for you, Ms...?"

"Jenkins. Martha Jenkins."

"All right."

"I have a message for you."

Chris raised her eyebrows. "Oh? From whom?"

"Her name is Aimee or something."

"That doesn't sound familiar."

"It's not from her, uh, she asked me to tell you that Dylan said the night has teeth?" Martha blurted out the last part.

Chris raised her hands, and time stopped. She slumped, and bending over, clawed at the table in front of her. Her heart drummed in her chest and sweat pooled at her lower back. She focused on her breathing, slowing it down from the gushing stream that spilled out like water running from an overflowing rain-barrel.

Chris shook, her fingers clenched, and her knuckles paled. She held her breath and counted to ten before she pressed out a sob and covered her face with her hands. No, she couldn't do this. Not here. She had to go. She straightened and wiped her eyes before pulling at her clothes, trying to erase what had transpired before releasing time.

"That's all she told me, but I can get you in contact with her," Martha said, her gaze flitting between Chris and the door.

"That won't be necessary, at least not for now. Thank you," Chris replied, surprised by how steady her voice sounded. "Have a good day," she added before snatching her bag and darting out of the classroom. She needed to get to the cave. Tonight. Darkness be damned.

Her mother had left without another word, and for once, she felt thankful for her tendency to dismiss people wordlessly. Chris hurried home, and back in her room, she threw her purse into a corner, snagging a poncho and her emergency pack before leaving the manor. She hadn't visited the cavern since she was a teenager, before the lessons that caused the fracture between Dylan and her.

They used to play there early on, and then just hung out, alone and without expectations pressing down on them. Gods, she missed her brother. Could this be? But Martha said the message came from a woman. Amy, was it? She frowned.

What game was this? What if this was a trick, and they lured her away as an attack on the Council? Could this be a trap by the Verlohren? Chris faltered and stopped.

No, how would they have known that sentence? It must be someone close to Dylan. But why? What did they want from her? She sped up and made it to the cave after another ten-minute march. Once there, she froze.

Night had swallowed the landscape, drowning it in inky blackness. A rustling nearby startled her, and she drew back, stumbling on a rock and losing her balance. Chris cursed low under her breath and shot up, wiping her hands on her pants.

She groaned. "Magic. Right." Chris ignited a fireball. If this was a trap, she'd burn them all down. The fire crackled in her hand and liquid heat suffused her arm. The flame lit the path ahead and allowed her to reach the cavern without another tumble.

Her footsteps resonated when she stepped farther into the grotto. Bats sped screeching, flapping their wings rapidly as Chris pressed her body against the wall, her heart galloping in her chest.

She exhaled and trod deeper into the cave, her steps guiding her along a path she'd almost forgotten. The trickling sound of water dripping off stalactites flooded her brain with memories of tinkling laughter and shouting competitions for the loudest echo.

Her heartbeat slowed and a somber heaviness spread through her. Whatever this was, she'd still never see Dylan again. Chris turned around a corner, and there it was, just like she'd remembered. She crouched low and shifted the orange and white rock to the side. At first, she stared at the folded sheet in their hiding spot.

It didn't seem aged and instead had the crisp whiteness and spring of new paper. Her hands quivered, but the fire held. She closed her eyes and reached out. Grasping the sheet, she unfolded it.

"What? *The Demise of Reason?*"

---

\*\*\*

Lance sprinted after Lara and Lily into the primary office of the Holding Center. "No one informed me of an inspection."

"What would be the point of apprising you of a survey? Then you would prepare, and we wouldn't see what is really going on here," Lara said.

"The Morgen family is upholding their part of the agreement," Anthony's voice thundered as he rose from his seat behind his desk once they entered the room.

"I don't doubt that," Lara drawled. "It's just been such a long time, and my sister here has voiced some concerns."

"What concerns?" Anthony asked.

"Apprehensions regarding the true… shall we say, purpose, of these Centers," Lara said.

Anthony strode forward and glared at them. "Our *purpose* has remained the same through the ages."

"Then you won't mind showing us around?" Lily asked. She feared what they'd find, given what she'd seen the other day. It had been hard to convince Lara to check up on this. Lara's lack of concern for the Verlohren or anyone besides her sister likely stemmed from her perpetual residence in that awful mountain. It had been too long since she'd ventured out. Lily had tried in vain to get her to come out and spend time among the Living, among the beings of Saltung.

"Of course," Anthony puffed. "If you would please follow us." He marched out of his office and led them to the main building into the courtyard of the camp.

"How many Verlohren do you hold here?" Lily asked.

"Between 500 and 1000," Anthony said.

"That's a lot of people. Not to mention, quite a range," Lily replied.

Lance scowled. "We do not count them."

"It hardly matters, seeing as we release them after their time with us is up," Anthony said.

"How do you make sure you don't always collect the same people if you don't count and identify them?" Lara asked.

"All you want is for them to suffer. It does not matter which ones of them do," Lance said.

"Suffer. That's such an ugly word," Lara said. "We are interested in their markings, in the intensity, quantity, and breadth of their designs."

Lance's forehead wrinkled, marring his otherwise smooth features. "For what?"

"That's irrelevant," Lara said.

Lily stared at the barracks at the other end of the enclosure. They were in urgent need of repair. Their roofs contained areas with loose and crooked hanging tiles. Some were bereft of even a single sheet and instead bore a gaping hole in the ceiling. Several windows had cracked or shattered glass panels and were boarded up with rotting plywood. The nearby trees were dead or dying and the grass surrounding the area stood in a dull yellow hue, inundated in the muddy puddles of foul-smelling water pooling on the surface.

"This is where you house them?" Lily asked.

"Yes. They are dead. No need to worry about their health," Anthony said.

"What is happening over there, in that gray stone building? That's new. I don't recall ever seeing that before," Lara said and headed toward it.

"Just a storage facility," Anthony said.

"It's out of order. There was a water leak and then a pipe burst. A lot of damage, and the building is covered in water stains and mold. It wouldn't to be wise to go there," Lance rushed out.

"That is the first time I hear about this," Anthony groused. "When did this happen and why was I not informed about this before?"

"Just last week," Lance said and hurried after them, still striding toward the storage unit. "You have been so busy with Christina's Initiation. I deemed it unnecessary to burden you with this nuisance and instead took care of it myself."

---

"All right then," Anthony said, holding Lance's gaze who tipped his head. "Right, right. Good thinking, my boy." He cleared his throat. "Let us skip that and move on to the Verlohren. We can go into their barracks, and you will see for yourself that everything is in order."

Lara agreed, and they all followed Anthony, with Lily trailing behind. Once the others had entered the first building, Lily stayed back and turned, sneaking toward the gray storage facility. It stood alone on a bank of pebbles. The outside seemed freshly painted, which could go in line with Lance's explanation. The wooden entrance had a pristine look as well.

Lily hesitated, but then gripped the handle and pushed down. Locked. She muttered a spell, and the door sprang open, creaking as she pulled it farther out and slid inside.

Before her eyes adjusted to the semi-darkness, she gagged. Urine mixed with sulfur, and the smell of burned rubber and flesh assaulted her nostrils. She inched forward and fire sparked in her hands. The boarded windows would prevent anyone on the outside from detecting her presence.

Lily groaned when light brightened the room, wishing she'd stayed with the others in the barracks. This was worse than she'd feared.

# two

Aimee flung the door open. "She spoke to her! Martha told your sister what you said."

Dylan dropped his pen and sprang up. "Seriously?"

"I'd never joke about that, especially since I'm still skeptical that this was a good idea."

"It was a great idea! If anyone knows about the text or can locate it, it's Chris."

"Uh-huh, but what will she do with it? She could use it against us! Has *that* ever crossed your mind?"

"She wouldn't do that." Dylan sat back down, eyeing the drawing he'd been working on.

"Oh no, you're not going to disappear in your art again when we're having a discussion."

"What's the point? We disagree, and we'll see who's right soon enough."

"Are you crazy? You love your sister, that's cool, and I'm not suggesting she'd do anything to harm *you*, but you said yourself she doesn't like the Verlohren. Why would she help us?"

Dylan smacked his pen on the table and rose. "Why wouldn't she? She's not a monster!"

"I never said she was."

"Sorry. Listen, this is... I'm nervous, 'K? I told you we'd grown apart, but I can't imagine she'd close her eyes and turn us away once she knows the truth."

"You're forgetting one thing."

"What's that?"

"As a loved one, she cannot see or hear you. How will you tell her anything when that's not possible?"

"That'll be your job."

"That easy, huh? Why should she believe me? There are limits. I'm not burning for you to make peace with your sister!"

---

"I didn't ask you to! There are outages and stuff that flies under the radar."

"How do you figure that?"

"Didn't you say you felt little to no resistance when Tom wanted you to tell his mom something? That you could get out some information?"

"That was *one* time. Almost a year ago! That's usually not the case."

"I'm sorry, Aimee. I don't want to put you in this position, but given what's at stake, don't we owe it to... all of us to try? Imagine what it would mean to have the heir of the Council on our side?"

"Yes. I know. Everything. I just don't trust her."

"You don't even know her."

"She considers us *defective*, Dylan! You said so!"

"Yes, but now—"

"What? When she finds out her precious baby brother is one of them, she'll change her tune? Dismiss everything she's ever learned? Turn her back on her family? Her birthright?"

"I'm her family, too," Dylan exclaimed. "Besides, she's not like that. Chris doesn't care about her legacy. And for the record, *I* did that. I rejected all they've ever taught me! I created a network of Living who help and support the Verlohren, who hire them and give them access to their money. How do you think I got the funds for this house?"

"I know, I know. But you did most of that while you were still alive. She's firmly in the camp of 'Living good–Verlohren bad.'"

"We will see. If you're right and she knows, I'm assuming she dashed to the cave, so she could be here any moment."

Aimee grunted and flopped down on the couch. "That was another dumb part of the plan."

"Hey! Stop being so mean."

"I'm not mean. I am the reality to your fantasy. You gave the heir of the Council of the Living the location of our home."

"Yeah. That might have been a bit..."

"Dumb?"

"Rash. I was gonna go with rash."

"Of course you were. Did you cook something?"

Dylan snorted. "It's in the fridge. Help yourself."

"Thanks. I'm starving."

"Tell me something new."

"Just wait until you've been dead for almost a decade," she said and pulled open the refrigerator door. "Ah, there it is," she said, and grabbed a bowl of chicken and rice.

\*\*\*

Chris halted in front of the house that had summoned her from the grave. At least that's what it felt like. The lights were on, chasing away the shadows of the night. She'd rarely been to this neighborhood, being one of the most destitute ones in Freit, it housed mostly Verlohren along with a few Living too poor to afford housing elsewhere. She once more contemplated the likelihood of this entire undertaking being a trap. Perhaps the Tarung were out to stage a coup? Chris chuckled. She sounded like Lance.

She crept toward the rear of the house and mouthed a spell to unlock the backdoor before slipping inside and easing the door closed behind her. Chris padded past the hallway. Her gaze trailed over walls devoid of mementos or decoration and in desperate need of a fresh coat of paint.

The silence inside made her shallow breathing resound in her ears, and she allowed fire to ignite in her palm. She stopped right outside what appeared to be the entrance to the living room. There was a woman walking inside from the kitchen, judging by the sandwich in her hand.

She stood a little taller than Chris, dressed in all black. Her dark hair tapered off at her shoulders and her tawny-brown skin glowed under the orange gleam of the light fixture.

Was this Amy? The woman gave no impression she was aware of Chris's presence, which seemed to forgo a sinister Verlohren plot.

"My brother and I created treasure maps for each other when we were little. I didn't expect to get something like this ever again," Chris said, entering the living room still unnoticed. She clutched a folded sheet of paper in her left hand, the right still set ablaze. "But this isn't his handwriting. Who are you?"

The woman in question startled and her sandwich fell to the floor. "Shoot." She uttered a low curse. "Do you always sneak up on people? Also, can the fire. It's a bit dramatic."

Chris frowned. "Can the fire?"

"Extinguish it. This is my home, and it's flammable."

"I'm threatening *you*, not the house." The flame burned.

"Not a fan of that either."

"Who are you? How do you know my brother, and what's all this *Demise of Reason* nonsense?"

"I told you so. But you wouldn't believe me. No, she'll come around. Do you see this?" The woman gesticulated at the empty sofa. "She's gonna set me on fire, or at the very least, she'll burn down the house. I shouldn't have worried about burning for you, she'll do it for me. Literally."

Chris stepped closer and gazed in the same direction, but there was nothing there besides a couch, a sofa seat, and a coffee table. "Who are you talking to? What does any of this mean? Are you... are you *crazy*?"

"Might as well be," she replied and sat down on the couch. "Can you please turn off the fire? You're in no danger here."

"I'm not defending myself. I'm—"

"Yes, yes. You're intimidating me."

"Right."

"Here's the thing, I'm already dead. So, what are you gonna do?"

"You're a Verlohren. I knew it! What's this about? You're going to kidnap me and extort my father?"

"Princess, *you're* the one threatening me, in *my* home, and your hand is on fire. Doesn't that hurt?"

"I'm *not* a princess!"

"All right. Do you prefer 'honorable heir of the Council of the Living'? Or just Lady Christina? Is there a special way us *defective* Verlohren must address you?"

Chris clenched her jaw. The flame in her hand grew as she edged closer to the woman. "Who are you?"

"Aimee."

"You're the one who sent the message."

"Half right. Your brother did."

Chris closed her hand and the fire died. "Dylan? He's... he's like you?"

"Defective?"

"Stop saying that!"

"Dylan is like me."

"Oh Gods," Chris moaned and cradled her head in her hands. "How can this be? He did nothing wrong. I mean, yes, he was advocating for... for the Verlohren. He didn't spend as much time meditating as he should have, but that's no reason for him to be..."

"Defective?" Aimee's gaze trailed Chris's pacing form. "Ow, stop that," she slapped the spot next to her.

"Lost. I was going to say lost. That's what you all are, isn't it?" She halted and caught Aimee's gaze.

"In a manner of speaking. What do you know about the Verlohren?"

Chris straightened. "Everything."

"Tell me. We can compare notes."

"You asked me here to discuss the Verlohren?"

"No, but it's a good place to start."

"First answer my question. What do you want from me?"

Aimee rolled her eyes. "I told you so." She waved her hands as if dismissing something she heard. "No, that's not the same."

Chris swallowed hard. "Who are you talking to?" Her heart trembled in her chest, and she struggled to breathe. She didn't want to listen to Aimee's answer, yet she doubted she'd ever desired anything more.

"Dylan."

Chris grabbed onto the backrest of the sofa chair in front of her, fighting the tremor that coursed through her. "This can't be. I don't believe you," she whispered.

"If that were the case, you'd already left or called your goons to arrest me."

"What?"

"The Council guards."

"They are not goons, and they are not under my command."

"As if they wouldn't come running if you called."

"I can take care of myself," Chris snapped.

"I'm not doing that. Really? You try, then. Oh, right, you *can't.*"

"I'm assuming that was you talking to my brother again."

"He said I should stop baiting you."

"If he... If what you say is true, and this isn't some elaborate trick to mess with my head—"

"Why would I do that? I'd invite the heir of the Council into my house to mess with her head? We just got through a raid with no major issues. Who would want such trouble?"

"I don't know you. You could be insane. Verlohren are..." She trailed off and remained silent before taking a deep breath. "You still didn't tell me what you want from me."

"Your help. We want your help."

"About this *Demise of Reason* text? I've never heard of it."

Aimee's head fell. "Oh."

"That doesn't mean it doesn't exist," Chris added in a rush. "I... I haven't read all the texts yet. We haven't gotten to the forbidden ones yet." Chris closed her eyes, disbelieving what had just spilled from her lips. Something *was* messing with her head.

"Forbidden texts?"

Chris pinched the bridge of her nose. "Do you mind if I sit down?"

"Go ahead."

She took a seat on the sofa chair. "I'm going through Initiation still, for another eleven months, to be exact. During that time, my father will reveal all the secrets of the Council to me. There's information that only the leader is privy to, and I'm about to start the first volumes of... that section."

"Why are these texts forbidden?"

"Some are private, accounts of the history of our family."

"It seems odd to keep that a secret."

Chris shrugged her shoulders.

"You're not in the habit of sharing any of this, are you?"

"Of course not," Chris bit out and rubbed her forehead. "But if my brother..."

Aimee held her gaze. "He's here. I'm not making this up."

"I just don't understand. The Verlohren are lost souls. You... you've done something that binds you to this place."

"Yeah, that's what we're all taught."

Chris sagged in her chair. "But you're saying that's not true. That means..."

"It's difficult, I get it. I still remember all they taught us, about the Verlohren and why they are here. But when you become one, you quickly realize none of that is true."

"But it's a main tenet of our society, and it..."

"It guides everything, yes, and if *that's* not true, then—"

"How do I know that you're telling the truth? This could still be some intricate scam. If my brother is truly here with us, we should test that. I can ask you something only he would know."

"Maybe."

"There's no maybe about this. He's here and you speak the truth, or—"

"There are rules, and they are part of why we believe all of this is a lie. As a Verlohren, you cannot communicate with your loved ones. They can't even see you."

"So you say."

"Well, you don't see Dylan."

"But all I have is your word!"

"All right. As I said, there can be no contact between a Verlohren and a loved one. There is stuff that I won't be able to relay to you. Something blocks me—"

"Blocks you? You specifically or any Verlohren who would attempt this?"

Aimee nodded with a small smile. "Any Verlohren who tries will encounter this problem."

"But you sent me his message," Chris argued.

"Yes, some things don't get trapped in the net, and we haven't figured out why. But I can guarantee you, there are aspects I won't be able to tell you. Mostly anything that relates to why he's still here."

"What does that have to do with me?"

"Let's shelve that for a moment, OK? How about we see if your test works instead, and if you're convinced that I'm telling the truth, we'll get into the rest."

Chris folded her arms. "Fine."

"I kinda need your question first," Aimee said.

"What did he call me when we were little?"

"Like a nickname?"

Chris nodded.

\*\*\*

Dylan frowned. "I had several nicknames for her."

"He says he had more than one," Aimee said.

Chris raised her eyebrows but remained quiet.

She scared the living daylights out of Aimee, showing up here out of nowhere, like some infernal ghost with a fireball dancing in her hand. All pale, with narrowed green eyes, her loose blonde curls falling over her shoulders. She had to believe them. Aimee still thought Dylan overestimated their chances, but she couldn't help hoping. That had always been her downfall.

"Kitty," Dylan said.

Aimee snorted. "Really? Kitty?" Her laughter died when she noticed Chris's face turn ashen and her gaze followed two fidgeting hands balling into tight fists in the woman's lap. She did a double take; were those sparks? "Please don't burn down the house. Or us."

"What?" Chris asked, her bright eyes wide.

"Your hands." Aimee pointed at them.

"Oh, right." Chris opened and closed them. "He's really here then?"

"Yes. I didn't lie to you. I wouldn't."

"You've never promised me that," Dylan complained.

Aimee waved him off. "Whatever."

"Will you tell me now what... why he's here. And how this relates to me?"

Chris's voice sounded so small; Aimee didn't relish being the bearer of the truth. "The traditions say that people who didn't live righteous lives, who have committed crimes are punished to exist as Verlohren."

"I am quite aware of that."

"We shouldn't tell her. This will only hurt her," Dylan interjected.

"You should've considered that before dragging her into this," Aimee snapped.

"What's he saying?"

Aimee opened her mouth to speak, but her throat constricted, and her breath stuttered with shallow gasps.

Heat spread through her body, and she gritted her teeth. "I can't say. It got caught in the net."

"What does that mean?"

"I told you it's impossible for a loved one to see or communicate with a Verlohren they'd lost. This also means I cannot act as a conduit, uh, a translator. Whenever his words relate to why he became a Verlohren, none of us can utter them when one of his loved ones is nearby."

"How could I have turned Dylan into a Verlohren? Because that's what you're implying, isn't it?" Chris darted up and paced.

Aimee braced herself. She couldn't remember wanting to do something less than uttering the next few sentences. "It's our loved ones who keep us here. It's not related to anything we've done. You know this is true because you said so yourself, your brother doesn't fit the traditional criteria."

Chris halted. "Is it because he… he died because of me?"

"Stop it! Just stop it!" Dylan shouted.

"What is she talking about?"

"She didn't kill me, but she thinks she did. That she's at fault but she's not."

"That's what keeps you here. You never told me," Aimee said.

"It doesn't matter. It's not like you're so forthcoming."

"Touché."

"Hello? I'm still here. What does all this mean? Because I killed him, he's stuck as a Verlohren?" She threw her hands in the air and resumed her pacing.

"I can't tell you anything about this, but yes, it relates to you. You are keeping him here, but it's not necessarily because of what you did while he was alive. It's what happened after." Sweat poured down Aimee's back and nausea welled up inside her.

Dylan grabbed her hand and squeezed it. "Stop it. You don't need to do this."

"Are you OK?" Chris asked and stepped closer to Aimee.
"I'm fine."

A shadow fell over Chris's face. She inhaled and closed her eyes. "I must leave."

"What?" Aimee and Dylan said at the same time.

"This is... insane. I can't... This *cannot* be true. You are some sort of con artist. I don't know *how* you've learned of that nickname, but you are lying. My brother is *not* a Verlohren. Whatever you want from me? You won't get it," Chris spat and scrambled out of the room.

Aimee gazed at a shell-shocked Dylan. "Wait, what just happened?"

"No idea. This isn't like her. She was concerned for you one second and the next she was all fury and full of mistrust."

"Glad I'm not alone in thinking this was odd."

"Definitely not. Chris is very steady. She isn't moody, and she always weighs her options. She's all about reason. I've never seen her act so irrationally."

"Maybe it was too much? This is a lot to take in for anyone, but in her position?" Aimee asked.

"Yes, but it shouldn't have happened so fast. This was a complete turnaround from one second to the next. Something isn't right here."

"What if it's related to the same underlying problem?"

"Go on," Dylan said.

"None of this is right, and something is at work that not only causes this, but that also doesn't want any change to happen."

"And who has more power to affect a difference than the future Head of the Council," he said. "We need to do more research. Chris will come around."

"That would be great, but I'm not sure it's up to her alone. Hey, don't be down. We'll figure it out somehow."

"Oh, it's not that. I just... I knew she wouldn't be able to see me, and I was prepared for that."

"But?" she asked.

—

"I didn't expect how painful it would be to see her, to hear her talk, but..." Dylan's shoulders slumped.

"You still can't reach her."

"Yeah."

***

Chris raced home without taking heed of her surroundings, and instead, she acted on pure instinct. Everything within her insisted she flee. Aimee lied. She must have. Dylan had moved on. There was no way her brother was one of *them*. The Verlohren were deceitful, dysfunctional, and as much a plague on society after their death as they were before. Dylan wasn't like that. He was kind, warm, and he cared. He cared so much, even for those horrible Verlohren. And now they used him to... to what?

She deflated the moment she closed the bedroom door behind her and sank to the floor. The familiar scent of lavender and vanilla washed over her, and Chris inhaled as if she'd been starved of oxygen. At last, her mind stopped spinning.

She didn't understand what had happened. One minute she was her usual self, shaken by everything Aimee had said, but in control, contemplating the effect of Aimee's suggestions, how, if true, it would change the world. Then a haze sank over her so suddenly.

Chris pulled her legs closer to her chest and put her head down. A memory was nipping at her, tempting her to touch it, to reach out and capture it. But when she tried, her heart sped up, much like it did at Aimee's place after she'd asked the woman if she was all right.

"Calm down," she mumbled, rocking back and forth. Where did this veil, this sudden darkness and irrationality come from? It had to be connected to the Verlohren.

Whenever this topic crept up, the hairs on the back of her neck rose and she felt the vein in her temple pulsate. She never liked them or approved of Dylan's attitude, or his quests, since that meant mingling with and forgiving delinquents. Deviants.

But were they? Aimee had seemed so normal. Funny. She didn't act like a criminal. Chris remembered her eyes pleading with her to listen, to understand and believe her.

But how could she when all of this went against everything she was taught? Were the teachings lies? Were they born out of deception, ignorance, or indifference? Did any of that matter? Did her father know? Nausea once more clawed at her. He couldn't know. That would mean...

Chris coughed and lowered her head into the crook of her arm. She'd been unreasonable. There was no way for Aimee to guess that nickname. Dylan had to have been there, and that meant that... She had to research this.

She hoped the forbidden section would shed some light and offer answers, though she still needed to figure out where this haze came from because she wasn't erratic. Ever. She would not start with that now.

The next evening, Chris marched along the cool, damp cobblestone corridors and headed to the basement of the Council. Her father had agreed to let her begin the forbidden text study early, laughing at her curiosity and ambition. Well, at least that was what he'd called it. She was glad he believed her and didn't suspect or detect the true reason behind her restlessness.

She unlocked the large, gray stone door and pulled it open. At last. She had been excited to gain access from the moment she learned of its existence. Now, though, dread and anticipation warred within her. What if Aimee had been telling the truth? What if this offered proof that she'd lied? Then Dylan would be ripped from her again.

Chris ambled into the room, surprised by the soft maroon carpet beneath her feet, while her gaze gravitated to columns of bookshelves. Her eyes widened when she stepped closer to the first shelf. *Are all those forbidden texts?*

She trailed her fingers over colorful spines, some with ancient runes she struggled to translate, while old, ornate scripts, equally hard to decipher, decorated others.

She'd taken a class on ancient cursive writing, but it remained the only subject in which she'd struggled.

Chris shuddered at the cold lingering in the room and stepped to the fireplace, adding wood and kindling before opening her hand, watching the fire leap off her fingertips and trickle into the fuel. She smiled at the crackling sounds and the soothing, earthy fragrance wafting in her direction.

She rose and returned to the shelf where she'd spotted a book that had the potential to answer some of her questions. Chris drew out a volume titled *Histories of the Morgen Line*. While leafing through yellow pages, she unfolded a sheet that stretched out to the size of a poster and depicted a drawing of a family tree.

She sat down at one table and spread the book out in front of her. The tree started with Tyler Morgen, the first Head of the Council of the Living, and followed his line for eight generations, until her grandmother, Louisa Morgen. They omitted all later-born children of each heir, only listing the Head of the Council along with their spouses and the next heir. The drawing also didn't depict her immediate family, and instead, the line ended with her grandmother. Chris folded the placard and settled in her chair to read the book. She might as well start from the beginning.

The first chapters covered familiar ground while offering a few more details Chris deemed irrelevant. She sat up straighter after reading the title of chapter five, *Ancient Superstitions*. That was new. She'd never heard such tales.

Chris unzipped her backpack and fished for her notebook and pen she'd brought along, figuring that her father might miss a book, though she doubted that now, given the sheer volume of texts down here. Either way, he'd be none the wiser of any note taking, and she needed information if she planned to show up at Aimee's again.

While scribbling down summaries and transcribing whole passages, Chris lost track of time, and never registered the clanging footsteps drawing near.

"My Christina with her nose deep in books, as expected," her father's voice boomed in the room's stillness, and she startled, scratching a line across her writing before slamming her notebook shut.

"Father. I did not hear you come in."

"Naturally. I just came by to check on you. What do you think of our little library here?"

"I'm not sure I'd call it *little*."

"Yes, you must have inherited your love for anything written from our ancestors."

Chris said nothing.

"What are you reading now?"

"A volume about the history of our family."

Anthony stroked his beard. "That is a good place to start."

"Father, these old superstitions—"

"Fascinating, are they not? What hogwash people believed back in the day before Tyler brought reason to Saltung."

"Right. It's just that I've never read anything about them, and they sound... odd."

"Our family values preserving histories, but why they kept that information?" He shrugged his shoulders. "Our citizens better remain ignorant, lest we revive some of these beliefs."

"There's no truth to any of this?"

"Truth? These are lies, embellishments or folk tales to make the poor happy." He frowned. "I'm surprised you would even ask such a question."

"I apologize, sir. I was merely curious what grandmother Louisa taught you about this, back then."

"I see. Much like you, I learned about this once I gained access to the forbidden texts during my Initiation. You and I are the only two beings in existence today with knowledge of the last remaining records of this drivel."

"There are no more oral renditions among the people?"

"I doubt it. No Living for generations remembers any of this, and if you ask me, the best course of action would be to toss these books into the fireplace."

Chris shuddered and strengthened her grip on the book.

Anthony's laughter once more rang through the room. "Don't worry, my Christina. I'd never commit such a sacrilege, at least not in your presence," he said. "I shall leave you to it. Do not stay up too long. It is already past nine."

"I won't. Thank you." Chris watched the retreating back of her father, heaved a sigh of relief and released her grasp on the book. "Burning books," she groused. He was joking, she hoped, but it would be wise to remain cautious. If this was all that remained of the histories from before the rule of her House, it presented the only chance to learn a truth that seemed to have gotten lost. At best.

\*\*\*

Year 302, Day 11

"It might've been some time since I was alive, but as far as I recall, it's customary to ring the doorbell when visiting, instead of just popping up in the middle of a person's living room. What if I'd been indecent?" Aimee squinted at Chris. "Wait. Can you teleport?"

"You're living with my baby brother, so I'd hope you wouldn't parade around naked."

Aimee folded her hands in front of her chest. "We're back to believing me again. Last time, I was a liar and a trickster."

Chris cleared her throat. "Yes, well, I've been thinking, and reading. A lot of reading, and—"

"In the forbidden section?"

Chris rolled her eyes. "Can we sit down? There are things I want to show you, and... Is Dylan here?"

"Dylan!" Aimee hollered.

There was a crash upstairs, followed by a loud curse before stomping footsteps rained down the stairs.

"You hear any of this?"

"Your vociferous yell? Yes, I'm not deaf."

"Never mind," Aimee said.

"What's uh, oh, Chris is back." Dylan bounced up and down.

"He's excited to see you again."

"He is?" Chris smiled. "Wait. Why could you tell me that?"

"Not sure. I didn't even think of it, but there was no pressure, nothing. I'm guessing it's not related to what holds him back, or the system is broken."

"You truly believe there's a structure in place that prevents me from seeing him?"

"Does any of that seem natural to you?"

"What do you mean?" Chris asked.

"Let's assume I am right, and the Living hold the Verlohren in place. You can see me because I'm not your loved one. Us being able to interact helps no one."

"Right," Chris said.

"But you can't see or communicate with Dylan. The person who'd need your help to move on is unable to even *hint* at his struggles with the assistance of others. How can this be natural? Now, if no Living could see any of us, or if we could just move on without this pit stop in hell, that would be one thing, but this here? It's... cruel," Aimee said.

"It's life," Chris replied.

Dylan sighed. "There go her teachings again."

"Hmm," Aimee voiced and pointed at the couch. "You're right. This is a conversation for which we should sit down. I have to get something to eat, though."

"You eat?" Chris asked.

Dylan snorted. "You have no idea."

"I heard that," Aimee called from the kitchen.

"My question?"

"No, your brother's being an ass."

"Oh," Chris said, sitting down in the now familiar sofa chair.

Dylan sat down on the couch and kept his gaze on his sister.

Aimee joined them a moment later and settled next to Dylan. "Yes, I eat. We have to consume a lot, and it gets worse the older you are."

"Your age when you die?" Chris asked.

"No, how long you've been dead." Aimee took a big bite of her cheese sandwich.

"How long have you been a Verlohren? Or is this too personal?"

"Doesn't matter," Aimee said after swallowing. "What have you got to show us?"

"I first would like to apologize."

"It's fine. Don't worry about it."

"It's not, but I'm glad you're not holding a grudge."

Aimee grinned. "You're welcome. Now, what did you find?"

"I ventured out to, let's say, unusual texts."

"The forbidden ones. You won't die if you call them what they are."

Chris furrowed her brows.

"If anyone should be sensitive about death, it's Dylan and me," Aimee said.

"Right," Chris murmured and ducked her head. She opened her bag, grabbed her notebook, and handed it to Aimee. "Here."

Aimee laughed. "What? No summary?"

"I thought you would want to read it for yourself."

"Are those your notes?"

Chris nodded. "I've copied some passages in their entirety."

Aimee opened the pad. "Wow."

"What's it say?" Dylan asked, leaning over the notepad.

"I can't read with your enormous head in the way."

"Excuse me?" Chris said. "Oh, Dylan." She chuckled. "He never had any patience."

Aimee bumped into Dylan's side. "Tell me about it."

"Hey!"

"Hush," Aimee said, and read. She didn't get far into the notes before she frowned and sought Chris's gaze. "Superstitions? That sounds more like an alternative history."

"Yes! Right?" Chris jumped out of her seat. "I had the same impression, and I asked my father if there was any truth to this, and he said no. Old folk tales to be kept away from the masses."

"Someone sounds bitter," Dylan said.

"Let's see." Aimee trailed her finger over a line in the notebook. "Here, it says that there used to be something like... I don't understand these terms. Vergehbing and Hailen? Do you?"

"No," Dylan said.

"They tell me nothing," Chris said. "But after reading more in the book, it seems to revolve around forgiveness and healing."

"For whom?" Aimee asked. "The Sattran?"

"I'm not sure there's any healing for them. Still, this is odd because it appears to imply everyone. These tales aren't about the Verlohren or the Living, not in that sense. It's more as if there's unity, a community that seeks forgiveness and healing."

"All right, but from what?" Aimee perused the notes. "Wait, wait." She rose and stepped closer to Chris. "This here? It sounds like it refers to the Verlohren."

Chris leaned in and scanned the passage. "Hmm, could be. I called you lost, too, though it's not a common term for you."

"Better than defective," Aimee said.

Chris withdrew. "I'm sorry."

"It's fine." Aimee waved her off. "I'm sorry, too. I don't want to keep bringing this up, and... we're grateful that you came back and that you even went through the trouble of examining these books, taking notes, and all. I'm not used to interacting with..." Aimee stuffed one hand into her pocket.

"The Living?"

Aimee nodded.

"It's all right. Given how most of us treat the Verlohren..." Chris worried her lower lip. "The way I left last time didn't sit right with me. It was impossible for you to guess that name, but..." She ran a hand through her hair. "I'm not high-strung or irrational, but that night I was both."

Aimee and Dylan shared a glance.

"It's understandable. It was a lot to take in." Aimee sat back down. "May I keep these notes? I want to compare them to the old texts we've found over the last few months."

"Oh? What texts? And yes, you may keep my notebook."

"Thanks. Well, some of them mention the *Demise of Reason*, and there are several references about other lost or misplaced tomes. Some may even have been hidden."

"How did you find them?" Chris asked.

"We have our ways," she said.

"Fair enough. Will you show them to me at some point?"

"I'm pretty sure I will," Aimee said with a small smile before returning her focus to the writing in front of her.

# three

Lance entered the mansion's library. "Christina! There you are."

Chris closed the book she'd been reading and covered her notes. "Hello."

He sat down in the chair across from her. "It has been difficult to get a hold of you. I miss you."

"The Initiation takes up a lot of my time."

"Even your evenings? I have tried to reach you over several days, but you were always out. No one seemed to know where you'd gone."

"I'm not in the habit of informing people of my every move."

"I did not mean to imply that. Your mother has been worried."

"Has she? And she's confided in you?"

"Why, yes? Diane and I get along splendidly. After missing you for the third time, I inquired about your whereabouts."

"I see."

Lance folded his hands and placed them on the table. "You have many responsibilities, and no one would dare begrudge you your... evening strolls, but it would be wise to remember who you are. Some neighborhoods in Freit are more dangerous than others."

"We've been at peace for decades."

"Yes, we have. Thanks to the strong rule of your father. The Verlohren are being kept in check and the citizens are happy."

"Kept in check," Chris muttered, tapping her pen on the table. "Do you plan to join more raids?"

"Whenever I am here, of course. It is my duty as your father's future son-in-law to help protect Saltung, most of all when it relates to the Tarung."

"You make it sound like we're at war."

"Are we not? The Tarung are gaining more followers as we speak, and they are not happy with how we treat them," he scoffed. "As if they were not all criminals."

"You just agreed that we have been at peace for decades."

"Yes, but this accord comes at a price, and we must enforce it. These raids are the only way to stop more of the Verlohren from joining the Tarung. If we did not, then more radical factions would form, and—"

"Perhaps they have a point. We are not kind to the Verlohren."

Lance leaned back in his chair and stared at Chris. "You sound like your brother. I did not expect the day would arrive when *you* are questioning Morgen policy."

"I'm not doubting my father's policies. I asked you a question. You said we are at war, but I doubt my father would agree with you."

Lance laughed. "You do not know your father as well as you think you do."

Chris narrowed her eyes.

"The Verlohren are trash, and their willful act of organizing and forming the Tarung... If our vigilance ever slips, they will invade our space, devour our resources, and injure our citizens."

"What about opening a dialogue?"

"I would be careful, Christina. Your father indulged Dylan's affinity for the Verlohren because he was not the heir of the Council. I doubt he would approve of this coming from you."

"I don't have an *affinity* for the Verlohren, but they are no threat, Tarung or not."

"That would explain your nightly excursions." He sighed. "You need to watch your back. These Verlohren are full of lies, and they will not hesitate to betray you."

Her eyes widened. She placed her pen on the desk but remained silent.

"Think about my words, Christina. I am worried about you. I have not shared my concerns with your parents, yet, and I suppose it would be best if this stayed between us."

"What do you want?"

"Your time. Your affection."

Chris gritted her teeth. "We can meet the day after tomorrow for lunch."

"How about we make it a recurrent date? Every other day we have lunch together. Your parents will be so pleased."

"Fine."

"Excellent. I shall leave you to your... studies," he said and rose. "Have a good evening, Christina."

"You, too," Chris replied, her gaze glued to his leaving form. This would complicate her plans, but she'd always juggled multiple, and at times difficult and time-consuming tasks without slipping. This wouldn't be any different. She needed to find out how he tracked her, though. She tilted her head, remembering an old spell book she'd seen and skimmed through during her time with the forbidden texts. She'd have to revisit that. There might be a way.

***

Year 302, Day 16

"Woah, Princess. You need to stop doing that," Aimee exclaimed and leaped back with her hand on her chest.

"Sorry, but I had no choice," Chris mouthed.

"Why are you mumbling?"

"Is Dylan around?"

Aimee motioned behind her shoulder. "He's in the living room."

"We should talk there."

"OK." Aimee gestured for Chris to go ahead and then followed her.

Dylan raised his head when they entered and put his pencil down. "She's back."

"Sit down." Aimee pointed at the sofa chair before sitting on the couch. "So?"

"Things are becoming more complicated than expected."

"What happened?" Aimee asked.

"I had to... improvise to get here. I'm afraid someone followed me the last several times."

Aimee leaned forward. "What? Who?"

"Lance, or one of his men."

"Who is Lance?"

"Her fiancé," Dylan muttered.

Aimee's eyebrows shot up. "You're engaged?"

"Yes, thank you, Dylan," Chris replied and rolled her eyes.

"Why is your fiancé following you or sending his people after you?"

"That's a good question," Chris said. "I'd seen a subterfuge spell in one of the... They also have spell books, apparently."

"I don't understand why you can't say forbidden section anymore."

"What if that's part of what's messing with her?" Dylan asked.

"Nah. I doubt it," Aimee said.

"What do you doubt?" Chris asked.

"Doesn't matter. So this subterfuge spell made you appear in my kitchen?"

"No. Teleporting is difficult and I'm not particularly... well-versed in it. It also costs a lot of energy."

"How did it work then?"

"It sort of makes people see right through you for as long as you cast it."

"Like invisible?"

"In a manner of speaking," Chris said.

"But you appeared out of nowhere before, too. So what's different with this?"

"I'd never cast that spell before tonight. You are just not very observant."

"Hey! This is our home. You can't be on guard all the time, besides, I'm already—"

Chris interrupted her. "Yes, yes. We know. No need to keep reminding us."

Aimee leaned back. "Do we make you this uncomfortable?"

Chris rubbed her hands across her pants legs. "It's not that."

"Then what is it?"

"It doesn't matter. Not with everything that I've discovered. There are more important issues to discuss."

"Ask her more about Lance," Dylan said and made a face.

"Not a fan, huh?" Aimee asked.

"You could say that," Dylan said.

"I can't say I'm fond of missing out on all your conversations," Chris groused.

Aimee cleared her throat. "So, this Lance guy. When's the wedding?"

Chris furrowed her brows. "The day of my thirty-first birthday."

"How convenient," Aimee said and chuckled.

"Excuse me?"

"He won't have to keep track of two different dates. You know, your birthday and the anniversary? It'll be easy to remember."

Dylan snorted.

"I don't want to marry him," Chris blurted out, frowned, and then slumped down.

"Wait, what?" Dylan said.

Aimee shrugged her shoulders. "Then don't. Won't you be the new Head of the Council, anyway? Who could force you to do something against your will?"

"It's not that simple," both Chris and Dylan said simultaneously.

"That's creepy," Aimee said, and at Chris's blank stare added, "you both said the exact same thing at the same time."

A sad smiled spread over Chris's face. "Oh. I wish I could see him."

"I'm sorry," Aimee said. "Why is it not that easy?"

"I'll be a shadow leader for four more years. Once I'm thirty-five, my father will retire, and then I take over as the sole Head of Council. Until then, he outranks me."

"Your father would force you to marry someone you don't want to be with?"

"No. I don't... He..." Chris trailed off. "We've never disagreed before, at least not openly."

Aimee's eyes widened. "Wow."

"No kidding," Dylan said.

"He loves Lance, both my parents do."

"Why don't they marry him then?" Aimee asked, and Dylan shoved her arm. "What?"

"This is not a joke!" Chris rose. "I've always done everything they wanted. Been the perfect daughter, and not because I tried. I didn't have any major issues with their plans for me. I wanted to learn, to study, and I've enjoyed every aspect of my schooling."

"But?"

"I... They were so focused on education that they left my personal life, what little of it I had, alone. Until Lance."

"And that's when you no longer agreed with their plans for your future?"

"Not at first. I didn't even register it because I was so absorbed in my studies. I thought Father kept inviting Lance because he wanted to mentor him."

"And now?"

"He claims he's loved me since we were teenagers. I'd never noticed him before Father introduced us."

"He loves you?" Aimee asked.

"He says so, but when he showed up at our library two nights ago, he clarified that he knows of my frequent trips, and that I'm visiting Verlohren. Or at least he suspects that part."

"That's not good," Aimee said.

"I'm sorry. He said he'd keep it between us if I have lunch with him every other day."

"I don't like this."

"It's just lunch."

"No, I mean, yes, that's not ideal, but it's the entire situation."

"Right," Chris said.

"And you're sure he won't be any wiser about tonight's trip?"

"Relatively, yes. Like I've said, I've never performed this spell before."

"When is your next lunch with him?" Aimee asked, rubbing the pendant around her neck between her fingers.

"Tomorrow."

"We'll know by then."

"Probably," Chris said. "In the meantime, this isn't the main purpose of my visit. I've found a copy of your mystery text."

"The *Demise of Reason*? Are you serious?" Aimee vaulted off the couch.

"Why wouldn't I be?"

\*\*\*

Year 302, Day 17

"We've read this text front to back several times over now. What are we waiting for? It's clear what we need to do next," Aimee said.

"Yes, but we're missing four pages." Chris leafed through the book.

"Stop being gloomy. That's my shtick. Besides, it hints at where to find the original copy."

"It won't be easy. This book." Chris opened it toward the end. "I don't trust it."

Aimee raised her eyebrows. "*You* don't trust a book?"

———

59

Chris jutted her jaw. "I don't have faith in *this* book. Who wrote it? There's no author. Why wouldn't anyone want to claim it?"

"They could have feared being persecuted for telling the truth," Aimee said.

"What truth? This book is full of riddles, and when it seems to have useful information for a change, the pages are missing!"

"Look, Princess, I've been at this for almost a decade! This is a huge triumph, just having access to it, having it here. It's not perfect, nothing ever is." Aimee raised her hands. "Let me finish. This was never going to be easy. We'll solve the riddles and search for the original text along with the artifacts mentioned in the book."

"We don't even know what those items are. This could be some elaborate prank," Chris said.

"It's not, OK!"

"Forgive me for being cautious!"

"Could you guys stop fighting," Dylan grumbled. "It's messing with my concentration."

"Tell your sister that!"

Both siblings glared at Aimee.

"This sucks."

"Indeed," Chris said.

"It'll be all right. We will get a hold of the original, and the missing pages could tell us what these artifacts are."

"Right. They might even explain the purpose of all of this," Chris said.

"That's the spirit."

Chris scowled. "That was sarcasm."

"Yes, and I chose to ignore it."

"You guys are horrible." Dylan placed his pen down. "We just need to get started. Go on the first mission and see."

"I agree with him."

"How convenient. You can tell me anything that he supposedly said, and I have no way of verifying it!"

"Woah, slow down, Princess."

"Stop calling me that!"

"I'm sorry. I swear, I won't lie to you, and never about Dylan."

Chris sat back down. "Fine. What did he say?"

"That we need to get started and see?"

Chris covered her face with her hands. "Of course he did," she complained. "I'm surrounded by children who will rush headfirst and without a plan into danger just to *see* what happens."

"Hey!" sounded from both Aimee and Dylan.

*\*\*\**

Year 302, Day 20

"Are you up for some sparring?" Terry asked, entering the library.

A book slipped from Chris's hands, and she bit out a low curse when she bent to pick it up. "I swear, you move so silently, it's scary."

Terry shrugged his shoulders. "Years of practice."

"I want to spar again, but I'm onto something here, and I'd like to finish that first. In an hour?"

He sat down next to her. "Sure. What are you looking for?"

"I've been doing research on the Verlohren."

"What for?"

"I'm not so sure anymore that our... that society's perception of them is accurate."

"That makes little sense. You've always followed the teachings of the House of Morgen, and our histories are clear on this topic."

"But what if that's not the entire picture?" Chris asked, tapping her pen on the notebook.

"What do you mean? You're not talking about the Tarung? They are dangerous. The Sattran?"

"All of them, but I'm mainly talking about the general Verlohren, not... not the rebels or the shadow ones."

"What does your research say so far?"

---

"It's frustrating. There's not much more out there than the regular talk: deviant, can't be killed, feeling pain, slow to heal, avoiding sunlight, attracted to wetlands. That kind of thing."

"Also, treacherous liars, thieves, and bound to sudden outbursts of violence?"

"Yes, but—"

"There are *no* buts, Chris. The Verlohren aren't your company to keep."

"Who says I'm keeping their company?"

Terry leaned back. "A figure of speech. You can't find any other information on the Verlohren because that's all they ever were. The dregs of society, both while they were living and now in death. Regular folks don't get condemned to such a life."

Chris lowered her head. "Right."

"Come on! Dylan used to talk about how misunderstood the Verlohren are, and perhaps this is your way of mourning your brother, and I'm all for that. But I'm afraid this will just lead to disappointment."

Her gaze fell. "I still want to read a little longer. Meet you in the dojo in an hour?"

"As you wish," he said and left.

\*\*\*

Year 302, Day 21

A small frown crossed Aimee's features. "This will be a long trip."

"Do Verlohren have any travel restrictions?" Chris asked. Weren't they sensitive to sunlight?

"What? No, we don't burn in the sun or avoid foggy lowlands. Those are old Living folktales. I'm concerned about you."

"About me?"

"Yeah, this will be quite the hike, and aren't you bound here with all this Initiation business?"

"Right, but if you postponed your trip by about a week, or let's say ten days, it wouldn't be a problem. Though we'd have to meet in Salbit."

"Huh?"

Silence.

"Again, huh? Is this about the convent?" Aimee asked.

"I'm surprised Dylan even remembers this. There are times during the Initiation where I must retreat to a sanctuary for meditation. The first trip is coming up soon, and it'll last a week."

"Won't they miss you there?" Aimee asked.

Chris smiled. "No, it's a solitary visit with the goal to live there in seclusion."

"What about food?" Aimee said and after a beat, glared at the empty couch.

"I have a kitchen and pantry there. They'll stock it before my arrival."

"And they wouldn't notice you leave?"

"Not with my subterfuge spell. It turned out to be quite successful. Lance was pleased that I'd listened and stopped my 'nocturnal excursions,'" Chris spat the last two words.

"I take it you didn't enjoy your lunches so far," Aimee said.

"He's... difficult to be around."

"Wait until you're married." Aimee rubbed her shin. "Ow, stop that."

"What happened?"

"Dylan's defending you. Asking me to stop being rude to you," Aimee grumbled.

"He's always done that," Chris replied with a small smile. "And for the record, I haven't decided whether I'll go through with the wedding. What you said, about me being the future Head of the Council? It makes sense. No one should force this on me!"

"Good on you," Aimee said.

"Yes, well, my parents remain uninformed of this consideration."

"One step at a time, Princess."

"I don't like how he talks about you."

"He knows about me?"

"No, not you, specifically. The Verlohren in general, but his real focus is on the Tarung. He keeps telling me they are dangerous and that we need to control them, or they'll take over and ruin Saltung. Have you... have you had any contact with the Tarung?"

"Nah, I prefer to be on my own. Stop it." She slapped the air next to her.

"Do you know anyone who belongs to them, or what their end goal is?"

Aimee frowned. "You're not by any chance a spy who is here to blow up the Tarung?" Aimee sputtered. "Knock it off. I'm not insulting your sister!"

"You were a bit, but I understand. You haven't known me that long and given my position, I'd say you have every right to be suspicious."

"There you go. See?"

"No. To answer your question, I'm not a spy. I have no interest in sharing anything we are doing here with anyone at home, or the school, and even less the Council."

"That's good."

"I just... During my entire education, they taught me that the Verlohren are bad, or, not bad, but... wrong?"

"Yes, remember, we're all taught that, but trust me, it's not true. Sure, there are some Verlohren who are not that trustworthy, but to be honest, there aren't too many shady people among us. This only gives credence to the idea that our loved ones keep us here. Criminals, the real bad ones, they don't have strong social or familial bonds."

Chris hummed in agreement.

"And about the Tarung, they're not terrible. They also believe things need to change, though they're more pro-active about it. They *demand* change, and they... I'm not sure. I doubt they will become violent, but there's a lot of anger among us. And pain."

"You're right. Hopefully, we will find a solution before the situation with the Tarung escalates."

"On that note, let's get back to work. We split up, so Dylan travels with Markus to get the original copy of the *Demise of Reason,* and you and I will go to the Thal mountains looking for the first artifact. Sounds good?"

"Why are we splitting up?" Chris asked. "Wait, Markus? You don't mean our gardener Markus?"

"Uh, yes. He says that's the one."

"Oh, wow. He's a great guy," Chris said.

"As for going in teams, we need to cover a lot of ground and it's easier in smaller groups. We already attract attention, and this would be even worse if people see you traveling with more than one Verlohren."

"But I can't see Dylan!"

"Yes, but other Living can."

Chris closed her eyes for a long moment. "Right. He'll be safe with Markus?"

"It's never safe when we leave the house," Aimee said. "But since... Well, you know? It'll be OK."

"Thank you."

"Sure, sure," she said. "Let's make a more detailed plan and also decide when and where we'll meet up." Aimee's head jerked up, and she spun around. "What? Are you serious?" She darted in front of the windows. "Shit."

"What's going on?"

"A raid, by your people," Aimee grunted, never taking her gaze off the approaching guards.

"That's impossible. I'd have known." Chris pursed her lips. "Lance."

"Your boyfriend's not as trusting as you thought he was, huh?" Aimee sniped.

"Hush. Come here, both of you. Gather all the materials that we need to hide and place them between us."

"Why?"

"Hurry! Do you want to get caught?" Chis almost shouted.

"Fine," Aimee muttered. "Dylan, find my backpack upstairs. It contains everything else we don't have down here." She flung books, maps, and notepads onto the coffee table. "Now what?"

"Is Dylan back yet?" Chris asked, while Aimee's gaze seemed to track his movements. Then a backpack appeared on the table, seemingly out of nowhere.

"Yes."

"Sit down, both of you. I need Dylan to sit next to you, and you must hold his hand. Whatever happens, don't move. Don't talk, and most importantly, do *not* let go of him."

Aimee sat down. "All right"

Chris stared at Aimee's left hand, laying open on the couch between her and an empty space. A space her brother occupied, but she couldn't see him. Or feel him. He was still lost to her.

"Now what?"

Chris started and turned her gaze to Aimee. "Give me your hand." She held out her arm.

Aimee hesitated before relenting and reaching out.

Chris released a harsh breath when Aimee grasped her hand. She'd expected Aimee's skin to be cold and clammy, but it wasn't. Instead, a warm, smooth grip intertwined their fingers. Not at all in-line with how Verlohren were supposed to feel. She made a mental note to contemplate this further another time and concentrated on casting the guarding spell.

"What are you doing?" Aimee asked, but Chris shook her head and clutched the woman's hand, hoping she'd get the message and be quiet.

Aimee narrowed her eyes but remained silent.

Heat rushed through Chris, flowing through her arm into Aimee, who shuddered but still said nothing. Her gaze fastened on Chris.

The door burst open and three men with heavy footsteps stormed inside.

"Spread out," Lance called. "This is where Lady Christina is being held."

Chris glared when Aimee opened her mouth before swallowing a sigh when no words fell from her lips.

Lance remained in the living room, his gaze wandering over the couches and bookshelves. He strode forward and glanced into the kitchen before returning and halting behind a seat, placing both hands on the backrest.

"Sir, the house is empty. No one in sight."

"Did you check all closets and attic crawlspaces?"

"I inspected them myself, and Frank is still searching the attic."

Lance remained quiet.

"Should we torch it?" the man asked.

Chris increased her hold on Aimee, willing the other woman to keep silent. More heat spiked within her and spread once again, making Aimee flinch.

"No. These animals could hide my fiancée in this shack somehow. I will not risk her life."

"Our intel was wrong, then?"

"No. They had followed her here for several nights, and there are two Verlohren squatting in the house," Lance said.

Aimee gritted her teeth and Chris tightened her grip.

"They could have taken her to a different hideout."

"Possibly," he said. "Go check on Frank."

He saluted. "Aye, sir."

"Where are you hiding, Christina? You are here somewhere," Lance grumbled. "Why are you spending so much time with this scum?" He stepped closer to a shelf and inspected the books.

"Sir, the crawlspaces are empty."

"All right. We shall head back home and confer with our investigators again."

"What about Lord Morgen?" Frank asked.

"What about him?" Lance's voice dropped a register.

"Shouldn't he be informed about this?"

"What makes you think he is not already aware?"

"Of course, sir."

"Let us leave this dump," Lance spat and marched out of the house, followed by the rest of the men.

The door fell shut.

Chris waited, she counted to one hundred in three languages before releasing Aimee's hand. "Thank you for being so patient."

Aimee nodded but avoided her gaze.

"We should finalize our plan another time. I should head back and be home before Lance gets there."

"You do that, Princess."

Chris winced but left. She understood Aimee's ire, but her stomach had plummeted at the ice that had fallen over the other woman's demeanor. When Lance had slammed the door, Chris's entire focus had rested on Aimee, though the woman hardly seemed to notice her.

Her dark mahogany-colored eyes had glinted with a chilling emptiness that Chris had never experienced before. She shuddered at the memory. Would Aimee still want Chris to accompany her on the journey to the Thal mountains?

Would they leave without her, and one time soon, she'd arrive at their house only to find it empty? What if Lance returned and set the house on fire after all? Should she put a protective spell on it? Or would that make them an even bigger target? The threat to their... not lives, but... She'd never seen Aimee's markings. Not that Aimee would have any reason to show her.

Chris cleared her throat and turned around. Her gaze once more trained on their house. She'd have to risk it.

She'd never forgive herself if she left them without protection and then they burned.

Chris had to admit that not all her information about the Verlohren was accurate, but that they healed slower and didn't die of their injuries still seemed a safe bet. Even Aimee had joked that they were already dead and couldn't perish again. That didn't mean they couldn't be hurt.

Chris worried her lower lip and raised her hands. She closed her eyes and channeled all her energy into the protection spell. The house lit up for an instant before once more standing shrouded in darkness. She smiled. Her inaction would never again make her brother suffer.

***

"What's wrong with you? Why did you kick her out like that?" Dylan asked with a frown spreading over his features as he crossed his arms.

"We need to forget about her. She's only going to create problems."

"Have you lost your mind? She is the reason we have access to the *Demise of Reason*, the text we've been hunting down for months, you for much longer on your own. Chris found that! She brought it here, even though this could get her into so much trouble!"

"I understand that she's your sister, and yes, she has helped us, but Dylan, the risk isn't only on her. Who will receive a harsher deal when this blows up? The future Head of the Council or two Verlohren?"

"I am still a Morgen."

"Too bad no one can vouch for that since your family can't see you."

"I'm well aware of that. You need to stop acting like I'm stupid."

"Then don't *be* stupid!"

"Nice, Aimee. And you wonder why you've spent the last eight years alone."

"I never asked you to join me! You're the one who followed me like a lost puppy when you ran into me at the market, babbling on about how great it is to meet a familiar face and if we couldn't work together, blah, blah, blah. That wasn't me!"

"You didn't put up much of a fight either!"

"You were a persistent puppy."

"Stop calling me a dog!"

"Look, I'm not saying this to hurt you, and it must mean a lot to be near your sister, but—"

"It's painful, actually."

"What?"

"She's here but we cannot interact. I notice the strain she's under, and she'd blame it all on the Initiation, and sure, that's part of it."

"But?"

"Chris is still torturing herself over what happened. How she didn't save me. Then there's Lance. I knew she never wanted to be with him, though it surprised me when she said that out loud. She's different when you're around. Less guarded."

"Sure," Aimee scoffed.

"I'm serious."

"If that's less guarded..."

"Right? Then again, you don't get to complain given how you act all the time."

"Whatever. Besides, I didn't like that spell. All the heat. It felt like my insides were vibrating."

"What are you talking about?"

"The magic she performed to hide us from Lance and his guards. You didn't feel it?"

"No."

"Maybe it's because you were holding my hand, while I was directly connected to her?"

"I doubt it. I've never felt her magic."

"Weird. I'd wondered if it might be a Verlohren thing or something."

"You could ask her if you'd deign to talk to her again."

"I didn't say I never want to see her again," Aimee grumbled.

"Either way, yes, this was a close one, but keep in mind that Chris protected us."

"From a danger *she* brought upon us."

"You said yourself that we're always at risk. This wasn't the first time we've escaped a raid. Remember the last time and where we had to seek shelter?"

Aimee shuddered. "Don't remind me."

"At least with Chris, we also have her fire power. When you guys go after the artifact, she'll be useful to have around. Your mission is much more dangerous than ours. You can't do it alone, and time is of the essence here."

"You're right."

"I should mark that in my calendar, the day Aimee said I'm right."

She threw a pillow at him. "Stop being such an unbearable smartass."

"You all right again?"

"I was never not all right."

Dylan laughed. "Sure."

"I'm hungry, though."

"Tell me something new."

"That it's old doesn't make it wrong."

"Go get some food then. I'm not your maid."

"No, but you're a much better cook than I am."

"Anyone is."

"True." Aimee rose and sauntered into the kitchen.

"Aimee," Dylan called.

She turned around.

"You're gonna take Chris with you, right?"

She grunted her agreement. "She'll be on the way, anyway. Might as well." Aimee shrugged and opened the fridge.

"Yeah, not to mention she'll probably save your ass a lot," Dylan said under his breath.

"I heard that!"

He gathered up their notepads and books. "Better not leave this lying around."

\*\*\*

"Christina! Are you all right?" Lance hurried toward Chris the moment she entered her parents' mansion.

"Of course. Why wouldn't I be?"

"We had received reports that several Verlohren had abducted you and were holding you hostage. I was about to organize another search party, this time with the mage sages in attendance."

"That won't be necessary, but I appreciate your concern. How did you say you've obtained the information about my non-existing abduction?"

"I did not. The intelligence section of the Council works best if few are informed of their sources and methods." Lance's gaze focused on her bag.

She crossed her arms. "Yet *you* are aware of them."

"It falls under the purview of my current role as the temporary commander of the Council guard."

"I see," Chris seethed. He'd rankled her during their lunches, but the pure nerve of this man! She couldn't fathom why her parents believed he'd make an excellent match.

Lance stood straighter. "I thought we had established a set of conditions, and that certain areas and… influences are too dangerous for you to expose yourself to, especially at night."

Chris frowned. "We agreed to have lunch together every other day. You are in no position to dictate my movements or associations."

"These are perilous times, Christina. We are to be wed, and it will be our duty to create the next line of Morgen heirs. How will this occur if you are injured, if you disappear, or even worse, if you were to die?"

"I'm not sure Verlohren can procreate," Chris said unmoving.

"There is no need to be glib. This is a serious situation."

"This isn't a *situation* at all. Our intelligence section received incorrect information. I wasn't snatched, and I've never been in any danger."

"Where have you been?"

Chris only stared at him.

"I shall have to inform your parents about these nightly excursions of yours," Lance said.

"Do what you must." Chris loosened her rigid grip on the strap of her bag before turning and heading toward her room, but Lance's next words froze her on the spot.

"I suppose you will not mind my guards returning to the Verlohren shack our intelligence section offered as the home of the would-be perpetrators of your foiled capture?"

Chris ground her jaw but didn't turn. Instead, she resumed her steps and strolled to her room. There was no reason to offer Lance more proof of how his words had rattled her.

She'd placed a protective spell on their house, and she trusted her magic, but success or failure also depended on the assault he had planned. If he made good on this threat, would he only bring the guards or the mage sages as well?

Chris paced in her room. Her parents were out and wouldn't return until the next day. There was no way to warn Aimee, aside from returning there, but given how she'd left? Still, she couldn't allow them to get hurt because they'd gotten into an argument.

Her subterfuge spell held, or didn't it? Lance likely knew of the place from when he had her followed earlier, before their lunch agreement. Yet, he kept spying on her.

—

She hated doing this, and she'd pay for it later, but there was no other option. She locked her room door, grabbed her bag, and heaved a sigh. Chris despised teleportation, aside from depleting her energy like nothing else, it made her queasy. She closed her eyes, turned inward, and teleported to the woods behind Aimee's house, having cast the subterfuge spell right before teleporting.

The moon shone high and bright, illuminating the landscape before her. Chris focused on the howling of an owl and the sound of the wind rustling through the leaves to distract from the nausea rumbling through her.

She took a deep breath and hummed. She had always loved the forest, its stillness away from all that was Freit, though she also enjoyed the woodsy smoke rising from the chimneys of several of the surrounding homes.

Aimee's house stood silently in the dark. There were lights on, but she couldn't detect any movement inside. Were they already sleeping? Not that she'd see her brother. Chris's shoulders slumped. She tried not to contemplate this situation, since it spread a heaviness through her that made her sluggish and yearn to sit in a corner and cry.

Time passed and Chris wished she could allow her flames to warm her. She hoped she wouldn't have to spend all night out here. The moment she chided herself for not bringing a book to read, the soft murmur of voices drew near. Were they coming through the woods?

Chris craned her neck to gaze into the coppice but only darkness greeted her at first, then flickering lights edged closer, followed by six Council guards, and, at the back, Lance.

She ground her jaw and stepped to the side.

The men crouched and crept over the field toward Aimee's house.

What were they going to do? At least there were no mage sages in sight.

Chris tracked their movements and trailed after them at a safe distance.

The two guards at the rear carried heavy backpacks, but she couldn't make out their contents.

"Commander, should we set up the perimeter here? The soil ahead is dry enough for the fire to grow and move toward the house. By the time it reaches its target, it'll already be strong."

"That is a good plan. Get started," Lance said and oversaw the guards pouring liquid zinder on the ground around the back of the property.

Chris halted and observed their progress. She scrambled for spells to extinguish a major fire, and her mind went blank. The habit of starting fires seemed to have drowned out any memories of useful counter-spells. Was it possible to use ice much in the same way? She was still lost in thought when a guard lit a match and flicked it on the ground into the saturated soil.

Bright flames blazed in the air and leapt forward, the accelerator speeding up the charge. The column of fire crackled and twisted as smoke billowed, and Chris fell back to avoid inhaling the fumes the wind blew in her direction.

The fire marched on before lurching as if it crashed into a stone barrier. It grew taller, but the forward momentum stalled.

"What happened? Why does it stop there?" a guard asked, inching closer to the angry shrieking but trapped wall of fire. The plumes climbed higher and trembled with their orange glow illuminating the night sky.

Chris raised her head and smiled. Her magic held. But what if this made it all worse? What if it showed Lance how invested she was in these two Verlohren?

Perhaps the house should burn? Chris worried her lower lip as her mind danced over spells and incantations, dismissing the first series of contenders, and instead dug deeper, trying to remember charms she'd only glanced at once and rejected.

Blinking rapidly, she smiled. Yes, that would work.

She raised her hands and whispered the incantation for the embild spell, one of the most invasive magics in her repertoire, and a tint darker than she preferred to venture.

It infiltrated the minds of her targets and created visual hallucinations. People would see what they wanted to see. Here, they'd perceive the house of two Verlohren engulfed in flames.

"Go closer. Light it up directly," Lance growled and followed the guards' trek to the house. They poured more zinder onto the wooden frames and once again struck a match that died as soon as it was lit. More matches met the striker but to no avail until the last one appeared to hold a flame.

Chris held her breath and drew closer.

The guard cupped the dancing ember and squatted to connect it to the accelerator, but instead of blazing, the fire died the moment it touched the wood.

"Finally," he shouted and faced Lance. "This should do it. The wind coming up will turn this into an inferno, sir."

Lance stood silent, his gaze locked on the house before he turned his head and gazed at Chris who flinched before she remembered he couldn't see her. He released a sharp exhale and returned his focus to the guards. "This won't kill the vermin inside, but it will make them scutter off, into the night and far away from my fiancée."

"Yes, sir. Should we continue the watch you'd ordered even though the house is burning down?"

"No, we will move those resources elsewhere. Big things ahead." He smiled and marched after the guards.

"What are you up to now?" Chris muttered, tearing her gaze away to check on the house again. Still no flames.

\*\*\*

Thal Mountains, Saltung
Year 302, Day 25

"Why are we working with him? He's vile, and what they are doing at those Centers, Lara, this is taking things too far!" Lily said.

Lara sighed. "You've always been such a bleeding heart."

"You weren't in that room. You didn't see it." She closed her eyes. "They were in such pain. I understand the markings are important and that there's only the one way, but this is torture. That's not better than—"

"No!" Lara jumped up. "Don't you *dare* say that! There's *no* comparison. Why would you even bring that up?"

"I'm sorry. I don't like Lance, and the idea of him getting married to Chris? It disturbs me. But when we went to the Center, and—"

"At your insistence! You wanted to check them out, and we did. Why can't you let it go? What other choice do we have? I'm sick of discussing this."

"There has to be another way. Hasn't the past output of the markings been enough? We don't need an increase."

Lara laughed. "That's not why they do this."

"What do you mean?"

"I didn't order this. They did this on their own."

"But why? They are already more powerful than the Verlohren. What we did made sure of that."

"It's what it always comes down to, Lily. Fear. They are afraid and they have the power to walk the path that fear demands."

"We could do something about it, though."

"That's not why we're here. There'll always be victims, Lily. We just have to make sure it'll never be us again."

* * *

Freit, Saltung<br>Year 302, Day 28

Chris wasn't sure how she'd be received when she returned to Aimee's place. She didn't even know if the other woman or her brother had been aware of the fire that, thank the Gods, refused to start the other night. Still, this encounter had made her realize that they needed a more efficient form of communication, and so she'd spent some time working on a solution.

——

She once more let herself in without knocking because, well, why break a habit, especially since she delighted in flustering Aimee. Though once she stepped inside, Chris wondered if that had been such a great idea, given how they'd parted last. Yet, Aimee once more surprised her by offering a greeting that indicated that nothing was amiss.

"Hey, what you're doing here? I thought you'd be knee-deep in preparations for your convent stay?" Aimee asked.

"What? Oh, you don't have to prepare much for a meditation session, especially one that doesn't take place. I'm assuming that's still the plan? To go there together?"

"Yes, Princess. That's still the plan."

"Good. Anyway, I thought of a more useful method of communication," Chris said as she pulled out a leather-bound notebook. "I've enchanted this, and well, I've made it that you and anyone of my blood line can read it, but only you will be able to write in it. Whatever you write, I see. I have the same copy."

"Oh, that's awesome." Aimee reached out for the booklet. "How do I know that you've written, though?"

"They open to the new page once we write something."

"Ah, OK. So, I just gotta place it somewhere where I'll be a lot, like on the coffee table here."

"That should work," Chris said.

# four

"I was about to leave without you," Aimee drawled, startling Chris, whose gaze had roamed across the seemingly barren clearing.

"And you complain about me sneaking up on people."

"Not people. Just me. Besides, I was sitting right under this tree there." Aimee pointed behind her. "Are you ready?"

"Why else would I be here?"

"I meant, no one followed you and all that?"

"No one noticed I was leaving, so it's safe to assume no one did."

"Famous last words and all."

"I'm happy to see you have recovered from your moody disposition."

Aimee laughed.

"How's… What about Dylan?"

"He's fine. He and Markus left yesterday, heading toward the Troken ocean."

"How will we know that they're OK?"

Aimee shrugged her shoulders. "If they show up at the meeting when we get back."

"Don't act so blasé. You care about him, and I *finally* recognized you. You seemed familiar from the start, but I just couldn't place you. Then I remembered. You taught Dylan for a couple of years. Right?"

"I was his tutor."

"I *knew* it."

"All right. Let's head out. It's a long journey until we get to our first stop, and though it's still in the woods, it's much closer to the mountain range. Any chance you can teleport us there?"

---

"That will be for emergencies only, if I manage at all given that we're moving into unfamiliar terrain." Chris fastened her backpack straps and marched ahead of Aimee, following the path into the Harrows Forest.

"I have faith in you, Princess." Aimee chuckled and followed her, unaware of the blush that spread over Chris's face.

A few sun rays wriggled their way through the thicket, producing flashing shadows on the ground. Along the trail lay fallen logs in various stages of decay, homesteads for wood beetles and spiders scuttling about, while a murmuring brook meandered through the nearby grove.

Chris inhaled deeply. She much preferred this march through the forest than her nocturnal jaunt and observation of would-be fire-starters last week. She should have told Aimee, but this would only lead to another argument, both about the deeds of the guards and Lance's role in it, and Chris's presumption to create a magical barrier around Aimee's house. Never mind that it had spared them both the agony of being burned and the loss of their home.

Aimee kept a steady pace, but her keen eyes reacted to every out-of-place noise.

"Aren't you worried about the Sattran? I've done more research and the Thal mountains are one of the areas that see the most activity," Chris asked after they had been hiking in silence for a while.

"Nah. We won't travel at night, and they'll avoid the sunlight as much as possible."

"Perhaps that's where these myths came from, that the Verlohren hate or avoid the sun."

Aimee grunted but said nothing.

Chris wanted to slap herself. Why did she say that? This would be a sore topic for someone like Aimee. She kept forgetting that Aimee wasn't like her—that she was a Verlohren. "I'm sorry. I didn't mean to upset you," Chris said after another stretch of quiet wandering through the forest.

"You didn't. I just don't like thinking about the Sattran."

"I understand."

"Do you? What do you know about them?"

"You're always asking me what I know."

"And you've yet to answer any of my questions." Aimee sounded amused.

"Fine. The Sattran once were Verlohren. Usually, Verlohren disappear after a while, according to our teachings, that happens after they've atoned for the sins that had kept them here."

"Of course," Aimee scoffed.

"You don't agree?"

"Not at all, but do continue. I want to hear the rest."

Chris grumbled. "The Sattran are stuck here forever because they refuse to atone. They reject to right what they've done wrong while alive. So, they haunt abandoned places, mostly far off from the Living. Some say they're cannibals, but I never believed that."

Aimee rolled her eyes. "Want to know my version?"

"Yes."

"I've already told you it's the Living who tie us to this existence, so it has nothing to do with anything *we've* done. There's no sin we need to atone for. We will move on whenever the Living who binds us lets us go. That still works for the Sattran, too."

"Oh," Chris exhaled and halted.

Aimee turned around and stopped as well. "What?"

"That's what I'm doing to Dylan? I'm keeping him here?"

"Yes, but let's not talk about that now."

"Why?"

"Because then you'll get all emotional, we'll fight and lose precious time. Not to mention that even trying to discuss this will cause me pain. Besides, I'm assuming you still wanna join me in looking for the artifact?"

"Yes, I want to help you find something we know nothing about."

"All right. Back to the story," Aimee said, and they resumed their travel.

"One last thing, though," Chris said.

"OK?"

"I don't want you to suffer, in general, but especially not because of me." Chris held Aimee's gaze.

"Oh. OK. That's… That's good. I appreciate it."

"Yes, well. Continue."

Aimee snorted. "The Sattran are Verlohren who have lost their minds."

"Excuse me?"

"We are bound to *you*, to the loved one who cannot move on. If they never manage to make peace with our passing, well, we're stuck here until they die, then we're released and disappear."

"To where?"

"No one knows, but everyone hopes it's better than here. Should be easy enough."

"You sound so bitter."

"Uh, because I am?"

"Being a Verlohren can't be easy, but—"

"No kidding, Princess. Think about how the Living see us, how they treat us, and what they say about us. Then you have the raids led by your wonderful fiancé—"

"He's not leading them."

"Not the point," Aimee growled.

"Go on."

"Our existence sucks. We are cut off from everyone we've ever loved. We have no influence over how long we are stuck in this limbo, and… We can't work our original jobs, only tasks the Living don't wanna do. There's no… We live, but we are *dead*. We don't take part in anything that used to make us feel *something*. Our bodies are crap, too."

"That sounds harrowing. I'm sorry. Growing up, that's not what we learned about the Verlohren. No written works tell that story either."

"They taught us all the same lies."

"Is everything our society believes about the Verlohren a lie?" Chris asked.

"Most of it. The Sattran, they couldn't handle it, and most of them have been Verlohren for decades. A lot of them were children when they died, and they don't grow. You don't age. Some of them… They never learned to adjust."

"What happens then?"

"They become shadows, or what we call the Sattran. The sun doesn't hurt us, though it can cause horrible headaches. We are dead, so our bodies don't work exactly like yours."

Chris shot a quick glance at Aimee. "Does this trip hurt you? If it's easier for you, we could sleep during the day and walk at night."

"No, I'm fine. I can handle the sun. Besides, traveling during the night through this forest or the mountains isn't safe, not for me, and even less for you."

"You always forget that I'm a mage."

"Oh, I don't, Princess. I never forget that."

***

They arrived at their first stop after several hours of hiking.

Aimee halted and pointed at an overhang strutting out below a flat stone surface that offered some protection from the elements. "We should set up camp here."

"How close are we to the mountains?" Chris asked, placing her backpack on the ground.

"About another day's walk, if we go the same pace we did today. You're up for that?"

"Of course."

"These woods are vast. Still, this is a covered area, and there's nothing quite like this ahead of us."

"I agree. We should stay here for the night."

"Great," Aimee said, opening her rucksack.

"You brought a tent?"

Aimee raised her head and her eyes sparkled. "Not a big fan of sleeping out in the open, or on the bare ground."

"Thank you. That didn't even cross my mind."

Aimee chuckled. "No worries." She unpacked the tent. "Help me set this up? Hey, you got a spell for that?"

"I don't think so. Besides, I rather save my energy just in case."

"Sounds like a plan."

They erected the tent and created a fire pit amidst a ring of stones Chris had scavenged.

"You're a convenient fire starter to have around," Aimee said, leaning against the wall.

Chris snorted. "I bet."

Aimee rummaged through her bag before handing Chris a sandwich. "Here. Do you eat meat? It's chicken."

"Thanks. I eat most things."

"Good to know."

Aimee laughed when Chris rolled her eyes and ducked her head. She would never say this out loud, but she was glad for Chris's company, and not just because she was a mage. Hiking left her alone with her thoughts, and that was not a comfortable space for her.

These last eight years, she'd hoped, ever since the day when... Aimee gritted her teeth. Since the moment she became a Verlohren and realized that everything they'd taught her was a lie, she'd searched for answers. They'd been scarce, in part because she'd never been great at making friends or interacting with strangers.

After several years of empty leads, Aimee had found a few clues about the *Demise of Reason*, and how this manuscript would hold all the answers, but she couldn't help wondering: what questions, and who had penned the text?

She'd acted as if she felt comfortable with the book and its riddles, because despite all her misgivings, she still wanted to see this thing through, and if she'd shown any doubts, Chris would never have tagged along.

She'd bumped into Dylan right after her research had yielded more solid leads. He'd been a welcome sight—another thing Aimee would never admit. His presence had made this entire ordeal more bearable. Her thoughts revolved less around death when either Morgen sibling was nearby, even though she didn't right away acknowledge that with Chris. Her eyelids drooped, and she yawned before scooting down into a more comfortable position.

They continued their journey the next morning, and by midday, they took a break under the last trees visible for miles.

Chris wiped her forehead. "Are you sure you're OK walking in this heat?"

"I'm fine. I'll tell you when it becomes a problem."

"Mmhmm," Chris said with raised eyebrows.

"I told you I won't lie to you."

"Right. What does your map say?" Chris scooted closer and leaned over the spread-out chart of Saltung.

"We are about nine miles away from the general location of the artifact. If everything goes according to plan, we should arrive in around three hours."

"Are you expecting trouble?" Chris asked.

"Always. Remember what you said about this area and the Sattran?"

"I thought you didn't believe Living information on the Verlohren."

"I don't buy their histories, but yeah, these mountains see a lot of Sattran activity. Most Verlohren avoid this place."

"Are they that dangerous to you?"

Aimee took a swig from her water bottle. "Not physically."

A fireball sprang from Chris's palm. "Do they like fire?"

Aimee coughed and sat up straighter. "I doubt it," she grumbled.

Chris smiled. "Good."

"That's one scary smile."

"Thank you!"

"Not sure that was a compliment," Aimee murmured and returned her container to her backpack. "Ready to go?"

Chris rose. "To the caves with the mystery item that might kill us? You bet."

"You're so dramatic. Dylan must get that from you. Little siblings always wanna be like their older brothers or sisters."

"Oh, you speak from experience?"

Aimee played with the pendant on her necklace. "No."

"I'm sorry. I keep doing this."

"It's fine. Besides, I'm pretty hard to kill."

"Ugh." Chris bumped into Aimee. "I wish you'd stop saying that."

Aimee held her gaze. She couldn't remember the last time someone seemed so concerned about her, and she wasn't sure what to do with the feelings that this realization unearthed.

***

After over three uneventful hours of walking, they arrived at the mountain area that hid the cavern the *Demise of Reason* had referenced. The sun dipped low, wending toward the horizon, and edged closer to setting than Aimee would have liked when they noticed a dark shadow on the side of a rocky outcropping.

"Are you sure this isn't a trap?" Chris asked.

Aimee trod toward the entrance. "No."

Chris crept behind her. "That's not reassuring."

"Only one way to find out." Aimee lowered her head, about to enter the cave when Chris grabbed her arm.

"Let me go in first."

"No way," Aimee exclaimed. "You're alive."

"Yes, and I have this." Chris conjured a fire ball in her palm.

"What if what's in there is immune to fire?"

"Something that's impervious to fire will hardly hide or live in a cavern. Such a creature would have very few natural enemies."

"You don't know that."

"Please, Aimee. I'm not helpless, and I have a feeling that I should go first."

Aimee groaned. "You Morgens and your feelings."

"Thank you," Chris said when Aimee stepped to the side and allowed her to press closer. Stillness engulfed her the moment she entered. Without the flame, she'd have been lost in total darkness.

"I'm behind you," Aimee whispered, touching Chris's back.

"Where to now?" she asked, raising her hand and waving her arm from left to right to reveal more of the surrounding area. The cavern walls were rugged, and sharp edges of stone hung low in several places. Despite the fire, cold air scuttered over Chris and she shuddered.

When she inched farther into the cave, she noticed granite pebbles near an oval shaped well close to the center of the grotto. They stepped closer, up to an ancient stone wall full of scribbled etchings depicting unfamiliar runes. The engravings were precise and done in a meticulous, cautious script that bespoke of the author's pride in their work. Chris glanced down before grabbing Aimee's arm. "Look!" She nodded toward the well and the pearly silver substance that swirled on its surface.

"What is that? Is our artifact in there?" Aimee asked.

"Perhaps. I can't read the text on the wall. Can you?"

"No. I've seen nothing like it," Aimee replied.

Chris shifted closer and raised her hand to better illuminate the drawings.

She traced her fingers over the carvings, trying to sound out the strange depictions. Something felt familiar, but she couldn't place it. Lost in thought, she missed Aimee's question, but spun around at a yelp followed by a low groan spilling from the other woman's lips.

Chris crouched down next to the fountain where Aimee had sunk to her knees. "What happened? Are you OK?"

Aimee held up her hand, the silvery substance from the well dripping down her fingers.

"You touched it!"

Aimee tried to open her mouth, but slammed it shut and whimpered instead. She slumped forward and Chris caught her, cursing as their hands intertwined and the liquid from Aimee's hand seeped into her skin.

"Damn it, Aimee," she slurred. Time slowed down, then popped, resembling a chewing gum bubble, only louder and with a shrill echo in her ears. Her vision blurred and her stomach contracted.

Pain bloomed in her neck and slithered down, raging through her body like a forest fire after months of intense draught. A bang filled the room, then everything went dark. Or were her eyes closed? Chris groaned, her eyelids fluttered open, and she scrambled to her feet.

"Aimee? Where are you? What happened?" Her voice sounded foreign and hoarse. She turned around, veering in every possible direction, but she was alone. Even worse, she wasn't in the cave anymore. She was in the middle of the Thal mountains, isolated, without supplies.

Why? Wait, what? Chris stared at her hands, then patted down her body. She screamed.

*** 

Aimee came to amidst loud buzzing in her ears. She rose to her feet. "Chris? Where are you?" She frowned. What was wrong with her voice? She cleared her throat and pressed a sweaty palm against her chest. Why was her heart beating so fast?

When she gazed at the setting sun, Aimee noticed the lack of pounding in her head. She took a deep breath and her gaze fell to her hands, but they weren't her own. She flipped around, for the first time noticing her surroundings. The cavern wasn't in sight, and she seemed closer to their rest stop from earlier in the day.

That didn't explain how she felt or why her hands looked like... She did a double take and groaned. These were Chris's hands, but then... Aimee sank to the ground.

They switched bodies, that substance... But why did it separate them and fling them away from the cave? Was Chris OK? How could she be all right, trapped in Aimee's dead body, deserted.

Dusk was approaching, and at night the mountains were teeming with Sattran. She needed to find Chris and hurry. Aimee jumped up, her body buzzing with an energy she couldn't remember ever possessing, and smiling, she broke into a sprint. At least she recalled the way.

\*\*\*

Chris cradled her face, and with tears streaming down her cheeks, she lay curled up on the ground, willing the banging in her head to subside. She'd never been this drained, and her stomach squeezed in an angry gnaw. Earlier, she'd tried accessing her magic, and even though she'd had little hope, given her current residence in Aimee's body, disappointment had still cut sharp at the hollow, unfamiliar void that lingered inside where magic would otherwise rise.

"How do you live like this?" Chris gasped and faltered, gagging at the acid rising up her esophagus. She had to get a grip. She couldn't stay here like this. She needed to return, find her way back to the grotto and hope Aimee would be there.

She'd at least know how to handle her body to make this agony bearable. Chris rose on unsteady legs, frowning when she realized that the sun was setting and she'd soon be alone, at night, in the godforsaken Thal mountains, without magic, surrounded by Sattran. She was going to die.

"You're already dead," she reiterated Aimee's words, words that had always filled her with sorrow and an ache she failed to name or define. Now, there was nothing. Just the awareness of the sluggish emptiness that radiated through her limbs. And sleep. She needed to sleep.

Chris thrust out her chin and slogged forward, one step after the other. If only she had her magic. Or her body. She felt weak and defenseless in Aimee's skin, and she could only hope she'd make it through the night. At least Aimee was the one with the map in her pocket, given that she'd have zero chances of escaping this nightmare without it.

Perhaps she should rest and find her way back tomorrow? She'd be liable to fall and crack her skull unseeing at night without her fire. Chris grunted and her gaze trailed over her surroundings. In the distance, she could make out the shape of a section of rock where she thought she saw a crevice that might act as a nook, protective enough to provide shelter for the night.

\*\*\*

Aimee bounced. How could Chris have this much energy and stay still? She charged forward before coming to a dead stop, panting and with her heart pounding with such a frenzy that she feared it might catapult out of her chest.

Wait. Was that? She tilted her head and ducked low. Murmuring chants rang through the night. The shadows were close by. Damn it. And she wasn't dead. Warmth spread through her, and she pulled at her collar. What was going on now?

Her hands glowed and tingled. She turned her palms up and inspected them. They didn't look any different. Aimee was about to rise when sparks trickled from her fingertips. "Oh shit," she stammered.
"Magic. Can I?" She concentrated and placed her right hand on her leg to steady herself while balling her left into a fist before spreading it open like she'd seen Chris do. Nothing happened.

"Ow," she cursed and gazed toward her other hand, which still rested on her thigh. Her eyes widened when she realized fire wept from her hand, burning a hole in her pants.

"Shit, shit," Aimee yelped and hopped up. Her gaze flashed over her surroundings, but there was no water in sight. Sand. Sand! Aimee fell to her knees and stuck her fingers in the sand next to the walking trail. She exhaled in a rush when the flames died. Magic sucked.

***

Thal Mountains, Saltung<br>Year 302, Day 32

She should have marched back in the dark. So what if she plunged off a cliff? Not like she could die. Chris lowered her chin toward her chest as burning hot shame crawled up her neck.

The stabbing in her brain had lessened overnight, even if sleep had proven to be elusive. The morning sun had made her eyes water and with its rise above the skyline, the drumming in her head had returned.

Chris stumbled ahead with weary bones but halted before almost sliding into two black holes in the ground, filled to the brim with a maroon-colored sap that emitted a hideous sizzle. She squatted to get a closer look at the substance and noticed tiny bubbles rising to the surface. Heat radiated off it, but she couldn't judge its temperature. Everything was numb.

Before Chris could further contemplate this lack of sensation, she grimaced when the smell of sulfur assaulted her nostrils. How hadn't she noticed that before? She choked and scrambled backwards.

Chris dragged herself back to her feet and lumbered around the bubbling pits. She wondered if Aimee had an idea what they were.

After an hour of hiking up slopes only to brace herself to avoid falling on her steps downhill, she pulled up her shirt and wiped her face.

She winced when looking down her body before tracing her fingers over the elaborate black swirls and lines of Aimee's markings slithering up her hipbone and along her side.

She grunted and sagged to the ground next to a rock formation offering shade, but it was too late. Chris moaned and clutching her stomach, she keeled over and vomited bile. Aimee had lied to her. She was not all right.

***

Year 302, Day 31

Aimee dashed back into the cavern. "Chris!" she called. "Are you here? Are you OK?" The cave still sat in darkness and Aimee crept along the walls until she reached the well, but now it stood empty.

She hesitated, but then dropped low and bending over its ledge, she glared into the fountain but found no answers. Aimee closed her eyes and leaned against its stony façade. Maybe Chris decided not to travel in the dark. Who knew where she'd been flung to?

Wired energy still rattled through her body and everything within her shouted to head back out and search for Chris, who was alone at night, somewhere in these mountains with no supplies. Without her magic. In the body of a Verlohren.

Aimee tapped her foot on the ground while her hands fidgeted in her lap. She had to stay here. There was no way of knowing where Chris had gone, and without light... Aimee paused and scrambled up toward the other side of the wall where they'd left their backpacks earlier.

She had brought... Where was it? She grabbed the shoulder strap of a rucksack, pulling it closer and yanking it open. A triumphant "yes!" spilled from her lips when her hands groped for her supplies. Right there. That would do.

Aimee shot up and slunk out of the cave, the unlit torch gripped in her hand. Outside, she scraped the stick against the stone wall of the cavern to ignite it. "There you go," she whispered.

Light bled from it, and Aimee wished she'd stayed in the grotto when her gaze fell to the floor and shadows swirled around her. "Damn it," she mumbled, stumbling backwards.

\*\*\*

Year 302, Day 32

The sun had climbed higher, and its rays burned unforgiving on Chris, who plodded forward, sweat soaked and panting. She had to make it back to the cave today. While she doubted Aimee would abandon her, there was no need to test that theory.

Relief flooded her when her current route sloped downhill, sure she'd collapse if she tried to force her body up higher terrain. Chris hoped she'd made it more than halfway back, wondering if Aimee had already reached the cavern.

The air became easier to breathe the farther down her path meandered, until Chris recoiled and stumbled before crashing to the floor. She scrambled backward when the rock in front of her soared up, halted, before crashing down.

"What the…" she breathed out when more rocks around her lifted, some twirled before tumbling right back down. There was no one nearby, at least as far as Chris could tell. Were they hiding? The Sattran? But this looked like magic, and the Verlohren had no magic. Her breathing quickened and dizziness overtook her, yet her body remained as listless as ever.

Chris spotted a way out and rose, darting forward, or trying to, she barely avoided another falling rock before tripping farther down the track. She wanted to go home.

\*\*\*

Year 302, Day 31

On the far side of the grotto, three Sattran twisted around each other in a tangle of mismatched clothes, wrapping their hands and mouths in scarves made of silken pieces of cloth, while strands of soiled fabric draped over their emaciated bodies.

The three moved as one, gliding over the sandy surface toward Aimee who had regained her footing and strode forward. With the torch secured in her hand, she waved it at the Sattran.

The figures shrieked and shied closer together. The tallest of them hissed and his hands stiffened into a claw-like gesture, drawn inward.

Aimee tread ahead, brandishing the fire from left to right. "Go away. You're not welcome here!"

A low buzz sang from the tallest Sattran's mouth, mingling in the air before dripping in complete harmony into the night, sending an icy shiver down Aimee's back. The hum grew into an almost melodic lament that tore at her heart. Her breath faltered, yet the rapid gallop in her chest continued its chase. Could this excitement harm Chris?

"Please, leave. I don't want to hurt you," Aimee begged. If only she'd been in her own body. They'd recognize her, and... She had no idea. She remembered nothing about interactions between Verlohren and Sattran, aside from a desire to be away from them.

Was it just the reminder of what Verlohren could become if they weren't careful, or was there a genuine danger? It didn't matter now since she was in Chris's body, and all they saw was one lone Living in the mountains, swinging a torch at them.

"I'm sorry, OK? We won't stay long. We'll get out of here tomorrow. What do you want?"

"You... wrong. Don't fit," the smallest of the Sattran stuttered.

"What?"

"Too big."

"I'm too big for what?" Aimee lowered the light, only to raise it again when they slithered closer. "Stay back!"

"Help..." they sang as one.

With what? There was no way to help the Sattran. "I'm not alone! I have a friend!"

"The fire."

"I don't understand what you want."

"Help," the tallest one shrieked, and then they were gone.

Aimee closed her eyes, counting to ten before opening them, her eyelids fluttering. "What just happened? I thought Verlohren don't have magic!"

\*\*\*

Year 302, Day 32

Chris groaned and fell to her knees. That was it. She'd perish alone in the dreadful Thal mountains. The sun once more raced toward the horizon, and only around two hours of sunlight remained. Her hands balled into fists, and she collapsed on her side.

"Oh Gods," she moaned. "I can't even die in this body." Her eyes welled up with tears. Would the Sattran come and get her? Didn't Aimee say the Verlohren avoided them? Why was that? Perhaps they *were* cannibals!

Her arms trembled when she tried to sit up and a cramp ripped through her left leg. "Verlohren don't feel pain, right, Father," she cried and pulled her legs closer to her body.

A sound… What was that? Chris raised her head. Was that? She crawled forward and staggered to her feet. "Aimee?" she croaked before clearing her throat. "Aimee!"

"Chris! Where are you?" Aimee shouted while fresh tears trailed down Chris's cheeks.

"Over here!" She managed a few steps before halting and catching her breath. "Please don't be a hallucination," she breathed and wiped her eyes.

"There you are," Aimee said in Chris's voice, but the cadence was off.

Chris sobbed and covered her face with her hands. "Oh, my Gods, I thought I'd die here."

"Not in this body," Aimee said.

"Don't joke."

"I'm sorry. This must have been hard for you."

"Are you kidding me? We switched bodies! I'm dead!"

"Uh, yes. I'm aware of that."

---

95

"How do we change this? Are we stuck like this forever?"

"I hope not."

"What's wrong with my body? I thought you'd be delighted to be alive again."

"At your expense? How... Seriously? Is *that* what you think of me?"

"Sorry. I'm sorry. I'm just in so much pain," Chris groaned, running the back of her hand over her eyes.

"I know. Come on," she placed an arm around Chris's shoulders. "Let's return to the cave. All our supplies are there, and you must be starving."

\*\*\*

They entered the cavern, Aimee dragging Chris along. As soon as they were within reach of the well, a torrent of light filled the air with blinding brilliance. The light, coming from a blue sphere in the middle of the fountain enveloped the entire grotto as the pattern in the glow changed from blue to red.

The transformation ceased, and the structure floated up and down akin to a balloon before crashing and shattering into jagged pieces. A dim glow emanated from the well, casting light on the immediate surroundings.

"I'm so done with this," Chris said, clasping Aimee's hand. "Wait, wait. I sound like myself!" She spun around, facing Aimee and grasped her face. "We're back! We're us again!"

"We were always us," Aimee drawled.

"How can you be so unaffected by this?"

"I'm not. But I undoubtedly got the better deal in this," Aimee said and rolled her shoulders. "Can't say I've missed this body."

"Wait, what is that?" Chris knelt next to the well and hesitated before reaching inside.

"What is it?" Aimee joined her on the floor.

"It looks like a book? The explosion of the sphere must have revealed it. Do you think it was hidden there the entire time?"

"There was nothing in there when we got here yesterday, or when I checked once I'd returned."

"Nothing but the weird substance you touched."

Aimee ducked her head. "Uh, yes, that."

Chris rolled her eyes. "All right. Should we get it out?"

"Yes! This must be our artifact!"

"You don't know that."

"No, but we can find out."

"How?"

Aimee drew nearer and stooped to pick up the book.

"You never hesitate, do you? When you want something, you just go for it. Consequences be damned."

Aimee canted her head, her gaze flitting between the text in her hand and Chris. "I'm sorry?"

"You're... You're sorry. Is that a question or are you apologizing?"

Both women rose.

"I don't understand why you're so angry suddenly. How else were we going to—"

Chris fell toward her and drummed with her fists against Aimee's chest. "You lied to me!"

"What are—"

"You are *not* fine. You're never fine! And yet you do all these things that—"

"I don't—"

"You're in *constant* pain. Everything hurts, and you're weary and have no energy. The headaches and nausea. Oh Gods." She sank to her feet, dragging Aimee along with her.

"You get used to it."

"How?"

"You were thrust into the body of a Verlohren who's been dead for over eight years. You went from being alive... to that."

"This isn't how Dylan feels?"

"No. It's not bad during the first couple of years."

"Don't lie to me."

"I'm not lying to you."

"But you said you're fine! And that's *not* fine!"

"Yeah, I can tell after having spent a day inside your body. It's… something. You have so much energy, and nothing hurts! Your magic sucks, though." Aimee frowned and fiddled with her necklace.

"What?"

"Never mind. That's another story. But what you felt, this… pain, it… it doesn't happen overnight. It gradually gets worse, and you adjust over time."

"That's Dylan's future if I don't let him go."

"Yes."

"I see."

"I'm sorry."

Chris laughed. "Right, but I'm not the one suffering. You're who has to exist in this state of constant—"

"Discomfort. That's what it is to me most days."

"That's difficult to imagine."

"I know. It's somewhat harder than usual, after having been you for a day."

"Will you be OK?"

"Yes, Princess. Stop worrying about me."

"You *really* need to stop calling me that."

"Then why is there a crown on your family's crest?"

Chris narrowed her eyes.

Aimee chuckled. "Let's have a look at this book, come on!"

"All right." She inched closer to Aimee who opened the text.

# five

"Terry, where are you?" Chris raced from the sparring room to the rumination section and headed to the library. "There you are," she said, and stopped in front of her friend and mentor.

Terry placed his book on the table. "How was your meditation retreat?"

"I came to talk to you about that, but well," she lowered her voice. "It's a secret."

"What is?"

"I didn't go to the sanctuary. I went, but I didn't stay."

"Why not? Did something happen? Are you all right? Your father—"

"He doesn't know. No one does, and I'd like to keep it that way."

"As you wish."

"Look," Chris said and placed the *Agaze Erbium* on the table.

Terry froze. His eyes widened for a second before his expression shifted back to impassive. "What's that?"

"A spell book."

"It looks old. Where'd you get it?"

"We… OK. I should start at the beginning. I met Aimee, and she knows Dylan, back when he was alive." Chris cleared her throat. "I met with her in Salbit, after I'd arrived. We went on a quest."

"A quest. For this text?"

"We weren't sure what artifact we were searching for. I'd found the *Demise of Reason* among the forbidden texts, which led us to this cave in the Thal mountains." She trailed her fingers over its cover. "Anyway, we discovered the *Agaze Erbium*, and it contains magic unlike anything I've ever seen.

"There are also stories in here. A kind of lore?" Chris opened the tome halfway to the middle and leafed a few pages back. "This here seems to talk about some kind of restoration. It's not always clear, because the language is old, and there are runes I don't recognize."

He held out a trembling hand. "May I see?"

"Are you OK?"

Terry smiled. "Yes, of course. I had a strenuous workout earlier."

"All right. Here, look." She handed the volume to Terry who grasped it, his knuckles paling. "What do you think?"

"I have to read first."

Chris fidgeted in her seat. "Right. Sorry."

He turned several pages, skipping to the middle before returning to the beginning.

"And?"

"I'm not sure. I've never heard of these spells, and I'm also not able to decipher everything written here."

Chris's shoulders slumped. "I'd hoped you could translate those runes or have an idea about the old language."

"I'm afraid not. To be honest, I'd not use or trust this magic."

"Why?"

"You don't know what these spells do, or who wrote the book. What if it's a prank, or even worse, it could harm you or Saltung."

"These spells don't seem dark."

"Something doesn't have to appear dangerous to be detrimental to you or your surroundings."

"Of course. I just… This book feels warm. Like it belongs, and the magic, it seems important."

"Perhaps this is a remnant of your journey. Are you sure this Aimee didn't orchestrate all this for you?"

"To what end?"

"I don't know. It could have been a scavenger hunt, and she wanted to impress you. You are the heir to the Council, after all."

Chris snorted. "I doubt that."

"You should tell your father about it."

"Absolutely not! And you won't say anything to him either! I only told you because…"

"Because you hoped I could help. Will you try these spells? What about the *Demise of Reason*? What will you do next with this newfound ledger?

She frowned. "I didn't say we were going to do anything. The *Agaze Erbium* is primarily a spell book. We've found it, and I want to do more research."

Terry chuckled and returned the manuscript. "Of course you do. Just promise me you will be careful. There's no telling the true purpose of this text. I don't want you to get hurt."

"All right. I promise," she said. "Wait, did you hear that?"

"What?"

"It sounded like a door creaking."

"No. I didn't. Must be your imagination with all this excitement." He rose. "Good night, Chris. I'm getting old and need my sleep."

"Right. Good night." She sunk into her chair and yawned. That hadn't gone as well as she'd hoped. There was no one else she could talk to about this, aside from Aimee. Maybe she had had more luck.

***

"We have a problem," Lily said.

"That's cryptic, especially coming from you, little sister," Lara replied.

"Back when everything was set up, everyone was in agreement, right?"

"Of course. It never would have worked otherwise."

"I thought so."

"You seem troubled," Lara said.

"Well, I said we have a problem."

"You did."

"Have you heard of a text called the *Demise of Reason* or a spell book, *Agaze Erbium,* containing lore?"

"What? No, and no such spell book exists anymore!"

"I held it in my own hands. It was an old, faded, battered copy, but the handwriting was unmistakable."

"Whose was it?"

"Elizabeth."

Thunder roared and soft patter morphed into the sullen sluice of thick, heavy raindrops. The wind howled with more cracks and flashes of light while steady downpour pounded the city. Lara raised her torch into the night sky and stared at the storm, but there was nothing to see, only darkness.

***

Year 302, Day 40

"Now with the original copy of the book, we know where all of this leads to, how many tasks we still have to finish, and so we should go for the—" Dylan started.

"Slow down. We need to plan this right. Besides, don't you think your sister should complete her research on the spell book first?" Aimee asked.

"I don't know. I... I thought she'd be the one saving your behind, not the other way round."

"Do you expect me to apologize for helping your sister or for getting her in trouble in the first place?"

"I... She's *alive*, Aimee. If anything were to happen to her..."

"Yes, and it's not like I don't worry, but you're not her keeper. She'll do what she wants, and she's not helpless. She made it back close to the cavern across a mountain pass covering who knows how many miles. In my body. She's tough."

"Yes, but I just... She's..."

"I understand, but again, not up to you. And she'd be livid if we moved ahead without her."

Dylan ducked his head. "Yeah, you're right. What's next?"

"We wait. Spells are within your sister's realm. We should study the text more and see if we can crack the remaining riddles."

Dylan laughed. "You just want to impress Chris."

"What? Oh, hush," Aimee huffed and grabbed the notes she'd been working on.

***

Year 302, Day 44

"May I.... You obviously don't have to answer, but you play a lot with your necklace. I've never seen such an emblem, and—"

Aimee chuckled. "Being unaware of a smidgen of knowledge is unacceptable?"

"Something like that," Chris said, laughing.

"The pendant itself was a present. From Sarah, uh, my girlfriend, back when I was alive."

"Oh."

"As to the symbol, Sarah and I grew up together. We were best friends first. She was an artist, working mostly with metal." Aimee clasped the locket before taking it off and handing it to Chris.

"It's beautiful."

"She gave it to me on my eighteenth birthday, right after we'd started dating."

"What does it mean, the image itself? Oh. Unless it's too personal, of course."

"Nah. When we were kids, we came across a snake nest and there were eggs, but they seemed abandoned and so we adopted them. We were ten," Aimee said with a small smile.

"That's sweet. Did you get to see them hatch or when they were babies?"

"We did. We were lucky because one afternoon, an egg cracked right when we got there." Aimee accepted the necklace when Chris held it out for her. "This was all we'd talk about for weeks. The cute, tiny snakes. My poor mom must have swallowed a million cringes. Snakes terrified her."

"I'm assuming that means the adoption fell through?"

Aimee laughed. "Most definitely. Anyway, this stuck with Sarah because her grandma had passed about a month before we'd found the nest, and the loss... It had devastated her. This adventure helped. Her grandmother had loved snakes."

"She turned the experience into a piece of art."

"Yes. It was a drawing first. I loved it the moment she showed me, but she didn't want to part with it. No matter how much I begged and promised that I'd frame it and hang it on the wall in my room."

"Until this," Chris said and smiled.

"Yeah. She'd engraved it onto this disk. I don't know how, but it was a sweet gesture, even if she hoarded the image for eight years," Aimee said in jest.

"I always thought Verlohren no longer had access to their belongings, back from when they were still part of the Living."

"Your brother changed that somewhat."

"Dylan? How?"

"He set up a network of Living who sympathize with the Verlohren and who help them. How do you think we got this house? He had tried to... He'd searched for something of mine for months because he wanted to thank me for... for being there for him after he'd passed."

A fond smile spread over Chris's face. "That sounds like him."

"When he couldn't find anything, he pestered me with specifics about random items I owned or stuff that held any importance to me.

"I never… I never expected he'd find this, and to be honest, I felt like I was sending him on a fruitless errand when I told him about this necklace."

"You didn't realize then how persistent he can be, huh?"

"Indeed," Aimee said. "He found this at a thrift store for sale. He gave it to me about a month before we contacted you."

"I'm glad he returned something meaningful to you," Chris said.

"Thank you."

"Here's to hoping he and Markus will be as relentless on their little errand."

"Very true," Aimee said.

"Are you ready to start?"

"Yeah, but are you sure you've translated this correctly?" Aimee asked.

"Yes."

"What if you turn us into animals? I don't want to be an animal," Aimee said.

They sat cross-legged on the meditation mat Chris had brought along.

Chris placed the back of her hands near her knees. "I won't turn us into animals, yes, my translation is accurate, no, it won't hurt us, kill us, or anything else."

"Is this necessary?"

"Do you still want to solve this mystery?"

"Of course!"

"It's necessary. This spell will reveal the next step, and yes, while there are other aspects to explore." Chris held up a hand to silence Aimee's interruption. "We are not ready. We both need to complete this spell since we found the *Agaze Erbium* together."

"I still don't see—"

"I know you are afraid of magic and—"

"I'm not afraid of magic!" Aimee sat up straighter.

Chris pinched the bridge of her nose.

"I just don't like it. It's… volatile," Aimee added and lowered her voice.

"All right. I understand, and having been in my body surely didn't help, considering all you've told me about your failed attempt to use magic."

"It wasn't a failed *attempt*…"

"The hole in my pants would suggest otherwise."

"Well, I was going to add that it was an accident."

"Right, but Aimee, I *am* a mage. I'm familiar with magic, and mine isn't volatile, at least not when I'm in command."

"OK."

"Do you trust me?"

"I do."

"Then please give me your hands."

Aimee held Chris's gaze before reaching out and grasping her outstretched hands.

She squeezed Aimee's fingers and closed her eyes.

"Should I do that, too?"

"Yes."

Aimee's eyes fluttered shut.

Chris murmured the spell. It was long, and in a language she wasn't overly familiar with, though she'd kept that information from Aimee. The other woman was skittish enough without knowing her insecurities.

The magic surged through her veins, comfortable and warm at first, but then it hastened and swelled, seeping out of her pores. Chris shivered and drew a deep breath, feeling the air fill her lungs. Steam rose and swirled in front of them. Tiny bubbles expanded, floating like incandescent diamonds, and shimmering red from the friction of air on water. Heat suffused her, and before she could process its force, magic settled like a balm on her skin, radiating through her.

A loud bang filled the room and flung both women backwards. Then nothing. A vast blackness faded in waves and the popping in her ears receded.

She opened her eyes to Aimee's groan. They weren't in the house anymore.

"So much for nothing to worry about."

"I don't know what happened," she said but Aimee didn't react; she didn't even look at her.

Chris rushed to stand. "Where are we?" Her gaze raked over the gray marble walls that rose around them, up high, as far as the eye could see. The slate stone floor beneath their feet had an odd buoyancy to it. Light shone down on them, but from where, she couldn't discern. The room was neither cold nor warm, but something frigid and almost menacing hung in the air.

"Chris? Where are you?" Aimee called.

She stepped closer to her. "I'm here."

"It's not funny. You magicked us somewhere and then disappeared? Take us back!"

"Aimee?" She tried to grasp Aimee's shoulders, but her hands passed right through her. "What is going on here?" Chris stepped back, shaking her head.

*\*\**

This was why she hated magic. Unpredictable, and it never did what it should. "Chris, come on! This isn't funny." Where was she? Was she truly alone? Was Chris here somewhere but lost?

Aimee stared at the marble walls encasing her before bursting into a sprint until she came to a skittering halt in front of the barricade. She raised her hands and hesitated, but then she touched the wall and groaned. A thousand tons of ice bit into her, seemingly freezing her to the spot.

"Aimee!"

She spun around at the shout. This didn't sound like Chris, but the voice rang familiar.

"Who's there?"

"Help me!"

Aimee clenched her hands and leaned back against the barrier, not registering how her frame shuddered at the contact. A stammered, "it can't be," escaped her lips.

"Help me!"

Aimee swallowed hard, then edged forward. One heavy step after another with every cell in her dead body rising to life and shouting at her. *Run. Get away.*

She licked her lips and quickened her pace. She needed to see this, she had to be sure… This was a hallucination. It had to be for how else… Aimee fell into a slow jog, the voice still ringing in her ears.

"No, Gods no. Please don't," Aimee wailed, sinking to the floor next to the twitching body of a woman. Her dark hair hung loosely over her face, but Aimee recognized the familiar jaw with its high cheekbones, the thin lips, and straight nose. The woman moaned and her eyelids blinked open. "Aimee," she slurred.

"Mom," she whimpered. Aimee grasped her mother's trembling hand and blinked rapidly to behold the dark, deep-set eyes of the woman who had been lost to her for nearly two decades.

\*\*\*

"Oh, Aimee," Chris whispered, who had chased after her and was now kneeling beside them.

This had to be a trick. How could the spell have brought them to Aimee's mother? She'd revealed nothing about her past, though Chris had tried to bring their conversations to Aimee's life and family only to have her change the subject. Was her mother even still alive? Was she the one who held Aimee here? Would that mean… If this was real and her mother died, then… then Aimee would disappear forever.

"Aimee," Chris said, but once more silence was her only reply. She wished there was a way to reach her, to comfort her.

What did this spell do? Wait. Did she still have magic? She hesitated, fear flooding her senses. Doing nothing wouldn't change what was.

She relaxed her posture and opened her left hand, willing fire to dance, but her palm stood barren.

Chris ground her jaw. "Why do I keep losing my magic whenever we're together?" That wasn't fair. This wasn't Aimee's fault, and nobody had forced her to join this or the last adventure. The spell wasn't even supposed to *be* an adventure. She'd promised it would be safe, yet here they were. Lost once more with no obvious way out.

Aimee lay with her head on her mother's chest and thick tears dripped down her cheeks. "I'm sorry. I'm *so* sorry, Mom. Please forgive me." She repeated this like a hymn, with the words seeping from her lips coalescing into a doleful chant.

Chris's heart buckled, and she closed her eyes, but the begging lament echoed in her mind.

"Don't leave me. Please don't leave me again," Aimee sobbed.

But her mother had stilled. Her chest no longer rose and fell with every quivering breath. Chris trudged closer and covered her mouth to stifle a sob at the sight of the woman's closed eyes and sallow, unmoving features.

Aimee cried out and teetered backward as her mother disappeared.

"Aimee? Where are you?" another voice called out from the other end of the room.

Aimee jumped up. "Sarah?" She ran toward the sound.

"Wait. Sarah's here, too?" What in the Gods' names was this place? She shuddered at the thought of what else they would encounter in this... prison. There had to be a way to get them out of here. But first things first. Chris tore after Aimee.

\*\*\*

Aimee wiped her eyes. Tears were useless, always had been, and they changed nothing. Sarah kept calling out to her, so she picked up her pace. There had to be a way. Or... Was she...

What if Chris never completed the spell and she was no longer tied to her existence as a Verlohren, and instead... She'd moved on? Was this what came after? Was this... hell?

Aimee plodded to a ponderous halt. Her breathing haggard and her head pounded. It figured hell wouldn't rid her of her physical ailments.

She scanned the room until she spotted a figure crumpled on the floor near the wall. "Sarah!" Aimee dashed ahead before falling to her knees next to the gasping woman. "Hell," she choked. "This is hell." She held Sarah's hand.

"Aimee," the name bubbled in a weak tremble from the blonde woman's lips.

"Shh, it's OK. You'll be fine."

"You've always... been... a terrible... liar."

Aimee laughed through her tears. "Guilty as charged." She refused to drop her gaze. She didn't want to face what awaited her. The same as before. Sarah's side drenched—crimson oozing into her cream-colored shirt. Too dark. Even though she didn't see or touch it, the stickiness remained on her fingers, much like her memories.

"I'm sorry," Aimee ground out.

Sarah shook her head.

"If I'd listened to you then, we'd never..." She blinked away moisture.

Sarah twisted and shuddered as a hard tremor gripped her body.

Aimee squeezed her hand and closed her eyes. "I'm sorry, I'm sorry, I'm sorry," she chanted. That was all she ever was. Sorry. Why should this be different in hell? Aimee bemoaned and bent down, lowering her head and arms onto Sarah's still chest. "I'm sorry my love wasn't enough."

After a minute, or maybe a year—time had slowed into a wide stretched yawn—a yell followed by a crash rumbled through the room.

A shiver trailed along her back, and she sat up. Stillness lasted for several trudging heartbeats before a scream tore at her. Aimee vaulted off the floor and bound after the voice. "Chris!" she yelled.

***

"Wait, what?" Chris frowned. "Wait!" She once more followed Aimee, cursing because her surprise had offered Aimee a wide lead.

Out of breath, she stuttered to a halt next to Aimee, who crouched over a seizing figure on the ground.

"No, no, no. This can't be. Come on, Chris! Don't do this to me," she faltered. "Please don't."

Chris bit her lower lip. She didn't want to step closer but felt drawn in. She slunk around Aimee and gasped. How could this be? This wasn't her. Chris pinched her arm. Solid. She was here. Real. Then who was that on the floor, convulsing in a seizure?

"Aimee," Chris's voice broke, and she licked her lips. She kneeled next to her. "That's not me. It's not real," she spoke with a force that chased a shudder through her body. Nothing.

Aimee didn't react. Instead, she seized the shoulder of the impostor, squeezing, begging her to open her eyes.

"I'm sorry my spell did this to you," Chris croaked and dropped to the floor. She bent her head and pulled her legs closer to her chest. "I don't know how to fix it or tell you that this isn't me, but I'm right here with you."

Aimee's wails made her heart hurt, but she wouldn't leave. She'd caused this, and she'd stay with Aimee, even if she never knew.

Wait. Hell? Why did Aimee believe this was hell?

***

"Wake up, please wake up," Aimee begged. "Why are you here? Did you die? Did the spell kill you? But why are you in my hell?"

Chris stopped twitching, but the torpor that fell over her body only increased the tension in Aimee.

111

Why did this *always* happen?

"Come on! Wake up. We need to get out of here."

Another seizure hit.

Aimee balled her hands into fists. All these tears. She was sick of them. Why couldn't she stop crying? She wiped her eyes, but a new sob clawed at her throat and broke free.

"I'm sorry I got you involved in all this. If I hadn't, you'd have gone to your retreat and meditated instead of getting lost in the mountains in the body of a Verlohren. When I'd found you," Aimee hiccupped, "I was so scared. I thought... I thought you..." She steadied her voice. "If I hadn't dragged you into this mess, you'd be safe, home alive, preparing to become the next Head of the Council. Even if you ended up marrying that *guy*, you'd be alive."

Aimee banged her hands on the ground, starting at the quaking she felt beneath her. "I never meant for you to get hurt. Please don't die." The floor quieted down, and Chris's body next to her followed along. She never opened her eyes.

"Why are you all leaving me?" Aimee cried. Grief swept through her like a tsunami threatening to shatter her foundations—collapsing her walls and allowing the flood to swell. Memories she'd kept at bay for a decade tore through her, drowning the glimmer of hope that had sparked inside her, sheltered from the deluge. Alone. She would always be alone.

She held Chris's hand and shivered at the coolness of the touch, standing in stark contrast with the warmth that usually flowed through her when touching her friend.

Darkness fell and Aimee didn't move. The floor beneath her grew colder, but the lethargy that had swamped her body glued her in place. She rocked back and forth but froze when a whimper filled the stillness.

"Hello?" She rose and cringed at the cracking in her knees. The dark cleared like fog, and she sighed at the by now familiar sight of gray walls.

"No, no, no," rang out from a distance and Aimee spun around, gazing at the floor where she'd found Chris. Empty. If Chris wasn't here and that voice... It *did* sound like her. Aimee hesitated before marching toward it.

"No, please. I'm sorry. I didn't mean it."

"Chris, oh my Gods! I thought you were dead. What is going on here, and who... Wait, isn't that your mother?" Aimee said when she reached Chris, who stood across a slender woman with long, curly blond hair, her face distorted in a mask of disdain. Neither of the women reacted to Aimee.

"Hey. So..." She sidled on and halted in front of Chris who didn't even blink. "You don't see me, do you?" Aimee shoulders dipped. "I don't understand any of this."

"Mother, please!" Chris begged.

***

"I lie awake at night wishing it was you who'd died," Diane sneered, her gaze boring into her daughter.

"Don't say that," Chris pleaded.

"He would have been a better heir than you ever could, but sadly, you were born first. Did you know that you almost died as a baby?"

"No," Chris whispered.

"Hmm, yes. If only I'd known, then, all that I... Not only would that have made Dylan the rightful successor, but you also wouldn't have killed him. He'd still be alive. My son."

"How do you—"

"Be quiet! I am *tired* of your whiny voice, your constant complaints, and your inability to show any drive or initiative."

"I'm sorry," Chris mumbled and drew her arms around her torso.

"What good does *that* do? Does it bring my son back? Does it change that you are the heir to the Council? Does it move your father to recognize what a sorry excuse of a daughter you are?"

"Mother, I, uh, I—"

"You what? Are you going to tell me you are sorry again? Or that I am wrong? I never wanted a daughter, but when you were born… Your father… You latched onto him the moment he held you. He loved you, at least until you killed Dylan."

"I didn't—"

"What? You didn't kill your brother? That's a rather bald-faced lie."

Chris wiped her eyes. "No, I… I never meant for him to get hurt."

"You never mean to do anything. That is your problem. You hesitate and then nothing happens. You play it safe, always have. You don't have the courage for change, for making a name of yourself. There's no ambition."

\*\*\*

"You need to stop listening to her. She's cruel and cold, and she's wrong! You're not like that. And for the record, Dylan *insists* you didn't kill him. Hey, I said that with you nearby!" Aimee kicked the floor. "Because you don't hear it."

"I'm sorry I am such a disappointment, Mother. I've done what you've asked of me all my life."

"Exactly." Diane laughed. "You *always* follow the rules."

"She might have a point there, Chris," Aimee said. "You are a bit of a stickler for rules, but the rest is nonsense."

Chris folded her arms. "That's not… Adhering to established procedures isn't a bad thing."

"It gets you nowhere. You will never be a true leader if all you do is obey the rules. It makes you pathetic, and odious."

"Woah, lady, that's harsh. None of that makes her unlovable or weak. You are nuts. Just go away. Leave! Is there something we need to do to make you all disappear again?"

"I know," Chris moaned, dropping to the ground.

"That's crap, Chris. Come on, don't let her walk over you," Aimee implored and sat down next to her.

\*\*\*

"I always knew, or at least I feared this. I understand that you're more attached to Dylan. He's like that. He draws people in." A small smile tugged at Chris's lips. "But... I still hoped that you'd love me, too."

"How could I?" Diane asked, towering over Chris.

She closed her eyes. "Yes, how could you."

"Mother's right."

"Dylan!" both women exclaimed at the same time.

"You killed me. Can you imagine? My big sister responsible for my death. You'd always been jealous, but I didn't expect you to take it this far. Did you hate me that much?"

"Dylan, please. Don't say that." Chris's bottom lip quivered. "I loved you. I've always loved you, and I've never been jealous of you."

He canted his head.

"All right. I envied your freedom. You were able to be who you wanted to be, do what you wanted. I coveted your freedom, your ability to withdraw from public life, to just be a face in the crowd, but I wasn't..."

He stepped closer to Chris who'd risen but seemed rooted to the ground. "Why did you kill me, then?"

"I didn't mean to... I... I'm so sorry, Dylan. I wish it'd been me, and I've cursed the Gods for taking you instead of me a thousand times..."

"I don't believe you."

"It's the truth! I never wanted for any of this to happen. I dream about that day all the time, and sometimes in my dreams, uh, I get it right, and you... you live."

"Dreams mean nothing," he spat.

Chris rubbed her eyes. "I know. I wake up and it's as if I lost you all over again."

Dylan sneered. "You think you have it hard? Try being dead!"

"Then why are you here? What are you? You are gone, and this place..." She stepped backward. "Whatever this is, and however we'll get out of here, there's one thing... You are dead!"

Dylan and Diane remained motionless with their gazes locked on Chris.

"We may have had our differences, and we weren't as close as we used to be when we were children, but *my* Dylan would never be this callous or cold." She glanced at Diane. "And you, Mother, you have been distant all my life. You don't show affection and you're demanding, but I refuse to believe what you said."

Neither of the two figures in front of her shifted or spoke. Their features grew more pallid.

"These are my fears," Chris mouthed. "You said everything that I've *ever* been afraid of. I'm at fault for your death, Dylan, but I didn't kill you. I need you to leave, both of you," she breathed the last sentence and closed her eyes. She rarely prayed, but in that moment, any help would do. She needed to be right. They couldn't be real.

Aimee's encounters must have been fake, too. The final one for sure, given that it wasn't her who Aimee had seen dying. Or was it real and she was a ghost? A Verlohren? But then her mother shouldn't have seen her. Unless she held no love for Chris. No, no, this was an illusion, a dream. She inhaled like she'd been starved of oxygen, then opened her eyes and a cry spilled from her lips. They were gone.

Chris fell to her knees and bawled until a soft, warm touch on her shoulder startled her.

\*\*\*

"Yeah, go away! Leave her alone!" Aimee hollered. "Dylan would never say that! Wait until I tell him. This isn't him! He loves you so much!" Aimee rocked back and forth on her heels.

Her eyes went wide when both Diane and Dylan disintegrated in front of her, like frozen statues shattering into myriad fragments, but there was nothing left. The floor where they'd stood remained bare. "What is this place?"

She crouched next to Chris and placed a hand on her shoulder, squeezing gently. "Even though you can't hear or feel me, I'm so proud of you."

"Aimee?" Chris wept as she twisted around and fell forward. "You're here! I can't believe it!" She pulled Aimee against her.

"Me neither," she mumbled and buried her face in Chris's neck before pulling back. "You can see me."

"I saw it all."

"What?"

"Your mom, Sarah, and... Well..." A frown spread over Chris's face.

"You. You saw me crying over..." Aimee leaped to her feet and scurried back.

"Please don't leave. I'm sorry. I tried talking to you, but you never heard me. I followed you and even tried to touch you, but—"

"Your hand went right through me."

"Yes," Chris said.

"Where are we? What is this place?"

"I'm not sure, but it's not real. My brother is dead, and I gathered so are your mom and Sarah?"

Aimee tightened her jaw but nodded.

"Then none of this is true."

"But why couldn't we see each other before, and now we can?"

"Perhaps because I acknowledged that it's all an illusion? Because I asked them to leave?"

"It's that simple?"

"I don't have any answers."

"Your spell did this," Aimee growled and paced.

Chris ducked her head. "I'm sorry."

"This is exactly why I don't like magic!"

Chris scrambled up. "I am aware of that! You've only said so a thousand times. Magic is bad, cannot be trusted, blah, blah, blah."

"Well, look at what it did to us. Where are we and how do we get back?"

"I don't know! And you're the one who wanted to find answers to your *delusions* about the Verlohren!"

"Delusions, huh?" She halted her pacing and marched toward Chris instead, stopping right in front of her. "Don't call them fantasies just because they make you look bad."

"What are you talking about?"

"You and your family. All the lies you've spread for centuries. For what? So you can stay in power? What about all the people, all the ones who suffer?"

"I *am* one of those people, too! I've lost my brother and bound him to this miserable existence that will only bring him pain. Don't you think I'd do *anything* to set him free? To spare him this suffering. What do you think of me?"

"I don't know! You've accused me of causing this, and I did, in the cave, but not now. It was *your* spell—"

"Here we go again." Chris pinched the bridge of her nose.

"You said the spell was safe!"

"I was wrong, all right? I'm not infallible, and neither are you, Ms. 'let's touch the silvery substance,' no matter that it was floating in a *well* in a *cavern* in the *mountains* while we were searching for a potentially dangerous artifact!"

"I said I'm sorry. What else do you want from me?"

"How about giving me the benefit of the doubt? I didn't mean for this to happen!"

"Yes, but magic—"

"Is a part of me, Aimee! What do you expect me to do? Rip it out? I can't. I'll always have magic and you hating it so much—"

"I don't hate it." She gripped Chris's hand. "I'm sorry. I'm just scared."

Chris rubbed the crook of Aimee's thumb. "So am I."

\*\*\*

"Does your magic work here?"

"No. I tried that right away," Chris grumbled.

"All right. What do we have so far? It's a room with no doors or other ways of entry. The walls don't seem to end, and you can't use magic. We were invisible to one another at first, and we were... We had impossible encounters with people who are dead or cannot be here."

"Right."

"It shows improvement, though. We can interact now, so that should mean we're moving in the correct direction."

Chris shrugged her shoulders. "Probably, but I honestly don't know."

Both women sat in silence.

"My perception of temperatures is off, but is it getting colder?" Aimee asked after a while, hugging herself.

"Yes," Chris said and shuddered. "I thought it was just me." Her palms touched the cinder block floor, and she cringed at the chill seeping into her.

"Let's get up." Aimee held out her hand to pull her up.

"Thanks." She put her arms around her chest and shuffled her feet. "This is... a problem."

"I'd say so." Aimee rubbed her hands together. "Check your magic again? That flame of yours would come in handy."

"Right." Chris cleared her throat. "Let's see." She closed her eyes and focused on her breath, suppressing an aggrieved chuckle at the memory of her students trying and failing to call forth their powers. Here, she could join them.

At first, there was only a void. The heady current of pulsing, warm power that infused her body whenever she invoked her magic lay dormant. Not even a glint. She was about to tell Aimee that nothing had changed when a flutter of energy trickled into her fingers.

Chris closed and opened her hands and miniscule flames sprouted from her palms.

"You did it!" Aimee shouted. "That's awesome!"

"Never thought I'd see you this excited about magic."

"Yes, well." Aimee scuffed her foot against the floor. "They're tiny, though."

Chris hummed in reply while her focus remained on the wispy lights in her palms. She'd never had to spend that much energy on keeping such little flames alive. Sweat dripped down her face as a faint shiver raked her frame.

"Are you all right?" Aimee asked, grasping Chris's arm. As soon as she touched Chris, the fire shot higher.

"Woah." Chris stumbled backwards to avoid the heat of the fire and lost contact with Aimee's hand.

"What happened?"

"Not sure, but when you touched my arm, the energy..." Chris bit her lower lip.

"I did that?"

"I think so." The words had barely left her mouth when a roar thundered through the room, echoing like wind gushing between houses and nestling under loose roof shingles. A wall of light burst through the floor, rising to form a dome-shaped barrier around them.

"That's bad." Aimee lifted her head. She stretched out her hand to reach the glow but stopped when Chris stomped her foot.

"Don't touch it!" she hissed.

Aimee cleared her throat and clasped her hands. "Sorry."

Chris held back rolling her eyes. This was becoming an all too often occurrence in Aimee's presence. "Touch me."

"What?"

"Touch my arm again. Like before." Chris winced. The effort of sustaining the flames drained her body and mind.

Aimee sucked in a quick breath, hesitated, but then reached out and rested her hand on Chris's forearm.

Chris gasped when her body shuddered, and a deafening noise exploded in the room. Her dry throat ached, and her vision blurred when the light barricade flashed while red and blue hairline cracks crawled from the inside out, encompassing the entire structure in mere seconds.

Aimee held onto her, the blossoming pain of her tight grip anchored Chris and allowed her to recite the same spell that had gotten them here. Darkness crept up, swallowing the light of the dome before a clanging sound spun around them.

# six

Freit, Saltung
Year 302, Day 44

Aimee woke to Dylan hovering over her. "Get off me! I'm fine."

"You were gone! You never said where you were going. All I knew was you were casting a spell with Chris, and then I come back home to this setup and neither of you in sight. I was worried about you," he said.

"Dylan's here?" Chris's voice shook.

"Yes. Your obnoxious brother is acting like he thought I'm dead." Aimee frowned. "For real dead."

"You shouldn't be rude to people who care and worry about you."

Dylan grinned. "She's right."

"You're only defending him because he's your brother. And you, hush."

"Not at all. I merely find rudeness offensive."

"Of course you do," she muttered while Dylan laughed. "Anyway, we're back after all. Congrats on not killing us, or better you, and me some more."

"Stop it. That's not funny. And yes, I tried the incantation, the one that got us there, and then... I don't recall. It was so loud, and..."

"I have no memory of what happened after the dome cracked either."

"This here showed up at the same time you did. It was on the floor right next to your bodies. You were both out for a minute, so I put it on the table."

Aimee turned around. "What? What do you mean it just popped up here with us?"

"You must have been gone all afternoon. It's after nine."

"What did he say?"

"Apparently, we were gone for half the day, but when we returned, this," Aimee bent over and picked up a book from the desk, "appeared right next to us."

Chris accepted the text from her. "Hmm." She inspected the faded and torn black leather band. It had no title. There was nothing, no words or symbols, no runes embedded in the volume's cover. Chris opened it and read the first few pages.

"And?" Aimee asked.

"Oh! You won't believe it, but this appeared because we completed a task."

"What? How can we complete an assignment we didn't even know we'd started?"

"Look, here it says, 'the Living and the Dead shall unite and perform the tasks of empathy and courage to receive the *Book of Sattran,* which is the first step to the ritual of Varstahnet, that shall reveal the true history of the land,'" Chris finished.

"I can hear what you've read, but I don't understand what you just said. And I've never heard or read of a *Book of Sattran*?"

Dylan scratched his head.

Aimee laughed. "Neither does your brother."

"I'm as confused as you are. If you think about it, though, before we got the *Agaze Erbium* from the well, it blew us away from the cavern, and we had to walk miles in the body of the other, then reunite in the cave for it all to reverse. We didn't find the book until after all of that."

"I don't know."

"We learned a lot about each other, how it feels to be the other. That's empathy."

"I suppose, and courage? What?" Aimee scoffed. "Because we dealt with all these imposters?"

"Are you always this cynical?" Chris asked.

"Yes, she is," Dylan said.

Aimee glared at him. "Shut it."

"I assume my brother agrees with me."

"You two are always ganging up on me, never mind that you can't interact with each other. You don't even see him!"

Aimee dropped her raised hands. "I'm sorry. This is a lot, and I'm glad we escaped from wherever *that* was, but…"

"What is it?" Chris asked.

"I'm not sure we should continue."

"What?" Dylan said.

Chris's eyes widened. "You're not serious."

"I am. It's too dangerous."

"Since when do you care about that?" he asked.

"Since it wasn't just two Verlohren on the line with nothing left to lose. Now we have other… things to consider." Aimee's gaze shifted between him and Chris.

"I am right *here*, so don't talk about me like that. Also, not a *thing*. I can take care of myself, and I thought you'd have realized that by now." Chris scrambled to her feet.

"I'm not doubting your abilities, or your courage, but you *are* alive. You can get hurt and die."

"You can get hurt, too. You feel pain, right? Physical pain, too? Because if I was hallucinating in the mountains, then—"

"Yes, yes. Of course, I do. I can get hurt."

"Right, so what's the difference? Don't you also heal slower than the Living do?"

"Yes, but we cannot die."

"A lot of things can kill me. It is my life, and my risk to take," Chris said.

"Since a lot of things can kill you, why add to the list when we don't have to?"

"You'll just give up? You'll never get your answer about the Verlohren, the Sattran, and our past. We'll never uncover the truth."

"The truth is overrated, especially if it's going to kill you. That's not worth it," Aimee snapped.

"It's worth it to *me*. I want to know the truth, and I want to help Dylan, and you. I want to fix this."

"You want to risk your life because you're feeling guilty about—" Aimee gasped for breath and tumbled over, moaning while clutching her stomach.

"Stop it!" Dylan shouted.

Chris hesitated, but then touched Aimee's shoulder. "What happened? Are you OK?"

"I'm fine," Aimee ground out.

"You don't look it."

"Remember I can't say certain things to you about Dylan?"

"Yes, but why did this hurt you?"

"I got close to saying something that relates to your... issues, and whenever that happens, and I intent to speak... It burns me."

"What burns you?"

She shrugged her shoulders. "Part of the mystery."

"The one you don't want to solve anymore."

"Chris, please, try to—"

She snatched the book and pulled it to her chest. "No. I won't accept this. I will continue on this path, whether you join me or not."

"That'll be difficult."

"And how's that?"

"What you read earlier, it talked about the Dead and the Living working together. That sounds like we both have to be in it for this to work."

Chris narrowed her eyes. "It doesn't name *you* specifically. Any Verlohren should do."

"Be my guest."

"You are *so* stubborn. I understand your concerns, and I appreciate them, but some risks are worth taking. Imagine how many people we could help. Imagine if things didn't have to be like this for the Verlohren, for the Sattran. Don't you want to help them?"

"Of course I do! How can you even ask that? But with you in the mix?" Aimee heaved a sigh.

"It's too much. I can't be responsible for… for causing another death."

"Oh, Aimee." She reached out and gripped Aimee's hand. "I'm so sorry. I didn't think of that. It doesn't have to be that way."

"No, but to prevent the same outcome, we have to quit now."

Chris tilted her head. "All right. Give it some time. Let things settle a bit, and in the meantime, I'll do some more research. Perhaps we can reconvene in a week or two? See where we are?"

Aimee patted Chris's hand. "OK. I make no promises."

"Thank you," she said and rose. "Contact me if anything happens before next week."

\*\*\*

Freit, Saltung
Year 302, Day 50

"I only see you with your nose stuck in a book these days. What happened to our training? We haven't sparred in a long time," Terry asked.

"You exaggerate. We trained two days ago."

"We used to spar daily, and before the last session, it was almost a week. What's going on, Chris? You're not in the habit to neglect a part of your education."

"Am I still such a novice with the staff or martial arts that I require constant training?"

"Training isn't just about instructions. It's about honing your skill, remaining flexible and strong. We need to establish and nurture the routines in our lives," Terry said.

"I don't see how I'm lacking in habits."

He sat down across the table from her. "Is this about the secret adventure and the books you've discovered?"

"Shh." Chris peered around the thankfully empty library. "You must realize that one doesn't blurt out secrets in public, for everyone to overhear."

Terry chuckled. "We're hardly out in the open. There's no one else here. Come on, tell your old friend what's been going on."

"It's complicated."

"Try me. I might be able to help you."

"Aimee wants to quit, even though we still have so much to do."

"Why does she want to stop?"

"She says it's too dangerous."

"Have you considered that she's right?"

"I knew you'd say that. Sometimes you must take risks, especially when what's at stake outweighs the potential danger to yourself!"

"And that's the case here, with these texts?"

"Yes! We are getting closer to the truth. I don't know who hid these artifacts or created the trials, but it must be for a reason, and from what I've read and researched, everything points to revealing the truth, a truth that someone or something has buried."

"Covered up by whom? And what truth? Is this still about the Verlohren?"

"Yes and no. It's about all of us, the Living and the Verlohren. We are all connected somehow, and these texts seem to reveal how and what happened."

"This all sounds like a fantasy or an elaborate hoax. You'd expect the person who started this quest would offer their name, or at least some hints to their identity. It's important to know the origin of your sources."

"Ordinarily, I'd agree with you, but in this case," Chris said and bit her lower lip. "Whoever created all of this, they were scared, or something or someone stood in their way."

"Do you believe this because it's what you want?"

"I doubt it. I much preferred life before I got tangled up in this mess. And now we're stuck."

"Maybe a break is for the best. Get back to the beginning and retrace your steps. Double check everything, and make sure you are on the correct path."

"Nothing else I can do, really. At least not until Aimee changes her mind."

\*\*\*

Lance placed his cup on the table. "Our lunches have been such a delight! They are a breath of fresh air from all the strain at work."

Chris held back a sigh. Most of her food lay untouched on the plate in front of her. "You seem to have taken over the leadership role of the Council guard permanently."

"Your father approves of my performance. With the threat of the Tarung rising daily, it makes sense to have a strong leader in charge."

"Has anyone tried to talk to them?"

"Talk to whom?"

"The Tarung. Has anyone attempted to open a dialogue and see what they want, and how we could settle this peacefully?"

He laughed. "Are you joking?"

She held his gaze.

"I see. One does not negotiate with terrorists, and—"

"They're not terrorists."

"They are attempting to overthrow your family. What would you call them, Christina?"

"How can you be sure that's their goal, if no one has ever spoken to them?"

"Their actions speak for themselves."

"All I've heard is that they are distributing information on the Verlohren, and—"

"Lies. Those are lies! Useless propaganda aimed at making the Living feel sorry for those parasites."

"Why shouldn't we have compassion for them? Their existence is dreadful, and the way we treat them only worsens their situation."

"They brought it upon themselves! Without their past sins, they would not be condemned to live as Verlohren. They would have moved on, like all the righteous and good people in Saltung."

"But—"

"That is not all. They could make amends, even in death, but they refuse to do that as well. What are we supposed to do? Let them infect us with their lawlessness and amoral behavior?"

"No, Lance. Of course not." She grabbed her fork and pierced the piece of chicken, almost sending it flying off her plate.

***

Lily hadn't returned home in ages. This was Lara's domain. Her sister reveled among the dead, among those who had lost all hope. She, on the other hand, had grown accustomed to the ways of the Living, their feelings and desires. She wondered what Lara would make of that. It had been her plan, though, for Lily to live amidst the Living, walk their path and help shape their policies. She'd done well in the past. Now, things were becoming more complicated.

She'd forgotten the acrid smell of sulfur that permeated this place. Lily wrinkled her nose and continued her slog down a meandering route along paths that most people only walked once. The black stone walls drew closer around her, and heat flared, drenching her flowing dress in seconds.

After a few more minutes, when the pathway broadened, she passed a house that had been built entirely of smashed glass. A young man sat on the floor, his contorted features faced the ceiling and a never-ending scream burst from his lips. Against expectations, the building dampened the noise of his shouts, and all Lily heard were the clinks and whirrs of the wind chimes that reflected off the polished porch ceiling.

She continued her journey until she arrived at her destination. Through the folds of the massive stone door, she stepped into an empty room, orange lighting marking the walls. There was silence, then the sound of a heavy door slamming reached her ears. Lara must have sensed her arrival. Good. They had plenty to discuss.

***

Freit, Saltung<br>Year 302, Day 56

"Yes! Finally!" Chris hurried back to the table. She slid the book onto the surface and nudged the binding open. Here it was. She should have realized sooner that after housing a copy of the *Demise of Reason*, the forbidden section would unearth other relevant volumes. If this didn't change Aimee's mind, nothing would.

She fell into the seat and pulled out her notebook and placed it next to the other two editions. The new text offered a cross reference to the ritual and described aspects that had been unclear to Chris before. The *Book of Sattran* spoke of a rite that needed to be completed to learn about the past. It didn't describe or even name the ceremony, and once more, Chris found herself confronted with riddles, but they seemed easier and more accessible than the ones in the *Demise of Reason*.

Her finger traced the text, 'The dead and the living, connected by a string, carved into a stone mountain at the dead center. That golden thread of light follows each life it touches until the distance is no longer seen. And it follows all things it is in contact with until it ends. With its own end—or the end of our world.'

She leaned closer and gazed at the jottings next to it. 'Is it time to stop? Is it time to go back? Can we trust this? The end? Are we prepared to see? Is the link safe? Is it close enough? All it's built upon is gone. All the survivors. Is this end real? Is this life real?'

The Well of Shadows

She wondered who'd added this, and if they ever found any answers to their questions. Was it still by the original author? Chris doubted that. The questions sounded like someone who had been where they are now, and then seemingly stopped. Or did they continue and fail?

When she read further, the text shifted to the ritual, and she grew excited when it appeared to revolve around establishing a connection. Another set of scribbles next to it seemed an addendum and recommended a protection spell.

Chris placed her pen on the table. What if Aimee saw this as just more magic that would create problems and hurt them? A ritual didn't have to include spells, though. She kept reading, and the more she read, the more she realized that yes, this would involve magic, at least if they added the protection spell which seemed like a must.

"Great." Chris suppressed a sigh. "There has to be…" She bent forward and browsed over more text, stopping when she reached another set of scrawls in the margins of several consecutive pages. "Wait, wait." She jumped up. No. This couldn't be. There was a way, but not one she had bargained for.

***

Year 302, Day 57

"Are you serious?" Aimee asked.

"Uh, yes?"

"That sounds promising. I'd be all for a ritual that offers answers. What's the catch, though?"

"Who says there's a catch?" Chris replied.

"Your face."

"Right. Well, the Book of Sattran focuses on two rituals. The Ritual of Varstahnet is the big one, the one supposedly offering all the answers. The one I'm talking about is different. It establishes a bond, but it also recommends casting a shielding spell before any of the rituals."

"So, the big rite reveals what really happened, and the other one creates a bond?" Aimee asked. "What's the problem then?"

"Yes, the protective spell connects us, and the ritual… binds the Dead and Living together."

"All of them? That's going to be a disaster," Dylan said.

"No, she means her and I. We'll be bound."

"Oh," Dylan mumbled.

"Yes," Chris replied.

"Binds us together how? And to what purpose? How is any of that different from the shielding spell connecting us?"

"The binding seems to allow for the sharing of vitality and abilities, while the protection spell is meant to fortify us against what is yet to come."

"I dread what's ahead, if such a spell is necessary. As for the binding, that means I'd have your magic at my disposal again, while you'd get to enjoy my dead body with all its glorious lack of energy. How is that helpful?"

"You'd have the *potential* for magic, though it would be difficult for you to access without proper training, and I doubt we have the time. The ritual is supposed to bind and reinforce strengths, so I likely won't have to deal with your energy issues."

"I still don't understand how this is supposed to help with the quest."

"I'm not sure that's its purpose. That's why there's a shielding spell scribbled in the margins. The binding… It'll be more like a test, like the ones we faced in the cave and the empty room. The protection spell will help, though given all we've experienced so far, I wouldn't be shocked if it was also part of the challenge."

"How reassuring." Aimee rolled her eyes. "Why would we do that? Sure, you're curious to learn the truth, and I was after this for years, too, so yes, I get being invested, but if that's all it does? If all we face is hardship and pain, why would we bother?"

"Because the truth is important!"

"To whom? Because it'll make you feel better about your family?"

"It's not about that. The truth *is* important for all of us, Living and Dead. Didn't you say the Sattran are suffering?"

"Yes."

"And the Tarung are getting stronger, and according to the Council, angrier. Learning the truth could help stop this conflict and allow us to find a better solution. Ending misery. Isn't that worth it?"

"In theory, yes. You're forgetting one thing, though."

"What?"

"There's no guarantee—"

"If this is about my survival again—"

"Not everything's about you, Princess."

Chris blushed.

"There is no guarantee we will learn the truth, or that the reveal is any better than what we are currently experiencing."

"What's wrong with you? Since when do you talk like this? I thought this was *your* quest. You were so passionate about it when we first met. What happened?" Chris asked.

"That's a good question. Woah, stop the death glare. She's right, and I'm not saying this because she's my sister. I know you were worried about Chris, about being or better, *feeling*, responsible again—"

"Dylan!"

"Let me finish. You'd sort of calmed down over the last several days, and now, when Chris first talked about a ritual that could help, you seemed all for it. So what happened? The spell you guys cast?"

"The magic *your* sister cast!"

"You're not usually this unreasonable. This is almost like that thing with Chris early on, when she accused you of being a con-artist and ran away," Dylan pointed out.

"That's not the same."

"What are you guys talking about?" Chris asked.

"It doesn't matter. Your brother has some weird delusions going on."

"Right, of course. Do you want to hear the bad news now?"

"Those weren't the bad news?" Aimee asked.

"No, and if your head wasn't stuck so far up…" Chris trailed off and relaxed her fists. "I still think there's something wrong with you, and I have a feeling Dylan agrees with me."

"I do," Dylan said.

Aimee stared at Chris but didn't say a word.

"Fine, have it your way. Remember after the empty room, when I said that according to the *Book of Sattran*, the one that arrived with us, we've completed a task?"

Aimee dipped her head.

"We signed a magical contract with both our trips, the caverns started it, and once we beat that task and followed up with the spell… We completed the pact."

"I signed nothing! *You* did the magic, so whatever this is, it's on you. You can deal with it."

"Stop being so awful," Dylan demanded.

"I wish it were that easy. It affects both of us, and if we don't continue, if we don't finish this quest—"

Aimee edged closer to Chris, stopping right in front of her. "Then what? I die?"

"No. I die, as in, the Living dies and the Dead… you burn."

Aimee swallowed hard. "You're lying."

"I'm not!"

"Yes, you are. You are so eager to persist you'll try any trick to change my mind. This is insane! We signed no contract, we agreed to no quest, and we surely did *not* agree to finish under penalty of *that*!"

"I understand this is upsetting—"

"You understand nothing! I wish Dylan had never contacted you. Even if that meant we'd never found the *Demise of Reason*. So be it! What good did it do so far? It almost killed us, and all the… all these *ghosts*." Aimee fell back.

"This is hard, it's difficult for me, too, but—"

"Dying is a walk in the park compared to burning! You have no clue—"

"I thought you opposed this because the risk is too high. That you didn't want me to die."

"I don't want you to die!"

"You're not acting like it."

"Sorry that I don't seem keen on *burning* for who knows how long."

"I don't even know what that means," Chris whispered.

"It's agony. The worst you can imagine? Multiply that by infinity. It traps you. You're locked up inside and all there is, all that exists, all you feel is pain."

Chris closed her eyes. "I'm not lying to you. We signed a contract, whether you believe it or not. And there will be consequences. Perhaps you'll change your mind when you get weaker, and…"

"Burn? Yes, Princess. I'm sure I'll notice that."

"You are unbelievable! That's not what I was going to say. I'm sorry, Dylan, but I can't be here anymore. I'll work on letting you go on my own, and well, if not… you'll be free either way soon." Chris glared at Aimee before darting out of the room and slamming the front door.

"I'd say you're horrible, but I know you're not. So, I will research what is going on and how to get you back to normal," Dylan said, grabbed his jacket and left the house.

"Whatever," Aimee whispered after the door fell shut for the second time.

***

Year 302, Day 62

An explosion reverberated through the streets and the air filled with dirt, debris, and the scent of burned rubber. The dust cleared and a cacophony of shouts and cries mingled in a wave of noise rattling in Chris's skull. She winced and raised a hand to her forehead, cursing when her fingers touched sticky redness. Her vision blurred, and she stumbled forward, rubble crunching beneath her feet.

"Christina! Where are you? Christina!"

Ripples of nausea rolled through her while the surrounding shouts resonated like an echo in her head. "Here," she breathed, trying to steady herself. Chris lumbered a few more steps toward the voice before she tightened her fists and accessed her magic to allow its flow to ease the hot pinpricks of pain tearing through her. She closed her eyes at the lull of warm energy soothing her body. How did people deal with pain without magic?

"I'm here," she called, cupping her hand above her eyes to shield against the blinding sun.

"Oh, my Gods, thank the heavens you are all right." Lance shook, grasping her hands. "I was so worried. I..." He swallowed hard and his eyes glinted. "They will pay for this! They almost killed you."

"Lance, calm down. I'm fine."

"You are bleeding... Your shirt." He motioned to touch her head, but then dropped his hand. "We need to get you to a physician."

"I'm all right. It's a scratch. I want to go home and rest."

"I am not sure that is a wise decision. Your father—"

"Is on a business trip, and I'm old enough to make my own decisions."

"All right. But I will accompany you back home."

Chris accepted his outstretched hand. "Thank you."

"I cannot stay since they will need my assistance in investigating this Tarung attack. Cowards," he grumbled.

"That's fine."

"It is not, but your mother will be home, so you will not be alone."

\*\*\*

Dylan shut the door behind him and raced into the kitchen. "There's been a strike near the Council."

"What?"

"People are saying the Tarung are responsible, that they'd wanted to assault the Council itself, but their attack failed and blew up between the marketplace and the Council."

"Is anyone hurt? Did people… Did someone die?" Aimee asked.

"Of course! How can an explosion in a public space not injure people?"

"Sorry, it's just… it doesn't sound like something the Tarung would do. They were making progress reaching out, and they'd even gained more Living followers. This might ruin all their hard work."

"How do you know this?"

Aimee scratched her head. "Uh, I may have reached out to someone who is a member of the Tarung. To see what they're up to and all that."

"Uh-huh, and who would that be?"

"Sarah?"

Dylan frowned. "Are you asking me or telling me?"

"I'm telling you, obviously. I talked to Sarah, and she told me a lot about them, their goals and methods. This doesn't fit."

"Mmhmm."

"What is it with you?"

"Nothing."

"What about… Do you know if… if Chris…?"

"No. I couldn't get close enough because the Council guards swarmed the area right away."

"Should I contact Martha and see if she heard anything?"

"Suddenly you're worried about her? Didn't seem like you gave a damn when you chased her out of *our* house last week."

"I never… Never mind. Forget it."

"I'm sorry. I'm worried about Chris, too, and I'm frustrated because I can't figure out anything about what's going on with you or how to fix it. Markus and I have gone over everything, and we've even spoken to most of his contacts," Dylan sulked.

"That's because there's nothing wrong with me."

He snorted. "Keep telling yourself that. But seriously, looking back to last week, does your behavior seem normal?"

Aimee rubbed her neck. "I'm sorry for the way I talked to Chris. She makes me so mad sometimes, but…"

"But?"

"It wasn't just that, all right? I don't like magic, but I trust your sister. I know she wouldn't lie to me, not about this."

"Then why did you say all these things? Last time, after you guys came back from that empty room, you wanted to stop because you were so worried about Chris, but you didn't act that way the other day. We could reason with you after the empty room, but last time, it was almost like you were a different person."

"I don't know! Everything was normal at first, and then the talk about spells and contracts and consequences. It was like this curtain fell. A haze? I got so angry and scared. I wanted it all to stop and for Chris to leave, to never speak of this quest again."

"And this all sounds like there's nothing wrong with you?"

"You might have a point."

\*\*\*

"Two visits home within a month. Careful, little sister, or I may get the impression you miss me," Lara drawled.

"Your intervention could have killed her! That wasn't why I came to you!" Lily exclaimed.

"Hmm, let me think about this." Lara put a finger on her lips. "Yes, right. You came to *me* with a problem *you* couldn't solve, and so I fixed it." She cocked her head. "And this is the gratitude I get? Your time among the Living might have addled your brain."

"I'm serious, Lara. That wasn't the deal."

"That's *exactly* what I'm upholding, dear. The deal, which is more important than anything else."

"Without her, we don't have a deal!"

"Because she's the last one?"

"Yes! You see the problem now?"

Lara shrugged her shoulders. "Her husband can continue."

"They are not married yet."

"Then make sure that changes soon."

"You overestimate my influence."

"And you seem to underestimate the consequences to us if you fail. If there's a breach of contract, or if there's no one to uphold their side of the bargain... Do I need to spell it out for you?"

"No. You don't."

"Then why are you still here? Go work on your lamb," Lara said, laughing.

Lily held her sister's gaze and clenched her jaw. This wasn't going as planned. Then again, when did it ever? Plans that fell to pieces seemed to be the story of her life. Wasn't that what led them here in the first place? Not that her sister would ever agree with such an assessment.

*** 

Year 302, Day 64

"I'm fine! Would you stop fussing over me!" Chris said with a scowl.

Aimee stuffed her hands into her pants pockets. "I'm sorry that you got hurt."

"Did you cause the explosion?"

"What? No, of course not."

"Then you have nothing to be sorry about. Besides, my favorite shirt suffered more than I did. There's so much blood on it from the tear on my head that I should probably throw it out."

"I am, though. I'm sorry for how I've treated you, last time, when..." Aimee scuffed her foot along the floor.

"I accept your apology."

"Dylan thinks there's something wrong with me. And for the record, he's the one who made me all crazy, hence the fussing."

"Right."

"I'm serious! He was so upset when we found out that you got hurt during the attack. What were you doing there?"

"Let's slow down. One thing after the other. Aside from being impulsive and hot-headed, what's supposed to be wrong with you?"

"Hey! I'm not that bad."

Chris raised her eyebrows.

"All right. Anyway, remember early on when we met, and you thought I was a con-artist?"

"I recall. I still cringe at the memory."

"That's how I feel about our last meeting. It seems odd, I mean, sure, at first I was a bit in denial, righteous anger and all that."

"Naturally," Chris said, laughing.

"But thinking back now, it was as if this… this veil dropped over me. I could not stop from reacting the way I did, as if something guided me. I wasn't in control, yet I was? I'm not making much sense." She rubbed her hands across her thighs.

"You are making perfect sense." Chris rose and paced. "After I'd gotten home, back then, I was calm again, but on the way there, I was still raging internally about you, and Verlohren in general. All the stereotypes and lies about your kind. They were bouncing in my head." She stopped. "I'll admit I had bought some of these ideas before meeting you and our adventure, my research and all."

"But you calmed down once you got home?"

"As soon as I entered my room, things changed. They became clearer again. Before, it was as if a haze had fallen over me at your place, and I had to run."

"Yes! I felt like running, too. I wanted our conversation to end. I *needed* it to end."

Chris sat down next to Aimee. "Exactly."

"I suppose that means Dylan is right."

"About what?"

140

"He should be back any minute. I'm pretty sure I can transmit what he has to say, but basically, we're connected somehow."

"What?"

"Yeah, that was my reaction, too. It's because of..." Aimee trailed off. "Wait, there he is."

"Great," Chris said, and blinked rapidly against the sting in her eyes. How she wished she could see him, too.

"Yes, she's fine, and of course I made sure and asked her all the million questions you requested. Look, I've already told her you think we're connected. Can you explain that again?"

Chris leaned back against the couch. She hated this. He was there, but still out of reach. She trusted Aimee, but this rankled her, and it hurt more than she wanted to contemplate.

"OK, so here it goes. According to his research, which he wants you to know took forever, and needed the help of one of Markus's sources, the shielding spell you put around us when Lance showed up already pointed toward a connection."

"How so?"

"I felt your magic."

"You did what? Why didn't you say anything?" Chris rose and resumed her pacing.

"Uh, because I had no idea that meant anything? Besides, I told Dylan."

"And he didn't deem it necessary for you to tell me?"

"He seemed to believe this was of no significance either."

Chris stomped her foot. "Dylan!"

"He's sorry?"

"I bet. Go on."

"I'd first suggested it's a Verlohren thing, but he didn't register your magic. I said it might be because I was the one directly connected to you, and we left it at that."

She glared at Aimee. How could her brother have forgotten this? He probably was daydreaming during those lessons.

"But that's not it. Our switch in the mountains and the empty room, all of it, it binds us."

Chris furrowed her brows. "I see."

"That's all you gotta say to this?"

"Well, what's done is done, and the incidents after the last spell would have led to this, anyway."

"Led to what? Why aren't you surprised?"

"Because unlike my brother, I paid attention in class."

Aimee snorted.

"I don't want to know what he just said."

Aimee raised her hands and failed at keeping a straight face. She cleared her throat. "OK, what did you pay attention to?"

"There are notes, stories and references of special connections between mages. They are rare, but powerful, and—"

"Let me stop you right there. I'm not a mage. I never was," Aimee said.

"That doesn't mean you didn't have the potential for magic back when you were alive."

"But there's no way to figure that out now. Though my mom... She dabbled in spells. At least the healing kind, and though I dimly recall some of her work, she didn't teach me her craft."

Chris settled back down next to Aimee. "She wouldn't have had to. You cannot teach a magical inclination. It is there, or it isn't. It would also explain why you could strengthen my magic in the empty room. Either way, this seems like the only explanation that makes sense. Dylan never had magic, and you said he felt nothing during my protection spell."

"That's all... I'm not sure you can count two cases as evidence."

"You'll be OK. You don't have to be afraid of this or magic."

"I'm not afraid of magic. I just don't like it," Aimee said.

"Right. We've established that." Chris heaved a sigh. "There's still a connection between us, no matter what caused it, and it has only gotten stronger. I'm sure this will be helpful during our quest."

"Yeah, probably. Also, not much we can do."

"Are you OK with performing the binding ritual after we cast the protection spell?"

"By *we* you mean you?"

"Yes and no. I will say the incantation, but it won't work without your presence. You are already a part of it, we both are, and if we don't..."

"I believe you, and yes, we will do both, the shielding spell and the binding rite."

"Great. I will prepare everything, and we should do it all here. There's no way to get away with any of this at the manor, and I'm not comfortable out in the open."

"I'd assumed we'd cast it here. Your house and the Council are kinda no-go zones for Verlohren."

"Right, the protection spells. I'd forgotten about those."

"How convenient," Aimee mumbled.

"I'm sorry. I sometimes forget, and—"

"It's fine. It's not you. I'm projecting."

"Oh?"

"The attack doesn't sit right with me. After you'd left last time and I'd calmed down, I reached out to... to Sarah and got some info on the Tarung."

"Sarah, your Sarah?"

Aimee nodded. "Wait, what? OK, be careful."

"What was that about?" Chris asked.

"Dylan's gotta go. He's meeting with Markus soon."

"Oh, OK. I didn't know she was still around."

"Hmm. Either way, their goal is to educate the Living as much as possible and eliminate or mitigate the stigma attached to the Verlohren. It makes no sense for them to plan or even execute an attack."

"If that's true, then I'd agree, but what if they did it but not as a sanctioned mission?"

"By some disgruntled members who don't like the pace or the way of the Tarung?"

"Yes. Any group is bound to encounter friction and disagreement among its followers."

"Sarah didn't mention any of that."

"How close are you two?"

"What?"

"I just mean, if you're not that close anymore and you suddenly contact her about the Tarung, why should she share everything with you? I wouldn't."

"I don't know. It's complicated."

"My point exactly."

"Still. Why would a group of Verlohren risk putting a bigger target on their backs? The Tarung are already in trouble because of their very existence. It makes no sense for them to carry out a strike, no matter what the Council says."

"Let's assume you're right. Who else would do this, and more importantly, who else would benefit from blaming such an attack on the Tarung?" Chris asked.

"That's the question, Princess."

"I've been thinking, given that this quest is more dangerous than we've anticipated, maybe it's time to train you?"

"What? But Verlohren can't use magic."

"Oh, no, not magic. More like martial arts, or self-defense," Chris explained.

"That's what I've got you for," Aimee said.

"Yes, unless we're separated or can't see each other."

Aimee shrugged her shoulders "All right. We could try it."

"Great." She jumped up. "Let's go outside."

"What? Now?" Aimee gazed toward the fridge.

Chris laughed. "You look like you're mourning the dissolution of you plan to get more food."

Aimee shrugged. "Well, I'm kinda hungry."

"You're always hungry. If we go by that, we'll get nothing done." Chris extended her hand and tugged Aimee to her feet. "Come on."

"Fine," she mumbled and followed Chris outside.

\*\*\*

Lily resented Lara for sending her on this senseless spying mission. Chris was spending more time with Aimee, but that didn't mean they were closer to finding the truth. Even if they did, Chris was the heir to the Council. Why would she destroy her own power? If only Dylan hadn't died. His death and fate were all that remained that could pit Chris against her family.

She stood in the clearing near Aimee and Dylan's house after conjuring up a glamor, watching the two women spar as her muscles twitched and she longed to join in.

"No, no, you take a step first, then drop the staff and block my blow," Chris instructed.

Aimee returned to her previous stance. "Let's try again."

Chris crouched and raised her baton. "Ready?"

"Yes," she said, batting her stick forward and meeting Chris's with a muted clang.

Chris parried the attack and dove to the side, swinging down and sweeping Aimee off her feet. She dropped her weapon and rushed next to her. "I'm sorry. Are you OK?"

Aimee rubbed her lower back. "Yeah. I'm fine. You just caught me off guard. How is kissing the ground all the time a lesson in self-defense? Shouldn't we be training without weapons?"

"I thought you'd enjoy the batons."

"They looked like fun, but let's try the regular stuff," Aimee said and leapt to her feet.

"Are you sure you're up for it?" Chris asked, canting her head.

"Yeah. Come on. You were the one going on about the dangers of our travels."

Lily groaned. Travels? Where were they going next? Maybe Chris would tell her later. Or afterwards. By the time she returned her focus to the pair training in the yard, Aimee had flung Chris to the ground and was hovering over her.

"I take it you've done this before?" Chris asked.

"A bit." Aimee laughed, which turned into a yelp when Chris grabbed her arms and hurled her around before straddling her.

"That's cheating. You could have told me that." Chris still pinned Aimee down.

"Right." Aimee cleared her throat, her gaze locked on Chris hovering above her.

Lily rolled her eyes. She'd seen enough.

\*\*\*

Freit, Saltung
Year 302, Day 70

"All right, let me see the list," Aimee said and opened the Book of Sattran to read out the information of the Varstahnet ritual.

> *"To call upon the next revelation procure:*
> - *Water from the clear flowing Eastern River*
> - *A waterlily's resident's liver*
> - *Stern Stone from within the Western Harrows*
> - *Leota root from the Northern dry lands*
> - *Babes feed from its milk from birth*
> - *Cinders are a Kefer tree's sole worth*
>
> *Only when assembled, they give way to the Truth which was altered."*

She looked up at Chris. "Uh, OK. I'm assuming you already have a plan for obtaining these items?"

"Of course. You and I will first go back to the Thal Mountains, while Dylan and Markus search for the Stern Stone."

"The Thal Mountains? What for?" Aimee whined.

"The text refers to the leota root, which is only found in the dry areas near the Thal Mountains, and since it grows high up, we have to climb."

"Ugh, why can't that grow somewhere else?"

"I don't want to go back there either, but our only other option is to send Dylan and Markus on this trip. They don't have magic. They're better off looking for the Stern stone in the Harrows Forest," Chris said.

Aimee grumbled. "Fine. But let's stay in our own bodies this time. No more touching strange fluids and all that."

"That was never *my* problem."

"Sure, sure. We gotta be on the same page, here."

"Just remember this when you once more register the urge to touch unknown objects."

Aimee frowned. "That sounds weird."

"Never mind," Chris said. "Are you ready for the protection spell and the ritual?"

"Now? I thought we'd go gather the ingredients for the Varstahnet rite first?"

"We could do it after, but it's safer to perform both before we head out to the mountains again. It'll allow us to locate each other if we get lost."

"But didn't you say that we might face a challenge again? What if that wipes us out and we can't leave tomorrow?"

"Then we'll postpone it by a couple of days. I want us to be able to locate one another."

Aimee tilted her head. "Is that part of the ritual that binds us?"

"No. It's a part of the shielding spell. It doesn't work for everybody, but our connection indicates that the protection spell will work that way between us."

"Because I felt your magic?"

"Yes. I'm sorry. I don't want to make you uncomfortable or put you in an awkward position, but I want us to be safe, and—"

"You worry too much." Aimee took Chris's hand. "I'm fine with this spell, the binding ritual and whatnot. You don't have to be so anxious about it. I've said I'd continue, and I meant that."

Chris smiled. "Good. Let's get started with the shielding charm first. Sit across from me and stretch out your hands." She sat down on the floor.

Aimee scooted off the couch and faced Chris.

"All right." She grasped Chris's hands. Her eyes closed before they snapped open.

"No, it will not hurt."

"Yes, but last time we... we went to that place. That room. I don't wanna go there again."

"We won't. This is a completely different spell."

"But it comes from the same place, this quest, and so there's a chance that this is another test or task or whatever."

"Yes, it has a similar origin, but it's not the same. It's a standard protection spell, and there's nothing unusual about it. I checked and researched it. It's safe."

"OK," Aimee breathed and closed her eyes.

Chris rattled off the incantation so fast Aimee couldn't fathom, but she felt it, the heat pouring from Chris' hands into hers, spreading through her body like a sugar rush and making her dizzy. A syrupy heaviness grew in her arms and legs, permeating her torso and forcing the air from her lungs. She gasped and a deep, frightened breath escaped her lips as her heart tightened in her chest. Her eyes flew open and widened.

"It's fine, you're all right," Chris soothed. "It's anchoring you to me."

"What does that mean, and why does it... hurt... so much." Aimee groaned, still holding on to Chris.

She frowned. "It shouldn't be painful."

"Whoever... told you... that... lied," Aimee pressed out.

"Terry said... Oh, no."

"What?"

"Perhaps it's because you're a Verlohren. I didn't tell him that when we selected the spell."

A spasm ran through Aimee.

"Let me try something." Chris once more closed her eyes.

The heat that had started as a pleasant wave and then transformed into a raging torrent eager to drown her in agony slowed down and merged into lapping ocean waves that trickled over bare feet on the beach. Her breathing ebbed, and her heart receded to its regular, languid cadence.

"Whatever you just did?" Aimee sighed and released her hold of Chris. "It worked."

No reply.

Aimee blinked and froze.

Chris rocked back and forth, her eyes closed, and her body drenched in sweat.

"What... Chris!" Aimee scrambled up and slid closer to Chris's shaking form. She hesitated, but then touched her shoulder, and when nothing changed, she grabbed onto both upper arms and shook her. "Come on, Princess. This isn't funny. What's going on?"

Chris muttered unintelligible sounds in a language Aimee had never heard.

"We got plans tomorrow, and I won't let you use this as an excuse to turn into a slacker. Besides, your brother will murder me if anything happens to you."

Chris's body trembled, but the rocking stopped.

"Is this an improvement? Come on! You said this would be fine and safe and all. You can't be wrong here."

Aimee shook her once more. "You're scaring me."

Chris's eyes flung open, and she gasped before sagging, falling toward Aimee who caught her.

"Hey. There you are." She pulled her close.

"Sorry," Chris murmured.

"Stop apologizing. What happened?"

Chris straightened and scuttered back. "Are you still in pain?" Her gaze roamed over Aimee.

"No. It eased shortly after you said you'd try something. What did you do?"

"You're not... Promise me you won't freak out."

"Oh Gods, don't start a sentence like that."

Chris picked at a loose string on the rug. "The protection spell established a connection between us, like I thought it would."

"And?"

"The spell apparently had two people of the Living variety in mind, so it... there was a hiccup, and it started to reject you."

"OK. But you fixed it. How did you do that?"

Chris dug her fingers into the carpet. "Remember when I told you that this spell would help us locate each other?"

"Yes, though I don't understand how that connects to whatever you've done to stop it."

"Our connection is stronger because... I had to do this, so please don't be mad."

"Your stalling and hedging make everything worse. You can't even look me in the eye and earlier you couldn't get away from me fast enough. What happened?"

"I, OK, so the connection between us is supposed to be like a thin thread, if you focus, you can pull on it and we could find each other again. When your pain started and I realized what was causing it... I had to fix it. The spell would have continued and eventually burned you."

Aimee's eyes widened.

"No, no. Not your kind of burning, though I'm not sure if this would be any better. You'd have been incinerated inside out. Is your version of burning worse than that because that's already gruesome."

"Quit. Stalling."

Chris licked her lips. "I allowed the connection to grow, and instead of a strand, it's more like a broad tree limb."

"Why is that a problem?"

"It might be intrusive, but it was the only way to channel the energy into me to stop your pain, and—"

Aimee jumped to her feet. "Wait, wait. Are you telling me you took the pain away by exposing yourself to it?"

Chris stared up at Aimee, her mouth opening and closing. "That's all you got out of what I said?"

"Well, isn't that the most important part? Do you think I prefer for you to endure suffering that was meant for me?"

"Stop it. Don't even start. I'm not a helpless damsel in need of protection."

"I'm not doing that at all. You might project your fiancé's attitude onto me."

"I'm not! You were the one who didn't want to continue this quest because you were so afraid for my life!"

Aimee raised her hands. "No, I won't let you derail this discussion by making me angry and turning this into a fight."

"Making you—"

"Chris, please. Come, sit down here," Aimee said before sitting on the couch and patting the space next to her.

She huffed, but joined her friend.

"This tree branch you've created, what does it do? How long does this last? Oh, and intrusive?"

"It lasts. There's a counter-spell, but to be honest, the way you reacted to this one, I don't want to try it."

"All right. What about the rest? Does it hurt you?"

"No, I mean, it can hurt both of us. You'd know if I'm in pain and I'd feel yours, but not at the same intensity. More like an echo letting you know the other is hurting or in danger."

"That's not bad."

"Hmm."

"What's bothering you about it?"

"The intrusive part, it's… It doesn't just work for pain." She cleared her throat. "Any powerful emotion we experience, the other will be aware of it."

"Like anger or hunger?"

Chris laughed and wiped her eyes.

"Hey. Why are you crying?"

"I don't know. I'm just… I should have known better, or I should have considered you being a Verlohren could throw things, but that would have meant telling Terry, and somehow, that doesn't feel right, and I go with—"

"Your feelings. Yes."

"And this time that cost you. If I didn't think of a way to fix it—"

"But you did. Stop beating yourself up over mistakes or problems you couldn't have foreseen, or even worse, things that never materialized. You suffer twice when you worry."

"Huh?"

"My mother used to always say that when I was little. Stop worrying, Aimee, it only makes you suffer twice."

"Or guarantees you suffer once."

Aimee cocked her head.

"Well, sometimes we worry for nothing, so when our fears don't come to pass, we suffered once in our imagination when we didn't have to, so you'll suffer at least once if you worry, even in situations where nothing bad happens."

"True. Can you apply this to yourself now?"

Chris bumped into Aimee. "I'll try." She sighed. "Are you still up for the binding ritual?"

Aimee's eyes crinkled. "Because we need an even deeper bond after the tree limb you just created?

"It's a different connection. I told you it lets—"

"I was just messing with you, Princess. I'm fine, and we can continue. Are you sure you have enough energy?"

Chris sat straighter. "Of course."

"All right. What does this entail now?"

"Thankfully, and unlike the big ritual, this one doesn't need any special ingredients. It's more of a really long, complicated spell that I have to recite while we—"

"Hold hands again?"

"Yes."

"Naturally," Aimee drawled and held out her hands for Chris. In certain aspects, magic was so predictable. She'd never admit it, but it might be growing on her a bit. At least Chris's version of magic. And here it was again, Chris's warmth seeping into her. She sighed.

"Close your eyes," Chris whispered.

Aimee followed suit.

\*\*\*

"No, no, you don't understand," Lily said, pacing.

"I understand perfectly. You're not keeping her in check, and because of that, they will ruin everything we've built. Is that what you want?" Lara stalked toward her sister. "You need to reinforce the magic!"

"Of course not. I just don't see the problem in them spending time together and training. That's better than going out exploring. The spells hold, both the original on the line and the one on Chris specifically. I've already checked that."

"If they did, they wouldn't be on this quest! What are they preparing for? Have you ever thought about that? People don't just train for the fun of it."

Lily opened her mouth, but Lara waved her off.

"You don't count. What else are you supposed to do? But now, during this important time, I'd expect you would take your duties more seriously."

"I am! Why do you think I spied on them?"

"Because I told you so. Otherwise, you'd be doing what? Sitting in your mansion, studying, or training?"

Lily folded her arms.

"And they were getting along?"

"Yes. They acted like... friends."

"That's bad."

"Why does that matter?" Lily asked.

"Do you ever read anything older, or did you forget all the ancient journals and tomes we've studied to prepare for this?"

"Oh."

"Yes, oh. We have disturbed the natural order of existence to increase our power. Do you think that happens without consequences? That there's no plan to force the path of the world back into its original course? That's what we're up against, sister, and I *need* you on board. I can't do this alone."

"I'd forgotten. You believe it then? Chris is part of…"

"How else would they have gotten this far? We need to stop them."

"But how?"

"We will send in the Zilal-ruh."

"That's overkill. I don't want Chris to die! We need her as the Morgen heir to uphold the contract."

"I told you before, her husband will do."

"She's not married yet!"

"Then I'd hurry and see that that changes soon," Lara barked.

# seven

The wind pushed against them, making their trip more tiring than expected.

"What did you tell your family? There's no retreat planned this weekend, is there?" Aimee asked.

"No. The next one is in a month. I told them I'm staying with friends. It's not as if I need to report home like a wayward child," Chris replied.

"You still live with your parents."

"It's difficult for the heir to reside elsewhere. They have additional security at the mansion, but it's also tradition, I suppose."

"Hmm. It can't be easy."

Chris laughed. "No, it's not."

"Wanna return to our cavern and spend the night there before climbing higher tomorrow morning?"

"You want to go back there?"

Aimee shrugged. "It's a shelter, and well, I never told you, but the night we switched, I may have run into a few Sattran."

Chris stopped. "What? And you're telling me this *now*?"

"It slipped my mind," Aimee mumbled and waved her off; her hand going straight to her pendant.

"How... ugh." Chris marched on while Aimee hurried to match her pace.

"I truly forgot. I wasn't trying to hide this from you. At the time, I was freaked out, but then I found you again, and the book, your spell, and that awful room... Next the haze happened, and I don't know, maybe my mind intentionally pushed this encounter down. I remembered right before the spell last night, but that took a lot out of me, then you and—"

"You're rambling. I'm not mad, OK? It's scary. This is the last place I want to be, much less spend the night, but we need to, and now the Sattran—"

"They hate fire."

"What?"

"I held them at bay with fire. You're a walking torch, so you can," Aimee made a shooing motion with her hands, "make them run."

"I'm *not* a walking torch."

"No offense. Burning hands better?"

Chris grumbled.

"I meant we're not helpless, and they weren't aggressive. They mumbled nonsense, and I don't know what they wanted, but they didn't seem dangerous. Just creepy."

"I hope so."

Although they didn't encounter any traces of Sattran on their trail, they set up guard for the night. Aimee took the first round with another torch gripped in her hand. There were moments she genuinely envied Chris's magic. The dripping water sounds in the cavern had given her a headache, or better added to the one the sun had already inflicted upon her, and she'd been grateful when it was Chris's turn to watch over them.

***

Thal Mountains, Saltung<br>Year 302, Day 72

In the morning, they continued their climb higher and were on the lookout for Leota roots.

"Did you have a nightmare last night?" Chris asked while digging through a few short thorny bushes.

"What?" Aimee halted her search. "Did I say something?"

"No. Never mind." Chris bent down to tear out a root. "I got one." She placed it in her knapsack. "Two more and we can head back home."

"Why did you think I had a nightmare, and why can't you look at me? You're all shifty and nervous. What's going on?"

Chris fiddled with the string of her backpack strap, swallowing hard to ease her dry mouth. Why had she brought that up? "I'm sorry. I'm being intrusive and I don't mean to be."

"How?" Aimee stepped closer to her. "Wait, is this about the spell? The connection you mentioned, and… Wait. Which one caused this? I'm assuming the spell."

"Yes. It comes from the link we've established with the protection spell." She cleared her throat, dropping her gaze. "When I was watching out for trouble, at first you seemed agitated. I got this nervous energy bleeding into me, but when you calmed down, everything went still." Chris bit her lip. "I was contemplating the ritual and wondering how Dylan and Markus were faring in their search for the Stern stone when this heaviness settled over me."

"What heaviness?"

"I felt sad suddenly, but it didn't seem to come from within me, and I… I thought it must have been you, and I remembered the empty room and everything, and I'm sorry. We should probably quit here and never bring this up again," Chris fretted.

"Stop." Aimee grasped her hands. "Your worry is making me anxious, not just watching you, but I feel it, here." She placed Chris's hand on her chest. "My heart rarely beats this fast."

"Oh," Chris exhaled, staring transfixed at her hand. She flushed, hoping that Aimee wouldn't notice or at least ignore the heat spreading through her. "Uh, I… I'm sorry?"

Aimee laughed and let go of her.

A few seconds ticked by without either of them stirring before Chris yanked her hand back as if she'd suffered a shock.

"I told you I was fine with all of this. It's not ideal, or rather, I'd prefer for us to not be so aware of each other, but I'm glad it's you, you know, if it had to be *someone*." Aimee dragged her feet along the rocky sand.

"Thanks?"

"You can stop turning statements into questions now. I'm serious, Princess. It's fine. We're good and all that. Let's get going, so we find the rest of the roots and head back home. I wanna sleep in my own bed sometime soon."

"Right." Chris's eyes fluttered as her gaze roamed over her surroundings, trying to snap out of the spell that Aimee's benign reaction had enveloped her in.

On their way down the mountain, Chris encountered a familiar, albeit unwelcome, sight. "Get down," she hissed and ducked behind a boulder. Aimee followed suit.

"What is it?" Aimee whispered.

Chris pointed forward. "Over there!"

"What? I don't... woah. Are those... Why are those stones *flying*?"

"No idea. This happened back then when we'd switched, but I had no magic, and... everything hurt. I just ran away."

"Neglected to tell me about that, huh?" Aimee smiled before bumping into Chris' shoulder.

"Right. Let me see if my magic can arrest them from here. If not, I can suspend time, and that'll freeze them so we can investigate further."

"Wait, what? Stopping time? I don't—"

"Hush. Not now. I need to concentrate." Chris took a deep breath and closed her eyes.

\*\*\*

Halting time. Of *all* the information not to share. Aimee pushed her tongue against her teeth to keep quiet. She wasn't mad at Chris about all the other stuff she hadn't mentioned yet, but the ability to stop time seemed kind of newsworthy and important, especially after the protection spell.

"We're not close enough. Come on." Chris grabbed Aimee's arm and pulled her forward.

"For your magic or to freeze time?"

"Stop being so grumpy about this. It didn't occur to me you needed a run-down of all my abilities."

Aimee grumbled but allowed Chris to drag her along.

"Stopping time is tricky and it doesn't always work. I can only do it if I'm close by. Don't worry, I'll unfreeze you."

Aimee stuffed her hands in her pants pockets. "How reassuring."

Chris chuckled and raised her arms, making the stones that still hovered above them freeze in mid-air.

"You did it!"

"Wait. You're not frozen? How is that possible?"

"I dunno. Maybe it's because of the protection spell or the connection?"

"I suppose," Chris said. "We should investigate."

"Agreed, but let's not do this for long, OK? We can still return to our previous camp place in the forest before nightfall."

"This might be important. We could always spend the night in the cave again."

"Never thought I'd hear you say that."

Chris reached out to touch the stone, but Aimee grasped her arm and pulled her backward. "Wait. Remember how touching stuff got us into trouble last time?"

"Right. But these are frozen."

"Yeah, I don't know."

"You said you wanted to go home."

"Yeah, but... Oh, whatever." Aimee raised her hand and touched the granite.

"Really?"

"I decide quickly."

"Apparently," Chris said and touched the floating stone as well.

The moment she did, a keening shout rang out. They jumped and tried to withdraw their hands from the rock, but they were stuck.

"What the..." Aimee pulled hard, but to no avail. "Can you unfreeze time while your hand is attached?"

"What good would that do? These things were gliding up and down. Besides, we'll run out in several minutes, anyway. I can't stop time longer than that."

"Good point," Aimee grunted and tried to loosen her grip, only to fail again. "But wait. Once your spell fades and we're still stuck, will we float with them?"

"No." Chris laughed. "I can keep halting time, though we still need to figure this out because while stopping and holding time isn't as exhausting as teleporting, it will drain me, too, eventually."

"Ah, good. That you can stop time again, not that it drains you."

Chris chuckled. "I understood what you meant."

Shuffling footsteps drew near.

"Didn't you freeze time?"

"Yes, but it's not covering all of Saltung, just about ten yards."

"Also helpful information to have!"

"I did say we have to move closer, so you could have assumed that distance is important."

"Never mind. What are we gonna do? Someone's coming and we're stuck. Can you still do magic with your other hand?"

"Of course."

Aimee's shoulders sagged. "All right. We're not completely helpless."

"Uh, Aimee," Chris breathed.

"What?"

"Are those... Are those Sattran? It's broad daylight. What are they doing here?"

She turned her head toward Chris's nod. "Oh, man. Those... They look like the ones I encountered outside of the cave."

Three Sattran glided closer, once more moving as a single unit. Colorful strips of mismatched fabric covered their bodies. "The fire and the earth," the tallest of them slurred.

"Are they drunk?" Chris murmured, but it resembled a shout in Aimee's head.

"No. They talk strange."

"The fire and the earth," the tall one intoned again.

"What does that mean?" Chris asked.

"Beats me. They mentioned fire last time, too."

"What else did they say?"

"I don't remember."

"Right." Chris cleared her throat. "What do you want? Are you responsible for us being stuck?"

"Fire and earth together. Truth."

"What truth? Who is fire and earth?" Aimee asked. "You could be fire, though how would they know you are a mage with fire hands?"

"I don't..." She sighed. "Whatever. Maybe earth refers to the stones?"

"And the truth?" Aimee added.

"Reveal truth," the smallest Sattran sang.

"Do they know of our quest?" Chris asked.

"Your guess is as good as mine."

"Truth. Now," the tall one lamented.

"How? We're not done with the quest. We don't even know the full truth yet," Chris said.

"Now. Truth. Fire and earth," the short one rasped.

"Maybe you're earth?"

"Why? Because I'll soon be part of it?"

"Don't say that!" Chris snapped.

"Truth. Free," the tall Sattran moaned.

"So we speak the truth and we'll be free?" Chris asked.

"Truth about what?"

"Heart," the tallest warbled before groaning.

"That's helpful," Aimee grumbled.

"It is, actually, but… You're not going to like it."

"Huh? You understand what they want?"

"I can make an educated guess."

"Wait." Aimee careened her head. "Where did they go?"

"What?"

"They've left again. They disappear from one second to the next. That is so rude! And now this bird is flying away! Wait, why is it able to leave while we're still stuck, and the stones aren't moving?"

"Huh, perhaps their motion is arrested for however long this takes," Chris said. "And quit being mad at the Sattran. Being out in the sun must have been hard for them. I remember how you felt."

"Hmpf."

"Stop sulking. They left enough clues."

"Verlohren don't have magic. How could they have trapped us here?"

"No one said they are responsible, only that they offered a potential way out," Chris said.

"Let's hear it."

"Speaking the truth from your heart will release you."

Aimee snorted. "That's dumb."

"Perhaps, but what's there to lose? We might as well try it."

"But what truth from my heart?"

Chris rose and straightened. "I can start, and… You could figure it out from there."

"All right."

Chris shuffled her feet and cast her gaze downward. "Being who I am, and the upbringing that I've had… I've never had many friends. Most people usually… They are after something whenever I meet them."

"I'm sorry."

"It's fine. I just… I didn't realize how lonely I was until I met you."

"Until you found Dylan again, you mean?"

Chris released a sound that rang somewhere between a laugh and a sob. "That, too, but no. I'm talking about you. All you've ever wanted was my help."

Aimee rolled her shoulders but remained quiet, unsure if she wished for Chris to continue.

"During all these lunches with Lance, he babbles about our future, and do you know what he's most interested in?"

Her gaze locked with Chris's. "What?"

"Me being the Head of the Council, and what that will mean for *him*."

Aimee scoffed but dropped her gaze. "You don't have to marry that guy."

"I won't."

"Does *he* know that? Do your parents?"

"No, but I'll tell them all when we get back. No matter how you'll react to what I'm about to say. That's not why I'm doing it."

"What? Telling me that people like to take advantage of you?"

"Are you always this oblivious?"

Aimee ducked her head. "Only when I want to be. When I *must* be."

"So you know where this is going."

"I might have an idea, and if… if it's *that*, uh, it's better you didn't."

"Then we'll stay stuck forever."

"You don't know that."

"This has been on my mind a lot, and I was slow to realize it because I've never…" Chris raised her head and stared at the sky. "Gods. This is not how I envisioned this."

"Chris—"

"Please let me finish. I told you how absorbed I've always been in my studies and my training. There weren't just no friends. There was no one else. No one of any significance."

"Your family, Terry—"

"Oh, of course. I'm not talking about those kinds of relationships."

"All right." Aimee once more tried to free her hand.

"That desperate to get away, huh?" Chris's voice carried a wistful undertone, but desolation clouded the sound.

Aimee's stomach sank. She leaned against the rock, shielding her face. "I don't wanna hurt you."

"Then don't."

***

Aimee laughed. "It's that easy?"

Chris joined in the laughter. "I can't speak from experience, so…"

"I really wish you wouldn't."

"You've made that clear, and I'm sorry. I don't want to force you to listen to this, and… I respect your right to react however you see fit, but in this situation, given we're stuck here, I need to say this."

"Chris—"

"I'm falling in love with you."

Silence.

Aimee once more hid her face. "I'm sorry, but I can't."

"Why?"

"I'm dead."

"I'm aware of that."

"Then you don't realize what this truly means. I have nothing to offer. There's no future. Everything… My entire existence depends on my best friend's whim, of whenever she forgives herself and lets me go… Once that happens…"

"You'll leave."

Aimee nodded.

"It hasn't happened so far, though. What about in the meantime, we could—"

164

"No! I'm not doing that to you."

"Why don't I have a say in this?"

"This isn't *easy* for me! You at least have a life ahead of you. All I have is… This here. This… you've *been* me. You know what it feels like."

"Yes," Chris whispered. "I'm sorry. I didn't think…"

"It's not that, I… I would if circumstances were different."

"You and your honesty," Chris pressed out. "Why don't you lie to me?"

"Excuse me?"

"All my life, I've followed the path set out for me. I did it because it was there. Yes, my parents wanted it, but… It was easy. There was a plan, and that was comforting. It took care of everything."

"I still don't understand how—"

Chris raised her hand. "I never had to choose something because there was only ever one choice, and that was fine by me. Since I've known you, all I've had were choices. I chose to follow you on this insane quest, knowing it might get us killed. I've chosen to decline my engagement and I know that once I share this with Lance and my parents, there will be a fight. I've chosen to keep going even when our path became more dangerous than we thought," Chris said. "I want to choose you."

Aimee sighed. "Chris."

"That's what I meant. Why don't you just lie to me? Tell me there can be a future, or we could pretend."

"And then what?"

"Let's not think that far ahead."

"It would hurt too much. It's better not knowing, believe me."

"Like I don't know what happened to you?"

"What do you mean?"

"You never told me how you died."

"Oh. It's... I don't like thinking about that. Much less talking about it."

"That's OK. I understand."

"But I want you to know."

"I'm here, if you ever want to..."

Aimee hugged herself with one arm. "I had just turned twenty-one, and a few months before that, Sarah was killed in an accident."

"I'm so sorry."

"Thank you. Anyway, she... I saw her. After she'd passed, uh, I ran into her at the marketplace. I thought I was imagining things, seeing what I wanted to see and all that."

"That's understandable."

"She... Sarah, she just stood there, staring at me. When she noticed I was holding her gaze, she frowned before flipping around to look behind her. I laughed hysterically. I still don't know why."

"It was a stressful moment. Maybe that was your way of dealing with it," Chris offered.

"Yeah. Well, by the time she turned back, I had awoken from my stupor and stepped closer. I called her name, and she cried. She dashed to me and hugged me. She held me so tightly, crying into my shoulder."

"I bet it was a shock for her, too."

"At first, I thought she must have survived the accident, and that they were wrong and had it all mixed up, though I knew that wasn't possible. I'd been there, I'd seen the blood..." Aimee's gaze darted to the horizon. "Sarah kept saying things like, she can't believe that I can see her and that it was a miracle."

"It sounds like one," Chris said.

"We walked to a nearby park, and there she told me everything. Her life as a Verlohren and how they usually can't be seen by their loved ones. After she said that, a shadow fell over her face."

"I'd think so."

"You picked up faster than I did. She vaulted off the park bench and withdrew. When I asked what was going on, she just shook her head. Then, after I pleaded with her for an eternity, she only said, 'I guess that means you never loved me.'" Aimee cleared her throat and her eyes shone.

"Oh, Aimee." Chris interlocked the fingers of their free hands.

"At first, I was too stunned and too hurt to reply, but then I swore I loved her. She eventually believed me. When I returned home, I told Mary about it, my best friend. The one who binds me here."

"Did she react badly?"

"No, though she wasn't sure what to make of it. I begged her to meet Sarah, to accompany me to our meeting the next day. She agreed." Aimee tightened her jaw. "When we got there, Sarah was nowhere to be seen. We waited for half an hour, then I suggested we leave. I thought I'd dreamed up the previous day and apologized to Mary."

"Did you really believe that?"

"Gods, it's been so long. I don't even remember. It was all so much, so many and conflicting emotions. Mary said we should give her some more time. I didn't want to, but Mary convinced me, so we stayed."

"Did Sarah ever make it to the meeting?"

"Yes. She ran to us, out of breath and bleeding. She said the Council guards were raiding the area, and that we needed to leave."

Chris closed her eyes.

"I didn't understand. At that point, I had thought little about the Verlohren. I didn't hate them or go out of my way to be rude to them, but... I was indifferent. It was their own fault they were in this predicament." A humorless chuckled left her. "I'd heard of the raids, but never seen one. I also wasn't afraid because they obviously wouldn't be after *me*. Then it hit me that they'd be after Sarah, but by then it was too late. The Council guards had arrived."

"I fear how this is going to end," Chris said in a low, monotone voice.

"I died. That's the short version of it."

"Please. Go on. Don't sugarcoat this."

\*\*\*

Freit, Saltung<br>Year 294

The gray-clad Council guards rounded up around ten Verlohren like cattle. They pushed and shoved them towards a transport wagon.

"What are they doing? Where will they take them? They can't do this!" Aimee called, rushing ahead.

Sarah grabbed her arm and pulled her back. "Let it go. They do this all the time. They can, and they will. There's nothing we can do."

"There has to be something! This isn't right. Look at them!"

Three of the Verlohren were elderly and hobbled forward, their faces scrunched up and their eyes wide. One of them, a scrawny, hunchbacked man, held onto the shoulders of a little girl, pulling her close. He mumbled something to another guard, who responded by smashing his elbow into the man's face before seizing the girl's arm and yanking her toward the carriage. She screamed and tears tracked soot-covered smudges down her cheeks. The other Verlohren wept and begged, converging on the guard who shoved the girl into the wagon.

"Let them go!" Aimee shouted. Shrugging off Sarah's hand, she sprinted toward the guards.

Mary and Sarah darted after her, begging her to stop, but Aimee didn't heed their warning and continued her pace.

She reached the guards while they tried to shuffle the remaining Verlohren into the cart, away from their fellow soldier who they were still swarming. "Let them go! They have done nothing!" Aimee cried.

The guard closest to her turned with his sword raised and without gazing at her, rammed it to the hilt into her upper stomach.

Aimee gasped, a broken stutter escaping her lips as she slumped to the ground and dropped her hands to her abdomen.

The guard grunted and pulled his blade back out.

She collapsed to her side and dust particles swirled through the air, while the man shafted his weapon and grabbed the last remaining Verlohren, tossing them into the wagon.

"Let's go!" he shouted.

"No!" Sarah screamed and fell to her knees next to Aimee. "Why did you do this?" she cried.

Mary plodded to a stop beside them, tears streaming down her face. She knelt and grasped Aimee's hand. "Please don't die," she sobbed. "I'm sorry I made you stay here longer. If I hadn't..."

Aimee squeezed her fingers. "It's OK..." Her breath gushed forth in quick gasps as red devoured more and more of her beige shirt, pooling around her and oozing into the ground.

***

Thal Mountains<br>Year 302, Day 72

Aimee wiped her eyes on her arm and stumbled backwards. "I'm free."

"Oh." Chris laughed. "Me, too! I told you it would work!"

"You did, Princess. Though saying 'I told you so' isn't a particularly attractive trait."

Chris scoffed. "Tell me that again when you've changed your mind."

"Chris." Aimee reached out, taking her hand. "I'm sorry, but that won't happen. I'd... It would be bad."

"We'll have to agree to disagree," Chris said curtly, withdrawing from Aimee's warmth. Her idea had freed them, but at what cost?

\*\*\*

"Mother, I did not expect you to be home."

Diane put down her book. "Where else would I be?"

"I wanted to talk to you. And to Father."

"Anthony will not be back until tomorrow. Did you forget? It's unusual for you to be unaware of his schedule."

"Right. I've been… busy."

"Yes, you have been absent a lot during the last couple of months. Poor Lance's pout sometimes reminds me of an abandoned child when he visits and finds you gone."

"I'm here to talk about that, actually."

"Go on."

"I… I don't… I won't marry Lance." Chris jutted her chin and stood straighter, her mother's forever complaint about her slouching posture ringing in her ears.

"Of course you will. We are in the midst of your wedding preparations. What on earth are you babbling about, Christina?"

"Why…" She opened her mouth and closed it. "The wedding is still over eight months away. Why would you already be in the middle of planning it?"

"Eight months is not a long time for such an event. You are the scion of the Council, not some commoner with no name to herself."

"Yes, exactly. I am the heir of the Council. I will rule Saltung once Father retires. It should be up to me whom I wed."

Diane laughed, reclining in her chair and dropping her head back a bit before straightening up and wiping a tear from her eye. "This… Is this a joke? It is a good one. We all know you will do as you are told. Just like you have always done. You are going to marry Lance."

"I won't. I am an adult, and heir or not, you won't force me into a marriage with someone I don't love. I'd rather reject my title."

Diane jumped out of her seat and stalked toward Chris, who froze. "What does love have to do with any of this? Do you think you are in a position to marry for *love*?"

"But... You and Father... I thought—"

"You thought what? That we were in love when we got married?"

"Yes?"

Diane closed her eyes. "In our position, love is not an option, and you better remember that. You marry the one who fits into the family and who has been chosen as your consort to rule Saltung alongside you."

"I'm sorry they did that to you, Mother."

Diane recoiled as if she'd been slapped, and her eyes widened staring at her daughter as one would gape at a mirage. "I don't..." She faltered before twisting around, her hand turning ashen when she gripped the arm rest of her sofa chair. "You will marry Lance, Christina. There is no way out."

"I won't marry him. If there's no way out, I'll make one." Chris left the room and then the mansion. She couldn't stay in this house any longer. She hadn't expected her parents to be happy about her announcement, and while she still had to tell her father, she hadn't foreseen her mother outright refusing her right to choose. Why would she do this if it had happened to her? Her first impulse was to run to Aimee and Dylan's, but then she remembered their last conversation and deflated. *The woods it shall be.*

Before she could disappear into the forest behind their property, Terry called after her. "Where are you running off to in such a hurry?"

Chris halted but didn't turn around.

He caught up with her, breathing hard. "I looked for you in the library and at the dojo and was on my way to ask your mother where you were when I saw you storm out of the mansion." He stepped to her side. "What's going on?"

"Mother... She's unwilling to see things from my perspective."

A low chuckle left Terry. "How is that new? You rarely agree with her."

"I still do what she says."

"True, too. What's different this time?"

Chris heaved a sigh. "I don't want to marry Lance, and Mother argues that it's my duty."

"You never wanted to marry him, but I always thought you would."

"Does *everyone* believe I'll do whatever my parents say or ask, no matter what I want?"

"Only those who know you."

Chris covered her face with her hands. "That's even worse."

"Where is this change coming from? Your adventures with Aimee?"

She spun around and confronted him, narrowing her eyes. "What do you know about those?"

"Woah." He raised his hands. "I only know what you've told me."

Chris kicked a pebble down the path. "Right."

"Talk to me. I want to help you," Terry urged.

"I'm not sure you can. It'll come down to... well, me standing up for what I want and not just toeing the line drawn by my parents."

"That scares you?"

Chris laughed. "No. I'm not scared. I'm terrified. I don't think I've ever felt like this, but..." She broke off and her gaze wandered to the woods.

"Go on."

"I'll lose either way, even if I win. Or especially then, and it's not just me."

"You're worried about Lance's feelings?"

Chris laughed. "To be honest, he didn't even cross my mind."

"Then how will you lose even though you win?"

"I... I made it clear what I want, but that, I cannot have because, well, it's not up to me alone. I accepted that, and even... even if I got it, it wouldn't last. It couldn't, but it's still better not getting what I want than accepting what I don't want. Does that make any sense?"

"A little. Besides, sometimes getting what you want is overrated. You think everything will be better and you'll live a happy life, but then you realize you fell for the oldest trap."

"Which is?"

"That another's life is better than your own. You never walked in their shoes, and—"

She snorted and Terry shot her a curious glance.

"Anyway. Yes, it can be advisable to avoid what you don't want, even if you're not getting what you want."

"Thanks." Chris smiled before leaning against him. "I'm glad you came looking for me."

"Always."

# eight

"You needed to talk to me?" Chris followed Aimee into the living room.

"Yes, uh, you've been kinda absent lately, and I... I wanted to check on things. How you are, and how your research is going, and so on."

"Right. It's going."

Aimee fidgeted. "Look, I'm sorry about what happened, and—"

Chris lifted her hands. "No, it's fine. I don't wish to discuss this. You've made your position clear, and I'll accept that. For now."

Aimee raised her eyebrows but remained silent.

"I'm frustrated. My mother didn't take my news regarding Lance too well, and..." She turned her gaze to the window. "My father has been restrained. He had this surprised look on his face, but he said nothing. He just left the room."

"And Lance? Did you tell him, too?"

Chris heaved a sigh. "Yes."

"That bad?"

"None of them take me seriously. Father hasn't even deigned to offer a response, and both Mother and Lance have assured me that of course I'm going to marry him."

"Wow."

"I'm not sure why I'm surprised. They assume I'll cave because that's all I've ever done."

"That doesn't mean you have to keep giving in. I'm not telling you what to do, but it should be your decision."

"Like with us?"

Aimee leaned back against the couch. "That's not fair."

"I'm not in a particularly accommodating mood. I've said this to Terry already, no matter what I do, I don't end up getting what I want."

"You will down the road. You'll find someone who's right for you."

"So you *are* saying I shouldn't marry Lance?"

"I didn't say that."

"What you said implied that I won't marry Lance."

"You told me that you don't *want* to marry him. I'm being supportive here. What else do you want from me?"

She narrowed her eyes and Aimee dropped her gaze. "I don't want to marry him, and I want... Even if I'm not getting what I want, I refuse to settle for something I *don't* want. At all. I had lunch with this man for months, and the idea of spending the rest of my life with him, seeing him every day..." Chris rose and ambled to the window. "I won't do it."

"Then don't."

"You make everything seem so easy."

"I doubt anyone has *ever* accused me of that," Aimee said. "I'm truly sorry, Chris."

"Yes, well. Not much you can do. Aside from what you refuse to do," Chris whispered, and a small smile spread over her face.

"You won't let that go, will you?"

"Why would I? You might change your mind, given that you want me, too."

"All right." Aimee clasped her hands together. "Let's move on to the quest at hand, freeing the Verlohren and all that. Bringing truth to Saltung."

Chris chuckled. "My research seems to indicate that our moment at the floating stone was our challenge from the binding ritual, the one the *Book of Sattran* spoke of."

"What does that mean? Did we pass?"

"We did. The ritual is now complete."

Aimee's brows furrowed. "It wasn't before?"

Chris shook her head.

"Magic is so weird. Anyway, how close are we to the ritual of Varstahnet?" Aimee asked.

"We got the Leota root, and the ash of the Kefer tree. All we need is the Stern stone, which they didn't find in the forest, but according to you, Dylan has another lead that he's pursuing. Then there's the water from the Als basin, which you said your mysterious contact can organize."

"What does this ritual do, anyway? I never solved that riddle."

"I'm not completely certain, but it'll reveal the truth, which then supposedly leaves it up to us to choose if we want to do the last step."

"Which is what?"

"I don't know. Did you expect any of this to be straight forward? I'm guessing after the revelation, there'll be a choice, and we'll decide," Chris said.

"What if it's an awful choice?"

"Didn't you tell me not too long ago that you suffer twice if you worry?"

"Sure did," Aimee said with a wry smile.

\*\*\*

Year 302, Day 91

Chris rubbed her temples. She wanted out, and this wasn't the first time she wished she'd been more rebellious growing up. If she'd possessed an ounce of her brother's tendencies to carve his own path, her family might not laugh at the very notion that she'd go against their wishes. "Say nothing more, Mother. I'm serious."

"How can I remain silent when you are determined to ruin your life?" Diane asked.

"If you'd open your eyes for *one* second, if I were more to you than the next heir to uphold the Morgen rule—"

"Christina!"

She released a deep breath. "Both of you only care about duty, about tradition, and what I want is lost, or it doesn't matter."

"What *do* you want?" Diane asked.

"I uh…" Her shoulders slumped.

"How can we *consider* an alternative path when you do not even know what it entails!"

"Don't act like you would ever do that! Even if I were to write out every little detail, you'd still..."

"You have never shown an inkling that following our traditions is not what you desire," Diane said.

"Perhaps you just paid no attention. Mother, Father," Chris said, and her gaze shifted between her parents. "I don't wish to marry Lance. I don't love him, and I cannot stomach even the idea of having to spend the rest of my life with him." She swallowed hard.

"Love is not all there is, and it might grow between you given time," Diane said.

"Like it did for you and Father?" she asked, staring at her mother who dipped her head. "Not everything changes with time," Chris muttered.

"What is all this nonsense?" Anthony spoke at last. "You will marry Lance, and that is not up for discussion. It *never* was. Your mother and I did not require time to *grow* our love as it blossomed from the start, much like between you and Lance."

Diane raised her head and held Chris's gaze for a second before offering a brittle smile. "Yes, dear."

"Lance loves you, and he has done so for years. He is a good man, and he is making great strides as the commander of the Council guard. His leadership has made the raids more productive, and we are close to crushing the Tarung once and for all," Anthony stated.

"How... What are you doing?"

"That does not concern you, my Christina," Anthony said.

"As the future Head of the Council, I should be in the loop about such significant plans. They affect all of us."

"You have a full plate with the Initiation and the wedding. Lance and the guards are taking care of the Tarung. There is no need to worry about that."

"I'm not worried, Father. I just want to—"

"Enough! This discussion is over."

Chris gritted her teeth. "Yes, Father."

\*\*\*

Chris yanked open the door and headed straight for Aimee's living room. "What happened? Your message scared me half to death. I left Terry in the middle of—"

"Dylan's gone."

"What?"

Aimee paced. "He was supposed to talk to one of his contacts about the Stern stone, and then come back, but he never did."

"Perhaps he is hanging out with a friend?"

Aimee glared at her. "He wouldn't do that. Not now. It was a straightforward trip and meeting. I already spoke with Markus, and Dylan should have made it home last night."

"He met with his contact then?"

"According to Markus, yes."

"So he got lost on the way back."

"He didn't *get* lost, not with his sense of direction. Why are you so calm? Don't you care about what happened to him?"

"Don't confuse being rational in a crisis with lack of care. He's my brother and I love him. Why do I even have to say this? Why do we *always* advance one step only to jump back two?"

Aimee only offered a blank stare.

Chris sighed. "Whatever."

"Maybe Lance and the guards took him. He could be in one of the Verlohren Centers. But that doesn't make sense given—"

Chris frowned. "Wait, what? What Verlohren Centers?"

"You remember the story I told you when… with Sarah and well, when I had that run-in with the Council guards?"

She shook her head. "Run-in? You mean when they stabbed and killed you? Yes. I recall that tale."

"After I'd passed, I'd started my research, not just to discover the truth behind the stories that people tell about the Verlohren, but also about the machinations of the Council."

"You make them sound like villains."

"Uh, your point?"

"Fine. Go on."

"I wanted to figure out where they were detaining Verlohren when they collected us like they did on that day. Where did they take all those people on the wagon?"

"What did you find out?"

"They have several Centers throughout Saltung, most in remote areas. I spied on two of them, but I never got close enough to spot what went on in there. The strangest thing, these wagons arrived and left with Verlohren, so they seem to release us again after a while."

"Maybe they consider it a prison of sorts?"

"Yeah, in which they throw you without a trial. Did you really never hear about them?"

"No! I haven't even heard rumors of this. To be fair, I never spent much time going anywhere, so I wasn't aware of raids where they take Verlohren in custody before you told me."

"Huh. All right. This is where I first thought Dylan could be, and wondered if you'd know about new raid plans, but then I discovered this. That's when I had to get you here. Follow me." She led Chris to the back door and onto the patio.

"What do you... Woah. What happened here?" She crouched down next to two pots with dead moonbeam flowers.

"I don't know. But look ahead toward the clearing into the forest."

Chris stood up and her mouth opened, but she just shook her head. In front of her lay a path of yellow, brown grass and drooping, dead weeds, amidst an otherwise blooming meadow. "It looks like this entity killed everything it touched or came in contact with."

"Given the condition of my poor flowers here, I assume that whatever did this was also in the house."

"You think it took Dylan? But why?"

"Don't know," Aimee said.

Chris sprinted forward. "We need to follow its trail and find out."

"Slow down!" Aimee grabbed her arm. "I can't believe this falls on me, but don't we need a plan? Wouldn't that be… smarter?"

"The longer we wait…"

"True. All right. Let's go," Aimee said, and marched ahead.

A small smile tugged at Chris's lips when she followed her friend. "What a shocker. You're up for a rash, unprepared, and potentially dangerous mission."

"Yep, but you started it this time."

"Well, sometimes circumstances demand that we reject careful preparation. Besides, I still have my magic."

They pursued the path of dead and dying vegetation deeper into the woods, and along the way they even encountered trees where half of the hanging branches seemed to have withered and died.

"Can you think of any magical creature that does this?" Aimee asked after a while.

"There are tales of spirits that bring death, but that's more related to the Living, not in the 'everything dies in their path' kind of way."

"Look, over there." Aimee pointed at the thicket behind a dried-up tree. Brown shriveled up leaves littered the ground surrounding a large trunk. "We are getting closer," Aimee whispered.

"Because of the tree? It could have also paused here or leaned against it," Chris argued.

"It's not just that. I… I think I can feel it."

"The creature?"

Aimee nodded but never glanced back at Chris. Instead, she headed for the undergrowth. "There's a cavern right behind this shrub."

She groaned but resisted the urge to stomp her foot. "Of course there is."

"Stop whining. Our track record with caves isn't that bad. This isn't the mountains either, no floating, sticky rocks digging up secrets and tearing out confessions," Aimee grumbled when they neared the grotto's entrance.

Chris glanced at her feet. "I'm sorry."

"Huh?" Aimee turned, but Chris avoided her gaze.

"I know you hated what happened, and I'm sorry... What I told you, that it made you uncomfortable."

"It's fine. You worry too much, and I believe I've mentioned that before, so yeah, it's true."

"I'm not worrying any more than appropriate. And for the record, just because you repeat something doesn't make it true," Chris said.

"Sure, Princess. Now, stop... not worrying, and come on. We need your light."

"Right." Chris stepped next to Aimee, channeling heat into her hands.

Aimee held out her arm. "After you."

Chris snorted. "Remember not to touch anything, no matter how shiny it looks."

"You could let this go, you know?"

"Nope. Now let's see who was dumb enough to kidnap my baby brother." Chris ventured deeper into the hollow; Aimee close enough that her arm bumped into Chris's back. "This is barren."

"I was gonna go with creepy," Aimee said, and Chris shuddered when her breath blew over her ear.

Before Chris could reply, a rumbling echoed through the cavern, followed by a steep drop in temperature.

Aimee huddled closer to Chris and the fire. "What's going on here?" she murmured.

Chris shook her head, her eyes fixed on the shadow crawling over rocks and stone nearby. "Out!" Extinguishing the flames, she grabbed Aimee by the arm and hauled her along until they had cleared the cave.

\*\*\*

"What the hell?" Aimee sputtered.

"Didn't you sense it? You said you did earlier."

"And you said you didn't!"

"Because I didn't then, but now, in there." Chris paced. "We must leave. We need a plan because this is much more…" She trailed off and fell back when the shadow they'd escaped from bled out of the mouth of a cave. Like molasses, it gurgled and slithered forward. Even though they were out in broad daylight and the sun shone high above them, a frost spread across the area. The shade grew and assembled into a towering creature with a narrow face, gaunt, black holes as eyes, and a mouth that hung open in a low hum that turned into the crescendo of a tortured scream.

Both women ducked their heads.

"What *is* that thing?" Aimee asked, withdrawing from it, and lining up next to Chris.

"It's a spirit?"

"That much I got with it not having an actual body and all," Aimee hissed and gestured wildly at the figure who had raised its head and roared.

Its arms swelled and a gray wisp swirled through its semi-transparent form. It lurched forward, and Aimee's gaze lingered on the plants and trees fading in its vicinity.

Chris widened her stance and closed her eyes while an incantation in a language Aimee didn't understand bubbled from her lips. When she opened her eyes, her pupils were blown. She raised her arms, and Aimee staggered and nearly fell under the pressure of the shockwaves that emanated from Chris and rippled past them before slamming into the still-approaching monster.

It halted, howling. Aimee tilted her head. That didn't sound like pain, more like... "Chris, I think it liked that. And look, it's becoming more solid!"

"What? How?" Chris grunted and hurled another spell at it.

This time, roots spurted out of the soil and snared around it, crawling up its legs and anchoring its feet to the ground.

"Good idea," Aimee said before she cursed under her breath. "That didn't last."

The creature tore through the branches and vines, ripping them out of the ground.

She grasped Chris's hand. "You need to teleport us out."

"No. This thing's got Dylan, and it could hurt him. We must get to him!"

"We'll be back for him. He's not gonna die."

"That doesn't mean he can't be in pain!" Chris shouted, glaring at her before attacking the creature again. This time, fire rained from her hands, incinerating the behemoth. Flames rose and feasted on its body. The gray wisp spun faster as the beast roared and thrashed.

Aimee jumped. "You got it!"

"No, no, no," Chris chanted and trembled.

"What is it?" She reached out and grasped Chris's shoulders. "Hey. Are you OK?"

Chris shook her head, her eyes wide and transfixed on the being.

Aimee followed her gaze and froze.

Instead of ashes, the monster had completely solidified and absorbed the flames. Its chest shimmered orange-red, and the wisp was gone. It set one thunderous step in front of the other, stomping towards them.

Aimee squeezed Chris's hand. "It's time to teleport."

"I can't. It requires a lot of energy, and after all this." She caught Aimee's gaze. "I'm sorry."

"OK, that's OK. We run? It shouldn't be more than two or three miles back."

"And then?"

Her gaze wandered from the creature to Chris. "We'll think of something."

"All right," Chris said, and they both turned but before they could break into a sprint, vines curled around their feet and locked them in place.

"What the..." Aimee gawked at her legs.

"It has magic," Chris shouted.

"So do you! Undo it!"

Chris blasted the tendrils at the same time the beast seized her and lifted her into the air.

"No! Let her go!" Aimee shouted while snapping the last remaining branches.

***

Chris struggled against its grasp, but the more she fought, the tighter it held onto her. She called on her magic once more, but before she could release it, the monster sucked it out of her. Aimee's screams faded, drowned out amidst the fog sweeping through her mind.

Her magic drained away at the speed of a river cascading down a steep waterfall. Every attempt at stemming the bleed futile, and instead it left her with an empty ache until all waned and her eyes fell shut.

She woke laying on a cold, wet stone floor. Her body ached, seemingly from the tips of her hair down to her toes. Her shoulders were locked while a stabbing pain drummed down her back from the base of her skull. She groaned and rose to her feet. She was no longer in the forest, instead, she stood barefoot in freezing water in a tunnel cloaked in dusk.

"Hello? Aimee?" her voice cracked, and she cleared her throat. Chris rose, unsure if she should head up or down given that the tunnel was just as dark in either direction. She was trapped in a shaft with no visible way out, so the route didn't matter.

Chris shuddered, and when no one answered, she stumbled forward. Her mind rambled in a trudging, uneven rhythm, and minutes passed before she remembered magic. How could she have forgotten?

She touched her chest and called upon her powers to warm her, but nothing happened. Once again, her magic had fled, and there was no Aimee to jump-start it. The splashing of water remained the only discernible sound as she waded through icy puddles to nowhere.

\*\*\*

"Let her go!" Aimee yelled again and stormed the beast.

It flipped around and threw Chris to the side. Aimee's eyes widened when Chris's limp body flew several feet through the air before crashing against a tree trunk and sliding down into the thicket below.

"Chris!" Aimee wanted to run and check on her, but that seemed to be what the entity was counting on, so she clenched her jaw and stood her ground, turning her attention back to the fiend.

The creature lumbered closer, and the soil trembled with each of its steps.

She had no weapons and no magic, though that hadn't helped before either. However, unlike Chris, she couldn't die. Aimee gritted her teeth. She needed to concentrate. Her worries wouldn't get them out of this situation.

The closer it drew, the more her stomach tightened. The energy of this being led her to places she never wanted to revisit—wastelands with nothing but loss and agony, and she'd be damned if she'd allowed this monster to drag her there.

"What are you," she mumbled, unable to shake the sense of familiarity this being evoked.

It halted in front of Aimee, at first, a standstill as both gazed at each other. Then it swung one arm, and in reflex, Aimee's left hand jerked up to block it. She braced for an impact that would knock her off her feet, but instead, it howled, and this time, the sound of pain rolled over her.

"That's odd." She pushed forward while it stumbled back.

Its heavy body almost crashed to the ground at the unexpected change in bearing. Aimee followed right behind, and though a part of her loathed to harm this entity—a feeling she'd examine later when she no longer feared for Chris's life— she had to end this. She needed to check on Chris and free Dylan so they could all go home.

She stretched her arms and grabbed onto its beefy limb, nearly recoiling at the trembling under her hands and the scream that thundered from its mouth.

"I'm sorry," Aimee pressed out but pursued the creature when it crashed to the ground, twisting, and turning in agony, yet unable to shake off Aimee's hold. "You need to leave."

She hovered over it, halfway leaning against its massive form, as the screeching that had been ongoing all this time changed and the lilt of the voice faded into a deeper rumble, a scream that petered out into a long, exhausted groan.

The being's body transformed and lost its corporeality and with it the wisp returned, floating, racing through its form, a gray trail ensnaring the amber that still suffused its shape.

Aimee's grip broke, and she fell into the shadows. She gasped for air as ice inundated her; her body stiffened to ward off the cold.

The shadow and Aimee registered at the same instant that they could move away from each other and vaulted in different directions. Aimee groaned at the air escaping her lungs as soon as her body struck the ground, while the figure, with a final wail that now resembled a wounded animal rather than a vicious beast, morphed into a mere shadow and slunk away.

"Chris," Aimee croaked and sprung back to her feet, racing to Chris's still form under the tree. She dropped to her knees next to her and wiped her palms on her pants before reaching out a trembling hand, gently touching Chris's arm.

"Wake up. Come on!" Aimee placed her fingers on Chris's neck, and she slumped as the dull trembling beneath her fingertips drained the backbreaking tension from her body.

She rocked back on her feet, and covered her face with her hands, swallowing hard.

What if she carried Chris home and contacted Markus to ask if one of their physicians would check on her? Then she could return and search for Dylan, although it would be night by then. She didn't want to leave him here, but Chris's condition... Aimee worried her lower lip. She hated feeling helpless, and this was the first time she truly wished she had magic. Wasn't there anything else she could do?

Suddenly, she remembered an old healing ritual her mother had favored, and while she hadn't thought of it in over a decade, it sprang to her mind now. An urge to try and save Chris invaded her head and spread like wildfire before doubts crept in. What if it made things worse? What if she hurt Chris? But Chris was already hurt.

"So I have no idea if this is going to work, and I hope it won't make things worse... in there, wherever you are. I'm not sure you can even hear me, but I just want you to know that I'm not trying to hurt you or anything, and uh, it's me doing this, so you're not in any danger. Please don't set me on fire, all right?"

Aimee slid forward and closed her eyes. She took a deep breath and then placed both hands on Chris's heart. The slow thudding beneath her palms calmed Aimee's nerves and she recited the ritual incantation, but after a few words, she froze.

A current, at first just a light tickle then small pinpricks that grew into an electric surge, infiltrated her fingers and cascaded through her, ricocheting like a pinball and stealing her breath. Her chest heaved and her normally shallow pulse banged against the veins in her neck as palpitations seemed to wrack her chest.

Chris remained unmoving, but the pallor of her face ebbed, and a flush crept up her collar.

The stream rose, a barrage of energy striking every cell in her body, barreling at them with an unbridled desire to beat them into submission. For what? Aimee couldn't say, but her mind clouded under the onslaught, and soon her only remaining thought revolved around the yearning to let go, to withdraw, yet she sat motionless, torn between her desire to help Chris and the instinct to avoid further pain.

\*\*\*

Wind howled and bounced off the walls when a roar neared. Chris didn't know how far she'd walked on the icy, wet floor of the tunnel, and so far nothing had changed. She stopped and shivered. Moving, while exhausting, had kept the cold somewhat in check.

Chris scanned both ways, but there was only emptiness. Perhaps it was too dark to see what lay ahead? A part of her rejoiced at the break in the silence that had clung to these tunnels forevermore, but fear spiked her heartbeat and sweat trickled down her back. This new shiver sprang from an altogether different well.

The roar swelled, seemingly in unison with the galloping in her chest. She licked her lips and gasped when a tumultuous wave of murky water flooded the channel and roared toward her.

Chris lifted her head. The waves filled almost the entire height of the tunnel, but if she could make it to the top, she might manage to breathe now and then. If only she had her magic.

She spun around and crouched down as if preparing for a sprint. The wave slammed into her with such force that she lost her breath. Icy water clung to her, and Chris tumbled through the liquid, trying to propel herself upward, but the spinning stream sucked her downward, and like a bouncing ball, she bobbled through the tunnel.

\*\*\*

The energy torrent intensified, raging through Aimee and tearing a trail of heat and pain through her that left her lightheaded. Sweat dripped down her neck, and she wiped her forehead on her upper arm, maintaining contact with Chris.

A low whine gushed from her lips, and she winced as a violent stroke thundered through her frame like lightning, choking her as it seared her esophagus.

The exertion caused her body to spasm, and as she felt herself slipping and ached to drop to the floor and curl up into a ball, the heat and energy abated. She fell forward and sobbed into Chris's chest.

"Aimee?"

Her head snapped up, and she hurried to wipe her eyes. "Chris! Thank the Gods, you're back," she hiccupped and cupped her cheek.

"What... happened? Where's the... creature?"

"It's gone."

"Dylan?"

Aimee shook her head. "I... I haven't searched for him yet. You... It flung you against a tree and you were unconscious. I first needed to get you back before..."

"Thank you," Chris croaked and closed her eyes.

"How are you?"

"I'm exhausted, sick of floods, cold, but otherwise OK."

"Floods?"

"Don't ask," Chris groaned and allowed Aimee to pull her to her feet.

"Ready to search for Dylan in the cave?"

"Yes. Let's get him back." Chris marched toward the cavern.

A dizzying relief washed over Aimee at Chris's restored energy and drive. This was how it should be.

***

"Quit fussing over me. It's exhausting. I'm fine," Dylan grumbled.

"This shadow monster sucked you dry! Eat something." Aimee handed Dylan a plate filled with sandwiches.

He accepted the offering. "At least you're sparing me your cooking."

Aimee huffed.

"And it wasn't a monster."

"You know what it was?"

"What it *is*, yes. I even have an idea why if affected both of you the way it did."

"How?"

"Unlike you, I was bedridden the last couple of days, and all I could do was read."

Aimee's eyes widened. "There's something in our books about it?"

"In the old collection, the ones we got through the exchange with Markus's friend, almost a year ago. Right after I found you," he said.

"The ones that were a bust regarding the *Demise of Reason*. I don't think I paid much attention to what was in there, aside from what wasn't."

"Obviously. I remembered something, and back then, this story intrigued me, and I wanted to draw it, but then other stuff happened and distracted me. Anyway, I picked up the book again, and while you and Chris were otherwise occupied, I read."

"And?"

"I believe the creature is called Zilal-ruh."

"Never heard of that before."

"It's supposed to be a myth, a being controlled by Death. It's an accumulation of tormented souls that never moved on."

"Sattran?"

"No, I don't think so. It might be the people who don't become Verlohren but who still aren't able to move on."

"But it became real! We could touch it. Spirits or souls don't just become corporeal!"

"It was created with magic, animated by magic, and then attracted to it because that's what fuels it."

"So when Chris attacked it with magic…"

"It strengthened it, allowed it to grow solid. She gave it a body."

"Wow. But why couldn't it bear my touch? It seemed in pain as soon as I grabbed its arm."

"It's only a theory, mind you. But as a Verlohren, you are devoid of magic. Even the Living still have traces of it running through them, though many cannot access it. Us, though? Empty shells."

"We're more than that."

"That's not what I meant." He laughed. "We are devoid of magic."

"All right. I still don't see how that caused it to hurt."

"It's a tortured, lost spirit, right?"

"Yes."

"I'm assuming it's in a lot of pain."

"That's a pretty safe assumption to make," she said.

"I thought so, too, and it leads me to my second hypothesis. Verlohren are no stranger to suffering, even torment, and you were protecting or defending Chris, so what you did wasn't selfish," he said, raising his hand when Aimee opened her mouth. "Yes. You like my sister and all, so you didn't want her to die, but that's still not self-serving. Either way, that, the lack of magic, and your… familiarity with agony, that was all you had to offer."

"I don't follow."

"I think you inundated it with your pain. Chris pumped it full of magic, and you transferred all the misery you've ever endured into it, the suffering you experience every day, and the terror that coursed through you at that moment. I doubt this creature had room to absorb any more pain."

"Interesting theory," Aimee said after a moment of silent contemplation. "Do you also have an idea what happened when I tried to use the healing ritual on Chris?"

"Indeed, I do."

"Of course. We've left you alone for too long."

"True. Anyway, Chris depleted her magic during the attack on the creature and so ran out of energy. I'm not sure she was conscious before that thing threw her against the tree," he said and tightened his hands into fists.

Aimee squeezed his arm. "She's fine."

"Yes." He cleared his throat. "When you attacked the Zilal-ruh, it also released Chris's magic back into you. I doubt that was by design, more like, it let go of everything to get away from the pain. And since you're... well, the empty shell bit, you became a reservoir for her magic."

"Wow. That makes sense."

"Yes, and when you tried the ritual, something within her latched onto you because she recognized her magic, and then she extracted it from you again."

Aimee frowned.

"What you described of the aftermath? It sounds like all your pain started when you touched Chris. You're not meant to hold that much magic, and then getting it out..."

"That's what hurt."

"Yes. You acted as a sort of conduit that allowed Chris to regain her magical energy in a semi-safe way."

"But she wasn't conscious. How would that have worked?"

"Automatically? There must have been traces of magic left that recognized its own kind when you touched her." He shrugged his shoulders. "You said it hurt?"

"More than anything else I've ever felt, especially toward the end."

"Wow. I'm sorry. I didn't realize it was that bad. You OK?"

She rubbed her face. "I'm fine. Just don't share this theory with your sister, K?"

"Why?"

"She's got enough to feel guilty about. Let's not add to it."

"You got it."

# nine

Aimee darted down a narrow corridor, panting, her hand pressed tightly against the bleeding tear on her side. One day she'll learn to shut her mouth, though it wouldn't be today. She'd been out to meet with a contact to discuss access to the Als reservoir for the ritual. Unbeknownst to both of them, their meeting place doubled as the next location of a raid.

Aimee clenched her jaw, both from the pain radiating through her and the memory of the Council guard rounding up Verlohren. Again. They shoved, pushed, and even slammed a few of them to the floor. What was the purpose of pushing down someone who spent their entire existence on the ground?

The Verlohren had never been a threat to the Living. Back when she was alive, Aimee had not been worried about them. She remembered being told old stories by her grandmother about the treacherous nature of the Verlohren, and how the Living needed to remain vigilant. How they gathered in rebel groups, ready to rise if the Living ever became careless. She'd been just a child then, but Aimee had recognized these tales as spooky legends recounted to hammer obedience into the next generation.

While alive, Aimee had barely taken notice of the few Verlohren she'd encountered. Most of them would slink into the shadows at the sight of a Living nearby. She remembered a few who'd begged for money or food. She still felt shame grip her at the memory of passing them on the street and thinking that it was their own fault while feeling outraged that they'd dare to beg for help.

The teaching that the Verlohren were the ones who not only caused their predicament but who refused to change, to move on, was the strongest tenet of their world.

Now, Aimee wondered why no one ever questioned this. It made no sense. Why would *anyone* choose such a miserable fate? To be hunted and spit upon, to always live amongst the dregs of society, to be cut off from all...

If she could leave... Gods, if only she could escape, that had been her wish throughout her entire existence as a Verlohren. Now, Chris's face unwittingly came to her mind, and she shuddered. For the first time during these wretched years, she wanted to stay, even if she'd never dare to go there.

She nudged the door to their house, and her arm, which seemed to be made of gelatin, struggled to press hard enough.

"Aimee? Is that you? What happened? You were supposed to be back hours ago. Chris is pacing a hole in the living room carpet." Dylan opened the door to the corridor and froze when he saw Aimee leaning against the wall. "Shit. You gotta call for Chris. She's not gonna hear me."

Aimee panted, her sticky hand still pressed against her wet side. "Chris," she tried to shout, but it rattled in a low, hoarse croak.

Chris rushed into the hallway. "Aimee?"

"She heard that?" Dylan asked.

"I could tell you were getting weaker and weaker, but I didn't... I was so focused on checking how you felt, I never noticed that you were getting closer. What happened?" She steadied her and guided the shaking woman back into the living room before easing her onto the couch.

Aimee grunted but struggled to form words. "Raid," she pressed out and collapsed against the cushions.

"Damn it," Chris cursed and crouched over Aimee, removing her cold hand to inspect the wound. "It's a deep cut."

Aimee mumbled an unintelligible whisper and passed out.

*  *  *

"Great. Of course this happens without me knowing enough about Verlohren physiology," Chris grumbled.

She dropped to her knees next to the couch and considered her options. Her connection with Aimee still buzzed like a hummingbird within her chest, so there didn't seem to be any immediate danger.

However, they needed Aimee fit and strong if they wanted to continue their quest, and Verlohren healed much slower than the Living did, which meant a great delay if Aimee's wound were to regenerate naturally.

Was it possible to heal a Verlohren? She'd never encountered a text that even hinted at such an occurrence. If it ever happened, she couldn't blame the mage in question for keeping it a secret.

She expelled a shuddering breath while one of her hands hovered over Aimee's side. Chris concentrated on her magic, then lowered her hand to the wound and poured all her warmth and energy into Aimee. A wall of resistance slammed down and cold seeped into her, but she gritted her teeth and pushed against the opposition that blocked her healing energy from reaching Aimee.

Her brows furrowed. She'd expected their connection to get rid of all mechanisms that separated them. Yet, here she was, thrashing against a shield that not only halted her magic but also soaked her with lead and ice, dragging her below the surface of Aimee's pain.

Chris worried her lip. Their link didn't allow them to experience pain or pleasure at the same or high intensity, but the throbbing that rippled through her from their bond paralyzed her and she swallowed hard. Was that because she was trying to heal Aimee, or did this mean the other woman was in agony?

She redoubled her efforts, and a tremble ran through her while sweat poured down her back. Aimee's wound grew warm, then hot, but Chris held on.

Old healing spells she thought long forgotten sprinted to the forefront of her mind and rumbled from her lips.

She bobbed back and forth, channeling more power into Aimee, more than she'd have to give to a Living. Her head throbbed and her mouth parched as more and more energy poured out of her and hemorrhaged into Aimee's still form.

The flapping wings in her chest slowed.

"Come on," she mumbled before pulling up her shirt to wipe her face. She touched Aimee's cheek, and the clammy, cold skin made her stomach drop. Nothing she'd done so far had even touched the surface. Was there no way? Was it truly impossible to heal a Verlohren? She refused to accept this.

Chris straightened and placed one hand on Aimee's chest and the other back on her wound. At least the bleeding appeared to have slowed, though it never spilled as fast as it would have had a Living received the same injury.

A hollow clanging sound caught Chris's attention, and she craned her neck to the side and noticed the *Agaze Erbium* had fallen off the table. Wait… Chris rose to inspect the page that had opened. Her gaze followed the shifting script and squiggly loops drawn in dark red ink. At first, she struggled to decipher the calligraphy which blurred for a second before clearing like mist. That was it. That spell, if this didn't work, nothing would.

Chris shifted her focus back to Aimee and murmured the words in the old tongue that she'd always toiled to pronounce, but now rang like a song from her lips. With her words came a heaviness that pierced through her, bored into her bones, and choked off the air that flowed through her.

Then all stopped. Nothing. Time screeched to a halt, trapped in syrup before it spun, and lead filled her again. She groaned.

More of her energy was sucked into Aimee. Her knees buckled, and she leaned forward, dropping her forehead onto Aimee's torso. "Please come back," she whispered.

There was no reaction.

Aimee continued to lay there, for once appearing as dead as she was.

Tears trickled down Chris's face. This was useless. She sniffed, then her head snapped up when the fluttering wings in her chest quickened.

***

Dizziness rolled through Aimee, and she shifted to lie on her side and gagged. "Chris," she croaked.

"Aimee," Chris cried and shuffled back. "Thank the Gods. How are you feeling?"

"Like I was stabbed. Again," she grunted.

Chris laughed and then hid her face in her hands when her laugh morphed into a low sob.

Aimee interlaced their fingers. "What's up? Are you hurt?"

Chris shook her head. "I'm fine."

"I doubt that," Dylan said.

"What do you mean?" Aimee asked.

"Dylan's here? How long has he been there?"

"I was here the entire time. I never left your side."

"What happened?" Aimee asked.

"She healed you."

"What?" Aimee ran her fingers down her now healed side. "How is this possible?"

"You're fine, and that's all that matters," Chris said.

Aimee sought Chris's gaze, who refused to meet her eyes. "What did you do?"

Chris flinched. "You don't like magic and I'm sorry, but I didn't know how—"

"Magic?" Aimee frowned. "I don't care about that. I'm worried about *you*."

"Oh." Chris dropped her head. "I'm fine. Tired."

"She channeled her energy, her life force into you to heal you, much more than she should have. I'm concerned about her. She just collapsed near the end," Dylan said.

"You really shouldn't have done that. This wouldn't have killed me. There's no reason for you to risk your life for me, Chris. *Ever*," Aimee pressed out.

"That's not up to you."

"This is unacceptable. I won't have you—"

"No." Chris rose and stumbled back. "There are certain things where I can't change your mind, even though you're clearly wrong." She shot her a dark look. "But this, helping you, saving you, isn't up for debate, so you might as well get used to it," Chris snapped.

***

Year 302, Day 102

Dylan settled down on the couch next to Aimee. "How are you?"

"I'm fine."

"You ignored Chris's message."

"I don't trust her—"

He recoiled. "What?"

"No, no. Not like that. I don't trust her not to put herself in danger, you know, to get hurt because… because she's trying to help me," Aimee whispered the last part and lowered her head.

"Oh, yes, well, then you'll have to end all contact with her," Dylan said.

Aimee's head snapped up and her eyes widened. "What?"

"When Chris… When she cares for someone, she doesn't just say 'oh, you're in trouble or in pain? Well, that's your problem.' She'll always try to fix it. That's who she is, though she'd forgotten that for a while. I imagine that after I passed…"

"Yeah."

"She doesn't have many people in her life who care about her, truly care, not just being interested in her position or what she can do for them."

"She told me," Aimee said.

He smiled. "Did she now?"

"You can stop that right there. It doesn't matter."

"Right. Keep deluding yourself. But I'll tell you one thing, it'll matter to Chris. It'll matter that you ignore her, and right after she healed you. When have you ever heard of magic being used to heal a Verlohren?"

"Never," she replied.

He flung the message book into Aimee's lap. "Like I said, stop ignoring my sister."

***

Year 302, Day 105

Chris followed Terry down a long, winding, shaky staircase. "Where are we going? Are you sure this is safe?"

"It's a surprise. As for safety, aren't you a mage?"

"Yes, but teleporting is a pain."

He laughed. "And dying isn't?"

She grunted and warily eyed the stairs while following Terry.

"I promise you'll like it."

"If you say so," Chris said. "You're lucky I trust you."

Terry halted and turned to her. "That... means a lot."

"Why are you so somber?"

He shrugged his shoulders. "I've been reevaluating a few things recently."

They reached the bottom and stepped off the staircase. "Like what?"

"My life. My choices. Why I'm doing... Why I've always done what I'm doing."

"Oh. You're thinking about... leaving? Don't the heirs retain their mentors until they take over as the Head of the Council?"

"They do."

"So you still got five years in you. Right?"

"It's not you, or—"

An incredulous expression washed over Chris's features. "You cannot give me *that* speech." She grasped his arm. "I can't handle another rejection."

"Another? Wait. I'm not rejecting you. I have no plans to leave you, but—"

"Then what were you talking about with your 'it's not you' speech?"

He stood taller. "Never mind. That's not important. Who rejected you?"

"Aren't we here for a surprise or something?" Chris whined.

"All right. Follow me." Terry took the lead.

Chris followed him down a tight stone hallway. Judging by the spiderwebs and dirt, this area of the Council's catacombs didn't appear to be frequented too often. "Are we even supposed to be here?"

"You *do* remember that you're the heir of the Council?"

Chris rubbed her arm. "Yes, but apparently that means nothing."

"All right, I might let a comment about one thing that is bothering you slide, but now you're asking too much. What's going on?"

"The same, really. I tried reasoning with my parents about… Lance. Not wanting to marry him. Strangely enough, Mother appeared to come around for a moment, but then Father crushed it. He's the Head of the Council and the family, and I shall follow traditions."

"But that's not what you want?"

"No. We've talked about this. I don't want to marry Lance."

"Are you sure?"

"What's with you? Of course, I'm sure. I don't love him, so why would I wish to marry him?"

"Your union would be beneficial to the Council and Saltung," he said.

"I don't care! My life should be more than that. My happiness or my will should count for something, too!"

"Traditions can blind people. Sometimes they don't realize that what used to be the right path ceased to be anything worth taking."

"And yet they still push you on it."

"Indeed. What will you do?" he asked.

"Aside from not marrying Lance?"

Terry laughed. "Yes, aside from that."

"I'm contemplating running away as a final option. They can't make me marry him if I'm not here."

"That's a somewhat radical solution to your problem," Terry said, turning to the right and clasping the keys in his pocket.

"Which is why it's my last resort. If I could offer an alternative…"

He unlocked the door and swung it open. "To Lance?"

"To everything. I don't have… There's no one else, at least no one my parents would deem an acceptable choice for me." Chris chuckled. "In fact, that one is as wrong as it gets. Doesn't matter, though, since it'll never happen."

"Are we entering the rejection story now?"

"In theory. It's basically the old tale of 'I don't want who wants me and the one I want…'" She shook her head.

"They don't want you?"

She offered a watery smile. "If it were that simple."

"Oh, Chris. I'm sorry. Come here." He hugged her.

Chris returned the embrace before pulling back and wiping her eyes.

"Anyway. What's up with this?" A flame sprung from her hand, and she stepped farther into the chamber. It appeared to be an old storage room. Full of boxes and crates with the obligatory dust and musty smell of decay.

Terry ambled toward one crate and pulled out a knife to loosen the lid. "I recall our last discussion. The addendum you discovered in that book of yours?"

She stepped closer. "The *Agaze Erbium*?"

"Yeah. Didn't it talk about the Chalice of Verspahen?"

"Yes, but neither of the books we've found offer any hints to its location. We're hoping that it's not a requirement to… well…" Chris ducked her head.

Terry chuckled. "I'm guessing you are performing some kind of ritual?"

She scuffed her shoe along a line of dirt on the ground. "You're careful, right?"

"As much as we can be."

"Good. That's all I ask for." He removed the lid and his hand disappeared in the crate to resurface with an ornate goblet in his grasp and a soft smile on his face. "This should help?"

"Oh Terry, is this… You found the chalice? How?"

"I may have done some reading after you left last time. The name of it rang a bell, but I didn't want to say anything in case I failed to locate it." He handed her the cup.

"Thank you! You don't know how much."

"I do. And you're welcome."

***

Year 302, Day 108

Aimee coughed. "Do potions always smell this vile?"

"Stop whining. First you take forever to respond to my message, and then you can't wait to brew this and complete the ritual. Dylan got hurt getting the Stern stone, again. Not to mention, we wouldn't have the chalice without Terry," Chris pointed out.

"It was the last ingredient, and he only bumped his head. He's fine, and he's fully recovered from his latest misadventure," she said. "And no offense to Terry, but what difference does it make where the Als water is stored?"

Chris huffed. "You truly know nothing about magic. Let me worry about that."

Aimee bumped into her. "That's what I do with everything."

"Anyway. Regarding the wellbeing of my brother, since I have no way of verifying that aside from your word." Chris raised her hands when Aimee opened her mouth, "Hush, I'll have to trust you given your obnoxious tendency to speak your truth."

"My truth? Truth is subjective now?"

Chris tilted her head and added more ash to the potion bubbling in front of her. "Yes and no. There are universal truths, but there are also aspects we hold as true without them having to be accurate for others."

"Like what?"

"Ice cream flavors," Chris replied and stirred the liquid.

"That's not truth, it's a matter of taste. There's no objective way to measure which one is correct."

"You're right. I just didn't want to bring up the first example that popped into my head."

"Why not?"

"Because you said you don't want to talk about it."

"Oh. Wait, you said you didn't want to talk about it," Aimee huffed. "You're killing me sometimes."

Chris chuckled.

"I'm sorry."

"Stop apologizing about this. You did nothing wrong. All you're doing is following your truth, and that it doesn't align with mine... Well, there's nothing we can do," Chris said.

"Is it supposed to bubble like that?"

"Yes. So far, everything is going according to plan."

Aimee scrunched up her nose. "What happens next?"

"I'll say the incantation once I'm done adding the last bit of Kefer tree ash and then I suppose we'll discover the truth."

"What about Dylan? I should wake him."

"Let him sleep! He's been through a lot recently, and he needs his rest. It's not like he can't learn about this when he wakes up."

Aimee snorted. "Fine, but if he's pissed, that's on you."

Chris laughed. "Sure, given that I cannot hear a word he says, that shouldn't be an issue."

"Lucky you."

"All right. I need you to be quiet, but we also have to be in physical contact for this to work."

"OK," Aimee said. "Hold hands?"

"No. The potion needs constant stirring while adding the last ingredient," she said while blending the draught.

"Hmm." Aimee stepped behind her. "How about I touch you like this?" She pressed the palm of her left hand against the middle of Chris's back.

"Oh," Chris breathed and stopped mixing the pot.

"I thought you had to blend this continuously?"

"Right," Chris mumbled, shaking her head, and resumed stirring while adding the rest of the ash.

"Ready?"

"Uh, yes, but remember to be still and quiet," Chris replied, closing her eyes and murmured the incantation she'd memorized. Magic thrummed through her, making her lightheaded, but Aimee's hand both supported and anchored her to the ground. She opened her eyes and marveled at the red and blue plume of smoke that rose from the cauldron.

Aimee coughed but remained silent.

"You can talk again," Chris said the same moment the house rattled.

"What the... What did you do?"

"What did *we* do! You're as much a part of this as I am!"

Aimee bent her knees and held onto Chris. "Semantics. The house is shaking!"

She grabbed Aimee's arm to steady herself. "You don't say!"

A booming sound rang through the room before the smoke cleared and the building stilled again.

"Now what?" Aimee asked.

"I don't know! It's not like I've ever done this before."

"But you're the mage out of the two of us."

"Yes, which is why I did the spell." Chris stepped closer to the pot and glanced inside. "Of course." She snorted and picked up a tome at the bottom.

"Another book." Aimee sulked and sat down on the couch. "At least this didn't burn a hole in my carpet or set my house on fire."

"Huh?" Chris raised her head.

"Never mind. What's this about now? More riddles?"

"No. It's a journal by," Chris said and licked her lips.

"Yes?"

"Elizabeth Morgen."

"The wife of Tyler Morgen? The founder of the Council of the Living and its first leader?"

"Yes."

"All right. Why am I not surprised that your family is involved? All those books? You had to inherit your obsessions with reading from someone."

"I'm not obsessed with books!"

"Sure." Aimee laughed. "Come on. Sit down and let's study this."

They read the book for a while and only stopped when Aimee raised her head and announced that Dylan had entered the room.

"You slept through your sister causing an earthquake and shaking the house," Aimee said.

"That's an exaggeration," Chris grumbled.

"Yeah, right. He's asking what we've found," Aimee relayed. "You wanna explain it, or shall I do it?"

"I'll do it. I'm assuming you'll be able to tell me any of his questions."

"Sure."

"After the potion and the spell, we found this journal written by Elizabeth Morgen, our great times-a-lot grandmother. We only read most of the first half so far, and... She says we need to decide how to proceed, but for this to be a true choice, we must understand the truth and the repercussions."

"Yeah. We haven't gotten to that part yet," Aimee said, and at Chris's raised eyebrows added, "he asked what truth and consequences."

"Elizabeth is long-winded and her speech pattern is formal, so there's a long introduction and conversation about what we already know about the quest and the premise for a Living mage and a Verlohren to embark on this journey together," Chris said.

Aimee snorted.

"What did he say?"

"He uttered a similar sentiment to what I said earlier, about certain affinities and maybe even tendencies running in your family."

"Right." Chris rolled her eyes. "Let's keep at it."

"Hey, you're going too fast," Aimee exclaimed after another ten minutes.

"Wait, wait… This can't be…" Chris turned away and pulled the book closer before thumbing through several pages, reading quietly for a couple of minutes before standing. "No." She closed the volume. "We're done."

"What? Come on! Some ingredients for the final spell sound challenging to get, and I'm not keen on killing a doe, but—"

"We need an Antward Stone, and there's only one location mentioned for it in all of lore, and there is no way you're going *there*. It's suicide."

"Yes, that's the place," Aimee said. "Dylan says that while it'll be difficult, we shouldn't just give up. He and I can go."

"No. There's more, and it's done, no matter what you both say."

"I didn't know you were in charge of this quest."

"I'm not, but the final spell needs my blood, and I'll never allow it."

"What's wrong? You're… Sit down. You're a second away from fainting."

Chris sat back down.

"I have no idea since she snatched the book before I could catch up! Look, your brother is worried, too. What's this about?" Aimee asked.

"Remember how... how upset you got when I told you we'd signed a contract and if you don't go on, then..."

"Yes, you die, and I burn. Is it something like that again? Then we have to continue either way."

Chris clutched the book closer to her chest. "No. We're not bound. It's up to us to decide. The truth is in here, but..."

"What is it?" Aimee asked.

"Only a Verlohren can obtain the Antward stone because only... one of you can go *there*."

"We know."

"It's the final part to be added to the spell, and once we do... *you*, not we. You must do it. The Verlohren who's been on the quest. You must add the stone at the end."

"And then?"

"You burn."

"You didn't react like that last time. What's the problem here, aside from the fact that I'm not in favor of burning."

"Back then it would have been a... a sort of punishment, and—"

"But it would have killed you if you didn't continue! That's extreme as punishments go."

"It is. That magic involved here... It's old."

"What's different, Chris?"

"Before, the burning would have stopped after a while. This... this won't. Not until..."

"Until Mary releases me or dies."

"Yes. So we're done. It's not worth it."

"What is the truth? Do you know? Was it in there? What would this spell do?"

Chris rubbed her neck. "If this... if what Elizabeth says is true, then everything we've ever been taught is a lie."

"I knew it!" Aimee called.

"They, my family… They made an arrangement with Death. Apparently, Death are twins. Lily and Lara. They… they offered a pact to make Tyler the ruler of Saltung, and to… Let me find it again." She leafed through the book. "Here it is. 'We created an enemy in the Verlohren, who used to be called Wanderden. Before Death cast the curse of Separation upon Saltung, they only existed as spirits, and they guided their loved ones on the path to reconciliation so that peace within the families may be established again.

'There had never been a Council or ruler before in Saltung because none was ever needed. We lived in harmony. Establishing an Other, a group that was different, separate, and could become the enemy was a crucial step in forming a Council and creating a leader. The Wanderden were already dead, so there was no actual harm done in making them corporal and cutting off their connection to their loved ones.

'They would still be released once their loved ones came to terms with their loss on their own or once they passed as well. The curse contains provisions to prevent the Verlohren from contacting or communicating with anyone who loved them, and even renders them invisible to them.'" Chris closed the book once more.

"That is… horrible." Aimee trembled. "I can't… This is so selfish and cruel, and…"

"Yes, but the price—"

"What would we get if we performed the spell?"

"We're *not* doing it!"

"Then give me the journal so I can read it for myself!"

"Fine." Chris made no move to hand over the diary. "We'd get the contract, the original document of the pact between my family and Death."

"The contract?" Aimee jumped up and paced. She ran her fingers through her hair. "We could prove to the Living that it's all a lie! That would end the raids, the awful treatment of the Verlohren. The Centers!"

"I doubt my father would let this happen."

She halted in front of Chris. "How is *that* up to him?"

"He's still the leader of Saltung and the Head of the Council."

"He's in charge because his great-whatever grandfather made a contract with Death to seize power! I'd say that invalidates his rule."

"He won't see it like that."

Aimee tilted her head. "Do *you*?"

"Why does that matter? It changes nothing."

"Maybe it matters to me," Aimee said.

She flung the book on the couch and stepped up to Aimee. "Do you really believe that I am on *their* side in this?"

She ducked her head. "No. I'm sorry. Yeah, yeah, yeah," Aimee said. "Your brother just called me an idiot."

"He isn't wrong," Chris sniffed.

"Yes, well, I still think we shouldn't dismiss this. Getting the contract would be huge. Not only could we use it to bring the truth to Saltung, but you're a mage. You could break the curse."

"You really don't understand magic. It's difficult to break a curse, and most of the time, you need the people who've cast it."

"Death."

"Yes. I highly doubt the twins would agree to this. They must have gotten something out of that pact as well or they wouldn't have agreed to it. I'm not sure there's a way to end it."

"Could you research it?"

"Sure, but what's the point? I won't *ever* complete that spell."

"You wouldn't have to. Didn't you say that was my job?"

Chris shoved Aimee. "This is no joking matter!"

"That wasn't a joke. I want to see if there's a possibility to break the curse before—"

"I don't know in what other language I must express this for you to get it through your thick skull, but I will *not* help you! I will *not* be a part of you burning and spending the rest of your existence in utter torment!"

"It's not your decision to make!"

"You need my blood, don't you? So what? If I say no, you're going to take it anyway?"

"What?" Aimee stuttered and fell back. "I'd never..."

"Which is why this is pointless. I don't care what any potential research says. Even if the spell were to be breakable, I will *not* sacrifice you."

"No, you'd sacrifice everyone else instead."

Chris flinched. "That's not fair."

"No, but it's true. I understand, OK? I don't want to burn. I'm no martyr or anything, but... how can we walk away from this knowing how many people would heal and find peace?"

"What if it was the other way?" Chris asked.

"What do you mean?"

"What if I had to add the stone and then die as the price for getting the contract?"

"That's not the same. I wouldn't die. I'm already—"

"Shut up! Stop saying that! It *is* the same because you won't be able to do anything anymore. You'll be catatonic, in a state of absolute torment and terror for the Gods know how long. Mary is thirty years old! She might live to be seventy or eighty."

"She could let me go before then. You could talk to her."

"There's no guarantee that it would work, and to find out, we'd have to cast the spell which I won't do. You still didn't answer."

"What question?"

Chris glared at her.

"'What if' scenarios are useless. There's no way to change things to where you'd be the one to have to add the stone and pay the price."

"You are avoiding the answer!"

Aimee stared at the ceiling. "It's different."

"It's not, but I get it. It's always different when it's not us. We're so quick and willing to sacrifice ourselves, but with…" Chris shook her head.

"If you know, then why make me say it?"

"To show you that your opposition is hypocritical because you wouldn't let me add that stone if I were in your shoes."

"Hypocritical? I'm trying to save an infinite amount of people from enduring this foul existence, from being cut off from their loved ones. From never finding peace!"

"But you move on. Eventually," Chris said.

"Some of us are here for forty, fifty years. Do you have any idea what state you're in if you've been a Verlohren for that long? You've seen the Sattran. Is that what you want for us?"

Chris closed her eyes. "No. I remember how it feels to be you. Does every Verlohren turn into a Sattran after a while?"

"I'm not sure," Aimee replied.

"Maybe you should research that before you accuse me of something awful and insensitive only to make me feel guilty for caring about you."

"Chris—"

"No. I'm done here." She grabbed the book and disappeared.

***

"Hey! I thought teleporting is hard and uses up too much of your energy!" Aimee shouted after Chris.

"You truly are such an idiot sometimes," Dylan said.

She sagged onto the couch. "Stop calling me an idiot."

"I will, as soon as you quit acting like one. I don't understand why my sister fell for you. I generally like you, but you are so emotionally challenged. I can't even imagine you having a relationship."

"Gee, thanks. I told her that, too."

"She's stubborn."

Aimee sighed. "Tell me about it."

"What are we gonna do?"

"We get that stone. Your sister will head to the convent soon, and we'll leave then. That gives us enough time to research and plan."

"Not to burst your bubble here, but even if we survive this little trip and come back with the stone, what good does that do when we don't have her blood? Or the rest of the ingredients since Chris conveniently took the journal with her."

"She'll be back, and then I'll make a copy of that list."

"And the blood? I don't see how you get that without using force."

"What is *wrong* with both of you? I'd never do that. I won't hurt Chris, but I have an idea."

"You think going against her will and getting the stone, performing the spell, and *burning* for the rest of your existence won't hurt her?"

Aimee clenched her jaw. "She'll get over it. I'm wrong for her and it would never work. Might as well take myself out of the equation."

"Wow. That's more messed up than I expected."

"What do you mean?"

"You're running away. That's your solution to what's between you. You refuse to give in, but you also don't want to see Chris move on and live her life with someone else."

Aimee cringed. "She'll do that eventually, anyway. And she should." She looked away. "But no, I don't want to be around for that."

"So all this talk about helping people, allowing them to heal and whatnot, that's a lie."

"Two things can be true at the same time."

"Sure, but that's not what makes you so adamant about this."

"I hardly think that matters. It's the right thing to do either way," she said.

"Tell Chris that," he said.

"Don't you dare. Not a word."

"How would I even?" Dylan spat.

"Oh." Aimee winced. "Sorry."

\*\*\*

Lily stormed into Lara's room. "Are you happy now? Their quest is over!"

"It is?" Lara jumped up. "You did it! Well done. I knew I could count on you."

"Don't look so pleased. Your monster didn't stop them, though it almost killed Chris, and—"

Lara scrunched up her eyebrows. "Why are you so attached to her? You've never been this worried about any of your other charges."

"She's different. Both her and Dylan. They are… or in his case, was kind."

"Kindness makes for an inefficient ruler. It only slows you down and prevents you from making tough decisions."

"What decisions? Like the experiments at the Centers Anthony and Lance designed? How are those part of an efficient way of ruling?"

"It's surely productive for us. Didn't you sense the increase in energy from the markings?"

"Yes, but we don't need that much," Lily argued.

Lara waved her off. "What stopped them if it wasn't the Zilal-ruh?"

Lily sighed. "Chris doesn't want to complete the ritual because it'll make Aimee burn."

"So?"

"Elizabeth apparently designed the final task in a way that demanded a total sacrifice from the Verlohren. She'd have to burn for the rest of her existence."

"I still fail to see the problem. Why is that stopping them?"

"Not *them*. Aimee still wants to continue, but Chris doesn't because… Well, she cares about Aimee."

Lara stared at her unblinkingly.

"She may be in love with Aimee," Lily mumbled.

Lara threw her head back and laughed. "A Morgen in love with a Verlohren? And they say irony is dead. This is delicious, and best of all, it solves all our problems."

"How is that?"

"It divides the only two of the current generation who can break the spell. Without them working towards a common goal, they won't succeed. Elizabeth didn't care about the Wanderden. She probably enjoyed setting this difficult task that exposed many demons between them, almost guaranteeing that they would fail."

"I doubt that was her objective. She gave them an option at the end. Do what's right for you or what's right for the community, the land. She hardly expected them to fall in love."

"That part doesn't matter. It just amuses me. A lot. Elizabeth's quest is still designed to disappoint, precisely because of the choice you've mentioned. When asked to choose between a personal sacrifice or the status quo that only hurts people you don't know or don't care about, who would elect the former?"

"That's a depressing outlook," Lily groused.

"No, that's reality. People are selfish. Even your Chris is selfish. She doesn't want the object of her affection to suffer, so she'd rather condemn everyone else to carry this cross. I might like her after all."

"Because that's what we did."

"Exactly," Lara said.

# ten

"That's not going to happen!" Chris exclaimed.

"What choice do we have?" Aimee asked.

"There must be another way to invalidate the contract. What about telling people the truth? And once I'm in charge, I'll not enforce our part of the agreement."

"None of that will work. People will think we're lying or that a bunch of Verlohren brainwashed you, and not to mention, you have *no idea* what your side of the deal even entails. The curse won't end because you ignore it. And—"

"No, I won't accept that. Not only is it suicide to go there, and I can't even come along to help, but aside from all that, you'll die if you add the stone," Chris said.

"I'm already—"

"Don't you dare finish that sentence! You will burn for the rest of your existence as a Verlohren. Do you know what that means?"

"I'd say better than you do."

"You don't have to sacrifice yourself for—"

"Is that what you think I'm doing? I want notoriety or recognition so that people know who I am? I don't care about any of that, and that's not the reason... Didn't you once claim that sometimes we must take risks, even if they are dangerous and can harm us, because it's the right thing to do? Remember?"

A muscle in Chris's jaw twitched.

"You convinced me of that, and then we did the protection spell and the binding ritual. Your life was in danger throughout this entire quest. You kept getting hurt. We raced after Dylan without a plan and fought that creature and almost lost. Those were acceptable risks, and this is not? Why? Because you still have some hope of living that fantasy of yours—"

"Stop."

"The truth hurts, Princess. Isn't that what they say? I'm *dead*, Chris. I wish I wasn't. I wish things were different, that we met back then, and... But that won't ever be, and I've made peace with that. You need to do the same."

"It's not about that," Chris pressed out through gritted teeth. "I've accepted your decision in that regard, even though I disagree, but I respect your prerogative to be wrong."

Aimee snorted.

"What I don't accept is you being in agony for the rest of your existence when it's unnecessary. Yes, the truth is important, and I'm not saying that it'll be easy to convince people of the true history of Saltung, of... of what my family has done. And without destroying the contract—"

"It'll be impossible."

"We need to try! Anything is better than you venturing *there*. The stone is useless anyway because even if you get it, you can't complete the spell alone. You need my blood, and as I've told you a million times, I will *never* give it to you."

Aimee's fingernails bit into the palms of her hands.

"Or did you change your mind and will force me after all?"

"We talked about this already, but sure, Chris. I'll stab you, put your blood in a vial and add it to the—"

"Sarcasm doesn't suit you."

"Melodrama isn't a good look on you either."

"Please let us try to find another way. The Tarung—"

"Are being hunted down like animals as we speak, by your fiancé."

"He's not my fiancé anymore, and you know that," Chris spat.

"Hardly the point."

"If that's true, then why did you bring it up?"

Aimee grumbled.

"I have no control over the Council guards. My father... He's still in charge."

"But you can influence our next steps. Are you OK with all these Verlohren suffering, and…" Aimee slumped down on the couch, placing her head in the palms of her hands. "I don't want to burn, Chris. I'm scared. I don't even have words… That's our worst fear, aside from turning into a Sattran."

"Then don't do it." She sat down next to Aimee and grasped her hand. "We will find another way. There must be a different solution. I can't…" Tears welled in her eyes.

Aimee sat up and pulled her close, kissing the top of her head. "I'm not sure what else we could do, Princess. We're running out of time. You remember your father's ominous warning about the Tarung?"

Chris sighed and hid her face in Aimee's neck.

\*\*\*

"This is everything we need?" Dylan asked, bending over the handwritten copy Aimee had transcribed.

"Yes."

"Let me see." He gripped Aimee's notebook and read out loud.

*"This final challenge brings forth the original pledge,*
*But with it, confront your heaviest gauntlet yet.*
*The Antward Stone will push you closest to the edge,*
*A doe's heart added to the Bound's blood is the safest bet.*
*The remaining ingredients are deceptively effortless,*
*Kathan root, red sepat, and Blum vinegar complete this set.*
*For the Verlohren, this ritual will be far from painless,*
*Only with the ultimate sacrifice can the conditions be met."*

He groaned. "It's no wonder Chris freaked out."

"Hmm." Aimee held out her hand for the notebook. "I found something else," she said, leafing through her booklet. "The journal also talks about a pendant that has been in your family for generations. It contains an orange-brownish stone fragment."

"Huh, that sounds familiar." He tapped his lower lip. "Could this be on a chain, like a necklace?"

"I suppose. Why?"

"My mom used to wear a pendant that fits. She'd only put it on during special occasions. Why did Elizabeth mention it?"

"She says to bring it with us on the journey to the Antward stone. It's supposed to be helpful."

"How?" Dylan asked.

"I have no idea, but I'd prefer to follow every word of those suggestions."

"That's probably a good call. I can look for the pendant when I get the shirt. Markus will disable the Verlohren detectors, so they won't notice my presence."

"Sounds like a plan," Aimee said.

"Do we have to... The heart of a doe?"

"I'm afraid so."

"That's awful. I don't wanna kill an animal."

"Me neither, but unless we're willing to collect all ingredients, we don't have to go after the stone either. We might as well give up," Aimee said.

"I'm not gonna quit."

"Then we get the heart of the doe."

He sighed. "I'll do it while out collecting Kathan root. You'll get the red sepat."

"All right."

"When are we leaving?"

"Whenever Chris next heads for Salbit."

"She'll kill us," he groaned.

"That she will."

\*\*\*

Freit, Saltung
Year 304, Day 114

"I've spoken with Lance, and—"

"He's accepted your decision to cancel the wedding?" Aimee asked.

"What? No. We didn't... I had other things on my mind. I won't marry him no matter what, so what he believes about that is rather meaningless," Chris declared. "I spoke to him about the Council's plan for the Tarung."

"And?"

"At first he was acting as if he can't tell me anything, 'need to know only,' and other such nonsense. Sometimes I think too many people consider my position as merely ornamental."

"Sounds like it," Aimee said.

"They've infiltrated the Tarung, and according to their sources, more attacks imminent. Weeks at the most."

"If they are aware of that, shouldn't it be easy to prevent these assaults?"

"Lance says that their spies only learn bits and pieces, not concrete plans."

"How convenient," Aimee griped.

"What do you mean?"

"I still don't believe the Tarung were responsible for the last attack. They have no motive, in fact, the opposite is true. Attacking the Living is suicide for any Verlohren organization. Your Council brings down any of our groups just because they exist, and they have done so forever."

"It's not my Council, but yes, it makes little sense for the Tarung to plan attacks on the Living."

"I reached out to Sarah again, and I brought up the possibility of fractures within their organization, that some people might not agree with their overall agenda or speed. She was skeptical but promised to investigate. I haven't heard from her yet, but I'm not convinced she'll find anything."

"What if the spies are the ones causing strife?" Chris proposed. "Do... do you see Sarah often?"

"Not making waves is part of their job description. I doubt the spies are there to cause trouble for the Tarung," Aimee said. "Unless, of course, that is their true purpose and Lance lied to you."

"That's one possibility."

"And I don't."

Chris picked at a string of the throw hanging over the couch. "Excuse me?"

"I don't see a lot of Sarah anymore. We'd tried to reconnect after my passing, but...," Aimee worried her lower lip. "I was too distracted, and maybe obsessed with finding answers to all these lies about the Verlohren. Pretty soon, we went our separate ways, but we've remained friendly, I suppose."

"That's..." Chris jumped to her feet and hurried to the window. "Why are there Sattran in your front yard?"

"What?" Aimee rushed next to her.

Outside stood six figures, dressed in lopsided, loose clothing, wearing way too many colorful scarves. As always, they hovered close together, forming a mass of withered bodies that swayed back and forth.

"How did they find us? What are they even doing in the city?" Chris asked.

"Only one way to find out." Aimee dashed outside.

"Wait!" Chris raced after her.

By the time they made it to the front, the Sattran had edged closer to the door.

"The fire and earth," one of them sang.

"That again," Aimee mumbled.

"They helped us last time," Chris pointed out.

"They speak in riddles worse than the damn *Demise of Reason,* and I'm so sick of this. If you can help, just say it!" Aimee shouted but lowered her head as the mass of Sattran flinched at her yell.

"I'm sorry. I don't want to upset you, but why are you here?"

"The stone. The earth produces the stone."

Chris stepped forward. "That won't happen."

"You mean the Antward stone? So we can get it if we go there?"

"Earth deliver stone. Fire burn," a different Sattran chanted.

"This is enough! Let's head back inside. We won't get the stone because we aren't suicidal."

"Fire. Earth. Stone," the Sattran vocalized together.

"But you said yourself they helped us last time. Why is this different? Because you don't like it?

"Because it's insane and not worth it! Can we perhaps delay this discussion until after I return from the convent? I don't want to worry about this while I'm there."

"Fine," Aimee grumbled and folded her arms.

"Thank you." She squeezed Aimee's arm. "Where did they go?"

"Who knows? They always do that." She canted her head and strolled out into the street.

"What is it?" Chris joined her. "What are those flickering lights down there?"

Aimee ground her jaw. "Torches."

"Another raid? Already?"

"Welcome to my life," she groused and clasped Chris's arm. "Let's go inside. You can do that spell thing to hide us if necessary."

"Wait, I want to talk to them."

"Are you insane? How are you gonna explain why you are here, at the house of two Verlohren? You do remember the last sweep you were present for, when your boyfriend thought we'd abducted you? What if he's part of this one, too?"

"Stop calling him that! Lance is *not* my boyfriend, and even if he was, what's it to you? Stop acting jealous while rejecting me at the same time!"

Aimee kicked a patch of dirt, her gaze focused on the soil. "You're right. I'm sorry. That's not fair."

The Council guards had drawn closer, and they heard their shouts and jeers while the sound of breaking glass and batons crashing into doors rang through the air.

"We need to get inside," Aimee urged.

"I will talk to them. I'm the heir to the Council. What are they going to do to me?"

"Tell your father about it, and then you have to explain what you were doing here, how you know me. Come on! This could endanger the entire plan."

"There is no more plan. At least not for now. And these incursions are going too far. I can say I was in the area to observe the raids."

"And then what?"

"I tell them to leave and return home," Chris said. "You need to go inside, though."

"This is…" Aimee released a mirthless chuckle. "Fine. Do what you want. I'll join your brother in hoping you won't get killed."

Chris frowned and turned to her. "You're being quite dramatic. They won't hurt me," she declared, and fire sprang from her hands.

Aimee marched back into the house and slammed the door shut.

Chris didn't have to wait long. A few minutes passed, and a group of Council guards paraded toward her. She'd extinguished the flames at this point.

"Lady Christina." The lieutenant bowed his head. "We are surprised to find you here. What has brought you to this area? These are Verlohren settlements."

"I wasn't aware I owe an explanation of my whereabouts or intentions to a Council guard," Chris sneered.

"Of course not. These are dangerous times. The heir to the Council should be secure, and frequenting these Verlohren squalors risks your safety."

"Do your raids improve the living conditions or security of the Verlohren?" Chris asked.

The guard laughed, while a few directly behind him snickered along. "That isn't our mission, Lady Christina. We'd gladly wipe them off the face of Saltung if they'd stayed dead. Even fire won't get them. Did you know that? You know all about fire, don't you?" He stepped closer while Chris remained still and held his gaze. "The Verlohren catch fire, and they burn, but they don't turn to ash. They just scream. And when the flames snuff out, they're still there. Like roaches. They never die."

"Who is burning Verlohren? Under whose order?" Chris asked while suppressing the bile that clawed up her throat.

"We do nothing but follow orders, Lady Christina. If Verlohren are burned?" He shrugged. "It's because our leaders have ordered it."

"You lie!" She was about to hurl further accusations at the guard when a crash from inside the house behind her captured her attention.

"You know anyone in there?" the guard asked.

"What?" She turned around. "How? I don't..." Another thud, followed by a loud bang and a shout, but by that time, Chris had yanked open the door and tore into the house. "Aimee? Where are you?"

***

"Get off him," Aimee shouted at the guard who'd dragged Dylan to the floor. They'd crept inside through the backdoor, and neither she nor Dylan had noticed since Chris had held their entire focus while they stood rooted in front of the windows, watching.

The guard shoved Aimee back, pushing her into a cupboard that struggled to contain its contents.

"Let go!" Dylan called and wrestled the guard off him before jumping to his feet and dashing to put the couch between him and the man.

"Aimee!" he cried as the scuffle between Aimee and the guard sent the cupboard reeling, and the plates and cups slid forward and crashed through the shattered glass before the unit fell. Shards scattered on the floor beneath the overturned sideboard. Beneath Aimee.

The other guard used Dylan's distraction and hauled him once more to the ground when Chris rushed into the room.

***

Chris burst inside. "What is going on?" Her hands sparked flames, high and bright. "Out! All of you! Get out of here!"

The guards scrambled to their feet, exchanged a quick glance, and bolted.

"Aimee?" Chris called and startled when she noticed Aimee's hand peeking out from under the fallen cabinet. She waved her hand in front of the locker, and it lifted off Aimee before it straightened and returned to its original position.

Chris crouched next to Aimee. "Hey." She gently touched her arm, but Aimee didn't stir. "Dylan. I know you are here. Are you alright? Can you get help? Some of your other friends? I'll move her to the couch and try to help her, but I'm not sure if last time was a fluke or if I can help her again.

"Is there... Do you have some kind of Verlohren physicians? If so, get one, but be careful. Wait until the guards have moved on."

She hoped he was here and heard her. Judging from the fight the other guard had seemed involved in, he'd been there. Now she could only pray he'd be able to get help.

"Come on. Let's move you to the couch." She levitated Aimee off the floor and onto the big chair. She placed a pillow beneath her head and paced. The last time she had tried to heal Aimee... It worked, but it almost didn't, and she wasn't sure if... But what else was there? She refused to do *nothing* or just sit there and wait for Dylan.

225

She had to do something. Chris glanced at Aimee's bruised face and the dent in her side where the cupboard seemed to have broken several ribs. There were lacerations across her torso, judging by the red leaking into her shirt. This would take forever to heal without magic.

She knelt next to Aimee and placed one hand over her heart and the other on her head. Once more, cold latched onto her, and the poor hummingbird thumbed weakly against her chest wall.

"Damn it. I should have listened to you," Chris mumbled, scraping against the walls that arrested her energy. The spell. Her eyes flew open. The spell from the *Agaze Erbium* that got her through last time. She furrowed her brows and recited the words, stumbling at first, but then they came back to her, and she finished the incantation.

Aimee trembled, then shifted before seizing.

"No!" Chris shouted, clinging to the thrashing body on the couch. "All right. Let's try this." She closed her eyes, called upon their connection, and visualized the strands between them, then pulled. Her world spun, and she sagged against Aimee.

The room in which Chris awoke was cramped, full of oddities and mundane items. Several chairs were stacked on a table, and next to it, a shovel leaned against a wall behind a wheelbarrow. Another desk stood in the corner and on top of it, on a bunched up blue blanket, lay a glowing orb.

The stone floor was littered with forks and spoons, but there were no knives. A tin case full of marbles rested on what appeared to be a beat-up nightstand. A broken vase joined the metal case, along with several silver coins. Light poured into the room from a window with a cracked glass panel.

Chris wiped her forehead and pulled at her shirt collar. Why was it so hot? She squeezed through another set of tables and stepped past more glowing spheres. This time, they were stuffed in bags and jackets. These orbs were smaller, but they shone just as brightly.

"Where am I?" she murmured and further inspected her surroundings. There were several mirrors on the walls, old, ornate ones, and more modern pieces with sleeker and darker frames. All of them were fractured. Gazing at the reflection inside made her head spin.

A low whine suspended all her movements. "Hello?" Chris asked.

The noise halted, yet in its stead, suppressed breathing rang out.

"I'm not here to hurt you," she said in a low, hushed voice, while her gaze trailed across the room. She turned and stopped in front of a writing table that stood barren. Nothing on top, and nothing... Chris checked below the counter and froze.

"Aimee! What's going on here? Where are we? Are you OK?

Aimee didn't answer, her gaze locked on a painting that rested against a chair in her line of sight. She rocked back and forth and uttered incoherent words under her breath.

"I don't..." Chris fell to the ground next to her, unsure what to do.

\*\*\*

"You're not real," Aimee sputtered, a mantra falling from her lips while she stared unblinkingly at the image in front of her. Her mother's favorite painting, in blue and green, raging waves crashing against the shore while gray skies and boisterous rain clouds obscure the sun.

This was her refuge, the one place she could turn to where the pain stopped, drowned out by the clutter of accumulations of a lifetime.

How did the shadow get here? She was safe. The only location where she had ever been protected. Not anymore. The specter had found her and would surely drag her back to the scorching pulsing, the sluggish pounding and bright light of her existence.

What did it matter that she was supposed to be a spirit? Helpful to Mary and with a purpose. No. It meant nothing because that wasn't her place. She was stuck. And now the shadow had spotted her, sitting in front of her. Yapping.

Aimee didn't understand the ghost's words. How could you understand a being that had no mouth? Where were these sounds coming from? And how did the shade get here? This was her sanctuary. No one knew about it, and no one could reach her here. She'd erected too many walls and barriers, created desolate wastelands and swamps full of treacherous traps and noxious fluid. No. This wasn't right. None of it made sense.

Aimee dipped her head in her hands and rocked back and forth. Her eyes were closed, so she neither saw nor heard the specter draw closer and touch her arm. She yelped at the sudden warmth imbuing her and jerked backward, pressing her body against the wall before she dared to open her eyes.

"Aimee, please come back to me," the shadow said, but no, not a ghost at all. Chris?

She licked her lips and closed her eyes once more, counting to ten, then she opened them again. "Is that really you?" Aimee rasped.

"Yes," Chris's voice broke, and she wiped her eyes. "Come on out of there."

Aimee reached for Chris's hand and when they touched, all went dark, then nothing.

\*\*\*

"What the…" Chris rose and looked around. They were back at Aimee's place, with the woman's still figure resting on the couch. No more seizures wracked her body.

"So it worked a little?" Chris sat down in front of the sofa. Did she dare access her magic and channel healing energy into her? She wasn't keen on revisiting that room, or ever seeing Aimee that frightened again, but she needed to try. She needed her back.

Chris once more hovered her hands over her unconscious friend. She rolled her shoulders and rested her hands on Aimee's chest and forehead. "Please work," she begged, calling on her energy, which she released without incantation and allowed to sink into Aimee through their connection.

She relinquished her grip on the torrent of power that churned within her before it poured downward. It was the only thing she'd never tried, never permitted. Her magic, while always present, existed under tight control, and Chris had chained it, refusing to *ever* allow it flow freely, too afraid of what effect it would have on her and those around her. But the energy level required to help Aimee by far exceeded the amount she could regulate, and so she surrendered and let go.

This time the energy flowed two ways, and parts of Aimee's mind, after absorbing her magic, flooded Chris, bringing with it images too fast to fully grasp, but most of all she felt the presence of a small child laughing and jumping into puddles of rainwater.

Chris blinked hard, raised her head and tried to navigate what seemed like stretched time, then flinched. Had she fallen asleep?

"Hey," Aimee croaked, shuffling into a more upright position while cupping Chris's cheek in her hand.

Chris leaned into the gesture and smiled. "Hey."

\*\*\*

Year 302, Day 115

Lara sat forward in her chair and swiped several books off the table before jumping up. "You said they were done!"

"Stop being so dramatic. I understand that you're angry—"

"Angry?" Lara stalked toward Lily. "You don't seem to realize or *care* what is happening here! If Chris and Aimee succeed in their little quest," Lara spat and drew back. She closed her eyes. "We'll lose everything."

"Maybe it's time for a shift?"

"Have you lost your mind? Change never helps, it never improves your life. It's a trap! It shatters all and you're left with… ruins."

"Not all change has to be bad. We altered Saltung, and—"

"Exactly! We were the creators of these modifications. No one forced them upon us, unlike what is going on now, all because you don't have the *guts* to do what needs to be done."

"What are you talking about?" She rose and stepped closer to Lara. "What did you do?"

"I have done nothing. Well, I talked to Lance, and he's more than happy to uphold the Morgen part of our bargain, with or without your little lamb."

Lily clenched her jaw. "You didn't!"

"Watch me." Lara chuckled when Lily stormed off and slammed the door.

***

Year 302, Day 115

A knock dragged Aimee out of her reverie. She sat up on her bed. "Come in."

Chris opened the door halfway and leaned against it. "Can we talk?"

"Depends. I'm still tired and I don't want to fight."

"That's not what I'm here for. I'm leaving tomorrow. Another session at the convent and this time, there'll be no adventure in the mountains to distract me."

"Because that was so much fun," Aimee grumbled and patted the space next to her. "Come here."

She sat down. "Thank you."

"Spending time with you isn't a hardship, Princess."

"Unless we're fighting, switching bodies, or are trapped in strange places. Not to mention, ending up in a cluttered room."

"I don't—"

"Sorry." Chris shook her head. "It's a lot to take in. We're… We're up against Death, and there's nothing we can do."

"We're *choosing* to do nothing."

"Didn't you say you don't want to fight?"

"We only settled on a delay for now, but that doesn't mean I'm gonna lie or pretend that I agree with you."

"No, you'd never do that."

"Don't sound so bitter."

"I *am* bitter. I thought finding out the truth, that you're not really dead but a corporeal spirit would—"

"I'm still dead. Yes, my original body is buried somewhere, rotten to bones at this point. It makes sense, and it explains why none of us had the injuries that killed us once we became Verlohren. Should have added that to my list of oddities."

"It's impossible to cover everything."

Aimee leaned back on her elbows. "True."

"Why doesn't it change things?"

"Because nothing's truly different. I'm dead. I have no influence over how long I'll be here and there's still no future."

"Then there never is because this isn't any different for the Living!"

"What?"

"We don't know when we'll die either. I might live to my eighties or nineties, or I might die tomorrow or in a month. None of us are guaranteed a specific time frame or length. How is that different from your situation? We also don't influence when we die, mostly."

Aimee frowned and worried her lower lip. "I never thought of it like that."

"I can tell," Chris huffed.

"But I'll leave for sure, and probably a lot sooner than you."

"Says who? For all we know, I could die before you ever stop being a Verlohren."

"Don't say that," Aimee's voice broke.

"It's no fun, is it, to contemplate each other's mortality."

"I never said it was."

"But you are always so quick to point out that you're dead and how you'll be gone soon."

"Because that's been my mindset for the last eight years. It's a hard habit to break."

"Would you leave someone you love because you found out they're sick and won't live for much longer?"

"Of course not!"

She held Aimee's gaze.

"But it's different starting a relationship with that outlook, and if I knew I was dying, I wouldn't want to start one."

"You cannot shield others from being hurt. Attempting to do that in a way that causes pain to whom you wish to protect, that's just illogical," Chris said.

"I never claimed to be logical." Aimee's gaze traveled to the ceiling. Should she tell her about their plan? How could she hide this from Chris? But she'd never agree and would probably try to stop them.

Dylan and she had comforted each other that they were doing the right thing, that sometimes, one must lie to one person to save many, to reveal the truth and break the contract that would alter the life of everyone in the land. How could they pass up on that? The price was high, but it seemed doable, and it would have been completely acceptable before meeting Chris. She was so lost in thought she missed the next question.

"What?"

"I asked if… if I may see your markings."

"Oh." Aimee internally stamped on the heat that spread through her. "Uh," she mumbled, sitting upright.

"You don't have to."

"No, it's fine." Aimee cleared her throat and folded her hands. "We keep them covered as much as we can. It's… I wonder what they do in the curse. I'm assuming the Wanderden didn't have them as spirits."

"Whatever their purpose, it's an efficient design."

Aimee snorted, relieved at the tension draining from her body. "You'd say that." She turned around, facing the other wall so that her back was turned to Chris and lifted her shirt, revealing the spattering of lines, sweeps, and curls darting up her side and spilling over her front and back.

They sat in silence for a moment with their breathing the only discernible sound in the room.

"They're beautiful," Chris whispered, and Aimee shuddered when Chris's finger trailed over one of her markings.

"Uh, sure, if... if they weren't a sign of the curse with likely some nefarious purpose."

"Right," Chris sounded distracted.

Aimee peered over her shoulder. "You all right?"

"Turn around."

"Uh." Aimee hesitated for a moment but then followed Chris's request. She tried to drop her gaze, to avoid holding eye contact with Chris, much like she'd tried and failed to convince herself that the woman across from her didn't mean that much. Weeks, months, and she knew they were all lies. But she couldn't, not only because she was dead and her future was uncertain, used to be precarious, but now she'd truly be gone. Not released, but inaccessible to Chris and it wasn't fair to—

"May I kiss you?"

Aimee's thoughts careened to a halt, and she clenched her jaw. "You shouldn't."

"Do you *want* me to kiss you?"

"Yes," Aimee pressed out; sure, she'd go to hell for this alone. The smile that broke over Chris's face physically pained Aimee, but that feeling drowned and helplessly trickled away the moment their lips connected. She gasped before dropping backwards on the bed, pulling Chris along.

Chris's hands slid under her shirt and up her sides. She pressed forward and deepened the kiss, a low groan bleeding from her lips.

Aimee trembled and decided to let go, to stop worrying about tomorrow and to enjoy this moment since it would never happen again. She drew Chris closer and nipped at her lower lip before once more entering the heat of her mouth.

Her usually weak sense of smell overcome by Chris's earthy scent and the nearness of her sent her heart racing. Her hands cupped Chris's cheeks, and she broke the kiss with a moan when Chris's hips rocked into her. Aimee bit her lip and slowed them down.

"We need to stop," she groaned and pressed her face against Chris's neck, letting her lips linger on soft, damp skin.

"I was hoping you'd take longer to recover to your senses," she grumbled, sinking further into Aimee.

"I'm sorry."

"I'm not. I have the better argument and we got time." Chis faced Aimee and pressed a quick kiss on her lips.

Pain drummed through Aimee, and she once more tightened her hold on Chris. Time was the only thing they didn't have, and what was even worse, Chris would hate her for this. A small and selfish part of her wanted to quit, to take what Chris offered so freely and walk away. But she'd never forgive herself if she did.

# eleven

Salbit, Saltung
Year 302, Day 116

Chris groaned as an explosion rattled her bones and her body hit the floor. There was fire all around her, and a dizziness shot through her that left her gagging. She tried to summon her magic to teleport out of the building, but healing Aimee and teleporting here late had sapped her energy, and now there was nothing left.

She coughed and pulled up her shirt to cover her nose and mouth. The putrid smell of smoke nauseated her, and her eyes teared.

Dull shouts rang in her ears. "Chris! Chris!"

"I'm in here!" she called, unsure who the voice belonged to, though it carried a familiar lilt.

The door burst open and with it, more smog infiltrated the area while tongues of fire licked around the frame.

She coughed. "Terry."

"Let's get you out of here." He sprang to Chris's side, taking her hands, and pulling her up. "Can you walk?"

She held on to him. "Yes."

He led her out. "Come on."

The fire had swallowed the entire first floor and most of the second story as well. A russet wall of heat hurdled their way and blocked every path out, while the beams of the house shuddered and groaned.

"There's... no way out... of here," Chris cried. "I can't... teleport us out."

Terry's gaze flitted around when a cracking sound echoed through the room and one of the ceiling struts broke and plummeted toward them. He raised his arm and the shaft disintegrated, raining ash on them instead.

"How... What did... How did you do that?" Chris stammered.

"Later. Let's get you out of here first." He held on tighter and teleported them out of the house.

"You're a mage!" Chris stumbled back. "You never told me. Why?"

Terry stared at her. "It's... complicated."

"You transformed the wood beam into ash, but you didn't say a spell. Just raised your arm." She paced. "We should be dead."

"Calm down."

"No! Tell me... tell me the truth. What's going on?"

He dropped his gaze. "You don't want that."

"That's *all* I want! Why do you think I've been...?" She sighed. "This is why I've been trying to uncover the history of the land!"

"The truth is sometimes better left alone."

"Who gets to decide that? I'm so *sick* of other people deciding what is best for someone based on their assumptions. That's so arrogant, and they are proven wrong almost *every* time. The truth is important, and yes, it may hurt, but it's vital to understand it. Only then can you make an informed decision about anything. Why do I have to keep explaining that to everyone?" Chris said before a coughing spell racked her body.

"Calm down. You were injured and you need to take it easy."

"I'm fine." She swatted at Terry. "Tell me!"

"It'll change everything, and it might even ruin..."

"Ruin what?"

"I never meant for any of this to happen, and I don't... I don't want to see you hurt."

"I don't understand."

He closed his eyes and his form dissolved in front of her, much like the rafter before, but this time there was no ash.

There was... Chris shook her head and rubbed her eyes before opening them. "Who are you?"

"My name is Lily, but... I've been Terry for you."

"You… What?" She scampered back. "That makes no sense."

"I'm…"

"Death. You are *Death*. Lily. That's one of the twins Elizabeth spoke of."

"Yes."

"So what? You murdered Terry and took his place for what? To stop me from finding out about your pact with my family? The curse you brought upon Saltung? You're too late! I read all about it."

"I did not kill him. I am, or I was, Terry."

"No, no." Chris jumped up and paced. "You're lying. This can't be. Terry… he's been around *all* my life. I've known him since I was a child, he…"

"Remember when your father bought you a glass bird from one of his trips and you carried it with you everywhere you went? How old were you? Five? You sat in your hiding place, admiring the figure when your cousin… oh, I forgot his name, he was playing with his brother and he fell on you, right there in your hiding place. The bird—"

"Broke," Chris whispered, having halted her pacing.

"You were devastated. You cried for days."

Chris licked her lips. "I don't… you… you've been there. My entire life. Why… Were you stalking me? For what?"

"I was watching over you."

"You are Death! You cursed the entire land for more power. To do what exactly? So you can play my mentor for almost thirty years?" Chris shouted.

"I wasn't always Death. When… When the contract was signed, we were mages, much like you, though more powerful."

"Who is *we*?"

"My sister Lara and I. We'd heard the legend of Death, and how…" Lily shook her head. "We wanted to be Death, but first, we had to get him out of the way, the original one."

"What? I understand nothing."

"Maybe I should start from the beginning. Why don't you sit down?"

***

Freit, Saltung<br>Year 0

Lara marched toward the mansion while Lily scampered after her, stumbling in her attempt to catch up.

"Is this the right thing to do?" Lily's voice trembled.

"Of course. We went over this. It's the perfect solution. Tyler needs us, and we need him," Lara stated.

"But is it wise? Can we trust him?"

"We only *ever* count on each other, Lily. Remember that."

"Then why are we doing this? There could be another way—"

"There's not. If we want power, we must take it. We stand no chance without this additional energy."

"Why is this so important to you?"

Lara halted and glared at her sister. "Are you joking? This is what we've been working toward our *entire* lives. Ever since... Don't tell me you'll bow out now."

"I'd never do that to you," Lily vowed.

"Good." Lara smiled and took her sister's hand. "We're here. Let's do this." She rang the bell and once the door swung open, a servant showed them to the library.

"Welcome to my home," Tyler Morgen boomed, his arms stretched out in greeting. "This is my wife, Elizabeth. Let us sit and discuss our plan."

"Thank you," Lara replied and shot her sister a meaningful glance before they sat down at the table across from the pair.

"How will all of this work?" Tyler asked.

"We sign a magical contract. Then, we will cast a curse upon this land that erases everyone's memories, present company excluded, about the role of the Wanderden. They will receive a new name, maybe something that has more of a negative connotation."

"How will that help?" Elizabeth asked.

"We both want something, and our plan offers a way to all that we desire. You wish to rule Saltung, and we... Let's not worry about the details, but what both of us long for is accomplished in the same manner. Our goals are aligned."

"How?" Tyler asked.

"The Wanderden will become outcasts, reviled by society. This creates an enemy, and your family will rise as the saviors, the ones who shall protect Saltung from their menace. People will be scared, and they will yearn for leadership. That's what you'll offer."

"How can we make them outcasts? The Wanderden are a central part of society and of how we all relate to one another," Elizabeth said. "It has always been that way."

"We will tell them a different story, or better, they will *remember* the new version of history and forget the old. After our curse, the Wanderden become corporeal, and they can no longer be seen by their loved ones."

"What should stop them from asking each other for help in talking to their families?" Tyler asked.

"The spell won't allow it. They would be in agony if they tried," Lily said.

"Why do they need to be corporeal for that? Won't that make them more dangerous to the Living?" Elizabeth asked.

"Yes, and that is by design. We will give them markings, runes, across their bodies that increase with age so you can recognize them. There has to be a clear threat for the populace, real fear, which will chase them right to where you need them," Lara said.

"How long will they stay like that?" Tyler asked.

"Usually, the Wanderden solve whatever issues that bind them here with their loved ones who cannot let them go. They travel together to the Isle of Wandth, or through the Thal mountains, and visit the Land of the Elders. They do their rituals, and then they are free."

"Nothing of this is new," Elizabeth stated.

"After the curse, people won't remember any of this, and such travel will become impossible. Not only will the Isle and the Land of the Elders beyond the Thal mountains disappear from all your maps and stories, but we'll also create a veil that prohibits travel there. The new version of the Wanderden can only be released once their loved ones let them go without assistance, or when they die as well."

"And no one will recall how things used to be?" Elizabeth leaned back in her chair. "Is that wise?"

"It's the only way to guarantee that this novel society will function how we envision and grant your family the rule of the land. That is still what you're interested in?" Lara asked.

"Yes, of course," Tyler said. "My wife has always advocated honesty. One might even say she's honest to a fault, aren't you, dear?" He squeezed Elizabeth's hand, who remained silent, her gaze never leaving the twins.

"Certain sacrifices have to be made. The Wanderden are dead anyway. I see no harm in these changes. A common enemy is the best way of bringing a society together," Tyler agreed.

"Exactly," Lara said.

"How long until you cast this curse?" Elizabeth asked.

"We already started preparations and should be ready within a moon's full cycle."

"Excellent," Tyler exclaimed.

Lara handed Tyler a sheet of paper. "We've prepared a list of what you'll need to accomplish in that time frame as well. We're not the only ones with tasks left to complete."

"Of course. That won't be a problem." He perused the writing in his hands.

\*\*\*

"All those people. All the suffering. For what? For power? Being in charge was more important to them than…" Chris collapsed on the ground.

"We need to get you to a physician." Lily took hold of Chris's arm to help her up. "Come on."

Chris shuddered and shrugged her off. "Don't touch me!"

"I'm sorry. I truly am, and you don't..." Lily closed her eyes.

"What? There's more to the story? What was in it for you, anyway? You said you were just two mages."

"I'm not sure why Elizabeth represented what happened in this manner, but no, we weren't Death then, but we wanted to be."

"How?"

"That's the other part she neglected to mention, though I don't recall if she knew about it. Lara likes to keep secrets."

"Your twin sister?"

"Yes. She doesn't trust easily, and..." Lily chuckled. "She'd be furious that I'm revealing my identity and telling you all this."

"Then why do it?"

"I'm so tired." Lily sat down next to Chris on the ground. "I've mentored almost your entire line since all this started. After we defeated Death, the original one, we celebrated for a long time. Then Lara got worried about your family holding up their end of the bargain, so I became the mentor of each new Morgen heir."

"How did nobody notice?"

"Oh, I was never the same person. I always showed up differently. For you, I became Terry," Lily said.

"Right." Chris pulled her legs closer to her chest. "Elizabeth revealed that the Verlohren are spirits turned corporeal, and the markings... it wasn't clear what their purpose was or is."

Lily sighed. "They aren't just a random manifestation of the curse. The anguish, the misery the Verlohren experience, it's feeding us. That's how we gathered enough power to defeat Death and take on his position."

"That is so awful."

"I suppose. We didn't see it that way. The Wanderden, back then, they were spirits, unfeeling."

"But you've changed that by making them corporeal, and I can tell you, they are in pain."

"Your friend Aimee?"

"Don't talk about her!"

"All right. I'm sorry. But yes, we were willfully ignorant. It didn't matter because their suffering didn't touch us. It didn't affect us."

"Nothing you say makes me feel sorry for you or betters your position. Quite the opposite."

Lily chuckled. "That's not my goal. Our relationship is in tatters and beyond repair. I'm not asking for your forgiveness or understanding, but I want you to know the truth. Didn't you say the truth is important?"

"Yes."

"Then that's what I'm doing. I'm sharing what truly occurred with you, as someone who was there when it happened. And there's one final part Elizabeth didn't realize. We weren't fully aware of it either."

"Go on," Chris said.

"The curse goes against nature. I'm not sure what is out there steering our lives or fates, but since we made those changes, there seems to be a growing resistance. We've noticed over time that most generations, definitely the most recent ones, have had a Verlohren and a Living mage who would have been able to attempt what you and Aimee have been doing."

"Getting through the quest?"

"Yes, though that wouldn't have been the only path. Two of you have always been capable of breaking the curse together. You are just the first to get this far," Lily said. "Not even the veil we've interwoven in the spell to blind the heir and their loved ones from seeking the truth stopped you. You've both overcome it and continued your journey."

"It changes nothing, though. We won't cast the spell to obtain the contract, and without that, no one in Saltung will ever believe us. It also means we can't break the curse."

Lily frowned. "That's odd."

"What?"

"I just... Why are Dylan and Aimee searching for the Antward stone as we speak?"

Chris jumped to her feet. "They are doing *what*?"

"I suppose they didn't tell you."

"No. I need to get home," Chris snapped.

"Wait. You're not strong enough. Let me help you."

Chris narrowed her eyes. "I'm not going anywhere with you."

"That's fair, but... allow me to recharge your magic?"

Chris stared at Lily for a moment before nodding.

\*\*\*

Berkan Mountains, Saltung
Day 116

"Chris is gonna murder us. Or set us on fire," Dylan said.

"You don't know the half of it." Aimee glanced around the edge of the cliff. "Why does this have to be so difficult to access?"

"Otherwise everyone would go there?"

"Nonsense. Why would they? The Living cannot enter this place anyway, so why make it so hard?"

"Perhaps they don't want to see us, or they wish to protect their stuff from thieves."

"Because anyone in their right mind would trek down there and steal from *them*," Aimee snarked.

"Uh, you do realize that's what we're here for?"

"Hush!"

"What? We're alone."

"You can never tell who's lurking around. You don't reveal your plan to your enemies before it's finished."

"It's moot to reveal it after it's done. They'd already know."

"Dylan, I love you, but seriously, now is not the time for such a discussion."

He grinned. "I love you, too."

"Figure of speech. Don't let it go to your head. You're bearable and all that."

"Hmm, sure. Much like my sister."

"Uh, yeah, well, I don't think she'll be that fond of me once we come back. Not to mention, I dragged her little brother on this insane mission."

"True. Which is why I said she'll murder us."

"She'll kill me. You're safe."

"She'll be mad at me, too."

"Yes, but she can't see you. How's she gonna hurt you?"

He smiled. "You're right."

"You brought the shirt and the pendant with you, right? I didn't get a chance to ask before. Did you have any problems sneaking into your old house?"

"I got everything, but I gotta say, that question comes a tad late. Also, not a problem to sneak into a place where no one can see you, especially when you have an accomplice who works there."

"True. Markus's been invaluable in all of this. What about the servants and other employees, though? They're not your loved ones."

Dylan shrugged his shoulders. "I avoided them. I grew up in that place."

"Look, over there." Aimee pointed toward a pitch-black corner at the edge of the mountain. "That's the entrance."

"How do you know? Could just be a shadow."

"I can feel it," Aimee mumbled and trod ahead.

"You are spending way too much time with Chris," Dylan groused and followed her down across slippery rocks while the currents of the ocean spewed briny water over their feet.

Aimee hunched over and bowed her head as she wobbly hopped from stone, nearing the spot she'd marked before. The wind gushed through the canyon walls and where they receded, a breeze blown by the outside gales wafted over them.

"You were right. This is an entrance into the mountains." Dylan hoisted himself up into the crevice. "A bit small, though."

"Move farther in and wait for me." Aimee climbed up.

"Chris's fire would be useful."

"That's why I brought these." She shrugged off her backpack and pulled out a torch, lighting it on the surface of the stone wall. Once the beacon lit their way, they followed the meandering path down into the mountain.

"Do you hear that?" Dylan's low voice rumbled in the space between them.

"It sounds like metal scrapping over stone."

"We really shouldn't be here."

"Agreed. What did the book say about the stone's location?"

"Only that it's guarded and at the heart of their realm."

"That should be fun," Aimee grumbled.

"If this is your idea of fun, you need a new, well, not life because you're dead and all, though technically we're spirits, not dead."

"Same difference." She raised her hand. "Wait. Do you hear that?"

"What? There's only silence," Dylan said.

"Exactly. The sounds from before, the grating against metal? It's gone."

They exchanged a glance before ducking simultaneously when hot steam rained on them from above. Tremors shook the ground, and they pressed closer to a wall to steady themselves.

Once the quaking stopped, they rose.

"Do you have the pendant?" Aimee asked.

"I already said yes," Dylan groused and furrowed his brows.

"Where is it?"

"Oh," he said. "I had the shirt tucked in with the other stuff in my backpack, but the necklace," he reached into his pants pocket and pulled out a silver pendant encircling a bright orange stone, "is right here. Wait a minute. Why is it glowing?" He held it out to Aimee.

"It didn't look like this before?"

"No. It was a dull, boring, amber stone."

"Are you sure?"

"I'd think I'd have noticed it gleaming. Or…" He cocked his head. "Trembling?"

"What?" She grasped it and her mouth fell open, but she remained silent when slight quivers rippled off the stone.

"The text said it would help us."

"And it started this here? You're sure?" Aimee asked.

"I would have missed the glowing with it being in my pants pocket, but I'm sure I'd have noticed those vibrations."

"True." Aimee held the pendant closer to the flame of her torch. She pointed it in different directions and the glow changed from a mute to a bright orange. "Could this guide us to the stone? Why else would it shine brighter in that one direction, but not the others?"

"You're right. We might as well follow it."

"Agreed." She headed toward the pathway the pendant had indicated. Nothing happened for a few minutes while they traveled along twining trails deeper into the mountain.

Dylan rubbed his arms. "It's getting colder. You feel that, too?"

"Yes," Aimee said before she yelped and slid forward, losing her footing on the floor that had shifted into ice.

"Watch out!" he shouted and sidled to a stop next to her, holding out his hand to pull her up.

"Thanks," she said. "The walls here also appear to be made of ice."

"Is it just me, or is it weird that we're facing the cold here? I was expecting heat."

Aimee chuckled. "There are stories about places like this composed of ice as well, though I doubt the cold will be all we'll encounter."

"That's a cheerful thought," Dylan mumbled. "You're ready to continue?"

"Might as well." Aimee inched ahead. They got a little farther before a howl echoed through the hallways.

He grabbed Aimee's arm. "This is making me uncomfortable."

"Why? We're dead already. It's not as if we can die again."

"There are worse things and conditions than death," Dylan replied. "What is that? It doesn't sound like any animal I know."

"That's not an animal," Aimee uttered the moment a strong wind squall knocked them off their feet.

"Oof," Dylan grunted. "I'm sensing a trend here."

Aimee struggled to regain her footing and rise. "As long as we can get back up."

"We should slide instead of walk," Dylan suggested.

"Sure." Aimee pulled him up before they slid across the ice surface with their heads down, heading deeper into the mountain.

After another few uneventful minutes, a creaking followed by a thunderous crash rang out.

He groaned. "What now?"

"We only just started. You knew this was going to be hard." She glanced at the glowing pendant again. "At least we're still heading in the correct direction."

"Just because I knew this was coming, doesn't make it any easier to deal with."

"All right. I'll give you that," she said and sighed at the sight in front of her. "What now?"

"There's no chance your torch can melt this?" Dylan asked.

"No way." Aimee stared at the blocks of snow and ice barricading their path forward. Another crack sounded out and when she spun around, more ice blocks formed behind them, cutting them off, trapping them in a narrow, freezing hallway inside a mountain.

"That's fantastic," Dylan groused. "We should have brought Chris along. Oh, wait. She can't go down here, and she'd never come here either, even if she could, because unlike us, she's not stupid!"

"Calm down!" Aimee marched toward the wall in front of them. She raised her hand and touched the ice. "It's softer than it looks," she said. "We should be able to dig through it." Her hands raked through the frozen slush and shoveled it out. "Come on. Help me."

Dylan stepped up to the barrier and followed her lead. They were silent while they dug their way out, inch by inch, ice and snow accumulating at their feet.

Aimee's hands hurt. Pins and needles turned into numbness, and she lost her grip on the ice several times. She panted, shivering while sweating.

"There," Dylan grunted and shoved at a remaining block of ice. "That should be big enough for us to squeeze through." He bent his head, clasped the straps of his backpack, and pressed through the fissure. "It's melting!" he called.

"What?" Aimee glanced at the pendant before pushing through behind him, and when she stepped on the other side, her feet were treading water. "Is this from the ice melting, or are we moving from ice to water?"

"I dunno, but I'm sure we'll find out. Onward, we go!"

Aimee narrowed her eyes. "Why are you suddenly so cheerful?"

"I'm not cheerful. More relieved? Not a fan of tight and enclosed spaces."

"Says the man on the path to the center of a mountain! Why didn't you say something?"

"What's there to say? It's gotta be done, so it'll get done."

"You still could have told me," she said.

"Stop grumbling. Come on. Check the pendant to make sure we're still on track."

"Way ahead of you. I did that before coming through. We're good."

"All right, then. Let's move." He marched on and Aimee followed him.

The water didn't rise or recede, and they kept their pace through one-inch-high water until the path in front of them forked.

"Which way?" he asked.

Aimee pulled out the pendant. "I should continue on one route and see how it acts. It's still glowing, and the intensity hasn't changed so far." At Dylan's acquiescence, she treaded on the path leading them to the right. With her eyes trained on the stone, she didn't notice branches snapping out of the wall and seizing her, drawing her close and pulling her against the hard, cold surface.

"Aimee!" Dylan shouted, rushing close but halting at her grunt of protest.

"Stay back."

The branches sprouted green and yellow leaves and shot off tendrils that snaked around Aimee, binding her wrists and sucking her closer to the rock wall.

"We gotta get you out of there!" Dylan yanked open his backpack. "Let's see." He dug through its contents. "Yes!" He pulled out a spear-point knife and unfolded it.

"How will... you... get me... out... if you... can't come here," Aimee pressed out.

"There's no other way. This thing is suffocating you." Dylan kept his gaze on the branches still rippling over Aimee and inched closer.

---

249

His gaze drifted to the other side of the wall, and he stopped to stretch out his arm into the hallway.

"What... are... you doing?" Aimee panted.

"Making sure there's no attack from the other side." He canted his head. "Though it could also be activated by me walking on the actual track."

"You think?"

"You really shouldn't waste your energy on sarcasm," Dylan said and halted right next to her. He raised his hand and cut through the first set of vines, only to watch several more spring off other branches and entangle Aimee. "Maybe not," he said.

"The torch," Aimee gasped.

"Right, wait, where?" He glanced around before he saw the torch had rolled to the side of the wall at Aimee's feet. "It got wet. I can't use that."

"Backpack," Aimee mumbled, her eyelids drooping while the vines and branches coiled tighter.

"Oh!" Dylan once more fished through the satchel and grabbed another torch. He lit it on the stone wall and stared at the bursting flames for a moment. "I don't want to burn you."

"Do... it," Aimee slurred.

He squared his shoulders and edged closer before crouching down to hold the flame against the bottom network of twigs and vines.

Like kindling they lapped up the fire and a crackling noise followed a muted sizzling as a low groan resounded through the hallway. The flames ate at the branches, and the leaves crumbled and turned black. A shriek pierced the air.

Aimee pushed and tore, twisting inside the tree's grasp and with a final lurch, stumbled forward, away from the burning, twisted, and marred branches. "Thanks," she breathed.

"Anytime. Are we to assume that this is the incorrect direction then?"

"Let me check." Aimee inspected the stone of the pendant. "It's dull, and there's only a minimal vibration to it." She held it toward him.

"Yeah. Didn't like this path anyway," he said and turned, heading to the other section of the fork.

Aimee followed and once reaching the passage leading to the left, the stone continued to glow and quiver. "All right then. Let's go."

Their hike resumed uneventfully until they encountered another crossroad, but this time with three new directions. One route continued straight ahead, the other veered to the left before going downhill, and the third led uphill to the right.

"Well, then. Where to next?" Dylan asked. "Do the thing with the stone again but watch where you're going."

"Really?" Aimee muttered.

"Sorry. I get testy when I'm nervous."

"It's fine. I'm gonna vote for the one that's going down. We entered here pretty high up, so I doubt wherever we're heading is leading up."

"What about straight ahead?"

"Nah. Doesn't seem right." She made a tight fist around the stone and crept to the left path heading down. After a few more steps, she peered the stone again, which continued to glow and vibrate. She emitted a shaky breath. "We're good."

Dylan entered behind her, and they continued their journey. "It's getting warmer."

Aimee pulled at the collar of her shirt but only grunted in response.

When they approached the end of the tunnel, a barrier made of cracked glass blocked their way.

"Of course." Dylan sighed and reached out to touch the boundary only to snap it right back. "Oh, this is cold!"

Aimee stepped closer. "What's that inside?"

Dylan followed Aimee's gaze. "Is… is that fire? Inside of ice?"

"It looks like flames, but the barrier doesn't seem to be ice." She picked up a piece of rock and smashed it against the wall.

"Do you think it's a great idea to crush glass, or whatever that is, to release fire?"

"Probably not, but how else can we continue?"

He groaned. "I was afraid you'd say that."

"We gotta break it." Aimee hit the wall again, and the rock tore a splinter through the already brittle surface. "Find another stone or something and help me." She spurred Dylan into action.

Wind gusts picked up around them.

He grabbed a rock and smashed it against the icy surface. They banged against the barriers for what felt like hours without any real headway, until a crack sounded and, instead of breaking through, they fell into an abyss full of dark chambers.

Aimee tried to pull herself up, but she slipped on the wet floor and tumbled back down.

"Dylan?"

"I'm here," he groaned.

"Are you hurt?"

"I landed on something hard, and it bruised my ribs," he winced. "You?"

Aimee checked her body, surprised by how cold she felt. When she dragged her hands over her arms, her numb fingers brushed over a sticky wetness. "I might have cut myself on my arm."

"Is it bleeding a lot?"

"No. We never do."

"That's a blessing here," he said. "Now what?"

"I'm assuming you brought torches, too?"

"Right. I forgot." He shuffled his backpack to the front and dug out a torch. Dylan stretched out his arms and inched forward until he ran into a hard surface where he ignited it.

Light bled from the head of the stick and lit up the room. There was still water on the floor, more of an icy slush than the clear, cold liquid they'd encountered earlier. Black stone walls rose around them with no passageway in sight.

Dylan waved his arm to light up more of the room. "Now what?"

"We'll have to climb up." Aimee raised her head toward the hole in the ceiling from where they'd fallen.

# twelve

"I can't believe we got away with that," Dylan panted while he rushed after Aimee to the clearing right outside of Freit. "How much time do we have?"

"Dunno," Aimee groaned and fell to her knees on the damp, grassy surface next to the cauldron Dylan had prepared before they'd left for the mountain.

"Are you sure you wanna do this?"

Aimee's eyes widened. "Why would I have gone through all *that* if I wasn't sure?"

"I meant you can still change your mind. There's still time before Chris—"

"No," Aimee ground out, ripping a strip of cloth from her shirt, tying it around her bleeding upper arm and fastening it with her teeth.

"All right." Dylan unzipped his bag and rummaged through it. "We got it all here," he said and pulled out a white shirt, a ceramic container, a bottle with clear liquid, and a knife he handed to Aimee.

"Thanks." She hissed when she cut her hand and squeezed blood into the cauldron.

"Why didn't you use the blood from the cut in your arm?"

"I... You gave me a knife, and... Whatever." She bandaged her hand before picking up the jar.

"Wait. You should add Chris's blood first."

"Good idea." Aimee grabbed the shirt. She wiped her blood off the blade before cutting out the stained fabric with Chris's dried blood and added it to the water. "This spell needs a lot of blood," she said before opening the jar and dropping in the heart of a doe that Dylan had captured and killed before their mission to retrieve the Antward stone.

"What's next?" Dylan asked.

"The Katheen root," Aimee said.

"Oh, right." He dug back into his backpack before holding up a brown package. "The red sepat is in there, too."

"Thanks." Aimee unwrapped the chopped root and deposited it in the cauldron with the blossoms. "You got the Blum vinegar?"

"Yeah. I stole that bottle from the pantry of the mansion when I got Chris's shirt."

Aimee snorted before unscrewing the cap and pouring half of the vinegar inside.

"There's only the stone left," Dylan said. "We really don't need to do this."

"And the incantation. I'll miss you, too, Dylan." Aimee grasped the Antward stone in her frigid hand. "With this I willingly restore what once was and should always be. I call forth the foul bargain that has cast a shadow over the land, and I shall accept the sacrifice. Bear witness!"

"Uh, Aimee, is that Chris barreling towards us?"

She lifted her head and clenched her jaw. How she wished she didn't have to do this. The knowledge that she'd disappoint and hurt Chris almost outweighed the fear of what was to come.

***

"No! Aimee, no, please don't!" Chris shouted while she sprinted toward the clearing where they had set up the incantation site. She was too late, but that didn't stop her legs and lungs from burning under the strain of her pace.

She never should have gone to the convent in the first place. Why did her conversation with Lily take so long? Why didn't she tell Chris earlier that Aimee and Dylan were after the stone? Worse, that they had found it. Shouldn't Lily have felt that? After all, she was aware of interlopers encroaching on her realm. Or did she deliberately hide this from Chris?

How did they get her blood? She'd never have gone to the sanctuary if she'd known that all they needed was the stone.

She had had nightmares about them going off alone and acquiring that blasted stone, but she'd dismissed those fears as irrational, since the potion would remain incomplete without her blood.

Why would they risk going *there* without a way to finish the spell? Yet, here she was, getting closer by the second, but she might as well reside on their crimson sun for she'd never reach them, not before...

Freezing time wouldn't work on Aimee. When she first learned that spell, it had thrilled her. Playing outside, laughing, and halting animals in their tracks. Everything stopped, even their breathing. She couldn't arrest time for long at first, and she still struggled to push past four minutes, but that was enough for almost anything she tried to accomplish. She couldn't believe that the spell would fail her again.

Why would Aimee do this? After everything? After the night they'd shared before she'd left for Salbit. Chris had assumed they agreed, at least with the ritual. Yes, Aimee had argued that they should carry on, but she'd grudgingly conceded that it was safer to find another way, or at least wait until she had returned from the abbey.

Had something changed in her absence? Did Aimee lie? Was all this talk a mere effort to dissuade Chris, to mollify her in the belief that they were safe? That she was safe. Though knowing Aimee, she'd argue that she'd never been safe. At least not until...

Her pulse thumped in her head, and she wanted to scream, but her body was too busy gulping and burning all the oxygen her lungs could deliver.

Even though she'd heard people talk about time slowing down in significant moments, she'd never experienced it herself. Not even when Dylan... Chris tightened her jaw.

Time stretched, but not by or through her will.

Aimee raised her hand in seeming slow-motion and the Antward stone glinted in the final sunlight of the day.

Damn her.

Damn both of them, and Tyler, and Elizabeth, and her father, and all the Morgen family who knew and did nothing.

"Stop!" Chris pressed out, surprised she could form words. Her heart thrashed so fast in her chest that her vision blurred while white lines and circles danced before her eyes.

But Aimee didn't stop. Chris was taken aback when Aimee raised her head and caught her gaze. She'd never seen her friend so grief stricken—wide, hollow eyes, her face pale and gaunt—as she slammed down the stone. A wave of red and blue light exploded from the ground and washed over them.

Chris slowed her pace, torn between her desire to be near Aimee and her fear of the same. She felt it, a buzzing like flies, but instead of swirling around her, they burrowed underneath her skin.

The hummingbird's steady fluttering quickened before it faltered and stuttered, much like Chris, coming to an agonizing halt the instant Aimee tumbled backward and crumbled to the ground like a shattered statue brought down by the hammer of an iconoclast.

She slackened to a stop next to Aimee, flinching at the sight of the twitching woman while similar cold shudders reverberated through her frame. She kneeled next to her, reaching out to pick up a white blouse on the floor, tossed right outside the incantation circle.

"That's how you got my blood," Chris whispered, balling up the shirt in her hand and peering blankly at the cut-out piece that bore the largest bloodstain. "I should have burned it after the attack on the marketplace."

She dropped the shirt as if the contact scalded her skin before she turned her head at movement in her peripheral. A scroll skittered down the gravel slope and without hesitation, Chris snatched it and spread it open.

She cringed at the words before her eyes.
This was it. This was the reason Aimee lay at her feet in agony, and why she'd remain like this for the next decades.

The contract between Tyler and the twins—the wretched curse that had created all their misery. She rocked back and forth and the knuckles on her hands paled.

Aimee had made a choice; she knew the price she had to pay, and while Chris respected freedom of will, this bargain never came close to resembling free will.

They were dragged into this adventure without knowing what it would entail and what price it would demand. Even less did they understand that only *one* person would be able to end it, who could procure this… document, this irrefutable proof of her family's crime.

The short-sighted, arrogant, and ignorant grasp for power at the expense of everyone else. And still it cost. Had this been part of the design, too? Did Elizabeth have a notion that the Living and the Dead might grow closer during this adventure?

Was this part of the test that she'd be willing to sacrifice Aimee? She'd failed because she'd never have chosen this. They could have found another way. There was *always* an alternative. Why didn't Aimee wait?

Her vision grew hazy, and she jumped up, throwing the contract away before stalking closer and igniting it with flames shooting from her hands. The smoldering parchment did not burn. Chris grunted and doused it with a stream of blue fire as tears spilled down her face while the scroll danced unscathed in the blaze.

Lily appeared with a low pop right next to her. "That's not how this works."

"Get away from me," Chris spat.

"I'm the last person you want to see, and I want to honor that, but I can help you."

"How? Can you undo what Aimee did? Can you make her burning stop?"

Lily's gaze found her hands. "That's more complicated, but—"

"Then I'm not sure how you can help," Chris growled and blasted the contract against a boulder before ripping the rock out of the earth. She levitated the stone and smashed it onto the treaty.

"Your magic alone cannot destroy the contract," Lily said.

Chris froze. She spun around, facing her. "The only other person who could aid in the contract's destruction... You. Or Lara. Do we need both of you?"

"You need the bloodlines of both parties that were involved in the curse's creation and who signed the contract."

"You and me. We can destroy the curse?"

"If that is your wish."

"Of course it is my wish! I'm bleeding out all my energy because what? I want to see how much it takes to knock me unconscious?"

"Take my hand." She reached out, but Chris hesitated. "Is this better?" Lily transformed into Terry, at which Chris recoiled.

She closed her eyes. "No, no. You can't be him. *Ever again.* Change back."

"All right. But you have to hold my hand," Lily said, her arm still stretched toward Chris, who released a shuddering breath and grasped the offered hand.

"I never want to see you again after this, in either form," Chris said. "What is the incantation?"

"There is no formal spell. Your need, your desire to destroy the contract and break the curse is enough, as long as the longing to annihilate it is present."

"Oh, it is."

"Good. Close your eyes and focus on your emotions. Imagine obliterating the scroll, ending the curse." Lily waved her hand, disintegrating the boulder.

This time, when the scroll burst into flames, purple smoke rose, and Chris coughed as the resulting sulfuric odor reached her.

A wailing scream filled the air before the contract disintegrated to ash. The ground shook, tripping Chris, and she stumbled when a hand grabbed her upper arm and steadied her.

"Chris. Are you OK?" asked a raspy voice she never imagined she'd hear again.

"Dylan?" Chris's eyes widened and her mouth slacked, but her body reacted on instinct, and she hugged her brother close, crying into his shoulder. "I'm so sorry," she sobbed.

"Hush. It's OK. It wasn't your fault." He stroked her back. "I'm sorry about the stone, and... I know how much Aimee means to you. She was so scared."

She cried harder and weakly punched Dylan's chest. "I... hate this. How... how could you do this? How could you let her do *this*?"

"There was no *letting* her. You know how she is."

"Now she's gone, and she's in torment. I can feel it," she choked.

"Yes," he said with a tremulous voice.

***

There was nothing. A stillness that boded anxiety. Then molten, liquid heat hemorrhaged through her veins, seeping into her bones and radiating through her body. A scream lodged in Aimee's throat, unheard and unanswered. Her eyes were shut tight, and as hard as she strained, her lids didn't budge; she couldn't even blink.

Still the fire raged within her, scorching her insides. Didn't people lose consciousness at a certain pain threshold? Would that also apply to her?

Never having been much of a crier, Aimee longed for the ability to shed tears. Perhaps the relief she pictured flooding her if she were to cry was an illusion, but that didn't stop her from craving the imagined release.

Regret didn't haunt her, at least not for what had led to this. Regret for leaving, for... abandoning Chris...

The ache emanating through her bit harder, jagged teeth mawing her flesh while her heart jittered, clenching in her chest. Her lungs struggled to pump oxygen through her body, worsening the sluggish exhaustion languishing her frame.

Coherent thoughts dangled in reach, but they were mismatched puzzle pieces, fragments that instead of forming an image, painted a picture so foreign and odd it rendered her mute in thought and in speech.

Even during her years as a Verlohren, she'd counted on an awareness of physical presence, that her body remained tangible; now, though, she tumbled through numb voids and the only sensation left was a forever expanding misery.

While Aimee was no stranger to pain, certainly not as a Verlohren where a certain level of discomfort lingered, the unabating anguish that now ripped through her belied any previous notions or fears of burning as child's play, a scratch on her shoulder that had already scabbed over.

The urge to flee grew, but with it came a persistent dread and a sense of desperation. How did one escape one's own body? She'd be stuck like this for however long it would take Mary to release her.

Once more her mind drifted to Chris. And Dylan. Now she could free her brother, and that belief almost convinced Aimee that she'd struck a worthwhile bargain.

*\*\**

Lily smiled, then furrowed her brows and wiped at the water dampening her face when she watched Chris reunite with Dylan. She never expected that her life among the Living would make her so weary. Or so weak. At least that's what Lara would call it.

Lily had first acted as usual—Chris's investigation a potential interference with their design, and she hastened to Lara's side as she had always done.

Lily had followed along or condoned, in retrospect, all of Lara's schemes and designs, her collaboration with the Living, and sending the Zilal-ruh to stop Chris and Aimee from bringing down their curse, their source of power. But now she had helped them destroy the very tenet that tied them to immortality.

For once in her existence, Lily had acted without consulting Lara first, and not just that, it was a decision she *knew* her sister would have rejected and forbidden. She raised her head to the sky, wondering where Lara was, and why it was taking her so long to appear. She must have felt the quake, the fracture that severed their creation.

When she lowered her head, her gaze fell on Aimee, who was staring into the night sky with wide-open eyes. Her body was wracked by tremors, and her tanned skin had taken on a sickly, ashen hue, while blood trickled from her mouth and nose. One of their most… gruesome additions to the curse.

Any Verlohren who tried to help another, sought to communicate in their stead with a loved one would burn, experience a state of catatonia accompanied by excruciating agony. When they'd designed this, they needed a guarantee that they wouldn't help each other and thus end their prolonged sentences as Verlohren. However, this state wasn't designed to last longer than an hour, still time enough to render some of them mad for the rest of their wretched existence.

Lily stepped closer before crouching next to Aimee. "You better be worth it," she whispered before pressing her hand against Aimee's chest. Lily closed her eyes and chanted in a language the present-day citizens of Saltung had long forgotten, from back when Verlohren had been Wanderden, spirits, guides, beloved by their communities, before their intervention, a language fluent within her still, filled with laughter and games from her childhood, then tinged with despair when the shadows came, back when everything collapsed, and Lara…

Lily ducked her head and gritted her teeth. Now wasn't the time to drown in memories.

She channeled the glow within her into a tight ball, willed it to travel down her arm before casting it away, and slammed it into Aimee's chest.

"What are you doing? Get away from her!" Chris shouted and hurtled toward her.

\*\*\*

Aimee had assumed she'd known misery, that nothing could be worse than being a Verlohren, but then she volunteered to burn. She thought there was nothing worse than the flames engulfing her senses, only to plummet from fire to a frozen cage. Maybe she'd conjured this by longing for relief and imagining the cool fall mornings of Freit she'd spent sitting under a tree in her parents' backyard.

The fire dwindled, and for a second she shed invisible tears, but then frost filled her, and with it her body lay in shattered glass. Smashed splinters invaded her cells, ricocheted and spilled ice that slithered through her veins and expanded them. She had to scream, but she no longer had a mouth. How was it possible that she no longer felt any physical part of her being and yet she was drowning in misery?

A bubble burst and light rebounded, blinding her, but it also eased the ordeal racking her body. She didn't trust this, though. Did water make the round after fire and ice?

After a moment of stillness and the tension it carried, more light shot through her, and instead of agony, it left a trail of warmth that expelled the ice and cooled the flames.

Her lungs expanded and… her hand. She could feel her fingers. Twitching. Aimee balled her hands into fists before spreading them open. She blinked rapidly, and while she was shrouded in dark, she could see. She could finally see. A sob tore from her throat and she rolled onto her side, weeping.

\*\*\*

"What are you… What did you do?" Chris fell to the floor next to a convulsing Aimee. "You're killing her!"

263

"I'm not," Lily pressed out. "You should feel the difference."

"What?" Chris's gaze traveled between Lily and Aimee, who still writhed on the floor.

"What's happening?" Dylan asked.

"I'm not sure," Chris said, trying to slow Aimee's violent shudders. "She's still in pain, but it's different... I can't..."

Lily slumped down on the ground, a couple of feet away. "Give her a minute. She's been through a lot"

Chris glared at her. "Yes, and whose fault is that?"

Lily's lips twitched in a small smile. "That's a good question."

"Ugh." Chris returned her attention to Aimee, who had stilled, but her eyes fluttered open before she teetered to the side, bawling.

"Aimee?" Chris's voice broke. She hesitated, but then reached out with trembling fingers and touched Aimee's arm, ran her hand up and down, whispering reassurances, trying to calm the sobbing woman. "Can you sit up?" she asked.

"Be careful," Dylan said.

Aimee grabbed her hand, clung to it for a moment, and then allowed Chris to pull her into a sitting position. "What... happened?"

"You... you burned, after... you'd finished the ritual and the contract appeared. I... We destroyed it."

"We?" Aimee croaked and cleared her throat.

"Uh, Lily and I," Chris said and shifted her gaze to the woman sitting across from her.

"Wait... Lily, as in, Death?"

"Yes. She... she also... What *did* you do?" Chris held Lily's gaze.

"I saved your friend."

"But how? Earlier you didn't want to, and—"

"No, that was *your* assumption. I said it's complicated. There was no way to stop the burning and restore her to the way she was before."

"But that's what you did! The burning stopped, and she's back to normal," Chris said, her gaze shifting between Aimee and Lily.

"Did I?" Lily asked and gazed at Aimee, who tilted her head before sitting straighter.

\*\*\*

One minute she was suspended in torment, the next she was back with Chris and Dylan. And Death, apparently.

Her heart drummed in her chest, much faster than she remembered it ever beating. Her head lacked its usual throbbing and overall, her body, while finally present and tangible again, was just there.

No soreness, no heaviness weighing her down. The tension in her neck that radiated down her back was absent as well. She almost... She felt like during the switch with Chris, when she was... "Alive!" Aimee jumped up and stumbled but caught herself before crashing back down.

Lily smiled.

Chris faltered. "What?"

"My heart." Aimee pressed her hand against her chest. "It's... it's much like it was when we switched in the mountains, and... I'm not in pain."

Chris took another step back. "Yes, you're no longer burning."

"No. There's no... The heaviness is gone. I have energy. This feels like you did." She stepped forward and grabbed Chris's hand, pressing it against her chest. "Do you feel it?"

Chris nodded and after a short moment, withdrew her hand.

Aimee canted her head. "Why are you walking away?"

"I... How... What does this mean?"

"I'm alive," Aimee said again before sagging to the ground.

"Hey! This is awesome!" Dylan crouched next to her. "I'm happy for you."

"How is this fair? What about you?" Aimee grasped his shoulder.

"Don't you dare feel bad about this! I'm fine. My death... It worked out. And now I even get to spend some more time with Chris. We can talk. Perhaps even with my parents. I'm ready, Aimee. You never were." He clasped her hand and squeezed it.

When both returned their focus to Chris, she had disappeared.

"What?" He rose. "Where did she go?"

"Give her some time," Lily said. "This is a lot to deal with."

"I'm undecided on whether I should kiss or throttle you," Dylan grumbled.

Lily laughed. "You should settle for neither."

"Why did you do it? Why did you save Aimee?" he asked.

Lily shrugged her shoulders. "It was selfish. A life for a life, and I owed Chris."

"What?" Aimee pushed herself back to her feet. "What do you mean by that? What life for what life? I don't want to owe you, and I'm not taking someone else's life just so I can live again!" She crossed her arms.

Lily chuckled. "So self-righteous. Don't worry, little one. You won't owe me. There was no other way. I couldn't stop you from burning because that was the price to pay for releasing the contract. We'd wanted to make sure that this never happened. Who in their right mind would choose to do *that*? And for the truth no less." Lily shook her head. "That's not a deal people strike."

Aimee raised one eyebrow but said nothing.

"Returning you to life, that was a sort of loophole? We didn't cover that back then because... I don't know. We didn't think of it, or was it we failed to imagine such a possibility?"

"Imagine what?" Dylan asked.

"The only way for me to bring you back to life was to give up my immortality. My energy halted the burning by reviving you. The Living don't burn. But I had to give a life to save one. Mine."

Aimee's eyes widened. "You... You gave up your immortality for me?"

"Don't worry. I didn't do it for you."

"But you did it for Chris. Why did you owe her?" Aimee asked.

Lily shifted into Terry.

Dylan staggered back. "What the hell?"

"I don't understand," Aimee said.

Lily transformed back to her own form. "I am, or was, Terry. Chris's mentor. I've accompanied her all her life, much like I did in various disguises for almost all Morgen heirs."

"And Chris knows," Dylan said.

"Yes. Our relationship is broken, and I expect nothing else. But... I've grown fond of her. Of the Living, and I... I'm so tired," Lily closed her eyes. "I want to be done."

"I'm sorry, though I probably shouldn't be given all you've done. All the suffering you've caused, but I... I can see that you are miserable, too. No one deserves that," Aimee said.

Lily nodded at her. "Thank you."

Aimee turned to Dylan. "Let's go find your sister."

\*\*\*

"How *nice* for you and how *touching*. What about me, little sister, huh? Have you ever considered what this will do to *me*?" Lara snapped, after popping up next to Lily.

"This isn't about you! How dare you? Chris almost *died*! As for what happened here, for *once* I decided solely based on what I *want*," Lily almost shouted and teleported them back to her house in the woods.

"You want to die? Why?"

Lily fell into a chair. "Immortality is overrated."

Lara snorted. "After everything we've been through, after everything we've overcome, and done, you're throwing it all away?"

"What is there to throw away? I babysit one Morgen heir after the other. I grow close to them, they keep up the lie we've built, and they die. Set this on infinite repeat. How is *that* living?"

Lara pulled out a chair across from her. "If you put it that way."

"And what's so great about your existence? You spend all your time *there*, in the dark, damp mountains, surrounded by shouts and shrieks of the dregs of society. The truly depraved."

"There are moments," Lara said and inspected her fingernails.

"I'm sure there are," Lily scoffed.

"But now you'll go. You'll die. Disappear," Lara uttered in a voice so low and hollow that Lily had to strain to hear her.

"Yes. After I live out this life, I'll finally die."

"You want to die? How can you say that! Why would you do that to me? What about us?"

"We've hardly spent any time together for the last, what? Two hundred years?"

"But they died, Lily! They died, all of them, and we said we never would!"

Lily reached across the table and clasped her sister's hand. "I know, Lar, I know. But perhaps living a meaningless life is worse than dying?"

Lara shook her head, trying to withdraw her hand, but Lily held on. "How... how can you say that?" she whispered.

"I've lived it. I'm so exhausted," Lily said.

"I'm tired, too." Tears welled in her eyes. "But what... What if we go *there*, after?"

Lily sighed. "Then we'd deserve it, but I don't think we'll end up *there*. And you, well, you're still immortal."

"For how long, though? New Verlohren will go back to what they used to be, spirits, with no bodies and no markings. Nothing to feed us anymore."

"Who knows? Maybe you no longer need it, but even if this is the end for you, too," Lily pressed her sister's hand, "our fear and pain, Lar, we've turned them into weapons, and we've hurt countless others."

Lara dropped her gaze to the floor.

"I can't do this anymore. It's not fair. Why make others suffer just because we did?"

"But—"

"I'm not saying anything could *ever* excuse or right what happened, but I'm not sure what we've done is the answer."

"I'm scared, Lil," Lara murmured.

"Me, too."

***

"Chris? Where are you?" Aimee called, flinging open her front door.

"Why come here? Wouldn't she have gone back home?" Dylan asked.

"It's a mixture between a feeling, our connection, and an educated guess."

"Care to explain the latter?"

"Chris is currently not… too fond of your family. After learning about what they did, and then Terry. I doubt she can bear being anywhere near the manor right now."

"You're probably right. Though she might have also gone into the woods," Dylan said.

"Nah, I doubt that." Aimee halted in front of her bedroom door. "Don't take this the wrong way, but… I kinda want to talk to her alone, and—"

"But you have no idea where she is!"

She glared at him.

"Or you do? All right. I wanna see my mom anyway." He patted her arm and left.

Aimee took a deep breath and pushed open the door to her room. "I thought I might find you here," she said and sat down next to Chris on her bed. "Are you OK?"

"Shouldn't I be asking you that?" Chris asked. "Now you got your entire life ahead of you again."

Aimee arched her brows. "Wasn't this what you wanted?"

Chris rubbed the back of her neck. "Doesn't matter."

"It matters to me," Aimee said. "Or was all you said before a lie? Did you only want me when you couldn't have me, when... there was no way for us to be together?"

Chris's eyes widened. "No! Of course not."

"Why are you so bitter?"

Chris laughed. "It's two-fold. Part of me is angry, no, furious with you. The other part is... more of an idiot."

"I get the anger part, and we should talk about that, too, but you wanna clarify the bit about you being an idiot?"

"When... you burned." She sighed. "You were gone, and I was livid. Beyond that. I don't think I've *ever* been so devastated, aside from Dylan's passing, but that was different, a different anguish. I couldn't believe you'd done that. You lied to me!"

"I'm sorry—"

Chris raised her hand. "I'm not ready to unpack all of this right now, but I went from *that* to you being back, then discovering that not only are you back, but you're also *alive*." She released a trembling breath. "And right before, all the... Terry, Lily, my family." She covered her face with her hands. "I assumed that... now that you're free again, what use do you have for me? I wanted to spare myself another rejection, learning that you being a Verlohren was an excuse and now, even though everything is different, nothing has changed."

Aimee bumped into her. "You *are* an idiot."

"At least I'm aware of it," she said and returned the gesture.

"Hey!" Aimee laughed and gripped Chris's hand, who offered her a watery smile.

# thirteen

Freit, Saltung
Year 302, Day 117

"You knew, didn't you?"

Anthony inspected the floor. "Yes."

"How long? How long have you known this?"

"Since my thirty-fifth birthday."

"What?"

He heaved a sigh. "My Christina, you would have been told as soon as you stepped into the role of the Head of the Council. It's the last piece of secret knowledge that is revealed to you."

Chris stared at her father. "How... How could you..."

"What? Keep it from you? Those are the rules, and—"

"No! You knew the truth! You *knew* that all our teachings about the Verlohren, about the Sattran... They are all *lies*. You knew, Father!"

"What would you have me do?"

"Change it. Release the true history, allow these people to heal, to—"

"It does not alter who they are. Why does it matter what binds them to this existence? The Verlohren, the Sattran, they are *scum*. They are roaches, leeches, who would drain the life blood—"

"They are *not*. Need I remind you that your own son is one!"

Anthony cringed. "There might be exceptions to that rule."

"How convenient. You care when it's one of your own?"

"Christina—"

"No. Not to mention, we have vilified an entire group of people based on lies that were spread to allow our family to seize and maintain power for centuries. How can you be a part of that? It's shameful."

"It's not my fault. I had no role in this."

"You might not have started it, but you perpetuated it by your silence. You benefited from it, from the unnecessary suffering of an endless number of our citizens. For what? Is power that important to you?"

"Might has to be wielded by the right people. The Morgen family has led Saltung to prosperity for generations. We have always been just and benevolent rulers."

"I doubt the Verlohren would agree with that assessment."

"There is no need to use that tone with me, Christina. It would behoove you to remember who I am."

"That's exactly the problem. You are my father, and I love you, but when I look at you now, all I feel is anger, betrayal, and revulsion. You disgust me. Your actions, or better, your inactions, they disgust—"

A slap rang out. Silence, aside from heavy breathing, filled the room.

"I'm sorry, my Christina, I'm so sorry."

Chris clenched her jaw and straightened her posture, fire licking into her palms. "You will never lay a hand on me again, or I will *burn* you to cinder. You will abdicate your rule and name me your successor. What you have done... What this family has done is beyond shameful. The suffering..." She swallowed hard as bile rose in her throat. She closed her eyes.

"As you wish," his voice trembled as he stepped back.

\*\*\*

Year 302, Day 121

Exhaustion lingered in Chris's very bones, and she longed to curl up under her covers for a half-century. Yet the list of tasks and obligations ahead seemed never-ending.

She missed Aimee. After their talk, everything seemed fine, and she'd returned home to deal with the aftermath of Saltung's realization of what had happened—that they now saw their deceased loved ones as members of the group of people they used to hold in utter contempt.

There'd been protests, and a good chunk of the population was joining the Tarung. The Council had been on lockdown, and with her father stepping down, it would be on her to resolve these issues.

She wanted to go back to Aimee, in part because doubts had once more crept up. About what? Chris wasn't sure, though blaming the entire situation and the turmoil rattling through Saltung seemed appealing.

She'd also avoided Dylan until now, fearing that any conversation would lead to him moving on, and she wasn't ready for that yet. She had just gotten him back. Chris groused. He hadn't really returned.

She was aware that he was stuck here because of her and that he'd rather move on and escape the miserable existence of a Verlohren. Would they change the name again? If only she could pause her brain, perhaps then she wouldn't fear jumping out of her skin any second.

Chris left her room and marched to the kitchen. Their cook greeted her before returning his attention to the steaming pot on the stove. She grabbed an apple and headed for her study.

Her eyes were drawn to the stack of books still resting on her desk, research material from their quest. Then, her thoughts drifted to Terry, or better, Lily, and she coughed. The piece of fruit she'd just swallowed lodged like a gnarled root in her throat. This had been another issue she'd compartmentalized, or suppressed, if she was being honest.

Images of her time with Terry flashed through her, and she stormed out of the room, racing passed the training area before coming to a slow stop just outside her mother's den. As she drew closer, the audible murmurs transformed into the modulated tones of her mother and the sweet, longed-for lilt of her brother.

She first listened to the sound of the voices without registering the actual words. For a second, she could pretend that everything was normal, returned to how it used to be before... But memories yanked her back into their net, and with their intrusion, words crystalized, and she frowned. Why were they talking about Aimee?

Chris stood straighter, hesitated for a moment before knocking on the door and entering her mother's den.

Dylan rushed to her and drew her into an embrace.

"Dylan," she mumbled, holding him tight.

"I never thought I would get to see my children together again," Diane said in a tremulous voice while a small smile tugged at her lips.

She withdrew from her brother and shoved her hands into her pants pockets. "Mother."

"You have been scarce these last few weeks, and now I understand."

Chris frowned. "Is this... You didn't know?"

"About the pact the Morgen family made with Death? No, dear. I did not. To be honest, there always seemed to be something off about the Verlohren, and the hardline Anthony pushed with the raids, but I did not expect this. Not... Dylan." Diane lowered her head.

Chris ran a hand through her hair. "But then why..."

"This is difficult to explain, but also to share. But having Dylan back, even if only for a short while... I do not wish to continue living like this."

She sat down next to her mother. "You're leaving?"

"I am not, but I will divorce your father." Diane laughed before wiping her eyes.

Dylan sat down, too. "Why is that funny?"

"It is not. I never dreamed I'd say these words aloud. I have voiced them in my head a million times, but it seemed forever out of reach."

"You never loved him?" Chris asked.

"No. My family... Your grandparents on my side, their only goal was to marry me to the Morgen heir. I was trained for that role all my life. There was never any other future."

"They didn't listen?"

"They never inquired about my wishes, but unlike you..." Diane patted Chris's arm. "I said nothing. I never declared my wishes, though to be honest, I did not identify what I wanted, merely what I did not want. However," she cleared her throat, "I could not even admit that in the privacy of my own mind without seeming like a failure, as if I was letting my family down."

"Is that why you were so angry when I said I wouldn't marry Lance?"

"It was the most bizarre moment; a flashback of what I had wanted, but never could have done, never would have had the courage to even suggest." She leaned back in her chair. "Your father would never have allowed you to decide for yourself, and your relationship with him had always been closer... than with me. I thought that if *I* pushed, then you'd at least have one parent left whom you didn't hate." Diane's gaze dropped to her lap.

"I don't hate you, Mother." Chris grasped her mother's hands, stilling the fidgeting. "I never have. I... You were always so removed, as if you didn't care. Unlike Father, who was involved in everything."

"You are the heir, and so it was his duty to attend to your education and training. My input was irrelevant, for sure to him, but I also never realized you were missing out on anything."

A sorrowful smile spread over Chris's face. "We see what we believe is there."

"For what it is worth, I am sorry. I never meant to give the impression that I do not care about you. I love you. In the end, I suppose I struggled to come to terms with my resentment toward the life I was forced into and my love for the children that grew out of this union."

"I can imagine," Chris said. "I'm sorry, too, for all the upset I've caused you."

Diane stroked her daughter's hair. "You were no trouble."

"To you," Dylan joked.

A teary laugh escaped Chris's lips, and she leaned forward and ruffled his hair.

A knock interrupted their laughter. At once, all three Morgens turned somber and faced the door.

"Come in," Diane called.

"Excuse me, Lady Diane. Master Lance is here and requests to speak with Lady Christina."

"Thank you, Thomas. She will be right out," Diane said and dismissed the servant.

Chris groaned and rose to her feet. "I so don't want to talk to him, but perhaps this time he'll get the message that I won't *ever* marry him."

"Want me to do it?" Dylan asked, cracking his knuckles.

She chortled. "No, thank you for offering, though."

"I was wrong to push Lance on you, not merely because it ignored your wishes, but I also misjudged his character. Be careful, Chris," Diane said.

She halted for a second, staring at her mother who had never addressed her this way before.

\*\*\*

Freit, Saltung
Year 302, Day 126

Chris curled up on the couch next to Aimee. "You never told me how you got the Antward stone and escaped that place alive."

"Yes, well, I didn't expect that'd be a topic you're keen to revisit."

"I'm not, but I'm also curious. Dylan only hinted at it and made some cryptic remarks about being thankful for a naked man?"

Aimee snorted. "It was bad. We didn't count on the weather being our worst enemy in there."

"The weather?"

"It went from hot to cold to ice and rain, lava, wind gusts, and overall misery. It even hailed at some point. Inside a *mountain*," Aimee exclaimed and shook her head. "Eventually, we crashed through a ceiling and had to climb back out to continue on our path. It was your mom's necklace that led us. Turns out, dear old Elizabeth had the Antward stone, or access to it, and she'd turned a piece into a pendant that was handed down in your family as an heirloom."

"The ugly one with the orange fragment?"

"Yes. It vibrated and glowed when we were heading in the correct direction."

"How did you figure this out?"

"Markesh told us."

"Who? All right. Start from the beginning and explain," Chris said.

***

Berkan Mountains, Saltung,<br>Year 302, Day 116

"Man, I wanna go home," Dylan groaned, pulling himself over the edge of the ditch. He reached out and hauled Aimee the rest of the way up.

"Thanks, and yes, that's the idea."

"Not really. Once we get the stone, the actual nightmare starts, especially for you."

"One step at a time." She consulted the necklace again. "I say we head this way." She pointed at a tunnel leading to the right.

They followed the winding path to the end without incidents and entered a large chamber. Burning torches stuck out of the walls in every direction.

"The stone is getting hot, and its vibration is stronger," Aimee said.

"That means it's close."

"I'm assuming so, but it's not like I've ever been here or done this before."

278

"Hmm," Dylan hummed and edged forward. "Look at this." He pointed at a lowered platform in the heart of the room. They had to stand closer to notice it, as it blended seamlessly into its surroundings. A cage of glowing silver metal and milky, crushed glass loomed in the center of the dais.

"Do you suppose the stone is in there?" Dylan asked.

"Why would they put the stone in a cage? I doubt it."

"One of you definitely makes more sense," a deep voice drawled from the enclosure.

Dylan jumped back. "Who's there? Who are you?"

"And it's not you," the voice added.

Aimee approached the crate and raised her hand.

"Don't touch it! You have no idea what'll happen. What if that's how he got in there and now he's stuck and luring us into the same trap?"

"That makes no sense," the voice replied. "If that had happened to me, I would warn anyone entering this room."

"Not if you're in on it and this is a ploy and you're just the decoy."

"You sound a tad paranoid," the voice stated.

"What's your name," Aimee asked.

"I have been called many names, but I prefer Markesh."

"That's an odd answer. Why would people call you by different names? Who has many names?" Dylan asked.

Markesh chuckled, and he seemed to shift because the noise of chains dragging over the stone floor echoed through the room. "I have a lot of different names because people gave them to me. Markesh is the one I've chosen."

"Your parents didn't give you a name?" Dylan asked.

"I don't have any parents," Markesh replied.

Dylan sputtered.

"Enough of this." Aimee leaned closer to inspect the material of the cage. "What is this stuff?" She touched it. The moment her fingers made contact, the torches brightened and turned red while an ululating sound filled the room.

"I told you not to touch it! Red! You made the fire go red! What's that noise?"

"Calm down, Dylan," Aimee said. "Oh, look!" She pointed at the enclosure.

The milky substance melted, draining off the crate. The silver metal shifted and withdrew, allowing them to see inside the cage.

A naked man with long, dark, curly hair sat cross-legged on the floor in the middle of the enclosure, his arms and legs bound to the ground in heavy metal chains.

"Who are you? Why are you naked?" Dylan asked.

Markesh laughed. "You ask a lot of questions. I've already told you who I am, and well, I was trapped here like this."

"You told us your name, not who you are."

"Ahh, you're not as stupid as you sound," Markesh said.

"Hey!" Dylan exclaimed.

"I used to rule this realm, but I became complacent and underestimated a threat until it was too late. I've been here ever since, locked up and chained."

"Wait, if you used to be in charge, who are Lily and Lara? I thought they were Death, but—"

He yanked on his chains. "Imposters!"

"How have they been able to—"

"A new system. I didn't notice," he groaned and hung his head. "They orchestrated it all right under my nose, but I was too busy, too concerned with..." He clenched his jaw. "It doesn't matter."

"So you're immortal?" Dylan asked.

"Yes."

"And they are not?"

"They are as well, in a manner of speaking."

"Explain," Aimee demanded.

"They cast a curse on this land that has altered the fabric of reality. No one remembers how things used to be, and—"

"One of my ancestors designed a riddle that we solved. We heard about the Wanderden and the deal my family struck with the twins."

"I see," Markesh murmured. "Do you also understand where their power originates from?"

"Let me guess, our markings?" Aimee asked.

"That is correct. The curse wasn't merely created to establish a new reality, but it also funnels energy off you lot to feed them."

Dylan's eyes widened. "We're the source of their immortality?"

"Not you, your pain is."

*** 

Freit, Saltung
Year 302, Day 126

Chris wiped her eyes. "That is so terrible."

"Are you OK? Why are you crying?"

"I'm so frustrated. My family did this. And that's not even all. Gods."

"What is it?"

"I'll tell you, but first finish yours. How did you get the stone?"

"There's nothing much left to tell. We told him about our plan, and well, he gave us the stone. He'd stolen it from them and hidden it. It was in the same chamber, so we got it and escaped."

"Markesh is still in that cell, in shackles?" Chris asked.

"We tried to loosen or destroy the chains, but they wouldn't budge. They were magical and had been dampening his magic for centuries, but he said that once things are restored, he should get this powers back.

"Do you think that's the case now? With the Verlohren no longer Verlohren, there will be no more markings on anyone new who passes, so their power source is gone."

"That might be enough, but those who are corporeal now remain so until they move on. That should still offer them some strength."

---

"Yes, but they aren't so miserable because they can see and talk to their loved ones," Aimee pointed out.

"That's true."

"What's going on? Why are you so upset?"

"I talked to my mother, and Dylan. I..., uh, sort of eavesdropped on them, not intentionally, mind you," Chris hurried to add.

"Of course," Aimee said with a small smile.

"It was a pleasant chat. My mom explained a lot, and that made it easier to release certain issues I... I clung to, and with Dylan there." Chris cleared her throat. "We made peace."

"That's awesome! Wait, Dylan... Is he still..."

"Oh, he's still here. He wouldn't leave without saying goodbye." She squeezed Aimee's hand.

"That's good. I'm... I'm glad."

"She didn't know."

"Huh?"

"My mom. She wasn't aware of the contract, or of... the Holding Centers," Chris spat the last name. "I'd asked her about that once Lance had left. It's worse than you imagined," she groaned and ducked her head.

"How? I don't..."

"Lance. I... Gods, he came by, right when we'd finished talking. He stood there, staring at me with this far-removed expression. It was eerie."

"What did he want?"

***

Freit, Saltung<br>Year 302, 121

"What are you doing here?" Chris asked.

"I..." Lance stood straighter. "I've talked to your father, and he agrees with me. Nothing that has happened should prevent our marriage. In fact, we should hasten the date to provide a united front for the people. It would be good for Saltung."

She gaped at him, unable to comprehend the words that left his mouth. Did her father truly... after the talk they had had? Could they have had that conversation before? Or was Lance lying? For what? How many times had she told him she wouldn't marry him, and now this?

"Christina. Answer me."

She blinked rapidly. "I will not marry you. What happened has no impact on my decision, and we've had this discussion several times. Nothing has changed, at least not in your favor. There never would have been a wedding before, and I surely won't wed you now."

"But Saltung—"

"I owe Saltung nothing. I owe you and my father even less. What both of you, what the Council has done, has been doing for generations!" Chris marched toward him. "I have no way to measure my abhorrence and loathing for you, for my father, and for anyone else who engaged in this, and—"

"If this is about the Holding Centers, the experiments weren't my idea."

Chris recoiled as if someone had physically struck her. "What are you talking about?"

His eyes widened. "Never mind."

She advanced closer. "Tell me. Everything!"

Lance avoided her gaze. "These Centers have always existed. The raids... The guards would arrest Verlohren and transport them to the Holding Centers. Once there, they became prisoners and worked for us."

"And?"

"It was the credo of the Council to ensure that the Verlohren not only feared us, but that we kept them down, drowning in misery."

"For what?"

"Preventive measures. People who are down rarely stand up to fight."

"Right. Back to these experiments. I ran into a guard who talked about burning Verlohren. I'd denied it at the time, accused him of lying, and he just laughed at me. He was right, wasn't he?"

Lance jutted his jaw. "It is not that simple."

"*Make* it so," she hissed.

"The Tarung worried your father. They had garnered quite the following among the Living. Every few decades one of these resistance groups would rise and the Council would crush it. This one was different."

"How?"

"They did not want to fight the Council, or the guards. Their entire focus was on convincing the Living that the Verlohren are not truly the trash and scum they are."

"How can you still believe this? After learning the truth—"

"A *version* of the truth that suits the needs of those degenerates. It is used to sow discord, to divide the Living, to allow the Verlohren to take over."

Chris pinched the bridge of her nose. "We're not talking about different perspectives or personal preferences. There are no *versions* of the truth. Something *is* true, or it *isn't*. Truth isn't up for interpretation."

Lance remained silent.

"Go on. My father worried about the Tarung."

"The mage sages suggested a potential solution, or better, a preparation for the war at hand."

"The war of the Verlohren against the Living?"

"Yes! Don't you see, this is where—"

Chris suppressed a sigh. "Just continue."

"The Verlohren cannot die because they are already dead. We understood that, but we needed to learn what would happen if we exposed them to situations and circumstance that are lethal to the Living."

She swallowed hard but motioned for him to proceed.

"We tested these conditions on them, to see what would occur."

"By conditions you mean maiming and torture," Chris spat, coughing to quell the wave of nausea that ripped through her.

"It was done as a defense!"

"Were they attacking you? Did you fear for your life?"

"We should all be afraid! They threaten our way of life. These creatures and their vile—"

"That's over now, anyway. There will be no more corporeal Verlohren."

"So they say. But that is a lie, too. They will lie low, and—"

"What happened to them?"

"What?"

"The Verlohren you tortured."

"They wouldn't die! We stabbed them, cut them open, chopped off their limbs. We even set them on fire, and they burn. Forever, if you let them, but they *won't* die." His voice trembled.

"You realize they do feel pain?"

"I can still hear their screams. The mage sages eventually silenced their moans and shouts. It was getting to the guards and moral was low, but after they fixed that issue—"

"Oh, my Gods," she croaked, digging her hands into her pockets.

"We even tried magic on them, but they won't leave. No matter what we did, they are just always there."

"Get out."

"What?"

"I n*ever* want to see you again."

"You're not serious! You are not thinking clearly. Those Verlohren you have been visiting must have put some sort of spell on you, and—"

Chris laughed and struggled to hold her tears at bay. "Did you forget? The Verlohren don't have any magic. There's no spell. Nothing. I just can't stand the sight of you." She bristled before turning and leaving.

***

Freit, Saltung<br>Year 302, Day 126

"Say something," she said and grasped Aimee's hands. "Please."

Aimee furrowed her brows. "I don't..." She winced. "There's a difference between... between hearing rumors and... and *this*." She withdrew from Chris, hid her face behind her hands and sobbed.

"I'm so sorry," she mumbled, rubbing Aimee's shoulders. "I had no idea. I swear, if I'd known, I'd—"

"I believe you," she whispered, rocking back and forth. "What happened to them?"

Chris tightened her hold on her friend. "They were all released. I've cornered one of the mage sages, and—"

"What?" Aimee sat up straight and stared at her. "Wasn't that dangerous?"

She smiled and cupped Aimee's cheek. "No. I can handle one or two of them. If they were all together, that'd be different, and I wouldn't do that. But it was just one. Tanja. We actually used to be close." Chris cleared her throat. "She didn't want to talk about it at first, but I wore her down, eventually. Not all of them were in favor of these experiments, but they remained quiet, too scared to make waves and have it blow up in their faces."

"Cowards!" Aimee jumped up. "They had magic! They could have freed these people or at least eased their pain!"

"It's... it's much easier from the outside, and—"

"Don't," Aimee pressed out, and her voice broke.

Chris's eyes widened. "What?"

"Don't rationalize this. Don't tell me you *understand* and can sympathize with what they did, not when... not when..." She turned around and inhaled harshly.

"I'm not. What they did was wrong, even if they had no active part in it. They *knew* what was happening, and they did *nothing* to change the situation. There were other ways besides an outright conflict or abandoning their position."

"Of course, but that's not my point. Even if they didn't dare to do anything about it, they stayed, Chris. They heard their screams and they suppressed them, and they stayed. They knew what they were doing. They understood the torture and terror... And they stayed anyway."

"I'm sorry," Chris whispered.

"Who ordered this?"

Chris's gaze dropped to the floor. "My father." When she lifted her head and caught Aimee's eyes, she froze at the icy glare that bored into her.

# fourteen

"Why do I feel like you're avoiding me?" Dylan asked, leaning against the door frame of Chris's room.

She placed her pen on the desk and turned her chair to face her brother. "Because I am."

"That's not like you, admitting what's going on upon the very first question."

"Perhaps I've changed?"

"You have, but that's not it." He canted his head. "What's up?"

She opened her mouth, then closed it and instead stood and paced the room.

"Oh, it's one of those topics." He trod fully inside, plopping down on Chris's bed. "Talk to me, big sister."

"I'm not sure where to start."

"It's more than one thing that got you all frazzled?"

"Yes, well, there's you, and then there's…"

"Aimee?"

She stopped, her shoulders dropping. "Yes."

He waved at her to sit down. "Come here."

"I don't want you to leave," she mumbled, still unmoving.

"I'm right here." He patted the space next to him until Chris relented and sat down.

"That's not what I mean," she replied and leaned against him.

Dylan wrapped his arm around her. "Yeah. I don't want to leave either. Not yet at least."

"How are you? Are you getting enough food? How's the exhaustion?"

He laughed. "I'm fine, and there's no chance that I'll lack food at the mansion. Don't worry about me."

"Did Aimee complain when you moved back in here? Have you seen her recently?"

"Nah, she understood. She actually went to see Mary."

"Oh. She never said. Then again..."

"You had another fight?"

"I didn't let it get that far."

"Huh?"

"I told you about Lance, Father, and the... the Holding Centers."

"That's a nice euphemism for what they are," he groused, pulling Chris closer.

"I told Aimee everything," she said.

Dylan closed his eyes. "She didn't take it well."

"No. I... She assumed I was rationalizing what the mage sages have done, or not done, the ones like Tanja who refused to participate. How it surely wasn't easy, and... She... Aimee told me not to make excuses for them, which I wasn't or didn't mean to."

"There's a time for reason, Chris, but that wasn't it."

"I know," she said miserably and ducked her head.

"What happened next?"

"She asked who ordered this, the experiments."

"Father. You told her it was him?"

"I wouldn't lie to her about this."

His eyes widened. "Wait. She was upset with you about what he did when you didn't even know these Centers existed, and even less about the torture?"

"Yes, no. I'm not sure! She... She glared at me, horrified, standing there like a statue, but her eyes, she... She was *so* angry."

"And then?"

"Nothing. I got up, mumbled some excuse, and ran away. I haven't seen or spoken to her since."

"Have you considered that her anger wasn't directed at you?"

"She didn't ask me to stay or go after me."

"You had dropped one of her worst fears into her lap, made it a reality, so she was probably too shocked, angry, and hurt to do or say anything."

"That didn't cross my mind."

"Yeah, and now, she's gonna assume the worst."

"What do you mean?"

"I have no clue what insane idea is going to take root in her brain, but it won't be a good one. She'll think you don't want her around anymore. And Gods, I haven't been over there in days either. She'll think we've abandoned her and moved on."

"She wouldn't. Would she?"

"You've met her. What do you reckon?"

"Oh Gods. What are we going to do?"

"We have to talk to her, though I should go first." He kissed the top of Chris's head. "I'll head over there right now. I might spend the night, but I'll find you as soon as I get back."

***

Doing nothing almost seemed easier when she was a Verlohren. Her body needed less attention, or better, it had fewer needs and desires. Aimee had been sitting on her couch for days, only getting up to eat or use the bathroom. She even slept there.

She wasn't sure what she'd have picked, being a Living once more or moving on as a Verlohren, had the choice presented itself to her. Not that she'd ever entertained such an idle notion before, for there was no way to return to the Living. Yet here she sat.

A body full of energy, shouting at her to move, to run, to do something. Anything, but sit on the couch and stare at the wall. She didn't doubt that she'd bounce back to a mindset that allowed movement, that enabled her to become active again. Right now, though, her mind raced along so fast that adding physical mobility to the mix seemed too daunting, and Aimee had given up trying.

She didn't blame Dylan and Chris for moving on, for getting away from her. They had never run in the same circles before, and now that Dylan could see his family again, where else would he go?

And Chris? Aimee closed her eyes. Being alive once more seemed enough of a struggle without delving into her tangled-up emotions about that.

Still. It would have been nice of them to say goodbye. She didn't even know if Dylan was here of if he'd already settled the situation with Chris and moved on. What was she going to do next? She could continue her studies. Or go back home, though there was not much to return to with her mother gone and her father in a perpetual drunken stupor. She'd seen and talked to Mary. They could pick up where they left off again. It would be nice to have friends again.

A knock startled her. "Yes?" she said but didn't move.

The door opened and Dylan stood in the room, allowing light to soak up the area from the outside.

"Why are you sitting here in the dark?" He closed the door and opened the curtains. "Much better."

"What are you doing here?" Aimee asked.

"No hello, how are you, huh?"

"I don't—"

He raised his hands. "No, don't worry. It's fine. This is on me. I didn't mean to be gone like this, or at least, not without sending word or telling you what's going on. It's just… It's been overwhelming, and…" His shoulders slumped. "You were all right when I saw you the other day, after your talk with Mary and all."

"Yes."

Dylan sighed and sat down next to Aimee. "I missed you," he stated to which she only nodded.

\*\*\*

"How is she?" Chris ushered her brother into her room. She'd spent hours pacing last night and had fallen into a restless sleep, only to wake up before the sun was even close to crawling across the horizon.

"Odd," Dylan said.

"I meant, how is she doing?"

"Wow. That's almost funny, though I don't think she's in the mood for such jokes right now."

"What? No. I didn't mean it like that. It wasn't a joke, and you know how she is. She can be quite... odd sometimes. Not in a bad way."

He yawned. "I'm not your audience for this."

"Did you get any sleep?"

"Not really. We spent the night talking, after she became coherent again."

"Is she sick? She's not taking care of herself now that she's alive, is she?"

"That's another topic you can pick up with her. Overall, you need to talk to her because what I said? That she would take all this the wrong way? Yeah, I was right."

"Should I go there today or is that too soon? Won't she suspect you notified me about this visit? Then she'll think I only went to see her because you told me to, and that's not the case, though it was you who figured out that she's suffering and it's all our fault. Why didn't I realize this, too?"

"Breathe!" Dylan laughed. "I'm too tired for your rambling.

Chris ducked her head. "I'm sorry."

"Besides," he waved her off, "she already knows."

"What? She knows what?"

"I told her you'd be by her place soon, too. That you had plans to visit her but that I'd gotten away first."

"Ah, OK. That's... That's not too bad. Right? Does she want to see me?"

"Gods, you're both such idiots. Go. Visit her. Talk to her. Don't give me any details, please," he groaned.

"What?"

"Never mind." He stood up. "I'm going to bed." He left the room.

***

After Dylan had left, Chris prepared herself and changed her clothes countless times, although she didn't understand why. Completely exasperated with herself, she finally strode to Aimee's place. The closer she got, the more hesitant her footsteps grew.

What if he was wrong and Aimee didn't want to see her? Or maybe she just wanted to talk to her to tell her she'd changed her mind and that there was yet another reason they couldn't be together? She would soon be the new Head of the Council, but not if she had a say in the matter. And that she did. But that was something she should sort out another day.

It also hinged on Aimee, if… if there still was something between them, then it would depend on what Aimee envisioned for her future. Perhaps she didn't wish to associate with anyone from the Council after all her family, especially her father, had done.

She took a deep breath and knocked on Aimee's door.

"Come in," Aimee called, and she entered.

"Hey," she said and closed the door behind her.

"Dylan said you'd stop by, but I didn't think it would be today."

"Oh, if now isn't a good time, I can come back tomorrow or another day."

"No, no. Come on in. I've just tried to wake myself up with a long shower. Your brother can be quite the chatterbox." She smiled.

"He was even worse as a little boy, constantly sharing his ideas and thoughts."

"I can imagine."

They both stood in the room, staring at the floor in silence.

"Uh, wanna sit down? Can I get you something to eat or drink?" Aimee eventually said.

"Sure. Some water?" She sat down and Aimee returned a moment later and placed two glasses on the table before joining her on the couch.

They both spoke at the same time.

"I'm—"

"Do you—"

"You go first," Aimee said.

"I'm sorry. I got lost in all that was going on, and while that's true, it was more than that. When… When we talked about… about the Centers and the…" Chris dropped her gaze. "The experiments, I just… I thought you were mad and that you were blaming me for not doing more, for not stopping them."

"Oh. Uh, that never occurred to me. I… I was livid, with your father, the Council, the mage sages, and anyone else who participated in this horror, but it had nothing to do with you. I believe you, that you didn't know about the Centers or the experiments. How could you have done something about an issue you didn't know existed?"

"But I should have been aware of this! I was the heir to the Council, and I should have known. If I was more thorough, researched more, I—"

Aimee laughed. "I don't think anyone could *ever* accuse you of not being thorough or not researching enough."

"Perhaps, but obviously I didn't do everything I could have done, or I was blind, or… willfully ignorant?"

"I don't believe that."

"Oh?"

"You are kind, and you care about others. Yes, you had your preconceived notions and stereotypes about the Verlohren, like most people do, or did. That's what we were all told, and so everyone grew up with these lies as the truth."

"Still… I should have been more open-minded."

"It was probably harder on you because you got a double dose of that big lie given your position and future."

Chris sighed.

"Anyway. You care about people, and your… father must have realized that. It makes sense he didn't share certain information with you."

"He claimed he couldn't have told me some of it until I had taken over completely at thirty-five."

"That could be how they've done it. Share most knowledge, but not all until you're the leader. But I wasn't just talking about that kind of stuff."

"You mean the experiments."

"I'm assuming this was a new part of the Centers?"

"That's my understanding. My father… He was concerned about a Verlohren uprising and wanted to be prepared to defend the Living."

Aimee scoffed and turned her gaze toward the window.

"It's not an excuse. I'm not justifying his behavior," Chris hurried to add.

"I didn't think you were. The whole mind-set is hard to grasp. The Verlohren were always oppressed and did nothing. Even the Tarung were more concerned with getting the Living to see them as more than vermin instead of planning to overthrow the Council."

"I don't understand how he got to this point either, and while fear can change people… This is just too much."

"This is exactly why I believe you were kept in the dark. They recognized you wouldn't fall in line and accept this. You are a powerful mage, and they needed you."

"You might be right."

"Do you… Will there be an investigation or a trial about what happened in these Centers?" Aimee asked.

"That would be my responsibility now that my father has abdicated. I'll decide, and then also oversee the proceedings. Perhaps that's why they aren't concerned with potential consequences since they assume there won't be any."

"Are they right?"

"No, though I haven't determined how to solve this issue. I need to do more research."

Aimee bumped into her. "Of course you do."

"What did you want to say, earlier," Chris asked.

"Oh, well. I was going to ask you how you... What you had in mind for... well, us?"

"I wasn't... after your reaction to my father ordering the experiments, or better, my assumptions about that, I sort of expected you no longer wanted there to be an—"

She failed to finish her sentence when Aimee pulled her near and kissed her. Her eyes fluttered shut, and she held on to Aimee's waist, drawing her closer and returned the kiss. She groaned and opened her mouth, reveling in the heat of Aimee's tongue.

She hadn't hoped for this, didn't dare, though every part of her longed to be with Aimee. She'd have settled for a friendship if that's all Aimee was ready for, but now, the entire world seemed to shift.

Aimee fell back against the couch and pulled her along, urging Chris to settle between her legs while her hands slid underneath her shirt as their kisses grew more ardent.

Chris's arms trembled and failed to support her weight and they both groaned when she lowered her body on top of Aimee's outstretched form.

Aimee broke the kiss and moaned, "I can feel you... you *ache*." Her hands drifted to Chris's butt and drew her in closer.

"The connection," Chris panted. "It's still there, and..." she groaned, her hips rocking against Aimee. She broke the kiss and trailed licks and nibbles down Aimee's neck, whose head fell back, her eyes closing.

"You don't understand what torture it was to stop after touching your markings, before..." she whispered.

"I didn't want to stop either," Aimee breathed. "Not stopping now, but let's move this to my bedroom?"

Chris halted her explorations and sat up. She rose from the couch and extended her hand to Aimee, who grasped it and led her to her room.

In there, she pushed Chris on the mattress while she remained standing as she undressed.

Chris's gaze was glued to Aimee's slowly emerging naked form, and she worried her lower lip once Aimee dropped her pants and climbed onto the bed, crawling towards her, clad only in a bra and panties.

"You're wearing too many clothes," she rasped before bending down and capturing Chris's lips once more in a fervent kiss.

"Whose fault is that?" She chuckled and lifted her torso so Aimee could remove her shirt before stripping her pants off as well.

Aimee crawled back up, peppering pale skin with kisses along her journey to once more be reunited with Chris's lips.

Her senses were overwhelmed with the heady mixture of Aimee's scent and taste, combined with the thrumming connection between them which allowed her to experience Aimee's arousal as well. She couldn't remember *ever* being this desperate for someone's touch, and she whimpered helplessly when Aimee removed her bra and liquid heat engulfed her breast.

She shuddered and moaned at Aimee's insistent tongue lavishing avid kisses to one nipple before licking a path to her other breast, this time sucking and placing little bites, which jolted Chris to anchor her hands into Aimee's hair.

After a seeming eternity that had strung Chris's body taut and saw her tremble with need, Aimee shifted and left Chris's breasts to meander south, kissing and licking along her stomach before trailing her tongue over the soft curve of her hip.

"Aimee," Chris panted.

She didn't reply but smiled when she encouraged Chris to lift her hips and pulled off her panties. She spread Chris's legs and moved to lie between them, lowering her head and darting her tongue along the side of her lover's heat, never once giving attention to the pulsating need that continued to throb between Chris's legs.

Her hands had found purchase on Aimee's sheets while her body shivered and trembled with the tension that Aimee insisted on escalating. Her heart thumped in her chest, and her body glistened with sweat while her hips undulated impatiently. "Aimee, please," she moaned, and her fingers tightened, clasping the sheets when Aimee's tongue leisurely ran up and down her wetness, twirling around her entrance before settling at the center of Chris's ache.

"Oh, Gods," she cried. Her hands shot to Aimee's head, and her fingers ran through dark locks as Aimee's tongue picked up speed.

Chris couldn't tell where her arousal ended and Aimee's began because their connection muddled them, mixed them, and poured an intensity over them both, judging by Aimee's helpless groans and the rocking of her hips against the mattress.

Chris felt everything; Aimee's pleasure at being this close to her as well as her ascending and gripping arousal at Chris's reactions to her ministrations.

Heat. Her entire body, consumed by ardor, pulsated with a tension that unwillingly evoked her magic, which spilled into the room and surrounded them both.

"Chris." Aimee drew back and released a shuddering moan. "What are you doing?" Her head dropped low, laying on Chris's mound for a moment, catching her breath.

"Don't stop," Chris begged, her hips resuming their motion. "It's… my magic. I… it escaped."

"I can feel it," Aimee groaned but heeded Chris's request and once more sunk her mouth into Chris's sex, sucking and licking until Chris grew rigid, a tremor rushing through her body as pleasure suffused her form and she sobbed her release.

\*\*\*

As a Verlohren, Aimee had had little interest in sex, though that had changed once she'd fallen for Chris. Still, her body had been too sluggish and weary to contemplate that aspect of intimacy for a prolonged period.

She wasn't sure if it was because she hadn't had sex in a decade, whether it was Chris herself, or tied to their magical connection, but perhaps it was the combination of all three that transformed this experience into something she could hardly fathom.

After guiding Chris through a series of aftershocks, she crawled back up her body and claimed her mouth in an eager kiss, delighting in the little groan that rushed from Chris's lips. She didn't even notice her hips had resumed rolling until Chris trailed one hand down her body and slid deft fingers with fast and sure strokes through her slick folds.

Aimee's eyes fell shut, and she shuddered and groaned, sinking onto Chris's fingers as once more their connection swelled, not only engulfing her in Chris's feelings but also sharpening her senses and drowning her in a haze of arousal that blazed through her veins.

"Gods," spilled from her lips when Chris pushed another finger inside.

Chris rose and sought Aimee's lips, licking into her mouth before sucking at her tongue while picking up the speed of her thrusts.

Digging her fingers into Chris's shoulders, Aimee broke the kiss and panted. Unable to hold herself up any longer, she dropped down and rested her head in the crook of Chris's neck, showering it with sloppy kisses.

Chris's fingers slipped out and rubbed rapid circles, making Aimee shudder and gasp, her hips rocking faster.

Aimee lifted her chest and strained, her grip on Chris's shoulders tightening as she chased her peak amidst fingers that seemed to understand her every desire before she fully realized it herself, or maybe their connection offered Chris such an insight.

Her mouth opened and Aimee's eyes fell shut when her body arrested before trembling and quaking in a blinding release that washed over her along with the soothing energy of Chris's magic. She sunk bonelessly onto Chris who withdrew her hand and painted gentle circles over Aimee's glistening back.

***

Year 302, Day 145

Chris and Aimee sat unmoving on the couch in Aimee's living room. The night was falling, yet neither had bothered with light. More minutes passed in silence before the unhurried opening of the front door resembled an almost deafening noise booming through the room.

Dylan rocked back and forth on his heels. "Hey."

Both women stared at him but didn't return his greeting.

"I already… I spoke to Mother, and I even had a chat with Martha yesterday," he said, smiling. "Uh, Father… He said, 'goodbye, son,' and patted me on the shoulder. Bizarre."

"I can't do this," Chris stammered and covered her face.

Aimee hesitated before reaching out and placing a hand on Chris's back. "I can head upstairs? Give you guys some privacy." She rose.

Chris sat up straight and seized her fingers. "No! Don't go!"

"All right." Aimee cleared her throat and settled next to her. "Sit down," she said, and Dylan took the seat across from them.

"This is hard, but—" he started.

"You know nothing!" Chris spat, leaning forward.

Aimee grasped Chris's thigh and squeezed.

"You're right. I can't imagine how this has been for you. I died, and when I came to, I was a Verlohren, lost, unable to communicate with anyone I've ever cared about. I could see you, but never reach you."

"I didn't mean—"

"I'm not mad at you. I believe you, and I wasn't trying to make it sounds like we're in a competition over who suffered more. I... I haven't experienced your side, and you don't know mine, but I'm sure we agree both versions sucked."

Chris laughed. "That's one way of putting it."

"You blamed yourself for what happened, and that's what turned me into a Verlohren, and I'm glad it did because otherwise, we never would have freed everyone. Things would still be as they always were since the twins messed with Markesh."

"It's a steep price to pay," Chris said.

"Maybe, but we all suffer at some point, and we rarely ever get to see what goes on inside another person. We cannot empathize with their pain, so it's..."

"Meaningless to quantify or qualify misery?" Chris asked.

"Yes!" He chuckled. "I've missed your ability to bring order to my thoughts."

"All right. Please don't take this the wrong way, but what in the world happened? How did you die, and why do you blame yourself for Dylan's death?"

Chris's eyes widened. "He never told you?"

"No."

"It's... It never came up." Dylan rubbed the back of his neck. "I also thought Chris had told you."

"Not a day I like to revisit." She flickered a wistful gaze between Dylan and Aimee. "We'd gone hiking. He'd badgered me for weeks to reconnect and do something we used to love as kids. I'd finally given in on one of those rare afternoons I had off. It started well enough, but as so often back then, we got into a fight."

\*\*\*

Dylan darted after his sister. "Stop! Why are you running away?"

"I don't understand you! How can you talk like that? We were raised in the same household, had the same lectures, mostly, yet it's as if you've grown up on a different planet!" Chris grumbled, halting, and facing her brother.

"You don't have to agree with your upbringing or the lessons you were taught. Why do you always follow the rules? You question nothing."

"That's not true! I have a lot of questions, all the time. I research, and—"

"What if your books are lying to you?"

"Just because you've lost your mind and run around with these criminals—"

"They are *not* criminals. They're merely dead."

"Then why don't they leave? Why don't they move on?" Dylan kicked a stone down the path. "I don't know!"

"Why are you so sure that you're right and all we've ever learned is wrong? You can't even prove it."

"Neither can you. All you've got are books, written by those in power who of course will recount history as they see fit."

"I get it. You had a friend when you were little who wasn't as horrible as the rest of them—"

"Leave Jim out of this!"

Chris exhaled in a rush. "Whatever. Believe what you want, and do as you wish, given that you've *always* done that." She stomped away, racing up the path.

Dylan didn't move. After a moment, he turned and stepped closer to the edge of the cliff.

Chris, still fuming, but unable to ignore her brother, doubled back. "Are you coming or what?"

"Whatever for?" he said without facing her.

"You're the one who wanted to do this. For weeks you've been begging me to go on this hike with you."

"Yeah, well, maybe I wanted to go on a walk with my sister. The one who used to love spending time with me, who would indulge her little brother by investigating the maps I'd drawn for our treasure hunts. The one who held me all night while I was crying after our dog died and Father told me to get over it? You remember her?" He turned around, and his face was flushed. "I miss her. Instead..." He waved at her. "There's this stranger. This carbon copy of Father," he scoffed.

"Don't you dare...," she shouted, fury rising and her vision blurring. "How can you even..." she said before pausing, her eyes wide.

Dylan, unaware that the grassy overgrowth had no stone surface, treaded sideways without paying attention to the terrain. He stepped into air and fell. "What... Chris!" he yelled, plummeting down the cliff.

"Dylan!" Chris cried, stopping time before sprinting to the edge of the bluff. She stumbled and prepared to pull the immobile Dylan up, but instead, she sank to her knees and sobbed. He had indeed frozen, but not on account of her halting time. She'd been too far away, so nothing but the hard, jagged stone floor beneath them had arrested his fall.

\*\*\*

Freit, Saltung
Year 302, Day 143

"It was an accident," Aimee said. "A tragic one, for sure, but you didn't cause it." She grasped Chris's trembling hand.

303

"If I didn't… if I hadn't marched ahead, my magic would have stopped him. He was too far away, and I didn't…"

"I also could've stood farther back from the edge or paid more attention to where I was going," Dylan said. "I've never blamed you for this, and I'm sorry."

Chris's eyes widened. "What?"

"I didn't mean what I said. You're not like Father at all. I was just so angry and hurt. You didn't seem to even want to consider my take on this. I had discovered more information that pointed toward all of our teachings being lies, and I'd planned to share them with you."

"Oh. I never knew."

"Of course you didn't. I hadn't told you yet, but I was going to, or I wanted to. But then, when you shot me down again, I felt like I'd lost you. As if we'd grown apart and there was nothing that could change that, that we'd never overcome this distance."

"I'm so sorry," Chris cried and hugged him. "I don't know why I was so angry all the time. Back then…" She shook her head. "It seems like a lifetime ago. So much has happened, and you were right." She touched his cheek.

"Yes," he mumbled with tears in his eyes. "I'm so happy we broke the curse and can have this conversation."

"Me, too. Though it won't last."

"It can't. I'm sorry, but I have to leave."

"How does that work?" Aimee asked.

"I'm not fully sure, but Chris is ready—"

"I'm not ready to let you go!"

"No, and you'll never be ready for *that*, but… you've stopped blaming yourself, or better, you're on the path there. You're prepared to heal, and I can feel it… within me, there's this draw, this pull that demands, begs, that I follow it?"

"To whatever comes after?"

"Yes."

"What if that's a trick? Lily and Lara are still around! What if this is their revenge for what we've done?" Chris asked.

"It's not. I have no idea where they are, if they have some sort of plan, or even desire for retribution, but this is *not* them. I can sense it. It's a… This pull is seductive, peaceful, and I long for it as well."

"So wherever you're going, it's… You'll be happy there?" Chris asked.

"I hope so. It feels that way. There's no fear, no doubt. I *know* it's tranquil and warm."

"I'm happy for you," Aimee said. "After never knowing what would come after we're let go, hearing this now, it's… it makes all of this a lot easier."

"Yeah. I had to share it with you. Whatever happens, you don't have to be afraid of what comes after this life," Dylan said.

"I'm glad that you're going to a good place." Chris shuffled closer to Aimee. "But they're still stealing you away from me." She cleared her throat. "Excuse me." She jumped up and rushed to Aimee's bedroom.

"When are you leaving?" Aimee asked after shifting her gaze from Chris's retreating back to Dylan.

"The plan was tonight, but I'm not sure. She's taking it harder than I expected."

"Are you serious? This surprises you?"

"Wishful thinking? I'm not shocked about how cozy the two of you are, though." He grinned.

"Hmm, yes, well, we had a talk, the other day, after you'd left, and apparently, there were a lot of misunderstandings and assumptions. On both sides. Once we worked through them, uh, yes. Well."

"In short, you slept with my sister."

"Dylan!" She threw a pillow at him. "It's not about that."

"Oh, I know, but it's always fun to see you squirm, even more so when you get flustered, which, yeah, still going on." He laughed and flipped the pillow right back.

"Hush! Don't be so loud. Your sister is liable to murder us if she's in there all upset because you're leaving, meanwhile we're out here laughing," Aimee hissed.

"You just don't want her to be mad at you."

"Duh! Have you met her?"

"Yes, I believe so."

"But seriously. Can you postpone your departure by a day? Let her sleep on this and talk again tomorrow?"

"Yeah. I'd already decided to do that. I'm assuming I'm still free to crash in my old room?"

"It's your house," Aimee said.

"Nah. It's yours. I've planned for that ages ago."

Aimee's mouth fell open. "You what?"

He chuckled. "Goodnight, Aimee." Dylan rose and pulled her up from the couch. "Let me hug you, please?"

"You idiot," she rasped and stepped into his embrace.

***

Freit, Saltung
Year 302, Day 203

"Come on! How much longer?" Aimee called.

"I'll be down in a second," Chris replied from the study.

"Only been working on this for two months," Aimee mumbled while settling in a chair.

A few minutes later, a flushed Chris rushed down the stairs, carrying a large tome.

Aimee pointed at the desk. "Let's hear it."

"Right." Chris slid into the chair across from Aimee, edging the volume on the table. She opened it and leafed through the first couple of pages. "You need to remember that this is a draft, and drafts are notoriously... fallible."

"Good Gods, you've been working on this for ages. I'm sure it's fine."

"It's a very complex issue, and I don't—"

Aimee crossed her arms. "Get to the point before I look myself."

She narrowed her eyes. "Fine, but you don't get to complain."

"Chris!" Aimee whined. "Get to it."

"I went over all the options, and well, I even considered the benefits and drawbacks of versions that aren't my personal first choices, but I'll get to those later."

Aimee raised her eyebrows but remained silent.

"I don't want to rule Saltung," Chris blurted out, fiddling with the pages.

"Yeah, obviously. So?"

She nearly dropped the book off the table. "What do you mean, obviously?"

"I haven't *just* met you, and it's… I never got the impression that you have a natural interest in leading, especially not the entire land, or even a city. You're not Council material."

She sat up straighter. "I was raised for that very position."

"Doesn't mean it fits."

"Hmm. You'd be OK with that?"

"With what?"

"Me stepping down as the Head of the Council," Chris said.

"Why wouldn't I be? Because I've had so many aspirations in life that included a potential leadership role of Saltung?"

"Be serious. This affects my future, and… well, I hope *our* future. I need to know you're fine with what I decide."

Aimee shook her head and grasped Chris's hands. "And I need you to listen to me carefully. I do not care what you do, as in, your profession. If you want to rule Saltung, I will support you, and I will do the same if you choose to step down and become a farmer or musician or whatever else.

What you do to earn your living doesn't matter to me. Though, I wanna add, I'm not partial to getting up early, so farming might rest on you, then."

Chris swatted her arm. "That's sweet, but it isn't about a profession. It's a social position that comes with power and responsibility. It would affect every aspect of our lives if I were to continue in my current role."

"I am aware of that. I've never cared for or striven for power. I'll be by your side if you're the ruler of Saltung, much like I'll be if you do something else. I'm serious about this, about us."

Chris blinked several times before clearing her throat. "Right."

"I get that this isn't easy for you to believe, given your upbringing, and the expectations of your parents, your duties. But I grew up differently. I was always allowed and encouraged to determine what I wanted to do with my life. I wish the same for you now. You get to select the path you want to walk on now, and I'll adjust."

"Even if it's something you hate?"

"I'm sure we'd be able to work out a compromise that would suit us both."

"OK, so yes. I don't wish to rule Saltung, but I also don't just want to hand it over to my cousin, or my mother."

"So there's no chance your father could return? I'm still surprised he just accepted this change."

Chris stared at the floor.

Aimee rubbed the pad of her thumb over the back of Chris's hand. "Hey. We don't have to talk about this. Not now, or not ever if you… if that is what you wish."

Chris released a humorless chuckle before raising her head and holding Aimee's gaze. "You're such a kind and sweet person, and I appreciate this more than I can express."

Aimee flushed.

"I suppose it's something I've first stewed over and then… kind of pushed down?"

Aimee tilted her head.

"I told you that my mother is in the process of divorcing my father."

"Yes."

Chris licked her lips. "I'd talked to him again, shortly after we... and after Dylan... left." She cleared her throat. "He's scared of me."

Aimee's eyes widened. "What?"

"He didn't say it outright, but it was clear. He... he said it's my job to clean up the mess I made, and that... that I broke the family."

"You didn't! That was entirely—"

Chris raised her hand. "I'm not upset about that. I'm not the one to blame here."

"What is it then?"

"When we were arguing, he rose and was about to leave. I wasn't done, so I stepped closer and he... he flinched, Aimee. My father fell back and recoiled from me because... because I was getting closer to him."

Aimee squeezed her hand.

"I know you don't like him, and I'm not expecting you to feel for him or anything. He's done horrible things, and I'm not defending him, but—"

Aimee smiled. "He's still your father."

Chris nodded as tears filled her eyes.

"Maybe this is more related to his view of himself."

"What do you mean?"

"Your father loves you, but he also knows that you are disgusted by him, or by his actions. He disappointed you."

Chris scoffed. "I doubt that matters."

"You never know. Emotions are strange, and it's hard to abandon a child. Even if he doesn't agree with what you've done, I still think he loves you. He knows he's failed you, and maybe your anger, your frustrations became too much for him to bear? Like he realized that your relationship is in shambles, and it hit him, so he... withdrew."

"I don't know. He never voiced any regret."

"It could be that he knows you wouldn't believe him anyway. Also, how does one apologize for what he did?"

Chris heaved a heavy sigh.

"Give it some time. I'm not saying there's any guarantee that your relationship will mend, or that you even need to try to fix anything, but holding a grudge and refusing to forgive will end up hurting you more."

"You're saying I need to work on forgiving him or I'll suffer? How can I forgive him? How could *you* even say that?"

"I don't love your father. We have no relationship, so there's no loss for me. I cannot change what he has done. The past is just that. It's gone, Chris. People can change, and I am not saying he did or that he will change, but it is possible. We only have this moment here, always. Spending it lost in hate or regret." She shook her head. "It'll ruin everything. In time, it'll seep into every fiber, every aspect of your life."

Tears she had held back earlier now spilled over her cheeks. "I don't know *how* to forgive him."

"That's OK. You don't have to do anything right now. That's why I said give it some time."

Chris sniffed.

Aimee leaned close and kissed her forehead. "I love you. We will figure this out."

"I love you, too. Thank you." Chris pressed a lingering kiss on Aimee's lips.

"All right. I believe we weren't done with our discussion. What do you have in mind for this new way of ruling Saltung?" Aimee asked.

Chris wiped her eyes. "Right. I researched different ways of social organizations, and I've also read all the remaining texts of the olden days. Before... before the twins, Saltung had no ruler. It was self-governed, and people solved disputes with the help of an arbitrator that both parties selected." She leafed through her book once more.

"What if they didn't agree on a person?"

"Then each could select one. Sometimes, there were up to four or five who ended up deciding together."

"What about laws? How were they enforced? Was there some type of guard?"

"I'm not sure. I suppose there could be a kind of peace force down the line. As for laws, we already have those, and they are not bad. I just... the Council would no longer be the main authority of all disputes."

"OK, I like that idea, but who will rule the Council, or do you plan on disbanding it?"

"A family shouldn't oversee the Council just because they came into power at one point. What if they don't want to rule or are horrible at it?"

"What's the solution?"

"People could volunteer for it and well, we could rotate. I also think it would be beneficial to have several people ruling together, and that they represent the different classes of Saltung."

"You'd have Verlohren on there?"

"Well, yes. Those who are still around and want to be on there, though it seems like most of the corporeal ones have made peace and moved on." Chris sniffed.

"I miss him, too."

"Yes. We... I'll be ready to talk about this soon, I think. But not now, please."

"Of course. In your own time." Aimee intertwined her fingers with Chris again. "What if no one volunteers? It's a lot of work and it takes people away from their jobs. They still need to provide for their lives."

"I thought of that, too. We might divert a stipend to them, as a compensation for their efforts. And I suppose, if no one comes forward, we can randomly select people. They wouldn't have to do it forever. Perhaps for a year or two? More like a stewardship."

"That's a great idea."

Chris smiled.

"Would you volunteer?"

"Gods, no. I was serious when I said I don't want to rule Saltung. Not even in this way. Still, I can't just walk away. There must be a transition period, and I'm not sure I trust the rest who could step in. Until this new system is running, I'll have to stick with it. But after that, I'm out."

"That makes sense. We don't want Lance deciding to be the next Head of the Council."

Chris shuddered. "I don't even want to contemplate that."

"Yeah. Let's go back to good thoughts."

"Yes, please," Chris said. "What about you? Would you volunteer once it's all set up?"

"Nah. That's not for me. I wanna go back to what I used to do."

"Counseling?"

"Yes. I have to finish my studies, but that shouldn't be a problem."

"I agree. This is exciting!" Chris bounced in her seat.

"So aside from what you don't want to do, what *do* you want to do?" Aimee asked.

"Study and teach magic."

"All right. No farm then."

Chris laughed. "No, no farm."

# afterword

The first university I attended in Germany had a "Frauen Bibliothek," a women's library, in the basement of their Liberal Arts building. To be honest, that was more my home than the university itself. I'd always been an avid reader, but I must confess that I hadn't realized that LGBTQ+ books existed until I stood in front of those bookshelves at the library. I devoured all of them, and most of these novels were English translations.

I do love a good romance novel, but I've always lamented that there weren't any books outside of that genre that told the adventures of LGBTQ+ characters, and yes, tales that included some kind of love story.

Today, such books thankfully exist, and I am absolutely delighted by this. However, I felt there can never be enough of them, so I decided to throw my hat into that well, too.

I sincerely hope you've enjoyed the result of my endeavor.

Thank you for reading.

# acknowledgement

Again, none of this would have been possible without the help and influence of my late mentor and friend, W.B. Gerard, who is missed beyond words and comprehension.

I'd like to thank my friend Tatiana for all her help in the creation and revision process. Without her input, this tale would be sorely lacking.

Juanita Barrett indulged me with an early brainstorming session when I told her I wanted to write a fantasy novel, but that I had no idea for the plot. She also helped me with the final proofing process.

Haley humored me when I was stuck, allowed me to tell her the plot, and together, we came up with a scene later on in the novel that remains one of my favorite moments in the book.

Rodna always finds herself on the receiving end of reading my stories, and unlike anyone else, she may not decline. Her unique perspective helped me rectify quite a few issues.

Kim received endless texts about sentence structure or concerning words I'd lost. She also refuses to let me get away with any bovine defecation.

Rebecca Taylor, thank you for all your help, for indulging me with a million "pick one" requests, for reading through a few scenes that bothered me, and for creating an awesome website.

I'd also like to thank Jennifer Jacobs for reading this and offering feedback.

My father, Leo, who taught me the idea of revision when he asked me at 15, after he'd just finished reading my twenty-page masterpiece: "So, and now you'll revise it and turn it into a real novel?" He also taught me about the creative power of our thoughts.

My mother, Rita, who supported all my, at times quite foolish, ideas, and who has gifted me with her unwavering love and support.

My sister, Sandra, who, like any great big sister, is responsible for shaping a variety of my loves, from skulls, to Roxette, and the Golden Girls. Ever the protective guardian of her little sister, Sandra has always been on my side.

My uncle Rudi and my aunt Angelika, who have both been a source of calm in any storm life has thrown at me.

There are many more people in my life who have helped and supported me along this road, and who have encouraged me in various ways. I am grateful for all of you.

Last, but not least, thank you Flo, Willow, and Silas. Without you, this would all be for naught. Thank you, Flo, for enabling me to follow my passion. You are a giant, and an inspiration to anyone who is lucky enough to know you.

# about the author

Sabrina has always written and used to tell her grandmother bedtime stories. She is a German native, and currently resides with her family in east Alabama.

For more information and updates on future releases of additional novels, check out her website: sabrinablaum.com, or follow her on Twitter: @BlaumSabrina

# publisher

Babette B. Publishing
300 Opelika Rd P.O. Box 581
Auburn, AL 36830

Made in United States
Orlando, FL
22 November 2021

10649639R00190